David crawled toward Maya, praying that she wasn't dead.

He cradled her head in his arms and held her, checking for a pulse. She was still alive.

Her eyes fluttered open.

"David." Her voice was weak and her gaze unfocused.

"Yes, I came for you." He looked all around. "Did you fall?"

"The man with the knife…he came after me."

"Where is Sarge?"

He'd have to deal with finding Sarge second. First he needed to get Maya to a safe place. "I got you now, Maya. You're going to be okay."

USA TODAY Bestselling Author

Sharon Dunn
and
Heather Woodhaven

Alaskan Protector

2 Thrilling Stories

Undercover Mission and *Arctic Witness*

LOVE INSPIRED

INSPIRATIONAL ROMANCE

Special thanks and acknowledgment are given to
Sharon Dunn and Heather Woodhaven for their contribution
to the Alaska K-9 Unit miniseries.

LOVE INSPIRED®

INSPIRATIONAL ROMANCE

Recycling programs
for this product may
not exist in your area.

ISBN-13: 978-1-335-47597-8

Alaskan Protector

Copyright © 2023 by Harlequin Enterprises ULC

Undercover Mission
First published in 2021. This edition published in 2023.
Copyright © 2021 by Harlequin Enterprises ULC

Arctic Witness
First published in 2021. This edition published in 2023.
Copyright © 2021 by Harlequin Enterprises ULC

For questions and comments about the quality of this book, please contact us
at CustomerService@Harlequin.com.

Love Inspired
22 Adelaide St. West, 41st Floor
Toronto, Ontario M5H 4E3, Canada
www.LoveInspired.com

Printed in U.S.A.

CONTENTS

Ever since she found the Nancy Drew books with the pink covers in her country school library, **Sharon Dunn** has loved mystery and suspense. Most of her books take place in Montana, where she lives with three nearly grown children and a hyper border collie. She lost her beloved husband of twenty-seven years to cancer in 2014. When she isn't writing, she loves to hike surrounded by God's beauty.

Books by Sharon Dunn

Love Inspired Suspense

Visit the Author Profile page at LoveInspired.com for more titles.

UNDERCOVER MISSION

Sharon Dunn

There is no fear in love; but perfect love
casteth out fear: because fear hath torment.
He that feareth is not made perfect in love.
—*1 John* 4:18

For Ariel, my beautiful, creative, funny daughter.

ONE

K-9 officer Maya Rodriguez took in a sharp breath as she stepped out onto the quiet upper deck of the Alaska Dream cruise ship. A fog had rolled in making it hard to see more than a few feet in front of her. Maya's partner, Sarge, a Malinois was by her side. He looked cute in his service dog vest. All part of the disguise for their undercover work. Though he was two years old, he was small for his age and breed, and people often thought he was still a puppy. Size was deceptive, however. Sarge was a top-notch detection and screening K-9. His nose could sniff out almost anything—weapons, explosives, even infectious diseases.

Maya's footsteps seemed to echo as she surveyed the boardwalk. Two nights ago, a woman had been murdered on this deck—an entertainment employee for the cruise line. There had been another attack on the ship as well. That victim, a female passenger, had been grabbed from behind. Her attacker held a knife to her throat, but she had managed to get away with only minor injuries. Both victims had similar profiles: young, dark haired, slender and attractive. Maya also fit that description, which was why her boss, Colonel Lorenza Gallo, had picked her for this covert assignment. Though she had been on the K-9 team for five years, this was the first time she'd been undercover.

The cruise ship owner was worried about losing business due to the attacks, so everything had to be on the down low. Ship security had not turned up any suspects or substantial evidence, which in itself was concerning. There was some speculation that the security team was covering for someone or just couldn't do a good job when it came to serious crime on board a ship.

It was so quiet Maya could hear Sarge's paw steps as he heeled at her side. Fear fluttered through her when her hand touched the hip where her firearm would normally be. No guns of any kind were allowed on board, which meant that if she was truly in danger, her only protection was her training and Sarge.

Though they were on the highest viewing area on the ship, she could hear the waves lapping against the hull of the ship. Despite it being June, the Alaska night air chilled her skin.

The clatter of footsteps caused her to whirl around. Her heart pounded. Sarge took up a position beside her, standing at attention and letting out a little supportive yipping noise.

A man and a woman in fancy dress emerged from the fog laughing.

Their expressions grew serious when they saw Maya and her dog.

"I was sure we would be the only ones up here in this

kind of weather," the woman said as she circled her arm through the man's elbow.

"Just thought I'd get a little air and solitude," Maya explained. She had seen on the ship's list of activities that there was ballroom dancing this evening. No doubt, the couple had just come from there.

Both the man and the woman drew their attention to Sarge.

The man tugged at the bow tie he wore with his tuxedo. "There's plenty of room on the ship. It's way colder up here than I thought it would be. Enjoy having the deck to yourself, miss."

"Ta-ta," the woman said. Their laughing and joyous mood resumed as they disappeared into the fog. Maya heard a door open and shut.

"False alarm," she murmured to Sarge. "They looked happy, like they were in love." She shook her head. "Some of us are just terminally single, right?" Maya continued to walk the deck looking for the place where the crime report said the murder had taken place. Though all the evidence of the crime had been removed, it often helped to retrace the steps of the victim. She had very little to work with based off the report written by the ship's security chief.

Crystal Lynwood, the murder victim, had worked for the onboard entertainment venues for less than a year. Her body had been found by the east entrance door. She'd been stabbed.

Maya located the door and reached for the knob, preparing to retrace the steps that the victim must have taken.

A hand grabbed her from behind and pulled her back. Judging from the strength he exhibited, the attacker was male. Sarge barked. The man kicked a deck chair in the direction of the dog. Maya heard a yelp of pain.

She felt herself being dragged. She crashed into another deck chair and then her assailant circled around and pushed her from the front until her back was against a wall. Before she could react, he slammed a fist in her solar plexus causing her to wheeze and gasp for breath.

He put a knife to her throat. With his free hand he pressed hard against her stomach. She was still fighting for air from the blow he'd struck. The attacker wore a ski mask.

She could hear Sarge but she could not see him. Why wasn't he coming to help her? As the K-9 barked, she could hear the noise of one object clanging against another.

"I'm going to make you pay for what you did." The man's voice held the threat of violence.

She could feel the pressure of the knife against her throat. Her hands were free. Though he had her pinned in place, she might still be able to get away. She balled her hand into a fist preparing to land a blow to his stomach. He pressed the knife deeper into her skin. She smelled the coppery scent of blood, and her skin stung from the cut.

"Don't even try," he warned.

Sarge's barking grew louder and then there was an odd scraping sound.

The guy shifted and let up pressure on her neck. In

that moment, his face was caught in one of the lights that illuminated the deck. She saw green eyes.

Some distance away, she heard footsteps. The attacker glanced to one side and then the other. He lifted the knife off her throat and then without another word disappeared into the fog. She could hear his retreating footsteps even as the other set of footsteps came toward her.

She didn't see Sarge anywhere—or hear him. Worry gnawed away at her. What had happened to her partner? She called his name. Now she heard the footsteps again coming toward her from the opposite direction the assailant had run to.

A silhouette of a man in uniform emerged from the fog. He held on to Sarge's leash.

"Did you lose your service dog, ma'am? His leash got tangled up with a deck chair and then that chair caught on another one when he tried to drag it and was trapped." The man stepped closer. "I'm the Security Chief, David Garrison." She'd noticed him when she'd boarded this morning. David Garrison was the one who had written the report that gave her almost nothing to work with.

Her chest hurt where she'd had the wind knocked out of her. The cut to her neck, though not deep, still stung. She held her hand out. Sarge jerked away from the man and ran toward her. She struggled to speak. "I—I was attacked."

David's voice filled with concern as he stepped toward her. "You okay?"

She managed a nod. And then kneeled and wrapped

her arms around Sarge. Holding the dog steadied her nerves. They both had had a scare.

Officer Garrison straightened his spine and squared his shoulders. "Which way? Where did he go?"

She pointed in the direction the perp had gone. David took off running. Sarge, who was trained to detect weapons and would pick up the scent of the fleeing man as well as the knife, would be able to track even more precisely than the security officer. She commanded him to go. He put his nose to the ground and then lifted his head and sniffed the air. A moment later, Sarge also took off running while she held on to the leash.

David Garrison's footsteps echoed as he darted all along the deck. It didn't take long for Maya and Sarge to catch up with him.

Her partner alerted on the west door that led down to the next deck. She swung the door open. Sarge scampered down the stairs. This floor was comprised of state rooms for the guests. The rooms had balconies that faced inward providing a view of the main floor where there was a pool and bumper cars as well as many shops. She had studied the layout of the ship from the maps provided on each floor, but it was massive. Ten floors of shops, restaurants, entertainment venues and staterooms. It was hard to remember where everything was.

Getting ahead of David, Sarge stayed on the scent, hesitating only a moment as they worked their way down the floors. He ran through the botanical gardens and then came to the door that led to the second deck which was mostly utilitarian and storage. Laundry and cooking facilities, as well as where the medical, administrative and security offices were held. When she peered over her shoulder, she saw that the security officer was behind them. He ran toward her favoring one of his legs with just the hint of a limp.

Sarge came to stand outside a set of double doors that were labeled Main Kitchen.

Maya commanded her partner to stop. The dog sat beside her feet. She turned toward David as he approached. "I think your man ran into this kitchen."

"Oh really. Your service dog knows how to track, does he?" Suspicion colored his words.

"He's protective of me is all." But even to her own ears, her excuse for Sarge's obvious expertise sounded lame.

David was at least six inches taller than her. Brown hair stuck out from beneath his cap. She had to admit he was good looking. Could she trust him to let him know she was undercover?

She caught herself. No matter what, she had to be on her guard. At this point, both passengers and crew were suspects. And she couldn't rule out members of the security team, especially because David's report had turned up zilch. Was he somehow involved?

"The kitchen is shut down at this hour. They start to prep for breakfast in a couple of hours. For sanitation reasons, your dog can't go in." He looked right at her. His eyes were blue. "Despite your dog's apparent talents, we do have regulations."

Okay, so David Garrison was way smarter than his handling of the investigation had let on. He was already suspicious of her story. And the blue eyes and the fact that he had appeared so quickly after her attacker fled probably meant she could take him off the suspect list. But he could still be covering for someone.

"I'll wait outside here with Sarge," she said. "My service dog."

"I can handle this. Why don't you go to the infirmary and get treated for that cut on your neck? I'll get a statement from you later, a description of anything you can tell me about the attacker. I'm sure you're pretty shaken up right now."

She detected the tone of challenge in his voice. He clearly didn't like a civilian interfering with his law enforcement duties.

"The cut is superficial. I can deal with it myself later. I'd rather just wait here and make my statement right away."

He stared at her long enough to make her feel uncomfortable. She didn't want to blow her cover after being on this boat for less than a day. She'd boarded when the ship had gotten into port in Juneau after leaving Seattle.

"Suit yourself." David pushed open the swinging double doors.

She could see him through the oval-shaped windows as he searched the place.

Maya sighed. She'd been running on adrenaline since the attack. But now that she had a quiet moment to reflect, all the fear she'd suppressed flooded through her. A knife had been held to her throat. She gripped the door frame trying to catch her breath. Sensing her change in mood, Sarge whimpered at her feet and stared up at her. She looked down at his mostly black nose framed by tan around his eyes. The dog was always tuned in to her emotions.

Sarge thumped his tail. His way of reassuring her.

She bent over and stroked his ears. "So glad you're my partner."

Maya straightened up. Her heart beat a little faster as she stared down the long empty hallway, wondering where the attacker had gone. Had he run into the kitchen as Sarge's nose had indicated or was he still lurking close by? As she stood alone in the corridor, she could not shake the feeling that she was being watched.

David Garrison switched on the lights and surveyed the entire kitchen. Stainless steel counters gleamed. The ship had many cafés and eateries, but much of the food was prepped in this main kitchen and then sent up to the other decks. In another couple of hours, it would be bustling with activity as breakfast preparation got underway.

He walked toward the ovens, checking underneath counters. As the ship's head security officer, even he was not allowed to carry a gun, only a Taser. Not being armed to do his job was an adjustment in comparison to the life he'd led as an MP in the army. David clenched his teeth. An IED had ended his grand military ambitions, leaving him with a leg injury.

He thought about the beautiful woman standing outside the door waiting for him. Something about her and that so-called service dog was really off. He wondered if she had noticed that he favored his left leg. He shook his head. Why did it matter anyway?

There were two doors on opposite sides of the kitchen as well as a service elevator for the transport of food. If the attacker had come through here, he could have gotten away. He searched the pantry and opened the service elevator. Finally, he checked the other door down the long hallway.

Well, if the guy had gone through here, he wasn't here anymore. David worked his way back through the kitchen. Now to deal with the woman and her dog…

She was standing in the hallway when he pushed open the door.

"Find anything?"

He shook his head. "What makes you think your dog would know where he went?"

"He was a K-9 before he became a service dog. He knows how to track and detect weapons."

Okay, so maybe that sounded believable. But why not just tell him that in the first place. "What did you say your name was?"

"Maya Rodriguez."

He wondered why she needed a service dog. She didn't have any apparent disability so it might be for emotional support or nonvisual condition.

"Maya, why don't I escort you and your dog back to your room, and you can tell me anything you remember about the attacker," he said. "If you feel comfortable with that."

She nodded. He turned, and they started to walk. It wasn't lost on him that with her long dark brown hair and youthful appearance, Maya looked like the woman who had been murdered and the passenger who had been attacked. Crystal Lynwood, the actress who had been killed, was still wearing an expensive gold-and-diamond bracelet when her body had been found by another crew member. The motive wasn't robbery, which made him worried that they were dealing with someone who was psychologically unstable. It frustrated him that he'd had pressure from the owner of the cruise line to do the investigation quickly.

As they walked, the dog took up a protective position wedging himself in between Maya and him. The canine's black ears stood up as he padded along.

"What did you say your dog's name was?"

"Sarge."

They took a flight of stairs, stepping out onto the promenade, the central part of the ship. The shops were closed at this hour, though some of the entertainment venues and midnight buffets were still open. "What deck are you on?"

"My room is on the sixth floor."

"We can take the elevator." He pointed off in a corner.

"This ship is so big. By the time I learn where everything is, the cruise will be over."

They walked past a music venue where the strains of Broadway tunes spilled out. "True, I think you could keep yourself entertained without ever going ashore."

They got into the glass elevator which faced outward and provided a stunning view of the dark rolling sea as well as the glaciers and mountains in the distance. Though he missed the excitement of the military, the thing he liked the most about his job was how the scenery was always changing. The last thing he wanted was to put down roots anywhere. This ship was his home now. That suited him fine.

Both of them stared out at the landscape. "Can you tell me anything about the attacker? You said he had a knife?"

She let out a heavy breath. "I only saw it for a moment. I would guess that it was more of a hunting knife than something you would use to cook with."

They were still waiting on the forensic autopsy for Crystal Lynwood. All he could conclude from the crime scene was that she had been stabbed. Just like with an airport, all passenger and crew had their luggage run through a screener. How had someone managed to smuggle a hunting knife on board?

The elevator came to a stop, the doors slid open and they stepped out into a carpeted hallway.

"I'm just down that way. Five staterooms away."

Maya seemed pretty calm, so he decided to press her for more information. The best time to do an interview was as close to the crime as possible. Trauma and time tended to distort memory. "What can you tell me about your attacker's appearance?"

"He was wearing a ski mask. Average height and build, nothing distinct about his voice."

Again, David felt a hiccup in his assessment of Maya. The way she was describing the perp was very cop-like.

She stood outside her room. Sarge sat at her feet and looked at David with probing dark eyes. One thing was for sure, the dog was protective of her.

She pulled her card key out of her pocket. "There was one thing about him that was distinct."

"What's that?"

She met his gaze. "He had green eyes. If I saw them again, I would know it was him."

Something about the way she looked at him made him want to lean closer to her. He squared his shoulders remembering that he was on the job. "That's helpful." Though he didn't want to tell her about the previous attack and Crystal's murder, both of which he was sure were committed by the same perp, she had given him significant information. "Why don't you try to get a good night's sleep?"

"Oh, I will," she said.

Again, something in the way she spoke suggested she intended to do the quite the opposite. Why did he keep going back to the idea that she wasn't being forthcoming with him? His dating history had created a natural distrust of women; they always ended up being deceptive in some way. And he understood that that colored every interaction he had with women. Still, he could not shake the gut feeling that Maya was withholding something from him.

She swiped her card key and offered him a smile. "You have a good rest of your night too."

She and her dog stepped inside. The door eased shut behind them. But he didn't hear the dead bolt click into place. Odd. After an attack like she had endured, most passengers would have secured every lock available.

David headed down the hall, turned a corner and continued to walk. He slowed and then stopped. Something was not sitting right with him. Maya Rodriguez was hiding something from him. He turned back around and headed toward the hallway where her room was. He got there just in time to see Maya and the dog headed up the hallway around a corner.

TWO

Maya hurried around the corner with Sarge in tow. She had one more thing she wanted to do before she could sleep— visit the place where the attack on the other passenger had taken place. And she had had to wait until David Garrison was out of the way. Really, he seemed like a nice enough guy, but if she had to be hush-hush about the investigation so be it.

In the report, the passenger had been able to provide no significant information about her attacker, but maybe seeing where the crime had taken place would give Maya a direction to go.

She was sure they were dealing with the same perp. And that that man had probably also attacked her. As she ran toward the elevator, she remembered what he had said.

I'm going to make you pay.

The words gave her chills. But they didn't make any sense. She'd boarded the ship only this morning. Why would someone already have an ax to grind with her?

She stepped into the elevator. The other attack had

taken place on the eighth floor solarium. Before the elevator doors closed, a man raced toward it and stepped on. Her heart beat a little faster. The guy was of average height and build. As they both stared straight ahead, she couldn't see what color his eyes were. All the same, being alone with a stranger in a closed space she couldn't escape from made her aware of the need to remain on guard.

"Which floor?"

"Eight, just like you." He stared straight ahead as the elevator numbers lit up.

Sarge let out a low-level growl and then moved so he was in between her and the man.

"Your dog is well behaved, I assume."

"When he wants to be." Maya hoped her comment would deter the man if he did have sinister intent. She glanced sideways at him, taking note of his indistinct appearance.

The ride up two floors seemed to take forever. Finally, the door slid open. The guy moved back to let her go first. She and Sarge stepped out. While she checked the map on the wall for how to get to the solarium, the man stepped out of the elevator and turned down a hallway. His footsteps faded. So he probably wasn't up to anything.

Maya let out a breath. The attack on the upper deck had made her feel vulnerable.

She found her way to the solarium which featured deck chairs facing floor-to-ceiling glass. They were in the forward part of the ship. The view at night was breathtaking. The fog had lifted, and she could see stars and a crescent moon.

There was only one other passenger. An older woman covered in a throw who had fallen asleep on one of the lounge chairs. Maya padded softly past her. The solarium wound around in a half circle. The report said the female passenger had come up here late at night for some solitude when she'd been attacked.

Though Maya wasn't sure how much stock she should put into the comment, the victim had mentioned that she had the feeling she was being followed at different times of the day prior to the attack. If that was the case, this perp stalked his victims waiting for the chance when they were alone and vulnerable. A *feeling*, however, was not hard evidence.

She walked around the solarium. She could no longer see the old woman. Up ahead was a door, and she reached for the handle. As she was opening it, a force pressed on her from behind propelling her across the threshold. Amid all the chaos, she dropped Sarge's leash. The door automatically closed. Sarge was on the other side, his barking muffled but intense. Pounding footsteps indicated that the man who had pushed her was right behind her. She found herself outside on a deck with a railing. A blast of cold air greeted her. There was a door at the other end of the deck that probably led back inside. The wind caught her hair and she could hear the waves beating the side of the ship. She turned to face the man who had pushed her. He lunged toward her. The ski mask he wore made it impossible to see his face.

She prepared to land a gut punch to her assailant. He anticipated the move, blocking her hand as she raised it, then pushed her against the railing. Cold metal pressed into her back. She kept waiting for him to brandish the knife, but he didn't.

Sarge was still barking on the other side of the door, and it sounded like he was flinging himself against it.

With a furious intensity she dove at the man, lifting her hand to grasp his mask. But he was too quick for her.

Her assailant swung her around and pushed her toward the railing. She felt the cold metal press against her stomach. When she looked down, she could see the turbulent water below.

He lifted her up, so she was on her tiptoes. The man was strong. Did he intend to throw her overboard? Her heart pounded as her hands gripped the cold railing. She tried to push away from it. Wind whipped her hair around across her face. He held her by the waist and neck. She locked her elbows, putting distance between herself and the railing.

He leaned close and hissed in her ear. "What are you up to?"

Desperation clawed through her. If she couldn't get away, she knew he'd throw her overboard.

A hand grabbed the back of her jacket and lifted her up. She saw only the sea rolling down below.

Please God, help me break free before he kills me.

The sound of the dog's barking alerted David to where he needed to go. Once Maya had turned the corner by her room, she could have gone in one of three different directions. He had wasted precious time looking for her. Though he had pursued her to find out why she'd lied to him, Sarge's urgent barking alerted him to the fact that she might be in some kind of danger again.

He entered the solarium where an elderly woman resting on a chaise lounge chair was just waking up. He ran around the half circle created by the solarium layout. At the other end of the solarium, he saw Sarge barking and bouncing against a door.

He raced across the expanse and flung open the door. Fear shot through him when he saw a man in a ski mask pressing Maya's body against the railing while she struggled to get away. Her front faced the railing while her hands gripped it. "Security, let go of her right now. Back off."

Turning, the attacker saw Sarge and David. He lifted Maya from the waist and pushed her over the railing. Before David could get to him, the attacker ran to the opposite end of the boardwalk through a door.

David made a split-second decision to let the attacker go and save Maya. He couldn't do both.

Maya's hands gripped the railing and David sprinted to where she was hanging on for her life.

"Hold on! I've got you." He reached down and grabbed her wrists.

He pulled her up, and she swung her legs over the railing, falling into his arms.

"I thought I was going to die," she gasped. "You saved me…again." She pulled away and looked up at him.

He felt a bit breathless when she gazed at him with

such gratitude. "Maybe we can still catch him." Perhaps it was just the energy he'd expended pulling her up that made him lightheaded. He turned his attention to the door where the attacker had run.

"We'll go with you." Maya tilted her head toward Sarge who was standing at attention waiting for instruction. "Sarge can help. People who are running in fear emit an odor that dogs can track."

"Let's go." He turned and pushed open the door.

"Good." She reached up and squeezed David's arm just above the elbow. Then picked up Sarge's leash and commanded him. "Go."

The dog took off running, leading down the passageway and out onto the floor where there were closed shops and seating areas. Only a smattering of other people were out at this hour. Most everyone was asleep or at least in their cabins by now. The dog stopped to sniff around a children's play area. Lots of places to hide.

David shone his flashlight all around the area but saw nothing. They kept searching, Sarge led them up another floor but lost the scent outside an elevator.

David stared at the doors of the elevator. "I guess that's it. I think he's vanished."

"But he's still out there!" she cried.

He picked up on the fear in her voice. He turned to face her. "You've been attacked twice."

"I think he followed me." Her hand fluttered to her head where there was a bruise. "How else would he have found me there alone."

"Maybe I can't catch this guy yet." The frustration he felt came out in his tone of voice. "But I can at least make an effort to keep you safe. If he's been follow- ing you, he probably knows which cabin you're in. The room next to mine in crew quarters is empty and there's an adjoining door." He didn't want another woman mur- dered, not on his watch.

"I suppose that would be wise. Sarge of course will stay with me." Her voice had become monotone. She was in shock.

"Of course," he said. "Let's go gather your things. I can arrange for a bellhop to meet us outside your door." He pulled his phone out preparing to make the call. "We can swing by and pick up your new card key first. I have the key to where they are kept for the crew and the authority to issue them."

She rubbed the cross necklace that she wore around her neck as though she were thinking about her options. And then she nodded as her eyes grew moist.

Compassion surged through him. "You've been through a lot tonight."

She squared her shoulders and lifted her chin. She swiped at her eyes.

He placed his hand on her upper arm, hoping the gesture would offer silent support. He remembered that she had touched him in the same way just a moment be- fore. Her touch had sent a spark of warmth through him.

Sarge let out a whimper of support. Maya smiled down at him. "He's my best buddy. What can I say?"

David made the call to the concierge station. The man who picked up agreed to meet him at Maya's room with a cart for transport.

After picking up the new card key, which took about

fifteen minutes, they walked through the corridors of the mostly quiet ship save for the few overnight janitors and people lingering after late-night buffets and the final shows of the evening. They came to her room. From the opposite direction, an older man was pushing a luggage cart toward them.

She swiped her card key, pushed the door open and stepped inside.

Though the door blocked his view of her, he heard Maya gasp. The dog barked in a rapid-fire fashion. He feared the worst as he moved to see what had caused such alarm.

THREE

Maya placed a hand on her chest and fell back against a wall as she stared at the total chaos that had become her room. Drawers were open. Clothes thrown around.

"Everything okay?" David entered the room. *"Whoa."*

Maya tried to take in a deep breath to calm herself. She waved her hand in a slicing motion in the air where Sarge could see it, a gesture that told him to stand at attention and be quiet.

"Robbery, maybe?" David stepped deeper into the room.

Was this connected to the attacks? "Have you had any recently?"

"There is always petty theft and pickpockets." He shook his head. "Breaking into a room is on a whole different level though. Do you have any jewelry or anything of value?"

Maya shook her head and stepped over to where the open drawers with the clothes hanging out were. Was somebody looking for something? Or was this meant to scare her? This did not fit the nature of the attack on the passenger or the murder of Crystal Lynwood.

She remembered the attacker had asked her what she was up to the second time he'd come after her.

The old man who had brought the luggage cart stood outside the door. "Looks like a break-in. Do you need help cleaning up?"

"I'll handle it, Lester," David said. "I imagine you have to get back to man the desk anyway."

"Yes indeed," the bellhop said. "If you're sure you don't want my help."

"We'll be all right. Thanks, Lester."

David's voice seemed to come from very far away as she stared at the mess that had been made of her personal things. Her purse was flung across the floor, its contents emptied. She'd hidden the purse in a drawer beneath her clothes. Maya leaned down to pick up her fake license and a credit card. Nothing in the purse would reveal that she was law enforcement. Ensuring that her cover wouldn't be discovered.

"I can dust for prints. We won't be able to do anything with the results until we're in port though," David said. "Maybe what we should do first is gather up your stuff and get you settled in the room next to me. At this point, I'm very concerned about your safety. I'm even more convinced that you shouldn't stay in this room."

Maya had to battle not to give in to the rising fear she felt. She was a trained officer used to dealing with violence and the unexpected. The hard part about being undercover was not having the direct support of the rest of the Alaskan K-9 Unit When she got a private moment, she would check in at headquarters with an update. There was no clear evidence to link the ransacking of the room to the attacks, but her gut told her they were related. "Yes, let's pack and get out of here."

As David helped her get her things in order, her head started to clear. Something about having him close made all of this easier to handle.

She picked up the items that belonged in her purse and put them back. She found the little sterling silver locket her grandmother had given her underneath a chair. Even though the chain for it was broken, she always carried it with her. Her *abuelita* still lived in Puerto Rico, so Maya got to see her only every couple of years. Because family was so important to her, having that distance between them could be hard even with her parents and siblings here in Alaska. Bottom line… if the motive for tossing the room was robbery, the invader would have taken the locket.

The entire contents of her purse had been dumped. Was he trying to figure out who she was? If it was the attacker who had come into her room, she supposed the fact that she had visited the areas where the murder and the other assault had taken place might make him suspicious about her. Maybe that was why he had asked her what she was up to. David probably was wondering the same thing.

"The door wasn't forced. Who would have the ability to break in here, anyway?"

David tossed the remainder of Maya's clothes in the suitcase that lay open on the table. He shrugged. "Lots of people. A staff member who had access to the card key. Someone who is computer savvy or has access to a master card key. Or perhaps even a passenger who stole a card key off a maid's cart. It doesn't happen often, but it does happen."

They packed up the remainder of her stuff and loaded it on the cart. David directed her to the service elevator which she noted required that he swipe a card key over it to get in. He pushed the cart while she held on to Sarge's leash.

They arrived at the lowest deck of the ship, where the staff and crew lived. David opened the room for her.

He pushed the luggage cart inside, helped her unload it and then left it in the hallway. "I imagine you're pretty tired."

"Exhausted," she said and then flopped down on the bed. Sarge sat at her feet. Because this part of the ship was underwater, there were no windows in the room.

"Make sure, the door is dead bolted after I leave." The security chief turned to go and then looked over his shoulder. "Remember, I'm right next door."

"Thank you, David, for everything." Though her body was fatigued, her mind was still racing.

He left, closing the door behind him. She rose and clicked the dead bolt into place. Before turning out the light, she took note of the side door that must lead to David's cabin. She slipped under the covers still fully clothed. Sarge lay down on the floor beside her. He would not jump on the bed unless he was commanded to.

She drew her feet up to her chest. From the crime report that she'd read, she'd made assumptions about David that had been way off. He was obviously extremely conscientious about his work.

Maya wondered how much longer she could keep from him why she was really on the ship. He knew that she had been to both the areas where the crimes had taken place and yet he hadn't pressed her. Probably because he'd seen how shaken up she was after nearly falling off the ship. He already suspected something was off with her cover story, and if she told him the truth it would be nice to have his help. She'd have to clear it with her boss, Lorenza, first.

Turning over on her side, she shuddered as she pulled the covers up to her neck. If the man who had attacked her twice was also the one who'd gone into her room, it meant she had an even bigger target on her back.

David slept fitfully. Partly because his leg hurt and partly because he was concerned about the attacks on Maya. He'd see to it that her old room was dusted for fingerprints. There were probably so many sets in that room that it would be hard to come up with anything conclusive. And maybe the guy had worn gloves. Frustration rose up in him. Chasing down fingerprints felt like a time-consuming rabbit trail.

Anyone who worked for the cruise line went through a thorough background check. That meant that the culprit was either a passenger or crew member with no previous criminal history. What would set someone off to start attacking attractive young women with long dark hair? And now the break-in made it seem like Maya was being targeted in an even creepier way.

He closed his eyes welcoming the fog of sleep as his mind finally started to shut down. His last thought was of Maya in the next room and how she had looked at him with those deep brown eyes.

He had long ago given up the possibility of marriage and kids. His own family had been so messed up by his father's alcoholism and adultery that he feared he would repeat the cycle. Even though he'd become a Christian after the IED had ended his army career, he didn't trust himself to be a good husband. He best served his God by staying single.

He drifted off to sleep with Maya's safety weighing heavily on his mind.

Maya woke up early so she could check in with her supervisor about everything that had happened. After showering and getting dressed, she grabbed her phone and prepared to video chat with her boss.

Though the connection was not great, Colonel Lorenza Gallo's face came on her phone screen. "Maya, glad to see you checking in."

Because the nature of undercover work was so uncertain, they did not have an agreed upon time for Maya to update her commander, only the promise that she would stay in touch and let her know if there were any new developments.

The screen glitched a bit. Maybe a room in the belly of the ship didn't have the best Wi-Fi connection.

Lorenza sat in her office chair at headquarters in Anchorage. In the background, Maya could see Denali, Lorenza's older husky lying in his bed in the corner of the room. Her boss put her face closer to the screen. "How is everything?"

"Things are *not* dull. I've been attacked two times since I boarded, and someone went through my stuff in my room."

Lorenza's eyes grew wide. "Are you okay?"

"Physically I'm fine. Just a bump on the head. Of course, I'm a little shaken emotionally."

The colonel ran her fingers through her short silver hair. "Sounds like we hit a nerve letting you go undercover. Do you think it's the same guy who killed Crystal and attacked the other woman?"

"Yes, I do. The first time he went after me it was with a knife just like with the others. The breaking into my room is no doubt linked to the other attacks. I'm concerned that he suspects I'm law enforcement and he was looking for some kind of ID in my room. Whether he figures out I'm a cop or not, my being here has caused him to escalate so maybe we can draw him out before anyone else gets hurt."

Lorenza's expression softened. "Maya, please be careful."

The maternal tone of the older woman's voice touched Maya deeply. "I will. I know how to protect myself. It helps that Sarge is with me." She reached over to rub her dog's ear.

"I want you back on land so you can give us a hand with everything we have going on."

"Thank you. The hardest thing about this assignment is being separated from the rest of the team. I miss working the investigations together. Have there been any breakthroughs in the other cases we're dealing with?"

When Lorenza glanced off to the side, Maya figured she must be looking at her laptop. "Actually, we might have something hopeful with our missing bride case. Someone called the tip line. A woman matching Violet's description was spotted in downtown Anchorage."

"Really." Maya felt her spirits lift. At least there was some progress with that investigation. Two months ago, a wedding party had been visiting Chugach State Park outside of Anchorage with a tour guide. The bride, Violet James, along with her bridesmaid, best man and groom all disappeared. The tour guide, Cal Brooks, was found shot dead. Maya and Sarge had been part of the K-9 search party that had been sent to track down the bridesmaid, and later, after their team rescued the terrified young woman, the groom and best man were located as well. Violet James was still at large.

According to the groom, Lance Wells, Violet had shot the tour guide because they were having an affair and Cal was about to spill the beans to Lance. Maya had found an engraved watch that belonged to Lance close to where the bridesmaid had been pushed off the cliff, which made her wonder if maybe the groom was not the innocent victim he said he was. Still, they needed more evidence.

"We're following up on the tip and seeing if there was any surveillance footage in the area where Violet was spotted," Lorenza said. "So, I'm hopeful we'll catch her soon."

Maya heard Denali let out a quick bark off screen. The noise caused Sarge to come to attention and whimper. His tail wagged when Maya looked in his direction.

She smiled at her partner. "You heard your buddy talking, didn't you?"

"I think some of the other officers must be on the floor. Denali always lets me know." A door opened off screen. Lorenza looked off to the side and said something Maya couldn't hear to whoever had stepped into the office. She turned back to look at Maya. "Hunter and Juneau are here. You want to say hi to them?"

Maya clutched the phone a little tighter. "I'd like that."

"Hey there." Hunter McCord's face came into view. Though she could not see him, Maya imagined that Hunter's Siberian husky, Juneau, was probably doing a sniff patrol of the office before greeting Denali.

"Good to see you." Her heart surged. She hadn't realized how much she missed the rest of the team.

Hunter offered her a warm smile. "How's the undercover work going?" For some reason, the image of David and his electric blue eyes popped into her head.

"Not as fun as working with you and Juneau." Hunter had been one of the other officers to conduct the search for the missing wedding party. He had since become engaged to the bridesmaid, Ariel Potter after saving her from certain death when she was held at gun point by a fellow dog breeder who regarded Ariel as competition that had to be eliminated.

Though the jury was still out, Ariel was convinced that Violet was innocent. She'd even received a letter from Violet saying as much. However, as a police officer, Maya had to go by what the evidence suggested. An innocent person didn't usually evade the police like Violet James was doing.

"Hopefully, you'll be back with the rest of the team soon," said Hunter. "Take care." His face was no longer on screen.

Lorenza reappeared. "Keep us in the loop, Maya. Check in when you can. I've got to get to a briefing."

"Okay, bye." She pressed the disconnect button on her phone, feeling a heaviness in her chest. The prospect of undercover work had seemed exciting to her at first. But she hadn't counted on the loneliness. Though she longed to be settled down and married, she didn't have anyone waiting in the wings. With the kind of hours she kept for work, dating was a challenge. She visited her parents and siblings who all lived in Wasilla as often as she could and poured the rest of her energy into work. The K-9 team was really like family to her. No wonder she missed them so much.

Her attention was drawn to the knock on her door from David's room.

Maya smiled when she opened the door. He liked her smile. She was fully dressed in jeans and a pink blouse. Her long dark hair had been pulled up on her head in a braid.

"Sleep all right?"

She nodded. "Sarge needs to go up to the doggie play area and do his business."

"I'll go with you."

"I'm sure I'll be fine. There's lots of people around."

His gut twisted. Her words, which almost seemed to push him away, reminded him that he knew she wasn't being forthcoming with him. If she wasn't a cop, she was hiding something else. Maybe she had some sort of personal connection to the attacker. "I'm going in the same direction."

She shrugged. "Okay." They hurried up to the dog exercise area.

Maya let Sarge off his leash to sniff around and do his business as well as introduce himself to the two other dogs that were there. As a rule, the ship allowed therapy dogs only on board, so the play areas were small.

She had brought a toy with her that she tossed. Sarge retrieved it and brought it to her so he could tug on it while she pulled. The dog growled playfully.

"He plays like a puppy," David said.

She smiled in response as Sarge whipped his head back and forth trying to get her to release the toy. "Some people think he's a puppy because of his size, but he's two years old."

"Yeah, his head looks almost too big for his body."

She let go of the toy and straightened, placing her hands on her hips. "Are you dissing my dog?" Her tone was playful.

"No, not at all," he teased back. "He's cute…in a big-head sort of way."

He liked how bright her expression was and the way light flashed in her pretty, dark eyes. The moment of levity between them made his heartbeat faster. "Let me take a picture of you two looking so cute together." He clicked on the camera icon on his phone and raised it up.

"That would be great. Send it to me so I can show how Sarge and I are having fun on vacation." She stood beside her dog.

A second after he took the photo, his attention was drawn to a scraping sound above him. He looked up just in time to see a huge pot falling straight toward Maya. He leaped the distance between them, pushing her out of the way as the ceramic pot and the plant it contained fell on the ground and shattered. The other two dog owners had grabbed their pets and scooted to the edge of the play area. The few people that were walking around or headed to breakfast stopped and stared. Their gaze going from Maya up to the next deck where the plant had been.

Sarge bounced up and down barking around Maya who lay on her stomach. David rolled off her. "You all right?"

She nodded as she pushed herself up. "Nothing is broken. I'm just a little stunned."

He jumped to his feet. When he looked up, no one was standing at the railing looking down. If the plant had been pushed by accident, it seemed like the person would have stuck around to apologize and make sure no one was hurt.

David took off running. Maya and Sarge were right behind him. He climbed the stairs two at a time to the deck above them. The plant had been one of three arranged outside an eatery that was meant to look like a French bistro with tables outside. There was a closed sign on the door of café. They were not open for breakfast, only lunch and dinner. This early in the morning no one was around.

The other two plants were pushed back from the railing. That meant that someone had to have lifted the pot and tilted it over the railing. Sarge was already doing his thing with his nose to ground where the third pot must have been.

They trotted down the boardwalk past shops preparing to open and where the lifeboats were secured to the outside of the ship. The area opened up to where passengers were doing laps in the pool. There were at least twenty people milling around or in the pool.

The scent of chlorine was heady as Sarge slowed his pace. He circled the pool coming back to where he'd started. Then he paced back and forth and lifted his nose.

Maya shook her head. "I think he lost the scent."

"I'm impressed with his skill…you know for just being a therapy dog."

Color rose up on her cheeks. "I'm hungry. Where is a good breakfast place?"

"Maya you've been attacked three times and your place broken into. I don't think it's wise for you to just randomly go out in the open on the ship. I know this is your vacation, but please, let me see if I can arrange for another security officer to escort you around."

Her lips formed a tight line. "For the whole time?"

"Look, it's a big ship, but this guy can't hide forever. I have some things I have to do for my job. Why don't I take you back to your room? I can arrange for breakfast to be brought to your cabin. That gives me time to see what I can set up to ensure your safety."

"If we just had something more to go on besides him having green eyes. It seems like once we are in port in a few days, he'll be able to slip off the ship."

David clenched his jaw. "True." She thought like a cop. Why didn't she just fess up to him? The evasiveness reminded him of past failed relationships. Maybe it was his own messed-up family life, but he'd always seemed to pick women who lied, cheated and withheld information. He hadn't dated since he'd become a Christian and he sure wasn't going to start. If Maya not being forthcoming triggered him that easily, it was only more evidence that he needed to stay unattached. "Let me take you back to your room for now. You okay with that?"

She nodded. They walked beside each other with Sarge pulling ahead as they went back down to the crew quarters.

They stood outside her door. "I'll swing by the crew mess hall to put in a breakfast order for you. They can bring it to your room. Then if you could wait in your room until I come by, that would be great."

Her forehead furrowed in frustration.

"I don't want your whole vacation ruined, Maya, but I don't want you dead either."

She sighed. "I know."

"Give me your number. I'll text you with the name of the person who will bring your food... Don't open the door until he or she says who they are."

After she recited her phone number, he waited until she was safe inside her room and he heard the dead bolt slide into place. After stopping by the crew mess and putting in the order for Maya, he hurried up the stairs to the security office. His morning duties had piled up while he'd stayed close to Maya, but it had been worth it to save her life.

David entered the security office. He made arrangements for another security officer to dust Maya's old room for prints and then he opened up the report that the night security officer had filed. It was the usual incidents. Someone who had too much to drink had become unruly, lost jewelry had been reported and missing toys that had been located.

One incident on the report caught his attention.

Woman, Brenda Littleton, age 25 reported that she thought she was being followed as she headed toward upper deck. Officer checked out her claim but found nothing.

Feeling a lump form in his throat, David called the reporting officer. He knew he would be waking him up, but his gut told him not to wait. The phone rang three times before the other officer, Hans Smith, picked up. "Hello, David. What can I do for you?" Hans's German accent was heavier when he was barely awake. One of the neat things about working on a ship was the international flavor of the crew he worked with.

"Sorry for waking you. I'm just looking over the report you filed for last night. Can you tell me what Brenda Littleton looks like?"

"Is that important?"

David swiveled in his chair. "It might be?"

"Long dark brown hair, pretty, slender," Hans said. "She's not married in case you're interested."

"No, that's not why I asked." A chill ran down David's spine. "Thanks. Try to get some sleep, huh."

He turned off his phone. He stared at the security monitors. Traffic was increasing as guests woke up and looked for things to do. A killer was still out there. Not only was he targeting Maya, but he had to assume that every young woman with long dark hair was still in danger.

FOUR

Maya was getting ready to call her boss to get permission to tell David who she really was when there was a knock on the door. Breakfast had gotten there faster than expected. David had texted her that the server bringing the food would be named Justin.

Maya turned back the dead bolt but kept the door shut. "Who is it?"

"Justin from the crew cafeteria. David Garrison put in a breakfast order for you."

She opened the door. Justin was young, maybe not more than twenty. Her heart beat a little faster when she noted that he had green eyes. Breakfast was laid out on a cart and covered with a silver dome.

"I can take it from here." She had to be careful. The last thing she wanted was to be alone in a room with a man who could be her attacker.

Justin shrugged. She stepped across the threshold and pulled the cart in. The young man stood staring at her just outside the door. The cart functioned as a barrier between them. She was already making plans to push it toward him if he tried to enter the room. Sarge had moved from his resting place on the other side of the bed to where he was visible to Justin.

"Cute dog." The tone of the server's voice indicated that he found Sarge to be the *opposite* of cute.

Sarge did not wag his tail.

"I like having him around," she said. "For protection."

Justin glanced at the dog and then at her. "You all right?" His forehead wrinkled in confusion.

Maybe he'd picked up on her fear. Maya didn't care if she was coming across as unstable—she wasn't taking any chances.

"I'm fine. Guess I'm a little bit hungry." She pulled the cart in farther out of the way of the door and prepared to close it. "Thank you."

Justin was still watching her as she shut the door and slid the dead bolt back into place. She lifted the silver dome. It looked like David had put in a full breakfast order for her: eggs, bacon, blueberry muffin and orange juice.

After portioning out Sarge's dog food for him, she settled in and ate most of her breakfast. Then she grabbed her phone and prepared to get in touch with Lorenza Gallo again.

Lorenza's face came on her phone screen but just like before the connection was not great. "Maya, good to see you again so soon. What's going on?"

"Listen, I've got a dilemma. The security chief for the ship has been sticking close to me because he wants to make sure I'm safe, which will make hiding my cover from him hard. And I'm pretty sure he knows I'm not just another passenger." She released a breath. "I know his internal investigation didn't turn up anything, but it's not because he's a clown. David Garrison is actually quite competent."

"Didn't we decide to keep him out of the loop due to the fact that he may have not been thorough in his investigation because he was covering for himself or some other crew member?"

"David has saved my life several times. The one thing I know about our perp is that he has green eyes. David has blue eyes. All of that is to say, I think he can be trusted and I could use his help. Plus, if he can't protect me he'll get another security officer to do it, which will make investigating and keeping my cover almost impossible. I might as well have David's assistance."

Her commander did not answer right away. She stretched and twisted a rubber band she had in her hand, probably mulling over her options. "I trust your judgment, Maya."

"Thank you."

"You caught me as I was on the way out the door. I've got another meeting to get to."

There hadn't been time to tell Lorenza about the potted plant that had almost landed on her. "Okay, bye." Maya pressed the disconnect button on her phone, relieved that her boss had granted her request. At least now she didn't have to be evasive with David. And keeping him in the loop would help with the feelings of isolation she'd been having since she'd taken on this undercover assignment.

A gentle knock on the door jarred her out of her thoughts. "Who is it?"

"It's David."

She walked over to the door and opened it. Maybe it was just her realization of how disconnected she felt from the people she cared about most, but there was something reassuring about seeing the handsome security chief in his crisp white uniform, his blue eyes filled with warmth.

Could she trust him with why she was really on the ship?

"How was your breakfast?"

"It was very good, thank you." Still, she was debating. A wall of tension seemed to go up between them.

"Look, I've got a full day ahead dealing with passengers' concerns. My junior security officer, Noah Lake, comes on duty soon. He has agreed to be your protection so you and Sarge can get out and enjoy the ship."

She could feel a tightening near her heart. She found herself thinking *but I'd rather be with you*. The notion surprised her as she thought David was a bit walled off emotionally even if he did seem to have a high level of integrity and competence where his job was concerned. She stared into his eyes for a long moment and then stepped back. "David, could you come inside? I have something to tell you."

David stepped into Maya's room. He hoped that she was going to tell him who she really was. He didn't like games or secrets. He saw himself as a straight shooter and expected the same of others.

"Please, have a seat." Maya gestured toward a chair and then sat on the end of the bed. Sarge took up a position at her feet. He cocked his head to one side and watched David as he sat down in a chair.

"What is it?"

She let out a breath and straightened her back. "I'm sure you're wondering why Sarge has skills that seem to go beyond that of an ordinary service dog."

"I wasn't wondering too much. I know you said he used to be a K-9, but I'm not buying it."

"Guess I didn't hide it very well," she said. "I am with the K-9 Unit out of Anchorage. As state troopers, we have jurisdiction over all of Alaska. The murder that happened on board took place close enough to the shore that we can investigate."

"So you're here to probe into the murder of Crystal Lynwood?"

"Yes, and the previous attack on the passenger, because the owner of the ship contacted us. Of course, he wants the perpetrator caught and put in jail, but he is also concerned that if the attacks continue his ship will get a reputation for being unsafe."

"My investigation was thorough." A note of defensiveness snuck into his tone. "The owner communicated to me as well the need to keep everything as low-key as possible." He shook his head. "Maybe the need to work quickly without drawing attention hindered my ability to give the case the depth of attention it needed."

"I know that you did the best you could with the restraints you had to work under." She stepped closer toward him. "And I can see that you want to catch this killer as badly as I do."

Her vote of confidence in him lifted his spirits. "Thanks."

She turned to grab her jacket that was laid out on the bed. "I'm sure your junior security officer would do fine watching over me, but I would prefer to hang close to you so we can work this case together. I understand you have regular duties you need to attend to, David, but maybe we can try to piece together who might be behind these attacks in your down time."

He nodded.

"I've seen the reports you filed related to the attack and the murder. But I need to examine them again. What we're looking for here are patterns. Maybe these attacks have been going on for a while, and they are just now escalating for whatever reason."

"I can give you access to those reports and maybe if I look at them it might jar my memory," David said.

"We also need to look at the staff and crew…maybe narrow it down to who has been here for both attacks."

"There were only minor crew replacements from the time we left Seattle. It could be a passenger too."

"Right now, there is a lot to consider." She blew out a breath. "We need to find a way to narrow it down to a male of average build with green eyes."

"That's not much to go on. Let's get started. You can shadow me in my rounds to answer some of the calls and complaints and we can talk."

Maya tapped a finger against her chin. "People are going to wonder why I'm following you. Let's just say that I am a reporter doing a story about security on a cruise ship." She slipped into her jacket then moved toward the table where Sarge's leash was. The dog was already in his service dog vest.

"All right that sounds like a good cover."

She clicked Sarge into his leash. "I'm going with the theory that my room was ransacked because the attacker was trying to figure out if I was a cop and was looking for some sort of ID. Maybe if he thinks I'm a reporter, he won't see me as such a threat."

"Maybe." David crossed his arms over his chest. "But in terms of appearance, you fit the profile of the other two women. I'm sure that's why you were chosen for the job." It impressed him that she had the level of courage to take on such an assignment, putting herself in harm's way to catch a killer. "One thing we have to keep in mind. If he's not coming after you, he might go after other women. Last night, we had a report of a women who thought someone was following her as she made her way to the upper deck."

"That does seem to be one of his favorite places. I wonder why? Crystal was killed there. And that is where I was first attacked when I went up there to check out the crime scene."

"I don't know…maybe the killer has some personal connection to that part of the ship. It's one of the places that is mostly unused at night," he said. "Too windy and cold even in June."

"Okay. What do we do first? Do you have business to attend to or can we go look at the reports…?" Sarge sat down at her feet and looked up at David.

The two of them were cute together, the big-headed dog and the beautiful dark-haired K-9 officer. "I have a couple of issues to deal with first—a missing purse and a complaint about apparent theft of supplies in one of the eateries."

"Sarge and I are right behind you," Maya said.

They hurried up to the passenger rooms where David interviewed an older woman who said her purse had been stolen while she was ballroom dancing. David took a description of the purse. On their way to deal with the theft at a restaurant, static came across his radio. He pulled it off his belt and pressed the talk button. "Officer Garrison, what is it, Noah?"

"Looks like we got an altercation in the bumper cars. Started out between kids who wanted the same car and escalated to parents, probably alcohol involved. You want me to handle it?"

"I'm close. I'll meet you there. Let's go see if we can settle things down." He turned off his radio and put it back on his belt.

"The fun never ends, huh?"

He liked the way her eyes filled with admiration. "I'm sure it's nothing like the calls you go out on," he said.

"It's all police work, right?"

"Let's go handle this." David took off at a jog. He was aware that the way he favored his injured leg would be more apparent. A wave of self-consciousness swept over him as he made his way through the hallways and corridors of the ship Yet at the same time, he found himself wanting to open up to Maya and tell her all the history that had brought him to living like a nomad on a cruise ship. She seemed like the kind of person who would listen without judgment.

As he rounded the curve, he wondered why he was even entertaining such thoughts.

Maya and Sarge kept pace with David as they came to the open corridor surrounded by shops and then entered the bumper car zone in the sports section of the ship. There was a crowd of people gathered around two men who were facing each other. Though they were not hitting each other, the combative stance—hands curled into fists, chests out—revealed the level of tension between the two men.

Noah Lake, dressed in his security uniform, entered from the other side of the bumper car area.

David turned toward Maya. "Why don't you and Sarge hang back?"

She commanded the dog to sit.

As he approached the two men, the glassiness in both their eyes told him they had been drinking. It seemed a little early to David, but some people thought of the cruise as a nonstop party. Noah closed in from the other side. Though things seemed relatively calm on the surface, he knew from experience that if alcohol was involved, violence could explode at any second.

In an odd way, his childhood served him well in his job. He was always ready for anything.

"Gentlemen, what seems to be the trouble here?"

He noticed then that the shorter man had a bruise on his cheek. Indicating blows might have already been exchanged. The taller man leaned toward the shorter one in a threatening manner. David was like a lion ready to pounce. His heart beat faster as he gave Noah a quick glance.

The taller man never took his eyes off the fellow with the bruised cheek. "This guy tried to take my son's bumper car."

"You liar." The man with the bruised cheek lunged at the other man.

David jumped into the fray and so did Noah as the passengers punched each other. David got between the two men and backed the taller one up while Noah did the same with the other man. "You have a choice here. I won't cuff you if you agree to go peacefully to a detainment area where both of you can cool off and sober up. If you give me any trouble, the cuffs go on."

A woman off to the side with her arm around a boy who looked to be maybe eight or nine spoke to the taller man. "Do what he says, Lee."

The taller man nodded.

"Okay, let's go," David said.

Noah and David escorted the two men away from the bumper cars. They walked past where Maya and Sarge were. Noah looked in Maya's direction. Her face blanched. How odd. Then Noah glanced back at David. It had never registered with David before that Noah had green eyes.

David felt a tightness in his chest. Any of the security officers on the ship would have easy access to card keys that would have allowed them to break into Maya's room. No one was above suspicion at this point.

He didn't like the idea of leaving Maya alone, but he couldn't make Noah escort the two men by himself.

There was too much danger of another altercation, and it would break protocol if he did.

As he glanced over his shoulder to see Maya letting a woman and her daughter pet Sarge, he realized he needed to get back to her as quickly as possible.

FIVE

After Maya let the woman and her daughter pet Sarge, she left the bumper car zone, found some outdoor seating and pulled out her phone. The K-9 sat at her feet on full alert. His ears stood straight up as he watched all the passers-by.

If David was taking those two men someplace where they could sleep it off, he wouldn't be able to answer his phone right away. She sent him a text asking if it would be okay if she came to his office and they looked through the police logs together.

Seeing that the other officer, Noah, had green eyes had sent chills through her. The change in David's expression suggested that it had registered with him too.

Maya put her phone away and looked up. She was in an open area of the ship where she could see the sky and the stacked decks with interior balconies where passengers had a view of the activities on the promenade below. She bolted to her feet. Maybe sitting out in the open like this wasn't such a good idea. It would be too easy to drop something from one of the balconies.

She remembered that there was a running track on the third floor of the ship which was one floor above where David's office was. That track was not exposed to the open area. She returned to her room, put on her tennis shoes and texted David about what she was doing. He still hadn't replied to the first text she'd sent, but she knew she needed to be patient. The man did have a job to do.

The run was relatively safe and would get rid of some of her nerves. Sarge as well needed to be exercised. Her place where she lived in Anchorage was close to a park. She often took her partner there to train and expend his energy. The confinement of the ship was hard on a dog who was used to a lot activity and space to move around.

Maya ran up to the third floor and located the track. She took off at a steady jog, seeing no other runners on the track. Sarge kept up with her as she increased her pace until she was gasping for air. The exertion felt good. She'd gone only about half a mile when her phone dinged. She stopped and pulled her phone out.

I'm in my office. Was waiting for Noah to leave.

On my way, she texted back.

After checking the map on the wall, she took off in the direction of David's office, taking several turns through corridors and then going down to the second floor. This part of the ship was like a labyrinth for someone who wasn't familiar with it. She slowed her pace realizing she was lost. She must have taken a wrong turn. Her heart beat a little faster and she knew it wasn't from the running.

There was no one in this part of the ship. She walked past several doors. The signs indicated that they were used for different kinds of storage.

She pulled her phone out and pressed David's number. It rang once.

A body slammed into hers. The masked man. He must have been following her. She caught the glint of a knife right before her back slammed against a door.

Sarge barked. The man turned slightly, threatening the dog with the knife. Sarge kept barking but backed up. The momentary distraction was enough time for her to lunge at the man, reaching for the hand that held the knife.

The man whirled around focusing his energy back on her.

Maya could see Sarge in her peripheral vision as the dog leaped at the masked man and latched onto a pant leg. The dog continued to growl and tug while Maya tried to extract the knife from the man's hand. First by pinching the nerves in his wrist and then clawing at the fist that held the knife. Her nails drew blood, but the man held on.

Laughter and the sound of many voices floated up the corridor from around the corner. The assailant lifted his head to the noise of people coming toward them. He pulled his hand away and pushed Maya against the wall with intense force. Her back slammed against the hard wall and pain shot through her, momentarily paralyzing her.

She watched in horror as the man yanked his pant leg away from Sarge's grasp and then kicked toward the dog's head. Sarge jumped away before the boot could find its target.

The attacker pushed again just as she straightened up. "You and your dog are in my way."

The man took off running as chatter and laughter from the crowd of people came from the other direction. Maya struggled to get a breath while her assailant's words echoed through her head. Now it was clear that he had figured out she was a cop.

At least ten people, some dressed in uniforms for work, came around the corner just as the man who had attacked her disappeared in the other direction. They were so focused on interacting with each other that they barely noticed Maya. As they walked past her through the narrow hallway, blocking the possibility of her chasing the masked man, she doubted she could catch him. Maybe security cameras would show where he had gone. Sarge had moved to sit at her feet where she was still using the wall for support.

The group of people made their way up the corridor and around the corner, their voices growing fainter.

Finally, she was able to take in air and get a deep breath. Her stomach still felt like it was tied up in knots. Sarge offered a supportive whimper. She reached down and patted his head.

Her phone lay on the carpet where she had dropped

it close to the opposite wall. She stepped across the corridor to pick it up.

David's voice came from far away. "Maya, Sarge where are you?"

Feeling the sense of relief, she ran toward his voice. She looked around for the sign that would indicate which hallway she was in but didn't see one. "David, we're here."

She heard pounding footsteps and then she saw him as he stepped into the hallway. The tall, handsome man in uniform was a welcome sight. A look of intense concern crossed his features.

He hurried toward her. "What happened? The phone rang—I picked up. I heard pounding noises and Sarge barking."

"It was him. The man in mask attacked me." Her legs felt weak. She fell into his arms and he held her.

"I was afraid of that. I knew you were close to the office, so I went looking. Maya, I was worried about you." His voice wavered from the intensity of his emotions.

His arms enveloped her. She felt safe now.

He pulled away but still stood close to her looking from her toes to her face. "Are you hurt? Do we need to get you medical attention?" His voice filled with concern.

"I'm okay physically. Just very shaken up."

"From now on, you need an escort 24/7. That's all there is to it."

She nodded. If even walking to his office was not safe, he was probably right. Still, she didn't like the loss of freedom and knew it would make conducting the investigation that much harder.

"He must have been following me and waiting for his chance. He'd stick out like a sore thumb with that mask on, so he must have put it on at the last second."

David gazed down at the beautiful dark-eyed woman, trying to take in what she was saying. The fear he'd seen on Maya's face when he'd come around the corner had sent a wave of rage through him toward the attacker.

She glanced up. "There's no security cameras? I thought we might be able to catch him on tape before he put his mask on."

"This floor is mostly for staff and crew. The security cameras are mounted in public areas that the passengers use."

Maya nodded. It was clear from her body language, the tightness in her features, that she was still shaken by the attack.

Why was this murderer constantly able to evade him? Wanting to reassure her, he purged the intense emotion from his voice. "My office is just a couple of twists and turns from here. Let's go sit down, maybe get you a hot cup of tea. We'll talk." He turned and started walking.

"A couple of twists and turns?" Her voice wavered.

He slowed down and offered her an arm for support when she struggled to keep pace with him. Sarge walked a foot in front of them.

"I don't know how you find your way around here," she said. "I keep getting confused especially on these two bottom decks."

"You get used to it," he told her. "The lack of windows on the bottom decks sometimes disorients people. The narrow hallways don't help either, but space is at a premium on the ship."

As she followed David, her mind returned to the case. "If we could figure out why he attacks the kind of women he goes after, that might help us narrow down the possibilities."

"Do you have any theories?"

He turned down another hallway, which brought them outside the security office. David swiped his card key over the locked door and pushed it open, stepping to the side so she could go in first.

She and Sarge walked in. Maya looked at the monitors. "Do you have a view of the entire ship?"

"Cameras are only set up in the public areas. I only have eight monitors—one for each of the decks where the passengers are. I can switch between cameras to show the different areas on each deck." He moved past her and placed his hands on the keyboard to show her how quickly he could click through the different parts of the ship. Then he pulled a chair out for her. Though the color had returned to her face, something about Maya seemed changed from this last attack. The threat was very personal.

He placed a hand on her shoulder. "It's okay to say you're afraid."

She massaged her temples. "I'm a police officer. I should be able to handle this."

"Everyone has a breaking point, Maya. I know I reached mine when I was in the army. How about I get you that hot cup of tea and you can take a moment to collect yourself?"

"Okay." She sat down and nodded, still watching the monitors.

He strode across the room to where there was a two-burner coffee maker. One carafe held coffee that was mostly bitter by this time of day and the other kept water hot. He grabbed a tea bag from the assortment and placed it in a coffee cup.

"You said you were in the military?"

The question made his stomach clench. But he was the one who had brought it up. Though it made him afraid, he wanted to open up to her. Maya had a tenderness that he had never experienced before. He poured the hot water into the cup watching it turn brown.

"I thought I was going to be a career officer." He turned and carried the steaming mug toward her. He placed it on the counter beside the keyboard. Sarge lay at Maya's feet, resting his chin on the toe of her shoe.

She lifted the mug and blew on it but didn't take a sip. "What happened?"

"An IED happened."

"Your leg? I noticed you favor it sometimes." She gazed at him before putting the mug down. "You really can't tell unless you're running."

Her voice held such a tone of compassion and non-judgment that the tightness in his stomach disappeared. "Thank you for saying that. I worked hard with the physical therapist to get back as much mobility as I could. I guess I have a memory of what I used to be capable of physically."

"Loss is never easy. I'm sure it was hard to reroute your career path."

The way she looked at him made his heart beat faster and that scared him. He jerked to his feet and turned away. "I don't mind it." He shrugged. "I like not being settled anywhere. The scenery and the passengers changing every ten to twenty-one days—it suits me."

"My job has some travel involved but I'm kind of a homebody." She let out a sigh. "I just had my thirtieth birthday. I thought I'd be married and with kids by now. That was always my dream."

Was she hinting at something? Though his feet remained planted, David felt like he was running a hundred miles an hour and the cavalcade of relationships that had turned sour played out in his mind. "Not me. I like being an unattached nomad."

Her expression changed as she drew her eyebrows together and leaned back. "Oh, I see. We all make different choices...have different dreams."

"Look, why don't we look through those reports? I can tell you off the top of my head nothing comes to mind that resembles these attacks and the murder."

"I just thought if there was something on a previous cruise, we could eliminate the passengers as suspects. You said crew personnel stays the same, right?"

"For the most part. Everyone has a contract, most of which run a year. People go on vacation or get sick, some people quit and we have to replace them," he said. "But I would say the core group of people stays the same."

"We're dealing with such a huge group of suspects.

There has to be a way to narrow our focus," Maya re-iterated.

"If we're assuming the attacks only started when we left Seattle. That means both passengers and crew members could be suspects." David shifted in his chair. Green eyes aren't that common, but I still think we're talking about hundreds of suspects."

"The upper deck where I was attacked that first night was a public area. Did the security footage show anything?"

He shook his head. "Nothing. And very little on the night Crystal was killed either."

"Almost like he is aware of where the cameras are."

Feeling a rising frustration, David shook his head. "All passengers and crew members have to have a photo ID, but I don't have software that would sort IDs for green eyes. We'd have to do that by hand. My onboard resources are kind of limited… Sorry."

"That's okay. We'll just have to do good old-fashioned detective work, right?"

He appreciated her optimism since he tended to be a glass half-empty guy.

"Right." David scooted his chair toward a computer. "I can look and see if there were any new hires for this cruise." He clicked the keyboard and looked at the screen. "We had one woman, a waitress named Tiffany Swarthout, who quit right before we sailed. There was not time to find a replacement."

"Okay, so that was a dead end."

Noah's voice rose above the static of the radio. It

sounded like he was running. "Purse snatcher fourth floor. Headed toward the third. Let's cut him off."

"On my way," David said. He bolted to his feet.

Maya got up as well, picking up Sarge's leash.

"Where do you think you are going?"

"With you. We agreed I shouldn't be alone, right? Sarge might be a help."

There was no time to argue the finer points of her staying in the locked office. So with Maya and Sarge beside him, David hurried through the corridors of the ship until he came to the elevator that would take them to deck three. They stepped into the elevator.

Maya stood close enough that her shoulder was almost touching his as they watched the numbers light up. Something about her being with him, working beside him, created a sense of peace he hadn't felt in a long time.

Even though he knew that she was a trained officer who could take care of herself, he felt protective of her. He only hoped he'd made the right choice in letting her come with him.

SIX

Before the number three lit up, Maya stepped toward the closed doors of the elevator. Her heart raced. This was what she loved about police work. The doors slid open, and she, David and Sarge all stepped out in unison.

"There are two or three ways he could go once he gets down here. How will we find him?"

"We block the most likely exit to the second floor. Noah will watch so he can't go back up. He's probably trying to blend in at this point. Which means he may have taken the money out of the purse and ditched it." David got back on his radio while he walked. "Do you have a description of our perp?"

"Yellow shirt. Red shorts. Young and athletic."

A man matching that description would be easy to spot. "Is there a chance he could slip into a cabin? Maybe Sarge and I could search," Maya said.

"No, the deal is you stay close to me." He softened his voice. "I don't want to risk you being attacked again. Plus, searching the cabins is a little more involved legally unless someone is in immediate danger."

His protectiveness touched her.

David came to the stairwell exit that led back down to the second floor.

"He could take the elevator down as well, right?"

"Sure," David replied. "The thing about a ship is he can't go far and his crime was probably caught on the security cameras. It would just be nice to wrap this up and get the purse back to its owner, but we'll catch the guy before we get to the next port."

He got back on the radio. "We're at the north stairwell."

"Far as I can tell he is headed your way based on where I last saw him," Noah said. "He's slowed down and he doesn't know I'm tailing him. I'm hanging back so I don't arouse suspicion."

David signed off and looked at her. "We'll wait inside the stairwell. He'll turn and run if he sees us."

They took up a position on opposite walls where they could peer out the window on the door that led to the stairwell. Maya studied the area. There was one hallway the perp could veer off into if he realized he was trapped.

A man matching the description of the purse snatcher came around the corner. David stepped out and identified himself. "Security. Put your hands up where I can see them."

Her heart beat faster as she and Sarge stepped out as well.

As she had predicted, the purse snatcher veered off toward the side corridor. She and Sarge chased after him, blocking his escape. Sarge barked only once, but the tone of threat was clear.

"You might want to put your hands up like the security officer suggested," she said.

The purse snatcher complied.

"Hands behind your back." David pulled out the zip ties that sufficed for handcuffs. "What did you do with the purse?"

"I ditched it in the trash."

"And the money?"

"Wallet in my left pocket. Am I going to jail?"

David drew out the wallet. "Theft is still theft even on a cruise ship. You'll wear an ankle bracelet and be confined to your cabin until we reach the next port where you will be taken into custody."

Noah came around the corner and headed up the hallway. "Caught him?"

"Yes," David said. "Thanks to Maya and her dog."

"Why is she hanging so close to you?"

"I'm a journalist doing a story on security on board a ship." It was the first time she'd had to vocalize the deception.

Noah stared at Maya long enough to make her uncomfortable. "You and your service dog make quite a team." His smile didn't quite reach his eyes. "The dog is pretty protective of you… I noticed earlier when I saw you."

What an odd thing to say at a moment like this. Despite the elation and excitement of catching the purse snatcher, she was reminded that a killer was still at large on the ship and she might be looking at him right now.

Her pulse sped up as Noah continued to study her.

Maybe he just wasn't buying that she was a journalist or maybe there was something more sinister going on.

She turned toward David. "Do you need to take this guy somewhere?" she asked, purging her voice of the fear that had encroached on her. Right now, no one with green eyes was above suspicion of being a killer.

David glanced over at Noah after noticing how Maya's expression had changed when he looked at her. Just because he worked with Noah didn't mean they could take him off the suspect list.

"I can take this guy in for processing if you want," Noah offered.

"That would be great." David handed the perp over to the other officer who escorted him down the stairwell.

"I'm too wound up to head back to the security office. We can go grab a bite to eat if you'd like." Maybe it was just the adrenaline from having caught the purse snatcher, but he found himself not wanting to end his time with Maya.

"Are you still on duty?"

"Actually, I was off hours ago," he answered. "Noah still has half a shift to finish and the night guy will be coming on in a couple of hours."

"I could use an early dinner since we haven't had lunch, but maybe we could order in," Maya said. "That way Sarge can eat too."

It would be safer for Maya not to be out in the open. "I like that idea."

They hurried through the corridors of the ship. David

stood outside Maya's door while she slid the card key across the reader.

"Let me have a look around before I leave you here alone to go change out of my uniform."

She stepped aside to let him go in first.

"If there is any kind of new smell in here, Sarge will alert to it." She kneeled and released the Malinois from his leash.

Sarge took off with his nose to the carpet while David checked the tiny bathroom, pulling back the shower curtain, and then he returned to the main room and checked under the bed while Maya opened the closet door. The dog sat back on his hindquarters and looked to Maya for further instructions.

"Just give me a minute to get changed," David murmured. "You can call into the staff kitchen and order something. I'm partial to the chicken parmesan." When she smiled at that last part, he added, "I'll give you the number code for staff to order. There should be a print menu for the staff kitchen in one of your drawers. Ask who the name of your server will be."

"Got it." After David gave her the five-digit number code for ordering, Maya headed across the room.

He had his hand on the doorknob that connected their two rooms. "Maya, remember to dead bolt the door until the delivery guy comes. And ask ahead of time what his or her name is when you order. Get verification that is the person at the door before you open it." He didn't like leaving her even for a moment. Hopefully, he would get changed before dinner even came.

"Will do. Those security measures make total sense." Maya moved across the room and dead bolted it.

David returned to his own room. His time in the military had taught him to live a minimalist lifestyle, which meant his cabin was tidy and uncluttered. He'd noticed that Maya tended to fling her suitcase open and leave clothes and clutter around. As he slipped out of his uniform and changed into something more casual, he wondered why he was even taking note of their different habits and tolerance for clutter. He hung the uniform outside the door so it would be picked up for cleaning and returned.

Then he knocked on the door that separated his and Maya's cabin.

"Come in. Food's on its way."

He opened the door. She had changed into an oversized orange sweater and jeans and she'd unbraided her long dark hair. It was the first time he'd seen her with her hair down. His heart fluttered at the sight of her. The faint smile she offered him only added to her beauty. Sarge lay at the foot of the bed. Maya had taken his service dog vest off. Though the dog was in a resting pose, his lifted head and straight ears suggested that he intended to be "on the job."

"When the food comes, my cabin is a little bigger and there is a dining area. Maybe we could eat over there."

"Sure, that sounds good."

"These cabins are below the waterline of the ship so I'm sorry we don't have a viewing deck or anything. Not exactly the same experience as the passengers."

"I don't mind. Dinner with you would be nice no matter what."

The comment caused him to flush.

A second later, there was a knock at the door. And a female voice announced, "Room service from the staff kitchen."

"Her name is Angie. You can get the meal if you want to. I'll stay out of the way."

Maya stepped out of view of the door.

David strode toward the door and flipped the dead bolt back. "Thanks, Angie. Much appreciated." He pulled the room service cart inside and then dead bolted the door again. "What did your order?"

"You said the chicken parmesan was good, so I got that too."

Maya held the door open for him while David pushed the cart into his suite. Together they placed everything on the little table and sat down. She called Sarge to come lie at her feet, and after saying grace, they dug into the meal.

David cut his chicken and took a bite, relishing the Italian spices and moistness of the meat. "Our staff chef does this so perfectly every time. Although it does taste a little different. I wonder if he changed the recipe."

Maya took a bite as well. "It's yummy."

They shared small talk about different calls they had been on in their jobs, laughing and enjoying each other's company. Maya was a hearty eater who seemed to enjoy the meal as much as he did.

Midway through their meal, his stomach started to

twist. He had the sensation of heat rising up his face. When he looked over at Maya, her face was red too.

"I think something in the food was off."

He ran for the bathroom. He heard Maya's footsteps and she hurried to her own bathroom.

As he flushed the toilet, a dreadful thought entered his mind. They'd been poisoned. Because they both had ordered the same thing, both meals had been tampered with. Still feeling nauseated and weak, he crawled out into the main room and reached for his phone to call the ship doctor.

Through the open door that connected their rooms, he could hear Maya being sick and Sarge pacing and whimpering.

He dialed the number and spoke to the ship's nurse even while his stomach threatened another eruption. "This is security officer Garrison. I'm in my cabin. I think I and a passenger have been poisoned. I need to arrange for transport. There is no way we can make it on our own."

The nurse promised a speedy response.

He clicked off the phone and lay on the floor on his stomach. Sweat broke out on his forehead. He prayed that they were not too late in getting the poison flushed out of their systems.

SEVEN

Feeling weak and nauseated, Maya awoke in a dark room. The last few hours had been a blur. Medical personnel had come for her and David. They'd been transported on stretchers. At some point, she must have lost consciousness or been given something.

Gradually, her eyes adjusted to the dark. There were curtains on either side of her hospital bed, and she was hooked up to an IV. The doctor must have flushed the poison out of her system by pumping her stomach.

A sense of panic made her more alert. What had happened to Sarge? Had David survived the poisoning? She tried to sit up, but the room spun around her, forcing her to slump back down. Her head sank even deeper into the pillow.

She padded the area around her on the bed. There must be a call button somewhere. She couldn't find it, and she didn't have the strength to roll on her side to see if it was on the tray beside her bed.

Footsteps tapped toward her.

"Nurse? Doctor?" Her voice was hoarse and faint. Her throat was raw from throwing up.

The footsteps grew louder coming toward her. A shadow appeared on the other side of the curtain.

"Nurse? I could use some help." She rested her hands on her stomach which wasn't churning anymore but still hurt.

Whoever was outside her curtain didn't respond. Instead he or she walked almost a full circle around her. They got to the place where the two curtains came together creating an opening.

"Hello?"

He or she continued to stand just outside the opening. Maya's heartbeat revved up a notch. She had a feeling whoever was on the other side of the curtain was not medical personnel. Having found out that she'd survived the poisoning, the attacker had come to finish the job.

She summoned all her strength to cry out. "Nurse? Somebody?" Her voice sounded weak. She wondered if anyone would even hear her.

A light came on at the far end of the room. The silhouette of the man outside her curtain retreated. But the footsteps were not rapid, almost as if the attacker were trying to appear casual as he made his escape.

Again, she heard tapping footsteps coming from the opposite direction that the attacker had gone.

A man pulled back her curtain a few inches and poked his head in. "Everything all right here?"

"I…" Talking still took substantial effort. She lifted her hand and pointed in the direction the assailant had gone. "Did you see a man leaving…that way?"

The man shook his head. "I was focused on you. I thought I heard you cry out."

She nodded.

"Is everything okay?" he asked. "I'm the night duty nurse. My name is John."

She nodded. "David Garrison? Is he okay?" She braced for bad news.

"He's three beds over and still unconscious from the sedation. Both of you had a rough go at it. But I think we got you flushed out fast enough."

She relaxed. David had made it.

"We took samples, but we won't know what it was until we can get it to a lab. At first we thought food poisoning, but no one else who ate the chicken parmesan got sick."

Her mind still felt foggy. She'd known right away that it was poison. That meant between the time the food had been prepared and then brought to her door someone had tampered with it. It was unlikely that a passenger would have had access to the crew kitchen. And how would they have known that she and David had put in an order? That meant that the attacker was a member of staff or crew. As her thinking became clearer, she felt a fresh wave of panic. "My dog?"

John shook his head. "I'm sorry I don't know anything about a dog."

She placed her hand on her chest. "There was a service dog, Sarge." The K-9 was well-trained enough that he would have remained in the room until he was commanded to do otherwise. Her fear was that the attacker had taken the opportunity to harm Sarge since he saw the dog as an obstacle to taking her out of the picture.

The nurse stepped toward her. "I can ask around

about the dog. Now why don't you let me take your vitals and then you can get some sleep?"

"I won't be able to sleep until I know that Sarge is okay. How long have I been out of it?"

"It's past nine p.m." John lifted her hand and put a device on her finger to measure her pulse. After he finished checking her blood pressure and her stomach sounds, he turned to go, promising to ask around about her dog.

Maya managed to get herself into a sitting position. She stared at the ceiling and tried to not let her mind wander to all the bad things that could have happened to Sarge. "David? Are you awake?"

"Hey," David's voice sounded weak and far away. All the same, it was a welcome sound. "I just now woke up. Still feel groggy from the sedative."

"Why don't you ask the nurse to open the curtains between us? Maybe they can scoot your bed closer."

"Okay. Just give me a minute. It takes all my brain and muscle power to push the call button and talk."

She let out a breath that sufficed for laughter. "I know the feeling."

While she waited in the near darkness, she prayed for Sarge's safety. The bond to her partner was just as strong as if Sarge had been human. The thought of anything happening to him filled her with despair.

It was hard enough to be away from the rest of the K-9 unit. To not know if Sarge was okay was heartbreaking.

She heard the patter of footsteps and the sound of

David's voice though he spoke in such a low voice she couldn't understand his words.

A few minutes later a different nurse, an older woman, and John were pulling curtains out of the way. Seeing David two beds over lifted her spirits. He offered her a wave and a faint smile.

Together the two nurses worked to get the empty bed out of the way and push David's hospital bed closer to Maya. They turned on the lights over her bed.

"Don't visit too long," John said. "Both of you need your rest. Your bodies have been severely traumatized."

"Any news on Sarge?"

"The dog was not in the room. We're still trying to track down what happened to him."

Her fear came back tenfold. Sarge would not have left the room on his own.

Once the two nurses were gone, Maya shared her theory that it was a crew member not a passenger who was behind the attacks.

David nodded. "I think you're probably right. If a passenger had been down in the crew area someone would have directed them to leave."

"How are the room service meals set up and delivered?"

"There is a board with room numbers up for delivery on it," he told her. "Anyone in the kitchen would have seen that. I think the food has a room number place card with it when it's placed on a cart for delivery. Might even be sitting on the cart for a while."

"So plenty of chances to sprinkle something toxic."

"We need to talk to the woman who delivered it,"

David said. "She's not a suspect, but maybe she saw something."

Maya adjusted her pillow behind her back. She could feel herself getting weaker from the exertion of sitting up. "The problem is the culprit would have totally blended in. Is it only the cooks and servers who go into the kitchen area?"

"All the staff and crew have access to that kitchen. Some like to cook their own meals because of dietary restriction or preferences. It could have been a crime of opportunity. The culprit was down there, saw that we had ordered a meal and grabbed whatever poison was available."

"It has to have been something that didn't alter the flavor of the food much. Nothing tasted off to me," she said.

"You hadn't had that dish before. It did taste different to me."

David's skin was pale, and his eyes didn't seem to have much life in them. "Are you feeling as tired as I am?"

He nodded. "I heard you talking about Sarge. I'll wait with you until we get some news."

She smiled despite herself. His desire to be supportive of her despite his weakened state touched her deeply. They continued to talk about the case as both their voices faded and the response time grew longer. Despite her concern for Sarge's welfare, the heaviness of sleep took over and she nodded off. Hours later she awoke in the darkness. David snored faintly.

Where was Sarge? Where was her partner?

* * *

The sound of voices at the far end of the room forced David to climb out of his deep slumber. In the dim light, he could just make out Maya in her hospital bed. The IV allowed her to sleep only on her back. Her hands rested on top of each other over her heart.

Footsteps came toward them.

Maya stirred awake lifting her head. "Who is it?" Fear permeated her voice.

"Not sure." Maybe her fear made sense. They were both in no condition to fend off any kind of an attack. He wouldn't put it past the assailant to take advantage of their weakened state and the lack of security around them.

He tuned his ears to the sounds around him. At least two sets of footsteps were coming toward them. Maybe that was a good sign.

A curtain was pulled back. John, the male nurse, stuck his head in. "Maya, I have a surprise for you."

She struggled to push herself into a sitting position. The curtain was pulled back even more revealing Noah and Sarge. The dog wagged his tail and whined.

Maya let out a cry of joy.

"It's against regulations to let a dog in here, but I thought we could let it slide for just a minute," John said.

Maya looked at Noah. "What happened? How did Sarge end up with you?"

The dog wouldn't stop wagging his tail and whining but he remained beside Noah.

"Just as I was getting off shift, I saw the call on the board that was from David's room number. You guys had already been transported. I went to the room and found your dog just sitting there waiting. When I called in to the infirmary, they said they would let me know when you two were out of the woods and awake."

"Someone else must have taken the call," John mused.

"Anyway, Sarge has been good company," Noah said. "He mostly slept at the foot my bed while I tried to get some shut-eye. Would have been here sooner, but I only woke up a bit ago."

Maya directed her question to the nurse. "Can he come over and say hello to me?"

"Sure," John replied.

Maya commanded Sarge to come over to the side of her bed that was opposite of where the IV was. The dog stood up and put his paws up on the bed and Maya leaned forward so she could get some doggie kisses. "I missed you."

David felt a sense of joy at witnessing the reunion between the two partners.

John excused himself, saying he had another patient he needed to deal with.

Maya commanded Sarge to get down. The dog returned to Noah.

The officer leaned over and grasped the leash. "I'll watch him until you two are released."

"Hopefully, that will be in a few hours. We really can't afford to stay here much longer." The one thing that was clear to David was that Noah could be taken off the suspect list. He had had an opportunity to take Sarge out of the picture and instead had made sure the dog was taken care of.

David signaled for Noah to come closer. He spoke in a low tone. "I need you to go back on duty. See if you can track down the woman who delivered our meal. Her name's Angie."

"I know Angie."

"Then if you can talk to the kitchen staff that was on duty when our meal was prepared, see if anyone saw anything unusual, if there's anything poisonous that is missing and if anyone acts suspicious when you question them. I'm not sure what would be in a kitchen that could poison someone so quickly. Cleaning products maybe."

"Got it. You two take care of yourselves." He left with the dog in tow.

Maya let out a heavy breath. "I wish Sarge could stay here with me."

"Why don't we both get a few hours' rest and then get out of here and see if we can track down our poisoner."

"I agree. We can't waste any more time. The killer is out there, and I have a feeling he is going to escalate as we get closer to catching him."

EIGHT

After getting a few hours' rest in the infirmary, Maya and David were released. They agreed that trying to work through the night with most everything shut down would be pointless though both of them were anxious to track down the poisoner.

They returned to their respective rooms to get more sleep so they could start the morning stronger and feeling more like themselves. Her stomach and throat still felt raw. She was going to have to eat very bland food for a while. At her request, Noah brought Sarge back to Maya's room.

Once the security officer identified himself, she opened the door. Feeling a rush of affection, she gathered Sarge in her arms. "There's my good buddy." She leaned back and stroked his soft head. "I missed you." Sarge wagged his tail and leaned into her petting.

"He's a good guy," Noah said.

She stood up and held a hand out to him. "Thank you for taking care of Sarge."

"No problem."

At least Noah was the one green-eyed crew member they could cross off the suspect list. "Were you able to track down the woman who delivered our food?"

"Yes. Angie said she didn't see anything out of the ordinary. I questioned the rest of the crew who were on shift at the time your meal was being prepared, and all of them gave the same report."

"So a dead end." Still, it helped to know that they weren't looking at passengers as suspects at this point.

She said good-night to Noah and closed the door making sure it was locked and dead bolted. Maya crawled into bed and invited Sarge up as well. Normally, the dog slept on the floor, but she'd missed him and the scare over harm coming to her partner made her want to be close to him.

Sarge snuggled in at the foot of the bed.

After taking the sleeping pill the infirmary had given her, Maya stared at the ceiling. Her mind raced with all that had happened. She'd have to at least text Lorenza about the poisoning and being able to narrow the suspect down to crew members. She wondered how things were going with the other cases the unit was dealing with. It wasn't just the missing bride/wedding party murder investigation that was on the docket. There were two other much more personal cases. Eli Partridge the tech guru who helped the unit out was desperately trying to find his godmother's survivalist family before it was too late. His godmother had cancer and her only wish was to see her son and his family.

Maya rolled over on her side hoping the sleeping pill would kick in soon.

The other investigation that was very personal for the whole unit concerned Lorenza's assistant Katie whose aunt ran the family reindeer ranch, which had experienced the theft of some of their stock as well as someone opening a pen and letting reindeer out.

Hopefully, she would be back on shore and ready to help out soon enough. She closed her eyes, as her muscles grew heavy and she fell asleep.

She slept through the night until she heard David's soft tapping on the door between their rooms.

"You up?"

"I'm awake but not ready."

"Look, I've got a security situation that requires my attention. Once you're ready, call me or get Hans to escort you. Text me and I'll let you know where I'm at on the ship."

"Okay." Though she felt groggy from the sleeping pill, she sat up. David still seemed to keep military hours. He must not have taken the sleeping aid.

Maya got up, showered and dressed. When she texted David, he said he would meet her in ten minutes at her door. She read her Bible and waited.

Ten minutes later, a text popped up on her phone.

I'm here.

She hurried toward the door, slid back the dead bolt and prepared to turn the knob. But then a thought occurred to her. How hard would it be for the attacker to steal David's phone or somehow make it look like the text had come from his phone?

She rested her palm against the door. "David, I need to hear your voice."

"Maya, it's me." Even with the barrier of the door between them, his voice sounded strong. His voice possessed a warmth that made her feel inexplicably drawn to him.

She opened the door. David smiled, making his blue eyes light up. Maybe she was reading into things, but something about him seemed different. With all they had been through together, she was starting to feel a deep bond toward him. She couldn't quite sort her feelings out. Especially since David had walls around his heart no one could climb over or break down, and he'd made it clear that he was a confirmed bachelor.

"I'm not sure where to start today with figuring out who is behind this," he admitted.

"I assume all staff and crew have photo IDs, right?"

"Yes, the IDs allow different crew members access to different parts of the ship. Just like a driver's license it lists eye color and all of them would be on file." David confirmed. As the two of them discussed their next move, they walked side by side through the corridor. "Green is not the most common eye color, but we are talking a lot of guys to call in for questioning. We'd have to sort through the IDs by hand, though, because I don't have software that would do that."

As they stood by the elevator waiting for it to arrive, his blue eyes locked on hers. Her breath caught in her throat. What was going on here?

The doors opened, and they stepped inside. "I suppose we could head to the security office and at least get an estimate of how many suspects we'd be looking at."

Maya was trying to concentrate on the case, but she couldn't let go of why her heart was fluttering every time David looked at her. Sarge, who had taken up a position between them, seemed to pick up on her change in mood. The dog shifted his weight and then lifted his chin and made a noise that was between a moan and a growl.

David gazed down at Sarge and the elevator rose up another floor. "What's up with him?"

"He's just asking me a question."

"About what?"

Her cheeks felt suddenly flushed. She stared at the wall. "David, do you suppose you'd ever consider having a home that wasn't moving?"

"This job suits me. I don't like the idea of being settled anywhere." The doors slid open. "Why do you ask?" He stood aside so she could leave first.

She noted the probing intensity in his expression when she looked at him. "Just trying to get to know you better. Even with all that has happened, working this case with you has been good." She stepped out with Sarge heeling beside her. Well, that was that. The little spark she felt began to wane. They were two very different people with incompatible ideas about what a good life looked like.

David moved to walk beside her. "You don't think you'd ever like living on a ship?"

With his question, her feelings swung back toward attraction. "The ship has been fun…in the short term even with the investigation putting me in peril. I'm kind of a homebody though. Besides, Sarge needs a place to run and train." His question made her wonder if maybe he was having some of the same feelings as she was. Hard to tell with this man, though.

David's radio made a crackling noise. He pulled it off his belt and pressed the talk button. "Yes."

"Missing child from the play area. Mom just called it in two minutes ago. Female three years old. Wearing yellow pants and a matching top."

The voice was not Noah's. It must be a different security officer.

"On it." David broke into a run.

She and Sarge kept pace with him as they hurried to the deck where the play area was. Once they arrived there, it wasn't hard to spot who the mom of the missing child was. The stricken expression on her face told Maya this was the woman.

There were people milling around the play equipment looking in nooks and crannies. A blond man in a security uniform hurried toward them.

"Hans what can you tell me?" David asked.

"We've locked down this deck, so no one can leave. The play area has been searched pretty thoroughly. I think the kid wandered off…or…"

Hans didn't say what everyone feared. That the child had been abducted. Maya assumed if that became the presumed theory, hiding the little girl would be hard given that they could probably lock the whole ship down and room-to-room searches would have to be conducted. She hoped it didn't come to that. Then another thought occurred to her, an even worse scenario but one that was more likely on a ship. What if the little girl had fallen overboard?

David scanned the play area and the shops beyond. "Obviously, we need to widen the search."

"Some volunteers have already started to spread out," Hans told him. "We've got an alert sent out. Any shop owners or passengers who see her will let us know right away."

"Lot of area to cover," David said. "Let's go." He took off at a jog, then looked back over his shoulder at her.

Maya waved indicating he should keep going. She'd be safe, Sarge was with her and there were plenty of people around.

She looked toward the mom who was clutching a stuffed animal to her chest. Maybe her K-9 partner could help out. Sarge was not a trained tracking dog but if he could follow the scent of a weapon, he might be able to pick up on that of a little girl.

Maya ran over to the mom. "Is that your daughter's?"

The woman didn't answer, but the teenage girl standing beside her did. "Yes, it belongs to my little sister Bess. We found it over there." The teen pointed toward a slide.

"If we could borrow the toy, my dog might be able to pick up the trail of where your sister went."

The teen nodded and lifted the stuffed animal out of the dazed mother's hands.

"Find my little girl. Find my baby."

"We'll do our best." Maya hoped her words communicated some degree of reassurance. She bent down and waved the toy in front of Sarge's nose. The dog's ear perked up, but then he sat back down on his haunches. Fighting off the disappointment, Maya kneeled so she was at Sarge's level. She wasn't going to give up that easily. Again, she lifted the toy to Sarge's nose. "Come on, buddy. Do this for me." She gave him the same command she used when he was tracking the scent of a weapon. "Find."

Sarge stood up. He wagged his tail as if asking her a question. She nodded and stroked his head. "You can do this."

Sarge stepped side to side and then put his nose to the ground. He took off toward the playground equipment ending up at the slide where the toy had been dropped and the little girl had last been seen. Sarge had the scent of the missing girl.

The dog yanked on the leash as he left the play area. Maya sprinted to keep up with him. The scent was probably fresh enough that it was still strong and distinctive. Sarge veered away from the main thoroughfare of shops and eateries down a side corridor, behind the establishments, where the employees entered and probably received deliveries to restock inventory when the ship was in port.

The dog doubled back and shot down a side corridor running even faster. Then he stopped and alerted beside a door. The sign indicated that this was the back entrance to a French bistro.

Maya glanced up and down the corridor not sure why Sarge had stopped. Praying he hadn't lost the scent, she was about to open the door to the back side of the café when she heard an odd squeaking sound. Sarge let out a single yipping bark.

He tugged on the leash. Straining toward the noise, they turned down yet another hallway. Up ahead a woman pushed a cart stacked with fresh folded table linens. The bottom of the cart was concealed by a fabric skirt.

Sarge jerked on the leash and yipped again.

The woman pushing the cart craned her head to look back at them.

"Could you wait up for just a second!" Maya jogged toward the linen cart while Sarge heeled beside her.

The Malinois shifted his weight side to side.

"Your dog seems upset," the woman said.

"Just excited," Maya explained. She lifted the fabric skirt and let out a huge sigh of relief. It was Bess. The little girl, all dressed in yellow, was asleep on the folded linens. Curly brown hair surrounded a round pink-cheeked face, and the child sucked on two fingers while she slept. Maya straightened up and spoke in a whisper. "You've been hauling a sleeping toddler around."

"What?"

"You must have had the linen cart close to the playground at some point."

"Yes, I parked it there while I went in to talk to a friend who runs one of the nearby shops." The woman looked a little guilty.

"No harm done. She must have crawled on when no one was looking." Maya lifted her head, searching for a sign or direction arrows that might tell her where she was. "If you could just tell me what this part of the ship is called."

"This is the east corridor hallway deck four."

Maya pulled out her phone and texted David.

Toddler has been found. Bring her mom. She texted the location.

Bess made a moaning sound and started to stir. Maya feared if the little girl woke up and saw only strangers she might be scared. All her concerns were allayed when she heard a sweet voice say, "Doggie."

Leave it to Sarge to break the ice. He wagged his tail but looked to Maya for permission to move. Bess poked her head out. When she looked at Maya her forehead crinkled. Her gaze wandered to the hallway and the feet of the woman who had pushed the cart.

"Bess, your mom will be here in just a minute. May I help you get out of there?"

The toddler nodded.

Maya reached in and pulled Bess out, setting her on her feet. The little girl took her fingers out of her mouth and pointed again at Sarge.

"You can pet him."

Bess giggled as she stroked Sarge's head. The dog leaned into the child's touch clearly enjoying the attention.

Footsteps muffled by carpet rushed up the corridor. Bess's mother ran toward them and swept the toddler up into her arms. She was laughing and crying at the same time as she held her child close.

David had been right behind the mom. Bess's sister followed, rushing toward mother and child.

"You scared all of us kiddo," the sister said.

After thanking Maya several times, the family headed down the hallway. The mom held Bess and Bess's sister patted her sibling's curly head as they disappeared around the corner.

"I'm glad everything turned out okay. Happy endings are always the best," murmured the woman pushing the linen cart. "I have to get back to work."

David's expression's glowed with affection as he looked toward Maya. "Good job."

"It was mostly Sarge's nose and instinct. He's always had a connection with kids." Again, when he looked at her, she felt that heart flutter.

"Maybe someday, you'll be married and Sarge will have some kids to watch over."

"I wouldn't count on it," she said. "Dating and being a K-9 officer don't seem terribly compatible."

"You never know."

She wondered why he was bringing up kids and marriage. As they stood there alone in the hallway and she felt the jolt of attraction between them, she had to remind herself not to read into the conversation. David had told her flat out that he was not interested in any kind of settled life.

"Are you hungry?" he asked.

"Starving."

"Let's go down to the crew kitchen. We're going to

have to cook our own meals from now on. Or eat things sealed in packages."

"That seems like a reasonable precaution," she agreed. "Maybe we can kind of casually ask around while we are making breakfast. I know Noah asked some questions of the crew that was on duty last night, but it never hurts to probe people's memories."

David fell in step with her. "Sounds good. We can poke around and see if we can find any possible sources for the poison although I suspect that if there was anything left of what was used, it's been tossed overboard."

"It's just a little two easy to get rid of evidence on a ship, isn't it?" She said.

"Yes, and bodies too. Not trying to be morbid. But in some ways a ship is a perfect place to commit a crime."

She kept pace with him. "Except that the culprit is trapped on the ship."

"Until we get into port."

As they made their way through the ship to the crew kitchen, Maya felt a tension in her muscles. They had to find the murderer. The clock was ticking.

By the time David and Maya entered the crew kitchen after leaving Sarge in the room, the early morning rush was over. His stomach growled. There were only a few stragglers and one chef cleaning up. Most of the people still in the kitchen probably had the day off or worked night shifts and could afford to have a late breakfast.

He turned toward Maya. "What do you feel like eating?"

Her face blanched. "What would be the safest?"

She must be remembering the trauma of the poisoning. "The safest would be dry granola bars, but I think if I make pancakes from scratch, we should be fine. The place is not crowded. Chef is just finishing up. We'll be the only ones in the kitchen so we can keep an eye on everything."

"Great, and I'll scramble some eggs."

He fired up one of the griddles while she searched one of the industrial-sized refrigerators. She returned with eggs and milk. He went to the pantry to retrieve the flour and baking soda. On his way, he flung open a cupboard where he knew cleaning supplies were stored. It seemed a futile activity to try to figure out what had been used to poison them. Once they could get the samples to a lab, maybe they would reveal something about the killer, but for now it seemed the best choice would be to try to narrow down the suspects.

He returned to where Maya was waiting for him.

"I got the eggs mixed up in a bowl. But I didn't want to pour them on the grill until the pancakes were close to being done. That way everything will be warm and yummy."

Maybe it was something about seeing Maya with Bess that had made him imagine pictures of domestic bliss in his head. She was just so different from any of the other women he'd dated. Yet although he felt drawn to her in that moment, he had to remind himself that he had a lousy track record where women were concerned...

More conflicted thoughts flitted through his mind

as they worked side by side. He mixed pancakes and poured them on the grill, watching them closely for the bubbling that indicated he needed to flip them. Their shoulders touched as she spread the eggs onto the griddle and scrambled them with a spatula.

"It smells good," she said.

Though he still felt that same spark between them now, he knew he had to let go of the idea that there could be anything but a friendship between as much as he enjoyed this time with her. Even a friendship would be strained by how often he was away at sea.

They finished cooking. David fished out some syrup that had not been opened as well as individual containers of orange juice that were sealed with a foil cover. All of the precautions reminded him that the killer was out there waiting for another chance to get at Maya and Sarge and that he didn't mind taking David out as collateral damage.

When they sat down to eat, only one other person remained in the kitchen, an older woman in a maid's uniform.

They bowed their heads while David thanked God for the food.

Maya stared down at her plate. "This looks so good. That was fun to cook together."

The warmth and affection that permeated her voice was a reminder that he needed to nip this in the bud.

"As work colleagues, Maya, I enjoy your company." His words held a chilly quality on purpose.

Her features hardened. "Yes, David. It has been good

to work with you and spend time together." Her voice had turned cold as well.

Just as long as she understood the boundary. He didn't want to hurt her or lead her on. Even if he did feel a special connection to her, they were two people from two different worlds. He couldn't fathom how those worlds would ever fit together.

NINE

Maya found herself grateful when their meal was interrupted by a text from the K-9 unit's forensic scientist, Tala Ekho. Whatever blossoming feelings she harbored for David, he had made it clear that he wasn't interested. Focusing on her work would take her mind off the disappointment she was experiencing. She reread the text.

We've had some developments in the wedding party murder. Call when you can. Want to keep you in the loop.

She looked up from her phone. "I have to make a ship to shore call. It would be nice if I could have consistent Wi-Fi, which I've noticed we don't get down here."

David finished up his last bite of breakfast. "Your better choice would be the internet café on deck six. I can escort you there."

"Sounds good. Let's pick up Sarge from the room on the way." Even as they spoke, Maya felt David's walls going up all around him. She'd breached some emotional boundary by expressing affection for him. She sensed though that it wasn't meanness that had made him become all brusque and businesslike, it was *fear*. And even though David had been crystal clear about where they stood, she found herself wanting to know more about why he'd shut her down so quickly. Was it just the incompatibility of their lives…or something deeper?

They loaded their dishes in the mostly full dishwasher and stopped back at her cabin room to get Sarge. As they walked down the labyrinth of the hallways, she told herself she needed to let go of her curiosity about David and focus on what mattered the most. Her work with the Alaskan K-9 unit. They headed up to the internet café, and once they arrived, the attendant provided her with log-on information so she could set up a video call.

While she sat waiting for the call to go through, David cupped his hand on her shoulder. "I'm technically on duty as of ten minutes ago. If I get called away, please wait here until I can come get you or send one of the other security officers."

She was surprised he had gone back to work so quickly. She still felt weak from the poisoning. But then again, wasn't that what she was doing too by getting briefed on the wedding party investigation? Maybe, like her, David had had no choice but to jump back into the fray. She hoped for both their sakes it was a quiet day.

Tala's face came up on the video screen. Her long dark hair was pulled back in a ponytail, and the round silver-framed glasses she wore seemed to make her brown eyes even darker and more intense. "Maya, so good to see you."

Tala worked out of Anchorage at the state crime lab. She handled most of the evidence pertaining to the K-9 unit's cases. Seeing anyone connected to her job tugged at Maya's heart. Especially after David's rejection. She missed being on land and working side by side with the team.

"Hey, Tala, what's up?"

"Lorenza wanted to make sure you were up-to-date on any breakthroughs with the cases we're working on," the other woman said. "We've had a big surprise with the wedding party murders."

"Oh really! Did they catch Violet James? Lorenza said they thought she'd been spotted in Anchorage."

"I don't know about that. You'd have to talk to Eli," Tala replied. "He was going to look at footage from where she was spotted."

Maya made a mental note that calling Eli Partridge, the tech guru who helped the team out, might be the next order of business. "So what's the development?"

"As you know, the groom and the best man have said all along that it was the bride, Violet James, who killed the guide and pushed the bridesmaid off the cliff, which made sense considering she seems to have gone into hiding."

"Her behavior would suggest guilt, yes," Maya concurred. "Even though the bridesmaid says it's totally out of character for Violet."

"Well, now that the best man and the groom are missing, Eli is trying to track them via credit card use."

"I hope he hits pay dirt soon."

"You and me both," Tala said. "So anyway, back to my big news. You remember how the groom Lance Wells and best man Jared Dennis claimed that when they were attacked in the hospital while a guard was posted outside their room, that the perpetrator was Violet?"

"Yeah… And I recall that the reason they were attacked in the first place was because the bride cold-cocked the guard, granting her access to the room." Maya furrowed her brow. "Why? Wasn't that how it all went down?"

"Not exactly. As it turns out, the guard never saw his attacker because the cameras in that hallway were disabled. The last recorded image is of someone in surgical scrubs and a face mask, an easy enough disguise to pull off in a hospital, so we couldn't ID anyone. However, there were some microscopic samples on the guard's uniform. Some hair and fibers that didn't match the guard's. The DNA matches the groom's."

Maya sat back in her chair. "Wow! This shifts the whole case. You know I had a gut feeling about the groom. There has been something fishy about Lance from the beginning, as well as his best man. How did you come up with a DNA match anyway? We checked Lance out when the murder of the guide first happened. He doesn't have a criminal record."

"That was one of the reasons it took me so long to match the samples. Violet and Lance gave each other an engagement gift of an ancestry test. Ariel was the one who told me about it. She still maintains Violet's innocence by the way."

"But if the bride hasn't done something, why doesn't she come out of hiding?" Maya's attention was drawn to David who had been pacing at the open entrance to the internet café. He was now talking on his radio, probably getting a call on something he needed to deal with.

"Motive is for the K-9 team to figure out. I just look at things under a microscope. Speaking of which, I need to get back to work."

Maya stared at the screen. "Thanks for the update. It was good to see you, Tala."

She hung up and the screen went black. When she looked over at the entrance to the internet café, David was gone.

That meant she was stuck here until David could come back or she would have to summon one of the other security officers. A wave of nausea suddenly roiled through her. Great. Her stomach felt like it was in even more turmoil than before.

To make matters worse, she was the only one in the internet café besides the attendant. Sarge lay at her feet. "I don't suppose you have anything on hand for an upset stomach?"

The attendant who looked like he was barely out of his teens looked up from his laptop and stared at her for a moment. She realized it was a bizarre question to ask someone who ran an internet café, but she would not be able to leave the café as per David's orders. Maybe the clerk had been sick at one time and had something around.

"No, there's a pharmacy down the first hallway to your right," he said.

She had a vague memory of having seen a sign with an arrow for it when she and David had come toward the internet café.

Her stomach churned again. She feared she was going to be sick. Had she been poisoned again? She stood up and tugged on Sarge's leash, glad that he was with her. This part of the ship was not a place with heavy passenger traffic. She saw only one other person walking away from her up the long corridor. As she read the signs on the doors, it looked like it consisted of places people would seek out because of particular needs. She passed a lost and found and also saw a sign indicating the infirmary was on this floor, which helped her orient herself a little. Her entrance and exit from the infirmary the previous night had been kind of a blur.

Maya followed the sign to the pharmacy. An older man was behind the counter. She found the shelf that contained medicine for stomach upset and selected a bottle. After paying the clerk, she texted David that she had left the internet café to go to the pharmacy but would head back there now. She didn't want him to return and worry that something had happened to her.

When she didn't get a text right back, she assumed he must still be out dealing with whatever the radio call had been about.

The pharmacy did have a public bathroom which she used to take some of the medicine she had just purchased. Afterward, Maya took the short walk up the hallway toward the internet café. She saw no one which gave her an uneasy feeling. Back at the café, the doors were still open, but the young clerk had disappeared. Maybe he was in the back room.

She checked her phone, but David had not texted her back.

She typed in another message.

Clerk is gone. Here by myself. Feeling a little vulnerable without you.

Her finger hovered over the send button. Sending such a text meant she was admitting something to David. She was a trained police officer with a K-9 partner who had her back, and yet she felt the safest when David was close by.

Maya pressed Send and sat back in her chair. She looked at the laptop in front of her thinking she should use the time to get in touch with the tech guru, Eli Partridge, to find out if he had made any headway in tracking down the missing groom and best man or in locating the bride. Her stomach was still doing a gymnastic routine while her hand hovered over the keyboard.

Then she heard approaching footsteps out in the corridor.

David hurried to deck eight where the call about an altercation had come in. This part of the ship had several hot tubs beneath a glass ceiling and a shuffleboard court and a virtual putting green. Several senior citizens were engaged in the shuffleboard game and he spotted four people in one of the hot tubs. Everyone appeared very relaxed.

His throat went tight. The call had come in as an emergency.

One older man playing shuffleboard looked in his direction. "Everything all right?"

David shook his head and turned to run in the direction he'd just come. "Just fine." He'd been set up, lured away from Maya.

As he increased his pace from a jog to a sprint, pain shot through his injured leg. He swung the door to the stairs open and hurried down. Once on the deck where Maya was, he ran as fast as he could to the internet café. When he got there, Sarge sat up in an alert stance. His tail thumped when he saw David. The clerk was behind the counter staring at his laptop. He looked up when David stepped into the café.

"The woman who was here?"

The attendant shrugged. "I went in the back to deal with some inventory. She left to go get something for her stomach." He pointed at the dog. "She must have come back while I was in the back room and then left her dog behind."

David's mind reeled. Was it possible the killer had managed to abduct or subdue her with Sarge so close?

"Did you see anyone else?"

The clerk closed his laptop. "Actually, I did. A guy came by twice and peered in like he was looking for something or someone. When I asked him if he needed help, he just shrugged."

"What did he look like?"

"I don't know. Average build, brown hair."

Pushing down a rising panic, David turned one way and then the other. "How long ago was that?"

"Five to seven minutes."

David could not piece together what had happened. The guy would not have come back looking for Maya if he already had her. Sarge was alert but not agitated. He looked at the dog. "Where did she go?"

Sarge wandered over to him and licked his hand.

"Hey." The voice behind him was more welcoming than a cool breeze on a hot day.

He whirled around to see Maya. She was extremely pale and clutching her stomach.

Joy surged through him. Even though she did not look well, he was glad she had not been harmed. "You okay?"

"Not really, I got sick and had to run to the bathroom. I don't think I am fully recovered yet from the poisoning."

"Oh no, so sorry to hear that." David took a step toward her. "When you weren't here, I was a little afraid something might have happened. The call I went on was a false alarm."

Her hand fluttered from her stomach to her neck. "Do you think our suspect made the call to lure you away, so I'd be alone?"

"Yes, and the clerk said a man came by here twice and looked in."

"Let me guess." She blew out an agitated breath. "He was of medium build, totally generic in appearance and too far away to notice if he had green eyes."

He hadn't asked the clerk if he'd noticed eye color, but since the young man hadn't mentioned something that distinctive, Maya was probably right. The near miss with the attacker was a reminder of how vulnerable she was. If she hadn't gone to the bathroom, if the timing of the clerk being in a back room had been different, David might not be looking into her beautiful brown eyes right now. "Glad you're okay. I was really worried."

"I did send you two texts."

He pulled his phone out. "There was no time to check them. I thought the most important thing was to ensure that you were not in danger." He looked at both texts. The first one was straightforward, just saying she had gone to the pharmacy on the same deck. However, the second caused a tightening in his throat. *Feeling a little vulnerable without you.* It was almost like she was admitting that she liked having him around. Maya could obviously take care of herself—as a highly skilled state trooper he figured she had all kinds of self-defense training. But did she feel safer when he was close? When he looked up from his phone, she stared at the floor as though self-conscious.

Against his will, his own face felt flushed. He smiled and shook his head. Despite how he tried to keep his defenses up, she had a way of getting to him. "It's nice to know you feel that way."

Her expression was glowing. Sarge, standing by her feet, wagged his tail.

He could at least admit that he felt an attraction to Maya. Even if nothing could come of it. He needed to keep reminding himself, and her, of that. His voice took on a businesslike quality. "I have some regular check-ins and follow-ups I need to do with some of the establishments that reported crimes. We have a bit of an employee theft problem in one of the shops. I need to pick up their surveillance footage. You and Sarge can come along with me."

The brightness faded from her features. "Sure, David. I need to make another ship to shore call to Eli Partridge sometime today—he's the tech wiz that works with the K-9 Unit."

"Some of the stuff I have to do is time sensitive." He stepped outside of the café and Maya fell in beside him. "We can work in the video chat when things are slower or maybe when I get off shift. I don't want you down here alone though."

"Sure, I get that. But I need to stay abreast of the unit's current investigations. Maybe we can come down here on your break or something."

"We'll work something out."

The whole conversation seemed stiff. Like they were both trying to avoid talking about their feelings by focusing on their respective jobs. Maybe they'd both crossed a line and the start of what might have been a unique friendship had become uncomfortable.

"Are you free to speak about the cases the team is working on? I might be able to provide some input. Sometimes just talking a case out can make light bulbs go on."

"You're right about that. It's hard not to be part of the investigation. Especially, the one involving a wedding party homicide. I was very involved when the case first broke."

"Tell me about it?"

She had a moment's hesitation about discussing the cases. "I would love to troubleshoot with you about them. But let me message my boss and ask permission first." She sent the text. "If she doesn't get back to me… as much as I would like to, I really shouldn't."

The fact the Maya respected the ethics of police work made him like her only more. Her phone dinged a few seconds later. She read the text. "My boss says it's okay to talk to you about the investigations."

As she shared the details of the case, the tension between them seemed to dissolve. He felt more comfortable when they kept their conversation work focused. And he did enjoy helping her as much as he liked it when she and Sarge assisted him.

However, as they made their way through the corridors and up to the next deck, he realized that her expressing her feelings in the text and the awareness that the same feelings were growing in him made him very uneasy.

TEN

Maya sat in the security office looking at all the employee records as well as copies of their IDs in the computer database. There was no way she would have the time to isolate the green-eyed crew members without sorting software. They had to find a way to narrow down the suspects even more. The attacks and the murder had taken place in different parts of the ship. Which meant they were dealing with someone who not only knew the layout of the ship but also could pinpoint the most isolated areas to find a woman alone, and at what time.

The question that rose to the surface for her was that if they were looking at someone who had been with the cruise line long term, there must be an inciting incident that triggered him to start trying to kill women and to have succeeded once.

Sarge relaxed at her feet while David sat in the chair next to her looking on a separate screen at surveillance videos from the store that was experiencing employee theft. The handsome security chief looked bored to death as he rested his chin in his palm and watched the screen. She noticed a little scar by his eyebrow and wondered what the story was behind it. A childhood accident or was it from the injury that had stolen his army career from him?

Though they seemed to stumble from one awkward moment to the next, she still found herself wanting to know more about him. Sharing with him about the wedding party investigation had eased the angst she felt at not being on land working the case with the rest of the K-9 team. She scooted her chair and leaned sideways so she had a view of David's screen. Not much happening; a customer moved around the store and the clerk remained behind the counter. "Like watching paint dry, huh?"

He clicked the pause button. "Not quite as exciting. How about you?"

"I'm wondering if you can pull up the crime reports from shortly before the murder took place. That would have been right before the cruise left Seattle or maybe a few days before. I don't know where the file is, and I assume it's password protected."

David pointed at her computer. "I can pull it up for you."

She scooted over to give him access to her computer. His fingers clicked on the keyboard. "Here, this is three days prior to the murder."

They both leaned forward to see the screen better, their heads nearly touching. He scrolled through the number of reported incidents, which averaged only about five per day. Mostly petty theft, minor injury and public intoxication, nothing overly violent. No report of a fight between a man and woman or between two men brawling over a woman, which was what she would be looking for. A man who had just been dumped or betrayed might seek revenge on another women if he was psychologically unbalanced. Some of the things the attacker had said to her made her believe that was true.

She shook her head. "No red flags there." She and David were huddled so close together that when she turned her head toward him, she could smell the soapy cleanness of his skin. The proximity caused heart flutters for her.

"I hate to say it. But I think we are going down a rabbit trail that won't open up any leads for us." David scooted away a few inches and turned his attention back to the screen where he had paused the surveillance footage of the store.

He was right. Her jaw clenched in frustration.

"I've had to look at surveillance footage for my job too. Maybe I could help you," she offered.

"Sure, a second set of eyes might help. We think the thefts are occurring during store hours, not when the store is closed. A quick skim through of the after-hours surveillance didn't show any movement."

He restarted the footage he'd been viewing and then reached over and handed her a disk. "This is for a different day. You can watch it on your computer."

After a few hours of watching footage that revealed nothing, Maya thought she might fall asleep. "Why don't we take Sarge to do his business and grab a coffee or I'm going to need a nap."

David chuckled. "Ah, the glamorous world of on-board security."

"I get it. Not all police work is exciting." She found herself enjoying his company even when they were doing the most tedious thing in the world.

David locked up the security office and they headed out to the play area for Sarge after getting coffee. They sipped their coffee and watched Sarge and one other dog play. The ship was alive and bustling with midday activity. Passengers heading toward recreational areas of the ship, or eating or shopping or visiting in the botanical gardens.

She smiled as a group of giggling preteen girls ran by. "It's like a little floating city."

"You could say that." He took a sip of his coffee. "Why don't we head back to the internet café so you can make that call. Looks like work is going to be quiet for now anyway."

David mentioning the call she wanted to make to Eli reminded her that sooner or later, she was going to have to check in with Lorenza and let her know what progress they had made in the shipboard case.

She took a sip of her coffee. "Might as well. You can listen in on the call since you have a gist of the investigation."

"I'd like that, Maya."

The way he said her name warmed her to the bone. Mentally, she kicked herself. Though she could not control her involuntary responses to having him close, she knew she had to let go of the idea that there could be anything between them.

"I know your job makes it hard to have a relationship, but you could date someone else who worked on the ship." She had to know why he was so opposed to anything romantic before she gave up completely on him.

"It's just that. I have a rotten track record with women. I do all right until things get serious." He sighed. "Sometimes you can't escape the things you learned from childhood even if God is a part of your life. My father was not a good guy. I'm afraid I might end up being just like him. I haven't treated women the way he treated my mom, but like I said, I always back out when it gets serious because of that fear." David's voice was raw with emotion.

She wasn't sure what to say.

He broke the silence. "Let's go make that call." He'd purged his voice of all the intensity from the moment before speaking in a monotone.

Whatever vulnerability he'd shown was gone, and he didn't seem to understand how his coldness affected her.

Maya knew she had to let her budding feelings of attraction go. David had made up his mind about what his life was going to look like, and it didn't include a relationship with her or anyone for that matter. She felt a deep sadness for him.

She glanced at Sarge and then drew her attention upward.

They were standing in the same place where the giant pot had been pushed off in order to kill her. She shuddered at the memory. Except for the near miss at the internet café, the assailant hadn't come after her since the poisoning.

David stepped a little closer and followed the line of her gaze. "He's not likely to do the same thing twice."

"I know," she said.

"My biggest worry is that if he's not coming after you, he might be spending his time stalking another woman preparing to attack her."

Fear twisted inside her. David was probably right. There was more at stake than just her own safety. They had to catch this guy before they got into port.

David and Maya made their way up to the internet café. This time they weren't the only ones in the café. A middle-aged woman wearing a swimming suit cover-up and sandals sat making a video call. David showed his ID so Maya wouldn't have to pay for the time wishing he had thought to do that the first time they'd been down here. One of the perks of working on the ship. Maya had already settled in front of a laptop.

David scooted in beside her. There was something about helping the pretty law enforcement officer stay engaged with her team's investigation that eased the frustration he felt about their search for the killer on the ship. These cases were far removed from the immediate danger that she and any other attractive woman on board faced.

Maya typed in the code that would allow her to make a ship to shore video call. She was sitting close enough to him that he could detect the floral scent of her perfume. If he was honest with himself, part of what was so appealing about helping her out was getting to be close to her. But he knew from experience that it took more than physical attraction to make a relationship work. David sighed, resolving just to enjoy this time with her and not open the door to there being anything more.

A man with a thin face and round black glasses popped up on the screen. "Hey, Maya. Good to see you."

It looked like the man was in some sort of cluttered office. There was a stack of books, file cabinets and computers in the background.

"Eli, how is it going?"

"It goes like it does. Always good to see your smiling face."

Maya tilted her head toward David. "Eli, this is security chief David Garrison. He's helping me out with the shipboard investigation. I've invited him to listen in on the progress with our cases on land. I value his input and experience."

The compliment elevated David's mood. His job could be pretty thankless and petty sometimes. He was glad Maya acknowledged his expertise.

Eli smoothed his hand over a mop of curly brown hair. "Nice to meet you, David." He turned slightly. "So let me guess, you're calling about progress with the wedding party murders?"

"Just thought I would check in with the source. Lorenza said that you might have a lead on our missing bride. Someone called in to the tip line about seeing her. You were going to look at some surveillance footage?"

"Yes, we think it is Violet James but in disguise—sunglasses and hiking hat low on her face. I had to watch the footage several times. She has some distinctive mannerisms and at one point for just a second, she looks at the camera, which means she doesn't realize it's there. She popped up again in the same area yesterday. We're not sure why she keeps going to that area of Anchorage. This is the second time we had a direct feed from that camera when she showed up. K-9 Officers Sean West and Gabriel Runyon were dispatched, but they were too late."

"I wish she'd turn herself in. Being in disguise suggests a level of guilt or wanting to hide, but why is she taking the risk and coming into town like that?"

Eli shrugged. "Who knows. To see someone she cares about? But she has no known relatives in Anchorage."

"If she'd just turn herself in, we could let her know that the groom and best man are under suspicion and missing now."

The tech guru nodded. "Exactly. It is hard to piece this together based on the way the people involved are acting. Maybe the groom, best man and bride were all involved in the murder of that guide and in pushing the bridesmaid off the cliff."

"The only one for sure we know is not involved is Ariel, and she insists Violet is innocent," Maya said. "But we can't believe her just because she's engaged to one of the K-9 officers until the evidence supports that."

David leaned closer to the screen. "So is there any more news about tracking down the groom and best man?"

"We're watching their bank accounts and credit cards. Nothing so far," Eli replied.

"Text me if there are any changes, will you?" Maya

said. "I want to hit the ground running with these cases once the one on the ship gets wrapped up."

"Sure thing." It looked like Eli was eating a snack or late lunch. He'd taken an apple out of a nearby container as well as what looked like slices of cheese.

"Eli, can I ask? How is your godmother?" She glanced at David and then looked back at the screen. "Only share if you feel comfortable."

David wasn't sure what Maya was asking about, but judging from the change in Eli's expression, the shadow that seemed to fall over his features, it was something pretty serious.

"Bettina is hanging in there through the chemo treatments, but we haven't been able to locate her son Cole and his family."

"Eli, I'm so sorry. I'm sure that weighs heavily on you knowing that the Seaver family is hiding out somewhere in the wilderness and your godmother may not have much more time."

"We'll just keep trying. What else can we do?" Eli turned sideways to glance at a stack of papers. "Look, I better get going. Work is piling up. I'll text you if there are any new developments."

"You got it," Maya said. "Stay in touch."

She clicked out of the video feed then sat back in the chair and let out a heavy breath.

"That sounds like some pretty heavy stuff Eli has been dealing with on a personal level."

"For sure. His godmother's only wish is to be reunited with her son and his wife and her grandson. They're survivalists. We think they might be hiding out in Chugach

State Park. But people who choose to live off the grid like that don't want to be found and that park is so big it really is like looking for a needle in a haystack."

The waver in Maya's voice indicated how emotionally connected she was to Eli and what he was going through. Really the way she talked about the whole K-9 team sounded like they had each other's backs, not just professionally but personally too.

The last time he'd felt deeply connected to other people and part of something bigger than himself was when he'd been in the army. With the exception of a few people on the ship, he wasn't overly social. He respected the other security officers, but didn't feel close to them.

When he saw how Maya lit up when she talked to one of her coworkers, he realized something was missing in his life.

"It's past lunchtime. Do you think you could eat something?" he asked.

"My stomach is growling. Maybe something bland like chicken soup and crackers."

"I know the perfect restaurant to get that," David told her. "And the perfect place to eat it so we don't have to worry about an attack."

"Lead the way."

He took her up a deck to a restaurant called Almost Mom's. Maya stared at the board posted behind the counter. While the service person waited for her to choose something to eat, David stood close to her. "Everything here is made from scratch and the chicken soup is their specialty. We can get it to go."

They ordered the food. It was late afternoon, and

most of the lunch rush had subsided. Only two people, a couple, sat at a table and no one but the two of them were waiting for takeout.

Once they had their lunch in a take-out bag, she turned toward him. "So where are we going?"

"You know that round ball on a crane-looking structure at the back of the ship?"

"Yes," she murmured.

"It's called the North Star and one of the perks of working on the ship is that I can go up in it anytime as long as they're not busy. It will give you a whole different view of the ship and the scenery."

"Sounds fun!"

He phoned ahead to the operator to make sure he would be there to lift them up. By the time they got to the deck where the North Star was, the sky had darkened in the distance indicating rain might be on the way.

The deck was deserted except for the North Star operator. David addressed the man. "Hey, Glen, this is Maya. I'd like to take her and her service dog up."

Glen glanced at the sky. "If the lightning gets too close, I'll have to bring you down. Should be nice viewing of the storm. Right now, it's pretty far away."

Glen walked over to his operating panel. The North Star was a pod-like structure with windows that went around the entire ball. The door slid open. David and Maya settled into the seats and he set the bag of food on the floor. "We can eat when we're elevated."

The pod door slid closed. There was a mechanical humming as the crane arm lifted them up.

Maya stared through the window while Sarge sat at her feet. "Wow."

Being able to share this experience with her made his own heart soar. The crane stopped. Their view was of the thunderstorm moving toward them from a forest across the water in the distance.

David reached down and pulled her soup and his sandwich out of the take-out bag. He handed the soup to her along with her crackers and a plastic spoon. They ate and watched as a sheet of gray indicating where the storm was moved across the landscape. The lightning and thunder were far enough away that it was not a danger to them.

Maya took several spoonsful of soup and then looked out through the window. "God is doing some beautiful work today, isn't He?"

"I do feel closer to God when I go up here. Such an exquisite world He's given us." A light rain sprayed against the window. He took a bite of his chicken sandwich. "How's your soup?"

"Really good. It reminds me of the soup my grandma used to make. Mom and I could never get it right. It needed a touch of Grandma's love."

"Has your grandma passed away?" he asked.

"No, it's just that she is still back in Puerto Rico. If I can swing it, I go back to visit her once a year."

"Why doesn't she move here?"

"The move and the cold weather would be really hard on her." She set her empty soup container down.

"That is neat that you have a close relationship."

She turned to look at him. "There isn't anyone in your family you're close to?"

His stomach clenched in response to her inquiry. He took a french fry from the cardboard container it was in and then offered her one, which she took. "Not all of us have families we like to talk about."

"David, I didn't mean to pry."

"No, you deserve to know. I've worked really hard to be a better man than my father was. And I think that I am in many ways. But it is still a struggle to have a relationship with my mom and sister. You and I are from two very different places and I don't just mean geographically." He felt like he was pushing her away with his words at the same time that he wanted more than anything to hold her in his arms.

Maya finished munching on her cracker. She stared out at the fantastic show taking place through the window. "Look, David," she said softly. "I know that the best we could hope for between us would be an infrequent friendship. All the same, I'm going to pray that you find community, a sort of replacement family, in whatever form that takes."

Until she said something, he hadn't viewed his life as lacking in any way. Maybe he did like his job because it meant he didn't have to belong to one place or person. "I never turn down someone praying for me. But I'm not unhappy living this way. It suits me. And I do have friends. We meet for a church service and give each other prayer support."

She studied him for a long moment. "I shouldn't try to dictate what your life should look like. I just know if my home was moving all the time with a rotating cast of characters, I would feel lonely is all. But like we've been saying all along, we are two very different people."

The storm in the distance intensified and drew their attention back to the window. They watched in silence as the sheet of gray moved across the water leaving a blue sky and clouds behind it.

David relished this time he had with Maya. It felt good just to sit beside her and watch the storm while rain splashed against their viewing window. Her suggestion that he might need a deeper connection to people bounced around his head. He'd always been kind of a loner and preferred it that way. But maybe he was shortchanging himself.

The storm shifted direction, now it looked like it might come closer to the ship. He signaled Glen to lower them to the deck. They'd just stepped out of the pod when his radio made a static noise. David pressed the talk button.

Hans's voice came across the line. "We got our first drunk and disorderly of the day. Neptune's Bar. Might need some back up."

"On my way," David said.

The time with Maya had been a brief reprieve. Back to real life.

ELEVEN

Maya and Sarge trotted along beside David as they headed toward wherever they needed to go. She had no idea which deck Neptune's Bar was on.

They stepped into an elevator. David's radio indicated someone was trying to reach him. He pulled it off his belt. "Yes."

"Looks like I got it de-escalated. Wasn't as bad as the bartender made it out to be."

"Okay, thanks, Hans." He took his hand off the talk button. Then addressed Maya. "It's only late afternoon. I'm sure there'll be more calls before the night is over. Since this is the last stretch of the cruise, you usually see a rise in alcohol-related incidents."

The elevator doors slid open.

"So what now?" Maya wondered if she'd been out of line in suggesting that David needed more community in his life. She had no right to think that his life needed to look like hers. Maybe her thinking there was something lonely about the way he lived was just her not being able to let go of the attraction she felt toward him. She was projecting things onto him. Like she could somehow rescue him from a desolation he wasn't even experiencing. Ridiculous.

They walked along a corridor that led to a solarium. "Are you getting tired of following me around?" David asked. "I know it's a shame to spend a cruise in a cabin that has no windows, but that would be the only other option I would feel comfortable with."

"Yeah, I think I would rather be with you than alone reading or watching TV."

They stepped out into the solarium with its floor-to-ceiling windows. Though it was late afternoon, the storm had moved closer to the ship, darkening the sky, so it almost appeared to be nighttime. Lightning flashed.

The four people in lounge chairs made an awestruck noise. One of them, an older man, jumped out of his chair as though the lightning might hit him.

Maya stared at the sky. "I think I liked it better when the storm was farther away."

"I'm going to have to do rounds on the outdoor viewing areas and decks to make sure no one is trying to get up close and personal with this storm. The ship's PA system will make a general announcement. I'm sure the captain was watching and knew the storm would head in this direction even if it looked to me like we were going to miss it."

"Yes, of course the captain is the one who makes the ultimate decisions about the ship." Maya had seen the ship's captain only at a distance when she had first boarded. She'd been so tuned into David's job responsibilities she'd started to think that he was the one running the ship.

"Procedurally, we always have to check on the exposed outdoor areas, make sure everyone is safe inside. Unfortunately, I don't have time to escort you back to your room."

"Sarge and I will go with you. I would prefer it that way."

David lifted a brow. "You sure?"

"I'm way better at being active and helpful than sitting in a room staring at the ceiling."

"Let's go then," he said.

Maya felt like she was in her element as the two of them checked several of the exposed viewing areas. The announcement came over the PA system that the storm had turned severe enough that everyone needed to be inside.

David led her to the outdoor pool. The waves hitting the ship had become intense enough that water in the pool sloshed over the sides.

She and Sarge fought to maintain balance. David on the other hand seemed to have no problem staying upright. It must be a learned skill.

"We've got one more deck to clear," he told her. "The rest of the night will be spent in the security room watching the monitors ensuring no one decides to be a daredevil until this storm is over."

Though the situation was serious, the thought of spending the night sipping hot tea or cocoa and being with David sounded appealing. Like the times she'd been on stakeouts with other members of the K-9 team. Bottom line, she liked working with David.

"Okay, let's go." she said.

As they hurried through the pool area, Maya peered back over her shoulder. No one was behind her, but there was a series of doors that led to other places. She couldn't shake the feeling that she was being watched. Still, this was not the time to search the area for the attacker. They needed to make sure all the passengers were safe from the storm.

The last deck they needed to clear was at the front of the ship on a lower level. When they got there, it looked like crew members had already removed the lounge chairs in preparation for the storm and the tumultuous waves.

"The deck wraps around." David pointed one direction and then the other. "Don't go far."

"I'll just check around the corner and come right back."

She and Sarge trotted around to the other side of the deck. No one was there. She turned back around to go rejoin David. Hit by a heavy wave, the ship tilted to one side. She fell backwards landing on her bottom and sliding across the deck. Sarge rolled and slid as well. The ship continued to be rocked by the waves. Her heart beat faster. Even though David was not far away, she realized the difficulty in moving on the deck in the storm made her vulnerable.

She reached out for Sarge's leash which she'd dropped when she fell. She saw a pair of boots. Sarge barked, but it was as if the wind picked it up and carried it away. Barely audible.

She got to her feet still unsteady from the motion of

the ship. She looked into the green eyes of the masked man. The mouth hole of the mask revealed the sneer on his lips.

Fear shot through her as her heart raced.

There were half a dozen entrances to this deck. He could have taken one of them once he figured out where she and David were going and then he'd waited for the moment when she was isolated.

The man lunged toward her. She backed up toward the railing. The attacker held up a knife and swung it at Sarge which was enough intimidation to keep Sarge from advancing toward the attacker.

"That dog is in my way." His voice held a menacing tone.

A second man emerged and grabbed Sarge's leash, dragging him. The man was not wearing a mask, but he had a bandana across most of his face.

Her heart wrenched when she heard Sarge's yelps of protest as the masked man came toward her. She doubted though that the sound would carry at all. Of course, they needed Sarge out of the way to get to her. He lifted the knife in the air. Her back pressed against the railing. "This time you're going to die. No dog to protect you." He swung again aiming to swipe across her stomach.

She rolled away before the blade could find its target, but the move put her in a vulnerable position. She was still having to deal with the motion of the ship. She turned sideways against the railing. The man lunged at her a third time, the knife cutting across her shoulder and tearing her jacket but not injuring her. A wave rocked the ship. The knife flew out of the attacker's hand.

She moved to subdue him with a blow to the neck. But he grabbed her wrist. Then he secured her other hand. His grip was like iron.

She tried to lift her leg to drive a knee into him. His hand let go of her wrist and clamped on her neck. She struggled to breathe and could feel herself growing weaker. A wave of water washed over the deck. The man's body slammed against her, but he kept his fingers pressed on her windpipe. He looked out toward the water, let go of her and stepped away. Another wave crashed against the boat. The attacker must have seen the wave coming and it could wash him overboard.

She lost her equilibrium and gasped for breath. She could feel herself being lifted up by the water. And then she was floating. She sucked in a ragged breath. She reached out. She was holding on to some part of the ship dangling in space. The ship rocked. She lost her grip. Then her body hit something solid and she saw the black dots that indicated she was about to lose consciousness.

Her last thought was that both she and Sarge were going to die.

David hurried around to the part of the deck where Maya and Sarge had gone. He'd been delayed when he had to usher a twenty-something couple off the deck who were filming the storm for their online travel channel. The man and woman had clearly had a couple of drinks and while the exchange was friendly their response in understanding the danger and heading inside had been slow.

He had assumed he would meet Maya at the front part of the wraparound deck. The storm was making the waves even more dangerous. They needed to get inside. He hurried to the side section of the deck. Fear took over when he didn't see Maya there. He checked the first door where she might be standing on a stair landing waiting for him out of the storm. No one was there. But that didn't make any sense. Why didn't she and Sarge just come and find him if she'd seen that no one was on that side of the deck? He never should have been separated from her even for a short time.

Fear overtook him as he ran toward the railing. He could see the rescue boats down below still hooked to the side of the ship. Maya had fallen into one of them. Her body was twisted at an unnatural angle. Was she even alive?

He raced toward the stairs. Despite how rocky the seas were, he took the stairs two at a time to get to the deck where the rescue boats were attached.

The ship was still listing side to side at intense angles. When he looked out, Maya's body rolled like a rag doll. He pressed the button that opened the automatic door that gave him access to the rescue boat. Climbing out to get to her proved a challenge on the unsteady sea. David fell into the rescue boat, landing on his knees, then crawled toward Maya praying that she wasn't dead. He cradled her head in his arms and held her, checking for a pulse. She was still alive.

Her eyes fluttered open.

"David." Her voice was weak and her gaze unfocused.

"Yes, I came for you." He looked all around. "Did you fall?"

"The man with the knife…he came after me."

David clenched his jaw. Mad at himself for letting her out of his sight. "You okay?"

She nodded.

"Where is Sarge?"

She shook her head. She opened her mouth as if to explain, but no words came out.

Something was seriously wrong, but she was still in too much shock to explain.

He'd have to deal with finding Sarge second. First, he needed to get Maya to a safe place. "I got you now, Maya. You're going to be okay."

He wrapped one arm around her. "Can you get up?"

She turned her head and stared at him as though she didn't understand what he was saying. Water sprayed against the side of the ship.

"We need to get inside, Maya."

When she looked at him, it was clear the paralysis of shock had set in. He wondered too if she might have some physical injury. "Are you hurt?"

Again, her response time was slow. She shook her head. "I don't think anything is broken."

Maya bent her head. Long strands of wet hair hid her face. The rescue boat creaked. He wrapped his arm around her back, cupping her shoulder and drawing her close.

She whispered the same words over and over. He

wasn't sure what she was saying until he bent his head close to her mouth.

"Thank you, David," she said several times.

He wasn't sure if he could trust her judgment about any injuries. Her back might be broken. While he still held her, David drew out his radio and called for the EMTs. "Help is on the way."

Within minutes the EMTs arrived. They crawled through and strapped Maya to a rescue backboard working together to get her on the ship and placed on a gurney.

David crawled back onto the ship as well. Before they could wheel her away, she grabbed his hand and squeezed. Her eyes had cleared, which was a good sign.

"I'm worried about Sarge. This attack was mostly about getting him out of the picture. There were two men this time. I'm afraid something may have happened to my dog."

Now he understood why she'd been unable to explain before what had happened to Sarge. "I'll do what I can." David watched as they took Maya to the infirmary to be checked out. He wasn't sure where to start the search for Sarge. So, the attacker was getting some help. Including someone else in your crime was risky. It suggested a level of desperation.

He walked a little faster. The first step would be to post a missing service dog report. The ship had its own "news" channel with viewing screens posted in strategic places. Any sale at stores, or special events on the ship were highlighted as well as weather warnings, and changes in arrival times for ports of call. If

Sarge was still on the ship maybe someone had seen him with his abductor.

His biggest fear though was that Sarge had simply been tossed overboard.

TWELVE

Maya watched the ceiling clip by as the EMTs wheeled her to the infirmary. At her request, they had undone the straps on the backboard. They'd taken her vitals right away, which they said were okay. The confusion and disorientation from the shock was lifting which was the most important thing. That meant she was getting better, not worse.

As she watched the designs on the ceiling and the light fixtures change, the thing foremost on her mind was Sarge. Could she even hope that he was still alive?

One of the EMTs put his head in her field of vision. "You doing okay, ma'am?"

"Better than okay." She sat up on the stretcher. If she had broken any bones it would have been obvious by now.

"Please lie back down. You've suffered a terrible shock…at the very least."

"You said it yourself. My vitals looked impressive." She jumped off the stretcher and moved from a walk to a trot.

The EMT came after her. "We need to have the doctor say you're okay."

She spoke over her shoulder as she moved into a jog. "Later. Right now, I need to talk to the head security officer, David Garrison."

Her jog turned into a sprint. She had to do everything to find Sarge. And she refused to let go of the hope that he was still alive.

She slowed a bit in her pace. She'd lost her phone in the struggle. How was she going to find David? He might be at the security office. She headed in that direction.

She passed one of the news monitors when Sarge's picture, which David must have taken when they were in the play area, came on the screen with info about a missing service dog. That had to have been David's doing. He'd gotten the word out pretty fast.

As she came to a more crowded part of the ship, she spotted Noah dressed in plain clothes. She ran toward him.

His eyes grew wide when he saw her. "Heard you had a bit of excitement."

"Can you phone David and find out where he is? I lost my phone. I need to get another one."

Noah took his phone out. "Sure, I can call him. What's the urgency?"

"Sarge is missing."

"Yeah that came across the boards. I take it you're not really a journalist?"

Now that she knew Noah could be trusted, she was fine with him knowing. "I'm a state trooper with the Alaskan K-9 Unit that works cases all over the state."

Noah nodded and then clicked the numbers on his phone screen. He addressed his comment to her while the call was being placed. "The security office can loan you a phone." Then he spoke into the phone. "Hello, David? I have Maya here."

Maya listened to the one-sided conversation and then Noah hung up. "I'm supposed to escort you to deck four where he is scouring all the public areas for Sarge. Hans and I are also going to do a deck by deck search and remain in radio contact."

"Let's go. I feel like we've lost precious time already."

She and Noah jogged through the commercial sections of the ship where the nightlife was just starting to pick up. Music spilled out of some of the venues, and she could hear dinnertime chatter as they sprinted past the restaurants. They found David on one of the enclosed decks, talking to the patrons who were resting in the lounge chairs, showing them Sarge's picture on his phone. Noah left, promising to get in contact as soon as he had any news.

Maya stood close to David when he stepped out of earshot of the lounging passengers. "Anything at all?" Her voice cracked when she asked the question.

David shook his head. "Nothing yet." His expression softened as he stepped closer to her. "How are you doing? Did you even make it to the infirmary?"

She avoided answering the question. "Sarge has to be my priority." Time was precious. The last thing she wanted to do was spend it being checked out by a doctor.

"I was hoping maybe one of the passengers had seen something. It's not that easy to deal with a dog who I'm sure was not compliant about being dragged away from you, but so far nothing. And no calls on the bulletin that went out over the ship's news feed."

Maya's vision blurred from the tears in her eyes. "David, I don't know what I would do without Sarge. Not only is he my work partner, he's my best buddy."

"I know how connected you and that dog are. We'll pull out all the stops to find him." David squeezed her shoulder. She knew he smiled to offer reassurance, but she saw fear behind his eyes.

Would all their efforts be for nothing? "Thank you." She was so glad he was here to be a support right now. It was the only thing that eased her worry over what might have happened to Sarge. "What's our next step?"

"We search every inch of the ship and keep asking questions. I already retraced where you fell into the rescue boat and searched that whole area and the path that the guy who grabbed Sarge probably took. Did you get a look at the second man?" David started walking and Maya fell in beside him. It felt strange not to be holding on to Sarge's leash seeing his ears bob up and down.

She shook her head. "For a moment. But his face was covered. His hair was sort of blond and was slicked back but obviously bleached because it was black underneath. Kind of distinct."

"I'll tell Noah and Hans to be on the lookout for someone matching that description. He might have been hired help. Since the attacker knew he couldn't keep Sarge out of the way and go after you. All the same, if we could track him down, he might roll on our attacker."

By the time they had searched all the decks as well

as the public spots in crew quarters and questioned hundreds of people, it was close to ten o'clock. Neither Hans nor Noah had found any sign of the dog. They'd stopped to get some takeout from one the cafés and headed back to the security office with heavy hearts.

Maya walked holding her take-out container. The aroma of sweet and sour chicken wafted up making her mouth water. They ate while they walked. She knew going so long without food would make it harder to think clearly and therefore conduct the search, but she didn't like slowing down for even a minute.

"While we're at the security office we can check the monitors to see if we can spot Sarge," David said.

"I want to keep looking." She tossed her empty take-out container in a trash can.

"We can cover a lot more ground via the security cameras. We need to switch up our tactics."

He was right. Searching the ship aimlessly could be a time waster when time was precious. "Okay."

They walked to the security office.

David unlocked it and pushed the door open.

"Is there anywhere else we can look to find Sarge, that we haven't already covered?"

David stepped to one side so she could go in first. "We could search the private cabins, but doing something like that involves some paperwork."

They stepped inside. "Maybe we can get the ball rolling on that." She settled in one of the chairs by the security monitors.

"Sure," David said.

Though she knew David would never say it, something in his tone of voice indicated that he thought Sarge was dead.

Maybe it would be a futile effort to keep looking, but she refused to lose hope. They watched the monitors for about five minutes seeing no sign of Sarge.

David swiveled his chair to face her. His voice filled with compassion. "Maya, I have some work-related things I need to take care of here in the office. But I'll still be watching the cameras. Meanwhile, I'm going to get Noah to come back on shift and keep looking for Sarge and asking questions. We will do everything we can to find him. If you want, Noah can come and escort you back to your room as well. You should rest."

"I think I'd rather stay here with you," Maya said.

David's blue eyes studied her. "Okay, there's a cot back in the break room. Why don't you try to get some sleep? You've been through a lot today, physically and emotionally. And judging from how quickly you got in touch with me, I take it you never got around to the doctor checking you out."

"You figured out I escaped from the EMTs?"

"Yes, I kind thought that's what happened."

She glanced in the direction David had indicated the break room was. Shuffling into the little room which consisted of a cot and blanket and file cabinets, she closed the door and clicked off the light. Then lay down, pulling the soft cover up to her chin.

Though her body was fatigued, sleep came slowly as worry about Sarge plagued her thoughts. She did finally feel herself drifting off.

Hours later, she was roused by David's voice as he shook her shoulder. "Maya, wake up. You're not going to believe what I just saw."

As he woke Maya from her slumber, David could not hide his elation. "While I was watching the monitors, guess who ran by on the screen?"

Maya sat upright. "Sarge! You saw my partner?" She'd gone from asleep to fully alert.

David stepped back and clicked on the light. He hadn't wanted to disturb her by turning it on. "Yes, in the stern of the ship where the wave pool is. Let's go."

Maya swung her legs off the cot and slipped into her shoes which she'd taken off before she fell asleep. "Do you suppose he got away from that guy who grabbed him?" She stood up.

"Maybe. My guess is if he did there were bite marks involved. If anyone comes into the infirmary with that kind of an injury, we have our accomplice. I'll call and send Noah over there to find out."

After making the call to Noah to check the infirmary, they hurried through the security office. David locked the door. The wave pool was three decks up. Both of them broke into a trot as they headed toward the elevator. "You say he ran across the screen?"

"Dragging his leash like he'd escaped," David said.

Maya let out a laugh and shook her head. "That's my buddy."

"I watched the screen to see if he ran back across it and then switched to the areas close to where he was last spotted but couldn't see him anywhere. The only way he could move to a different deck was if he got into the elevator with someone or waited until a stairwell door was open."

"And since there is an all-points bulletin out on him, the second he was spotted someone would phone it in."

Maya was right. Anyone who saw the dog would know to call security. But at this early a.m. hour most people were sleeping.

Once they were on the deck where the wave pool was, David led her through a corridor that was used by staff and crew but not the public. He needed a card key to open some of the doors, but they would get to the pool that much faster.

They came out to the open area by the wave pool which was turned off at this hour. Surfboards for passengers to use were stored against one wall. The air smelled like chlorine. The pool area had a glass sky dome and lots of plants all around the deck. David walked the perimeter until he found a tropical plant that served as a sort of landmark. "When I saw him on screen this is the way he ran. Past this plant and off in that direction." There were six different entrances that led to the pool that surrounded the seating area around the pool. Four of them did not have doors.

Because the screen had shown only a portion of the pool area, Sarge could have gone down any of the corridors that didn't have doors. The most efficient thing would be to split up and do a search of each of the possible escape routes, but he couldn't risk Maya being attacked again. He needed to stay close to her.

Each of the entries would lead to a different part of the deck. They had a lot of territory to cover. Sooner or later though the dog would have to come to a closed door and turn around.

"If he's close and can hear me, Sarge will come when I call him."

"Let's be methodical and work our way down each corridor."

Maya pointed toward the hallway closest to them. They hurried down that corridor which led to a book store and snack shop, both of which were closed. The hallway then opened up to a wider shopping corridor which gave them an open view of the area. The retail shops would all be locked up at this hour. Unless her K-9 partner was hiding behind a plant, they would see him.

She called out Sarge's name. Her voice was filled with anguish.

"At least we know he's alive," he said quietly. "We'll find him, Maya. By morning, people will be wandering the ship. He'll be spotted."

"As long as those two men don't get to him first."

"Let's keep looking." His thought was that if Sarge didn't turn up soon, it might be more productive to watch the monitors from the security office. Noah was already on duty, but he could wake Hans and send him out to patrol the deck where Sarge most likely was.

They continued their search through a hallway that had little boutique shops that opened up into a courtyard which featured some kids' playground equipment and benches for sitting. There was even a hot dog vendor cart, and an ice cream truck which was a golf cart that pulled a trailer behind it. Both carts were shut down and covered with a tarp.

David's radio indicated he had a call. He pulled it from his belt and pressed the talk button. "Go ahead, Noah."

"No one came into the infirmary with a dog bite, but I spotted a guy in one of the casinos that had the hair Maya described. Blond and slicked back. He fessed up right away that he'd been hired to take the dog for money. Apparently, he has gambling debt that's through the roof. He let the dog go when he was told to kill it and said he just lied to the other guy that he did the deed. He never saw the man who hired him. The communication was via text, different number every time."

So, his theory that the second guy was hired help had been confirmed but it was a dead end in every other way. "Thanks for the good police work, Noah."

"No problem."

David turned his attention back to the search.

Maya continued to call her dog and checked all the places in the open area Sarge might be. "Maybe he's hurt and can't come to me."

"We'll work the other corridors and then we'll go farther out." He pulled his phone out of his pocket. "I'm going to get Hans out of bed to help us with the search." When the other officers were on duty they could be reached by radio, but during off hours he had to call them.

His phone rang. It wasn't a number he recognized, but it had come in on the emergency line. The ship did not have a dispatcher. David clicked on the talk button.

"Chief Officer Garrison Alaska Dream security," he said.

It was a woman's voice filled with anguish. "My husband and I are here with a young woman who was just attacked."

A tight knot formed at the back of David's neck and his mouth went dry.

"Ma'am, I'm on my way. Where are you?"

"The little enclosed lounge off the upper deck. The young woman is quite upset. She said the man had a knife. If my husband and I hadn't heard her scream, who knows what would have happened."

David sucked in air through his teeth. "Was he wearing a mask?"

The woman didn't answer right away. He heard mumbling as if she was talking to someone. "She says yes, he was wearing a mask."

"Stay where you are. On my way." David clicked his phone off.

Maya's voice had become flat. "There's been another attack, hasn't there?"

David nodded. "I need to go take her statement. You'll have to come with me."

She grabbed his arm. "No, I want to stay here and keep searching for Sarge. If the man just attacked that woman, he's not on this deck."

"He fled the scene Maya. We don't know where he is."

Her expression was filled with distress.

"He could be on his way here."

"And he might have assumed both Sarge and I are dead and that's why he felt free to attack that woman."

She had a point. While the killer was focused on Maya, the attacks on other women had stopped. "All we know is he is roaming the ship. I just can't take a chance with you wandering around alone—look what happened when we split up for just a few minutes. Please, Maya, we can't delay."

She blew out a breath. "Fine. I'll go. But on the condition that you can get Hans or Noah to come get me and help with the search?"

"Deal. I'll make the call as we head up to the upper deck. It shouldn't take more than fifteen minutes for them to come up and escort you back down here to continue looking for Sarge.

It will be helpful to my investigation if I heard what this victim had to say anyway," Maya said.

"I agree. Let's go."

On their way up in the elevator, David made a call to Hans who didn't pick up. He then tried Noah via the radio. David explained the situation. Noah promised to be on the upper deck as fast as he could get there.

The elevator doors slid open and they stepped out onto a quiet part of the upper deck. The storm had passed and there was a light breeze beneath a starry sky.

Maya stayed one step behind him as he hurried to the lounge where the victim was. He could tell her mind was on finding Sarge, but knew he could count on her professionalism and focus once they began the interview. Traumatic incidents like this attack tended to become less accurate and fuzzier the longer the victim waited to do the interview. He prayed that they would come up with some new evidence that would lead them to the man with the knife.

He opened the door to the lounge where a young woman with long brown hair was being held by another woman who looked to be in her forties while a man who was probably her husband sat close by.

The woman with the long hair looked up when David and Maya walked in.

"I'm head security officer David Garrison. Can you tell me your name?"

"Hannah Stevenson." The woman glanced at Maya as if seeking an explanation for who she was.

Maya stepped forward. "I'm helping officer Garrison with this investigation."

The vague explanation seemed to satisfy Hannah.

David pulled out a notebook. He took a chair opposite the young woman. "If I could just ask you a few questions…" He noted the fresh scratches on Hannah's bare shoulder. "And then we will take you down to the ship's medical facility to have you checked out."

Hannah was dressed in an off-the-shoulder gown that sparkled.

"Were you just ballroom dancing?" Maya asked gently.

Hannah brightened at the question. "Yes. It was crew night to have the ballroom. I work at the information desk."

The attacker, who they knew was a member of the crew, had probably been at the ballroom as well, scouting for his next victim. Since he may have assumed that both Maya and Sarge were dead, he felt free to continue going after women.

"I know this has probably been very frightening for you," Maya said.

"Yes," Hannah drew her attention to the older woman who still had her arm wrapped around her back. "If these two hadn't come along when they did... I don't know what would have happened."

"Is there anything you remember about your attacker? I know you couldn't see his face."

"He was in a tux. Unless he was a waiter in one of the higher-end restaurants, he must have been at the ballroom as well." Hannah rubbed her bare arms.

The man who had been sitting close took off his jacket and draped it over the younger woman's shoulders. "This is a terrible thing to happen. Hannah is our daughter's age."

"Is there anything at all you remember?" David asked. "Did the man say anything to you?"

"Yes, he said, 'All you beautiful women are alike.'" Hannah shuddered and the older woman drew her close.

That sounded like a man who had been hurt by a woman.

Noah popped his head in. "I'm here to give Maya a hand."

"We're just finishing up," said David. He hoped the comment would communicate to Maya that is was okay for her to go. "Unless you have any more questions Maya?"

Maya rose to her feet. "I'll catch up with you later Officer Garrison. We'll talk."

David did not fail to catch the tinge of emotion in her voice. She was torn between doing her job and finding her partner. He knew Maya was keeping things formal in front of the witness and the passengers. Still, he wished he could have offered his support for finding Sarge by giving her a hug.

As he turned his attention back to Hannah, a debate was raging in his head. She had been able to get away, but maybe the next woman wouldn't. So far, the attacks and even the murder had been kept mostly under the radar. David knew for the safety of the female passengers that the time had come to issue a public warning about being alone on any of the decks, and maybe even close off this upper deck since the killer seemed to that location. But he also knew that when he called the cruise line owner he would meet with resistance. Once the announcement about taking precautions was made, some people might want to disembark and get their money back when they got into port.

He escorted Hannah down to the infirmary. The older couple stayed with her.

David headed out of the infirmary with a heavy heart. He had some important decisions to make before morning, but first he knew he needed to get some sleep, at least a couple of hours.

He texted Noah to let him know he was returning to his cabin but would be up in a couple of hours. Then he asked about Sarge.

The reply text came just as David opened the door to his cabin.

No sign of the dog. We will continue the search. Maya refuses to give up.

It felt like a knife had gone into his chest. More than anything he wanted to be with her to help and to console. But going without sleep for so long meant he would be no good to anyone.

All the same, there was no place in the world he would rather be than with Maya. He hated seeing her so torn up.

As he fell asleep, he prayed that Sarge was okay.

THIRTEEN

Maya sat in front of the monitors feeling her eyelids grow heavy. When she and Noah finally had to call the search for Sarge off, Noah had agreed to let her into the security office so she could watch the screens for any sign of her dog. She promised to call him if she saw any sign of Sarge. As long as David was getting some much-needed sleep, Noah would be there to guard her and help in finding Sarge.

She watched the screens and clicked through the various areas on the deck where the wave pool was. Then she searched all the other areas on the ship that had security cameras. The only thing she saw was Noah walking a patrol on an empty deck.

Sarge just had to be *somewhere* on this ship. What scared her though was that maybe he had been taken again. It just seemed like a dog on the run would be spotted sooner or later even with most of the passengers asleep.

As her eyes closed, her head snapped back and then forward. Resting her cheek on her hand she laid her head on the counter by the keyboard. Maybe if she took a power nap, she'd get her energy back.

The next thing she was aware of was the smell of fresh coffee. She raised her head. David was standing beside her and had placed a steaming mug on the counter by her.

He smiled.

She laughed. "You seem really perky."

"I only needed a couple hours sleep to get my mojo back. Looks like you got a little shut-eye too."

Maya self-consciously wiped her mouth, wondering if she'd been drooling in her sleep. She glanced at the clock on the wall. It was four in the morning. She'd been asleep for an hour. "Not on purpose."

She stared at the screen. Still no activity. She knew that as soon as the hour was reasonable, she was going to have to call Lorenza and let her know Sarge was missing. The thought made her feel even more hopeless.

David took a sip of his coffee. "In another hour the morning kitchen crews will be in full force getting ready for the breakfast crowd. Then you'll see the shop owners opening up. There is a rhythm to life on the Alaska Dream."

"That sounds kind of neat. It's like a floating village…and you are the village constable."

David laughed and sat down beside her. He ran his hands through his hair and let out a heavy breath. "As soon as the hour is decent, I'm going to need to call the owner and have a serious talk. He wanted all of this to be under the radar as much as possible. But given that last attack on Hannah, I think we will have to put out a general warning for women to not be alone on decks or anywhere they might be vulnerable." A muscle ticked in his jaw. "It may cost me my job, but the safety of the passengers has to be my top priority."

"I couldn't agree more." As she stared into David's blue eyes, she felt a deep admiration for him. "But a tough choice all the same."

David nodded. He pointed to the dorm-size fridge with the microwave on top of it. "I think we have some precooked sausage and egg sandwiches I can heat up if you're hungry."

"Sure, that sounds good." While he pulled food out of the little freezer and put it the microwave, she drew her attention back to the security screens. Maya took a sip of her coffee, enjoying the warmth and taste, then leaned forward to study each picture more intently. A man in a chef uniform walked across one of the screens. "What if Sarge has been taken to crew living quarters. Is there any way we could see that, at least the hallways, dining hall and laundry?"

"There are no security cameras in the crew area. We can search it on foot." He set a sausage sandwich on a paper plate in front of her. "First breakfast."

"Okay good, that's what we will do."

David turned his chair, so it faced her. "You know, Maya, I want to find Sarge as badly as you do, but at some point, we might have to accept that he's not on the ship anymore."

Though his comment was spoken with great tenderness, it still felt like a knife through her heart. She did not want to face that possibility. "I think it's too early to give up. If he's running free, he would have shown up somewhere or been spotted. I think the attacker saw him and grabbed him." She touched her hand to her heart. "I feel it in here. He's still alive."

He nodded. "Okay, we'll keep looking. If I get security calls, I'll have to deal with them."

"I get that," Maya said as the heaviness of despair filled her. "I just think that someone would have to have a really black heart to kill a dog or throw it overboard. The accomplice couldn't bring himself to do it."

"We are dealing with a man who has killed a woman."

The tightness through Maya's chest was so intense that she laid her palm on her heart. Nothing David was saying was untrue—she was just having a hard time accepting it.

They finished their breakfast and coffee. No security calls had yet come in. "Let's go search the crew area." She stood up and gave a final glance at the screen. Movement caught her eye. Sarge dragging his leash raced across the screen. "Did you see that?" She pointed to the screen where she'd seen her dog. "He was there! Where is that?"

David looked at the screen. "That's the corridor by the botanical gardens and the kids' activity room. But it's not on the same deck as the wave pool. Wonder how he got up there."

Feeling a joy she almost couldn't contain, Maya moved toward the door. "Let's go get him."

They raced through the ship, passing early rising passengers and crew members getting ready for a day of work. Once they got to the botanical gardens Maya called out Sarge's name. She heard barking but could not see him anywhere. They were in a jungle.

Both of them moved toward the sound of Sarge's barking.

"Why isn't he coming to me?" She couldn't contain her excitement.

The botanical gardens were beneath a dome. The room was kept warm to aid the growth of the tropical plants. The air was thick and humid. Maya pushed past the plants, running ahead of David.

Sarge's barking got louder as she hurried around a display of orchids. The K-9 was there tied to an iron bench. Something clicked in her brain. When they'd seen Sarge on the screen he'd been running free. He could not have gotten to the deck alone. "This is a trap." Sarge had been used as bait to lure her there. She turned to warn David, but all she saw was his arm on the floor sticking out from a bush. Her brain barely registered that he'd been knocked out when the masked man jumped out from behind a lattice wall of flowers.

Maya screamed. Sarge barked and jerked on his leash. The assailant came at her with the knife. She dodged out of the way, then reached her leg out to try and hit him behind the knees so he would fall to the ground. He avoided her and raised the knife above his head. As the knife came toward her shoulder, she blocked the move by grabbing the man's wrist and then landing a blow to his stomach with her other hand. She pressed on the nerves of his hand to try to get him to drop the knife.

As they struggled, she was only inches from the

masked man's face. His eyes held a wild dancing quality. "You're going to die."

She reached up with her free hand to grab his mask.

He stepped back to prevent her from seeing who he was. The distraction gave her time to bang the hand that held the knife against the wall. He dropped the knife and grabbed his wrist.

A moaning sound came from where David had been disabled.

The attacker tilted his head and then took off running still holding his hand, probably frightened at the prospect of having to fight two people. Maya hurried to free Sarge, taking note of where the attacker had gone. David, who still seemed wobbly on his feet, came and stood beside her. "You okay?"

David nodded.

"Sarge can track that knife," said Maya. "The trail is still hot."

"Let's go."

With Sarge taking the lead, they sprinted through corridors and down a deck. The direction they were going felt vaguely familiar. Then she remembered, that first night when she'd been attacked this was where Sarge had taken her. They ended up outside the same main kitchen on deck three.

Sarge alerted.

David opened the door. The place was busy with crew preparing breakfast. Grills sizzled and the smell of bacon was heavy in the air.

The dog whined. David let go of the swinging door and peered down at the trash can outside the kitchen.

He pointed. "I'm going to need an evidence bag."

Maya peered into the garbage can where the knife had been tossed.

"I can probably find something in the kitchen to use as an evidence bag. Let's go in and see if we can find a man with green eyes."

Maya had a feeling that the perp had probably passed through the kitchen out a back entrance or the service elevator just like the first time. They entered the kitchen where David retrieved a plastic bag to store the knife along with some disposable gloves used to handle the food. While he questioned the busy kitchen staff, Maya wandered around the counters making eye contact with every man of medium build. The attacker had been dressed in black pants and a gray shirt. No one here was dressed like that. Though it would have been easy enough to don a white chef's smock. None of the men avoided her gaze. None of them appeared to have green eyes.

David came over to her. "From talking to the folks in here, there is a ton of crew traffic this time of day. No one going through was a strange face. You know what that means?"

Her mood lifted. "Our suspect works out of this kitchen. That narrows down the possibilities substantially." They were getting closer to catching this guy.

"I'll grab that knife, and we can go look at employee records."

After retrieving the knife from the garbage and placing it in the bag, they hurried back to the security office to look through employee records. They stopped to grab some food for Sarge. Once in the security office, David found some containers for the food and water. Sarge ate heartily. Maya sat down on the floor beside him and rubbed his ears. There hadn't been time to show how happy she was that he was safe and sound until now. "I don't think he's been fed since they took him. Poor guy."

Sarge stopped eating long enough to lean into her touch as she petted his back and front shoulder. "So glad to have you back on duty, buddy."

The dog wagged his tail.

Maya drew her attention back up to where David was tapping the keyboard and scrutinizing the computer screen. "This shouldn't take long. We are looking at thirty guys who work out of the kitchen. We can eliminate anyone who is not of average build. I'm going to print out all the employee IDs, which will list their eye color." He pushed several buttons.

She heard a printer running but wasn't sure where it was kept. David opened a cabinet underneath the counter and pulled out a stack of papers. He divided them and handed her a stack.

The IDs were printed out in black-and-white but referenced eye color. Maya sorted through her stack coming up with two men whose eye color was listed as green. She studied each picture ID feeling a chill run down her spine. "I got two."

"I got two possibilities as well." He reached over for her stack. "So now we text each of these four men saying we want to question them. I won't say why, just that the security office wants to talk to them."

"Do you have an interview room?"

"No, but there's a small conference room in one of the administrative rooms that will suffice. Let me send out the texts."

Maya knew that a smart criminal would show up for the interview and tell lies. She'd had some training in watching body language to figure out if a man was being honest in his answers. "I'd like to help with the interviews."

Again, David offered her his forty-watt smile. "Of course, that goes without saying. Your help has been invaluable."

He sent off the texts. All four men responded, and a time was set up to interview each one of them. Maya, Sarge and David left the office on several calls, including a case of a teenage boy stealing from a shop and that of an older man who had lost his wallet. As they worked together, Maya was struck by how compassionate David was in dealing with the teenager and the senior citizen.

Once Hans was on duty to take the calls that came in, they hurried to the interview room. The first two men came in. David asked each man the same set of questions about their whereabouts at the times the attacks had taken place along with some other inquiries that might expose their guilt.

For the most part, Maya remained silent and simply studied the reactions of the men. From the moment they came into the room, she watched their expressions when they saw her. None of them showed any sign of recognition. She did see a little fear in one of the men's eyes when his gaze landed on Sarge as he sat at attention beside her, a very normal reaction. Despite his size, Sarge could be intimidating when he wanted to be. He seemed to understand that that was his role for these interviews.

The second suspect left, and they waited for the third man. The interviews were set up to last twenty minutes. Five minutes went by.

"Who is it we are waiting for?"

David sifted through the stack of papers and pushed one across the table. Maya stared down at the black-and-white copy of the photo ID, Joel Morris. They waited for Joel. Five minutes passed then five more.

"Our number three suspect is not going to show," said Maya.

"No, he's not." David tapped his fingers on the table. "And unless he has a real good reason for not showing, it kind of makes him look guilty."

Then the fourth suspect came in for questioning. David interviewed the man for only five minutes and then told him he was free to go. That crew member clearly was not culpable.

They were both thinking the same thing. Joel Morris was the man they were after.

FOURTEEN

Though it seemed like a futile activity, David, Maya and Sarge all hurried down to the crew living quarters to Joel Morris's cabin. If Joel knew they were on to him, he was probably hiding out somewhere on the ship. Maybe it would have been smarter to track down each of the men and question them. Hard to say.

They came to the door of Joel's cabin. David glanced in Maya's direction. "You and Sarge be on high alert? We know what kind of violence he's capable of. Just in case he is in his cabin…"

"We're ready for anything," Maya said.

He knocked on the cabin door. "Joel Morris, this is David Garrison, head of ship security. We need to talk to you."

A groggy male voice came from behind the door. "Joel isn't here."

Must be Joel's cabinmate. "Sir, can you please open the door? We need to talk to you."

David heard some shuffling and banging and an expletive. All the cabins had only one exit. The man wasn't going anywhere.

The door swung open and a disheveled man with uncombed hair stood on the threshold. He blinked over and over again.

"Sorry we woke you up, but we need to ask you some questions about Joel Morris. Is he your roommate?"

"Yes."

Maya stepped forward. "And can you tell us your name?"

The man lifted his head and blinked several times. "I'm Wayne Hawkins."

"When was the last time you saw Joel?" David asked.

"The reason why we make such good roommates is because we work opposite shifts. He starts in the early morning and I work the concert venues at night as a bartender." Wayne ran his hands through his messy hair. "We haven't run into each other for like a day."

Maya stepped sideways so she was visible to the man. "How long have you been his roommate?"

"Eight months."

"Have you noticed any changes in the last week or so," she asked.

Wayne tilted his head to the side. "Right before we left Seattle, he was pretty torn up about his girlfriend finding someone else and then quitting the ship."

"How torn up?" she murmured.

"He threw things around the room, put a fist through the wall and called her every name in the book." He shrugged. "I guess I should have reported it."

"Can I ask what the girlfriend looked like?" Maya spoke up.

"She was way out of Joel's league. Supermodel material."

"Did she have long brown hair?" David asked.

"Yes," he answered.

Now they had a motive for the attacks and the murder. Joel was going after women who reminded him of the one who had betrayed him.

"We're so sorry to have bothered you. I know about late night shifts," David said. "Hope you are able to go back to sleep. If you see Joel or hear about where he is, you need to get in touch with me right away."

"Wow, that sounds serious. What's going on?"

"We need to question him about some incidents that have taken place on the ship," Maya explained.

The roommate's eyes grew a little wider. "Yeah, I saw that bulletin about women needing to be careful about being alone. Seriously, Joel might be the guy who's going after women?"

"We can't say anything at this point," David said. "It's just very important that he get in touch with us. If he does return to the room or you see him, please let us know."

Wayne tugged on the collar of his baggy worn T-shirt. "For sure. I'll do that."

"Thanks again," Maya said.

The roommate moved to close the door.

"Hang on." David caught the door. "Does he have any favorite places he likes to go on the ship. Entertainment venues? Sports things?"

"Honestly, we don't talk that much. The one thing I do know is that him and his lady love used to meet on that upper deck at night cause it usually is not very crowded."

Now the attacks on the upper deck made even more sense.

"Sure. I'll let you know right away if he comes around." Wayne said. "Anything else?"

Maya spoke up. "Is there something of Joel's that we might borrow that would have his scent on it. A T-shirt he wore recently or something like that?"

Maya was one step ahead of him, David thought admiringly. The next thing to do in locating Joel was combing the whole ship to find him. Using Sarge to sniff him out would make that search much easier.

The roommate turned sideways staring at the clutter in the cabin. "Give me a second... I'll find something." He stepped away from the door. They could hear him rummaging around.

The guy returned with a shirt which he handed to Maya.

David piped up. "Can we ask that you not touch, put away or dispose of any of Joel's belongings?"

"Sure not a problem."

"One more thing. Is there anyone else who Joel was close to who might be able to shed some light on where he might be on the ship?"

Wayne shrugged. "He kind of kept to himself. Maybe someone in the kitchen he worked out of would know. To be honest with you, I always thought he was a little out there and then after his breakup, he kind of scared me. I don't blame the lady for breaking up with him."

"We'll be back in touch."

The roommate closed the door.

"I'm going to get all of the ship's security team on duty for the search. If we can't track Joel down, the next step is to put out a bulletin to the public. Something that says, 'Have you seen this man? He's wanted for questioning in some crimes on the ship.' We have to be careful not to imply any guilt or the case could be thrown out once it goes to court."

Maya held the T-shirt they'd been given. "Sarge is trained to track weapons, but a dog's nose is a hundred times better than anything we could do."

"Let me make the calls to Hans and Noah and then we'll get started."

"That sounds good," said Maya. "I need to call my boss and let her know that we have a suspect and are searching for him. Once we have in in custody, the K-9 Unit will make arrangements to transport him when we get into port."

Both of them made their respective phone calls. Within minutes, they were ready to begin a shipwide search.

As promised, David got the rest of the security team on board with what needed to happen. Hans would help with the search and Noah would go down to the kitchen that Joel had worked out of to question his coworkers to find any leads on where he might be hiding. Maya placed the T-shirt by Sarge's nose. The dog stood at attention and licked his chops.

Maya gave the command and they were off and running. The search took them through the ship but dead-ended by the wave pool.

"The scent of the chlorine might be messing with Sarge's ability to track," she said. "Let's pull him out of this area and see if we can get him back on track. He needs to find a fresh scent."

Maya steered her partner into a corridor and then placed the T-shirt under the dog's nose again. Sarge whimpered.

"He's confused," Maya said. "I'm not sure what's happening." She rubbed the Malinois's ears. "I wonder if the scent is bringing back how he was treated by Joel. Being abducted is just as traumatic for a dog as it is for a person." Maya put her face close to Sarge's and rubbed his ears.

"Poor guy," David said.

She looked up at him. "What if we just keep walking and searching? Maybe he'll pick up on something."

After several hours, both David and Maya admitted to feeling discouraged. They stopped to grab hot dogs to eat and got a container of water for Sarge.

David's radio made a static noise. He pressed the talk button. "What is it?"

Noah's voice came across the line. "Been asking a lot of questions of Joel's coworkers. Not coming up with much, but several of them did mention that he liked to go to movies when he wasn't working."

"Okay, we'll head over to the movie theater. Thanks, Noah."

"All the kitchen crew knows we're looking for him. They are the ones most likely to recognize him anyway," Noah added.

"I agree. Putting something out to the public might

cause unnecessary fear. Stay in touch." David clicked off his radio and looked at Maya. "We're headed to the theater."

"I have no idea where the theater is."

Maya's heartbeat clicked up a notch when David said they were going to search the theater. Maybe they were getting closer. There were a thousand places someone could hide on this ship. If Joel didn't return to his cabin though, where would he sleep? On a deck chair?

So far, from what Noah had indicated Joel didn't have friends who might let him hide in their cabin. That meant he probably had to stay in the public places. Though, a crew member might know of some tucked-away places no one would think to search.

They hurried past a corridor of shops and turned down a side corridor where the signs indicated the direction of the theater. There was even a marquee out front that advertised two movie choices: a classic Western and a kids' movie. When they checked the movie times, it looked like the Western had started twenty minutes ago.

They entered the back of the dark theater. Sarge heeled beside Maya. The movie flickered on the screen. Though it was hard to see, it looked like the theater was maybe half-full. If Joel Morris was in here, how were they going to find him and keep him from fleeing? Maybe they could wait until the film was over and watch the people come out. The movie had started only twenty minutes ago though, and there were two exits at the front of the theater by the screen through which someone could escape unnoticed if they wanted to.

David pointed, indicating that she and Sarge would take one aisle and he would take the other. "No flashlights," he whispered. "We don't want to give him a chance to get away."

Maya wasn't sure if not using flashlights would make a difference. Even in the dark, David's uniform was easy to spot and Sarge as well would cause a panic to Joel Morris if he barked. As she worked her way down the aisle, row by row, no one seemed alarmed. Though some people glanced in her direction most kept their attention on the film.

A gunfight scene erupted on the screen which made it impossible to hear anything else. When she was nearly to the first row, Sarge tugged on his leash indicating the back of the theater by the main exit they had come through. Though her eyes were still not completely adjusted to the lack of light, she thought she saw a figure—she could not tell if it was a man or woman—get up and slip out.

She hurried back up the aisle. A woman holding the hand of a small child had gotten up and blocked her way.

The woman whispered, "Do you know where the bathroom is?"

"Nice doggie," the little boy said.

"I don't know where the bathroom is. Scuse me," Maya moved to arc around the woman and child so she could reach the exit where the person had gone. She stepped out into the bright lights. Plenty of people were walking around the shops and places to eat. She scanned back and forth. None of the men seemed in a hurry and no one looked like Joel.

A man walking casually with a hat pulled down low over his face caught her attention. She and Sarge ran toward the man but when he looked in her direction, she saw that it wasn't Joel.

Maya led Sarge back into the theater. She didn't see David anywhere.

The man sitting at the end of the row she was standing by tugged on her sleeve. "He went that way in a hurry."

The man pointed to one of the two exits at the front of the theater. With Sarge heeling beside her, Maya hurried toward the exit. David must have seen something. She pulled the curtain aside that blocked the exit and stepped into what appeared to be a dark hallway.

Sarge pulled on the leash and yipped. The level of excitement he exhibited suggested that his powerful K-9 nose had picked up on something.

"Wait." Maya fumbled for her phone to turn on the flashlight app.

Sarge got even more excited. She shone the light all around. They were in a wide hallway that looked like it was used for storage. There were lots of boxes, totes and movie posters. Now that she had some light, she could see the door at the other end of it that led back outside.

Sarge yanked on the leash. At first, she thought he was headed toward the door, but then he lunged at a stack of totes. The totes started to wobble.

A man jumped out at her from behind them and lunged at her. She dropped her phone as she twisted to get away. Sarge barked. The dog had grabbed hold of the man's pant leg and was tugging.

Though she could not see, it was clear this had to be Joel. Maya struggled to get away when the man grabbed her arm and twisted it behind her back. He pushed her arm up so far it hurt. He leaned close enough that she felt his hot breath on the back of her neck. "I've had about enough of you."

A door slammed somewhere. The attacker pushed her hard from behind. The impact of hitting the floor knocked the wind out of her. Was she hearing David's voice or just imagining it?

David returned through the theater exit door when he realized after a quick search that Joel had not gone out the door but had probably hidden behind the boxes. When he shone his light, he saw Maya falling to the floor and Joel kicking Sarge to get away from him. The dog yipped in pain.

The perp took off back toward the theater. Someone must have heard the ruckus because the lights were on and people had gotten out of their seats. The movie continued to flicker on the screen. Joel got around the people by jumping over seats.

"Stop, security!" David yelled.

Joel pushed the people attempting to stop him out out of the way and disappeared into the main corridor. David hurried up the aisle as folks stepped aside so he could get to the main exit.

Heart pounding, David stepped out into the busy thoroughfare. A lot of passengers were strolling around.

He could see quite far up and down the corridor. Of course, Joel would stop running and blend in. There had been nothing distinct in what Joel had been wearing. All neutral colors meant that he would blend into background pretty easily. David studied the shoppers and clusters of people for at least a minute before giving up hope of finding Joel. He radioed the other two officers letting them know the last place Joel had been spotted. David spoke into his radio. "He had on a beige shirt and gray pants. He was wearing a black baseball hat but it fell off in the fight he had with Maya and Sarge. Medium height, medium build, brown hair."

Noah came on the line. "He might try to grab another hat somewhere to hide his face, right?"

"Maybe. If you could keep searching, I'll send Hans into the security room to see if he can spot anything on the cameras in this area. I'll be back to help as soon as I make sure Maya isn't hurt."

After signing off, David turned and raced back into the theater toward the exit by the screen. He could hear Sarge barking even before he pulled back the curtain to see if Maya was okay.

One of the moviegoers standing close to the exit curtain said, "We tried to get in there to help that woman, but that dog won't let anyone close."

When Sarge saw David, he stopped barking and wagged his tail. David dove down to the floor and gathered Maya in his arms. Sarge licked David's face and whined.

She opened her mouth, but no words came out. Was she in pain. Had she broken something?

He drew her closer. David addressed the three people who had pulled back the curtain and were peering in. "Can someone call for a medic?"

"Sure," said an older man.

"I'm okay." Her voice was shaky.

"Hey." Joy surged through him when she looked at him. "You're back."

"Did you get Joel?"

David shook his head. "Hans and Noah are still searching."

"I'm sure they need our help." Maya tried to sit up but fell back down into his arms. She was weak from the fight she'd been in.

"First, we need to get you checked out and make sure it's nothing serious."

"That is precious time that we'll lose."

"True. But I don't want you passing out because you have some sort of serious injury going on. If you need to rest a few hours, so be it. Sarge and I will continue the search."

She smiled. "Yes, Sarge seems to have taken a liking to you." She reached out to pet the dog. Sarge responded by licking her cheek.

The EMTs popped their heads in, a man and woman who looked like they could have been twins, both blond and slender. David knew the woman's name was Vicky, but her male partner must be a new hire. "We got a stretcher for her."

"She was pushed hard," David said, looking back toward her.

"Did you hit your head or anything?" Vicky dove in

with a tiny penlight which she shone on Maya's eyes. "Pupils aren't dilated."

"Is it even worth it to take me back to the infirmary?" Maya touched her arm and winced.

Vicky sat back on her toes. "It's always good to have the doc check you out. What's going on with your arm?"

"He twisted it really severely and then when I fell forward it took most of the impact."

"Might be fractured." The male EMT stepped closer. "Why don't we get her on the stretcher?"

The medics both rose to their feet and pushed the stretcher into the storage/hallway area.

As Vicky and her partner lifted Maya, she grasped David's sleeve. "Take care of Sarge for me."

"Will do. I'm sure he will be a help. I'll check with you in a bit or you can text me when you are given the okay to be released. Don't leave the infirmary alone."

As she was laid on the stretcher, she lifted a hand to indicate she agreed. He assumed that with medical personal around the infirmary and all of the crew on the lookout for Joel that Maya would be okay. He prayed he wasn't wrong.

FIFTEEN

Maya heard her phone beep that she had a text while the doctor, a woman with a grandmotherly disposition, checked her out. It was clear that the shipboard medical facilities had limited equipment. After doing an X-ray which showed no break, most of the doctor's examination involved asking a host of questions and turning Maya's arm and inquiring if it hurt.

Maya wondered if the text was from David. Maybe they had tracked down Joel.

The doctor held a penlight vertical in her hand. "Maya, I'm going to move this light across your field of vision. Please follow it with your gaze."

Maya complied with the doctor's wishes. "I didn't hit my head."

"I don't want to take any chances," the doctor said.

Maya shuddered at the memory of the attack as pain shot through her arm again.

"I think we are looking at a sprain for the arm. Ice it and try to limit use that would cause further damage." The doctor stepped over to a computer that was in the room and typed on a keyboard.

"Okay. Can I go now?"

"Your body and mind have been through a lot with this altercation. Why don't you rest for a little bit and then I will feel comfortable releasing you?"

Maya nodded. Once the doctor left the room, she reached for her phone which was on the rolling table by her bed. The text was not from David as she had hoped. It was from Poppy Walsh, another K-9 officer that Maya worked with.

Have an update on Katie's case with her aunt's reindeer ranch. Call me when you can.

Since the text had come in only a few minutes ago, she could probably catch Poppy. Maya pressed in the number. When she had gotten the temporary phone from the security office, she'd given the new number to Lorenza to forward to the rest of the team.

Poppy picked up right away. "Maya, good to see your name and number pop up on my phone."

The other woman's chipper voice reminded Maya that she longed to be back on shore with the rest of the team. "You did just text me a few minutes ago."

"So I did. Lorenza has made it super clear in the briefings that we need to make sure you are updated on our cases. She wants to ensure you hit the ground running when you get back on dry land. You are coming back, right? You haven't fallen in love with a handsome sailor or something?"

Maya's mind immediately went to David. "No, no handsome sailors on board."

"It's like I hear a smile in your voice. You *have* met someone?"

"Someone I like a great deal, but it's an impossible situation. I assure you as soon as this investigation is wrapped up, I will come ashore and be ready to dive back into my regular work."

"Good to hear," Poppy said. "Anyway, just wanted to let you know what is going on with that reindeer farm that Katie's aunt owns."

Katie was Lorenza's assistant. "Did the surveillance equipment you guys put up show something?" The ranch had suffered harassment, and reindeer had been let out of their pen. All but one was eventually found and then another reindeer was stolen.

"Yes indeed," Poppy said. "We caught a man in black with a hoodie covering his face running around the storage area and the bunkhouse on the ranch. Or should I say sneaking around, because his body language and the time of day all suggest he was up to some kind of mischief. Lorenza thinks if we can catch this guy, we'll get to the bottom of what is going on."

"Obviously from the way the guy was dressed, he didn't want to be identified. Any idea who it might be?"

"Not sure. All the people Katie and her aunt suggested might have something against the ranch had alibis that put them elsewhere."

"What's the team's next move then?"

"Lorenza is posting some private security guards by the place," Poppy said. "We think given the history of theft and destruction of property the guy in the hoodie will come back."

"Let's hope so. At least that's progress, huh?"

"Yes. How are things on board the ship?"

"Well, as I'm sure Lorenza has kept you up to speed. We have a suspect, but he's hiding out somewhere on the ship. He's a crew member so he knows all the good hiding places, and this is a big ship." As she spoke to Poppy, an idea occurred to Maya. Joel did know the ship really well. So wouldn't he go someplace the security cameras weren't likely to spot him, especially after he'd been tracked down in the theater? It seemed like he'd go deeper into the less public parts of the ship.

"Sound like you're getting close to bringing him in," Poppy said.

"We're concerned that once we dock tomorrow morning, he'll slip out into the general population. That doesn't give us much time. I would hate to have identified him as a very prominent suspect only to lose him out in the wide world." Maya felt some of the tension ease from her body. Talking with Poppy about the case, hearing her team member's encouragement, renewed her strength. She and David and the rest of the security team were going to catch this guy.

"I know you Maya, once you narrow in on a suspect you are like a dog on a scent. I bet before too long you'll be telling us that your suspect is in handcuffs and ready to be brought ashore."

"Thanks, Poppy. I needed that pep talk."

"That's what I'm here for."

Maya heard a male voice in the background like someone had come into the room where Poppy was. Her teammate's voice got fainter and Maya could no longer discern what she was saying. She figured she must be talking to the man who had entered the room.

Poppy came back on the line. "I got to go. Lex is here with Danny. We're going to make a picnic lunch and head to the park so Danny can play."

Lex was a park ranger that Poppy had recently worked with on a poaching case in Glacier Bay National Park. They had been romantically involved ten years ago, but it had ended and Lex had married someone else. Lex had lost his wife and been left to raise his son Danny alone until he was reunited with Poppy and they'd rekindled their romance.

Poppy was a year older than Maya. The fact that her colleague had found true love gave Maya some hope that she shouldn't assume that at thirty she was facing a life of singleness.

Maya said her goodbyes to Poppy and hung up.

The nurse popped her head around the curtain. "I heard voices in here. The doctor's orders are that you rest then we'll check you out in a bit."

Still gripping the phone, Maya nodded. "Okay."

The nurse's head disappeared, and Maya waited until the footsteps had receded before she put in a call to David to share her theory about where Joel might be hiding. He didn't pick up, so she texted him. She stared at the phone, half expecting an instantaneous response.

Though her mind was spinning with what to do about catching Joel, she leaned back and shut her eyes. It surprised her how easily sleep overtook her. She woke up in the dark. The nurse must have come in and shut the lights off. When she checked her phone, which had slipped out of her hand when she nodded off, she saw that only a half hour had passed. David still had not responded to her text.

An empty feeling invaded her awareness. She had to admit that getting a text from him lifted her spirits even if it was just about the case.

She could hear whispers and footsteps growing closer. She was reminded of the last time she was in this infirmary and she had wondered if the man they now knew as Joel Morris had come in to do her harm but been scared away. The footsteps grew louder and then took what sounded like an abrupt turn. More hushed voices landed on her ear.

Her phone pinged. She looked at her screen expecting to see David's text response. Instead, the message was from an unknown number, though it was crystal clear to Maya who had sent it.

I'm coming for you Maya. I know who you really are. You are in my way.

Again, she heard approaching footsteps pounding intensely as they came toward her. This time they did not veer off.

Fighting off a sense of defeat, David sat down on a bench to check his texts and email messages. Maybe Hans had spotted something on the security monitors or maybe a call had come in from a passenger who'd seen Joel. Sarge sat at David's feet and gazed up at him.

He had to admit the dog had found a way into his heart. He reached out and stroked the K-9's ears and muzzle.

The only text and missed call was from Maya. She hadn't left anything on voicemail, but he was happy that she'd sent a text.

I'm thinking that Joel knows this ship really well. He's going to go somewhere the security cameras can't see him.

True. But where to start? There were parts of the ship that even some of the crew didn't have access to. The engine room for instance. Only the captain and authorized maintenance people could go in there. Joel might steal a card key to get in there to hide. But that seemed like a lot of work and too much risk of being caught. The laundry facilities and other public parts of crew quarters did not have cameras. So that was a possibility. Hans so far hadn't spotted anyone who looked like Joel on the security cameras though it would be nothing to find a hat to cover his face from view.

Maybe he could brainstorm with Maya and come up with a plan. He dialed her number, but it went to voicemail. Maybe she'd turned it off and was sleeping.

He called the desk at the infirmary.

Someone picked up right away. "Alaska Dream infirmary. How may I help you?" A woman's voice came across the line.

"Can you check on Maya Rodriguez for me? She's not answering her phone."

"One second. Stay on the line. It's a short walk."

David heard footsteps and then the nurse spoke up. "She's not in her bed."

David swallowed hard to push down the rising panic. "Do you think she might have left?"

"Maybe, but the doctor requested to check her out one more time before that."

David stood up from the bench. "Maybe she just went to the bathroom or something. I'm on my way there. See you in five."

Sarge whimpered.

"Let's go, buddy. I'm afraid something might have happened to Maya. We sure wouldn't want that, would we? Since we both care about her."

He trotted along toward the infirmary when his phone pinged again. He breathed a sigh of relief. The text was from Maya.

Meet me in the hallway outside the back of the infirmary.

It was easy enough to reroute and head to where Maya had said she was waiting. He and Sarge stepped into a hallway that had three doors connected to it. All of which, judging by the signs on them, held medical supplies. He slipped past the first door and called Maya's name. Maybe she was in the adjoining hallway. Her descriptions of places on the ship could be a little wonky because she didn't use the same lingo that the crew did to describe locations.

Sarge sat on his back haunches and growled. The dog started to turn back in the direction they'd just come.

David had only a moment to register that the door

they had just passed was slightly ajar before a jolt of electricity hit his back and he crumpled to the ground. The last sound he heard was Sarge yelping as though in pain.

After realizing that Joel might be coming for her while she was in her hospital bed, Maya had slipped out and hidden in the first place she could find, a closet on the other side of the curtain from where her bed was. It wasn't until she was hiding that she realized in her haste that she had left her phone behind.

Not wanting to draw attention to herself, she waited in silence. When she didn't hear any more footsteps, she returned to her bed. Her phone had been stolen. She hurried to the front desk.

"Did you see anyone come or go through here? A man with brown hair—he may have had a hat on— average build?"

The nurse shook her head. "No, sorry. But the security officer should be here by now. He was on his way to talk to you when you didn't answer your phone."

Maya's heartbeat skipped up a notch. "Is the front entrance the only way in and out of the infirmary?"

"No, there is a back way where we keep our supplies. I'll show you."

The nurse led her past the curtains that served to divide the three hospital beds to a door which she opened. "It goes around the corner and then into a hallway."

"Thank you."

Maya hurried around the corner. She gasped at what she saw. Sarge lying prone, his legs jerking spastically.

David flat on his face, not moving. And a man kneeling over Sarge holding a Taser. Joel Morris.

She had no gun, no weapon of any kind, but she didn't care. Joel had hurt, maybe killed, the two beings she cared about more than anything else in the world.

"Stop right there."

Joel lifted his head. Green eyes caught and held the light. She moved toward him but hesitated when he bolted to his feet. Facing her as he backed up, he aimed the stun gun at her. Where had he gotten that? Both Sarge and David were shaking and immobilized from the jolt of electricity they'd received.

She held her hands up and backed far enough away that the stun gun wouldn't reach her.

"You will pay for thinking you could catch me, detective." He stepped toward her. His hand on the finger of the stun gun.

There was noise up the hallway—the sound of people, maybe coming this way.

Joel lifted his chin at the noise, turned and ran in the opposite direction, disappearing around a corner.

Maya chased after him. She entered a long hallway but Joel was nowhere in sight. She ran back to where Sarge and David lay. There were no people in the hallway. They must have turned down a different way. At least the potential of a crowd had scared Joel away before he could hit her with the stun gun.

David had stopped shaking but had not yet sat up. Sarge's legs still spasmed.

Maya grabbed David's radio off his belt and notified Noah where Joel was headed. She jumped up and ran down the hallway where she had just come from, call-ing for the nurse, and then returned to be with David and Sarge.

David was sitting up but looked very pale. Her K-9 partner had stopped quivering but still lay on his side, making yipping sounds that indicated he was in pain.

She handed David's radio back to him.

David's hands were shaking when he took the radio. "Thank you."

Maya drew her attention to her partner. She made soothing sounds. She petted his head and then along his back and stomach. Despite the pain and shock he must be going through, Sarge's tail thumped on the carpet when she touched him.

"Poor guy," David said. "It takes a while for the ef-fects of the stun gun to wear off. I still feel like I am vibrating from the inside."

She rested Sarge's head in her lap. "And it doesn't make any sense to him." Part of police training at the academy involved being zapped with the stun gun, so Maya knew what it felt like.

The nurse came around the corner. "What hap-pened?"

"These two were hit with a stun gun."

Her eyes widened. "Well, let's get you to an exam room." She looked at David. "Do you feel well enough to walk?"

"I'll be fine. It just takes a bit to feel normal. I don't need a doctor to look at me."

"What about the dog?" The nurse's voice filled with compassion as she stepped closer.

Maya stroked Sarge's head. She hated seeing him like this. "Let's just give him a minute. The stun gun doesn't do any permanent physical damage. I guess I yelled for you because I was so afraid when I saw these two just lying on the carpet, so disabled."

"Okay, then," the nurse murmured. "Let me know if you need anything." She headed back down the hall.

"I heard you talking to Noah," David said, reattaching his radio to his belt. "Maybe he'll spot Joel."

"The only reason that creep is coming out of hiding is to come after me and you. So far Hans has not spotted him on any of the security cameras."

"He knows the ship pretty well and he must be finding ways to avoid the cameras."

She nodded. "He must have a hiding place. Any ideas?"

"After I saw your text, I thought about that." David shook his head. "He would have access to all the areas that are for the crew members only. But there could be an empty cabin he managed to get into."

Sarge lifted his head and whimpered. Joy surged through Maya. "Hey buddy, welcome back." She rubbed his ears.

David reached out to pet him. "He growled right before the attack. Things could have been a lot worse if he hadn't been with me."

Sarge got to his feet and licked Maya's cheek. "I always feel like he has my back. I couldn't ask for a better partner. How did Joel get a stun gun anyway?"

"Hans texted me a while back that he'd taken off his belt to jump into a pool to help when a developmentally disabled who had been drowning started to pull the life-guard under with him. When he put the belt back on the stun gun was gone."

"That makes our perp that much more dangerous."

Both David and Maya petted the now fully revived Sarge. Their hands touched. Maya gazed into David's eyes as she felt a spark of awareness between them. Maybe it was just because she'd seen both her dog and the man she had to admit she cared about deeply in such a vulnerable state. All the same, she could not deny she had feelings for this man.

David slowly stood up "Come on, the three of us have a job to do." He held a hand out to help Maya to her feet.

When he grasped her hand, warmth spread up her arm and was like a zap of electricity to her heart. She glanced at him and quickly looked away, feeling her cheeks grow hot. Why did he make her feel like some sort of shy junior high girl?

David had turned to head up the hallway. She reached out for his arm, touching his elbow. "I'm just glad you and Sarge are okay. That was pretty scary to see you both lying on the floor like that." Her voice sounded breathless, but she didn't care.

David studied her for a moment. The blue sparkle in his eyes grew a little duller. "All in the line of duty, right?" His voice had no emotion at all.

Just like that he threw cold water on her feelings. "Yeah…right…sure." Her tone of voice did not hide her disappointment.

SIXTEEN

As he turned to head up the hallway, David cringed at his icy response to Maya. She had merely expressed that she cared about him…and that scared him. What would it mean to open his heart to a woman? It meant he could be hurt again. Not a chance he wanted to take.

Until she'd come into his life, he had liked his floating world with the ever-changing scenery. He'd felt a sense of purpose in knowing it was his job to keep the people on board safe. Now everything had gone sideways because if he was honest with himself, he cared about her too.

The realization made David walk even faster as if he could outrun his feelings.

"Slow down… Sarge and I can't keep up with you."

"Sorry, I'm just thinking that time is running short for catching Joel." That wasn't entirely true. Even though he was frustrated by the guy's ability to evade them, the fast walking had nothing to do with the manhunt they were in the midst of.

Maya and Sarge came alongside him. "So how do we find out if there are any empty cabins in the crew area?"

"We can check with the lady who makes those assignments. She's one deck up in a little administrative office."

As they walked side by side toward the elevator, he kept stealing glances in Maya's direction. Despite all his resistance, she had somehow managed to tap into some part of his heart that he'd thought had gone dormant. The part that wanted to love and give.

They rode the elevator up and David led them to the information office. The woman behind the desk smiled when she saw him. Juanita Dickens May was a woman in her sixties who had worked for the Alaska Dream cruise line in some capacity since she was twenty. David always felt like they understood each other in wanting to call the ship home and she had become a substitute mom for him in many ways.

"David, always good to see you! I have cookies I made myself in the crew kitchen if you're interested." Juanita stood up. "They are just in the back room."

"I wish I had time. We're kind of in the middle of something that can't wait."

"I've been watching those bulletins up on the newsfeed. I hope you catch the predator who has made it unsafe for women to be alone on the ship." Juanita drew her attention to Maya and Sarge. "Looks like you have some help with your search. Would your dog like a treat?"

David smiled at the offer. Juanita had treats for everyone of every age and species.

"It's better that the dog not have anything right now," Maya said. Sarge sat down beside her and looked up at Juanita.

The older woman studied Maya and then glanced in David's direction. Juanita was not dumb. She'd probably figured out that Maya wasn't just a passenger with a service dog. "You've done a good job, David, at not triggering panic but keeping passengers safe."

The compliment warmed him all the way to the marrow. "Thank you, Juanita. Which brings me to the reason we're here. We need to check on cabin vacancies in the crew quarters."

"I don't have to look. I can tell you right now that there are no vacancies in the crew quarters. Some have only one person when there is room for two. We were full up when we left Seattle. We had only one person quit last minute."

That one employee must be the woman who broke up with Joel. "Can I get her name and contact information?"

"Sure." Juanita bustled to her keyboard.

"Maybe it would be worth it to make a ship to shore call to the ex-girlfriend. She might be able to shed light on where Joel would be hiding."

The older woman handed David a printout. "When you're less busy, we'll have to grab a bite. See you at church on Sunday."

David took the printout. "Thanks, Juanita. For sure, we'll get a coffee or something soon."

As they left the office, Maya piped up. "They have a church on the ship?"

"It's kind of informal. There are about thirty of us who meet in the all-purpose conference room. We have a guitar player and Juanita has a beautiful singing voice."

"That's neat. You do have fellowship. Here I thought you were some sort of lone ranger Christian."

David laughed. "There's a lot you don't know about me."

"And Juanita is kind of like your shipboard mom." Maya's voice got quieter. "You have a nice life here."

Had Maya come to a place of acceptance that there couldn't be anything between them? Somehow that made him really sad. The turmoil he felt caused his stomach to twist into a knot. "Maybe when all this is over, and Joel is behind bars, you can take a cruise and actually enjoy yourself."

"That sounds fun. I'd like that. If I can engineer some time off work and save the money."

"I think as a thank-you I might be able to talk the owner into comping you."

Maya stopped walking and faced David. "I'm not sure why you're inviting me?"

He was quick with his answer, realizing how misleading the offer had sounded. "As a friend and as a thank-you for all your help." At the same time, there was a part of him that wanted a chance to see her again once the case was wrapped up and things calmed down. He clenched his jaw. It felt like his emotions were swinging one way and then the other, making it seem like he was teasing Maya, which hadn't been his intent at all.

Before she could respond, David's radio buzzed. He pushed the talk button. "Go ahead, Noah."

"I've searched all the possibilities in crew headquarters, laundry, storage, even the dining hall and kitchen. There was some evidence in one of the linen storage closets that someone may have slept in there, but no one, including the roommate, has seen any sign of him. However, all the other crew members know to be on the lookout for Joel."

"I doubt he'll come back to that linen closet now." David took a deep breath to stave off the mounting frustration. "Look you must be tired. Why don't you get some shut-eye?"

"I just need an hour or so and then I'll come back on duty."

"Let me know when you are rested and ready. Over and out." David put his radio back on his belt. He stared at the piece of paper Juanita had given him and read the name Tiffany Swarthout. He'd seen the name before when they'd been looking to see if any employees had quit. "Let's make this phone call. Right now, it's our only lead for finding Joel before it's too late."

As David, Maya and Sarge returned to the security office to make the call to Joel's ex-girlfriend, Maya found herself wrestling with confusion about David. He'd invited her back to the ship when things would be more relaxed while making it clear that the invitation was purely platonic in nature. Given her feelings, she wasn't sure if she could just be his friend. It led only to heartache to hold out hope that when a man said he wanted to be friends that perhaps it could turn into something more.

When they entered the security office, Hans was still watching the screens.

"You look wiped. Why don't you take a break?"

"Good idea." Hans rubbed the back of his neck and turned his head side to side. "So do you have any new leads?"

David held up his phone. "I'm hoping this phone call might help us narrow down our search. It's Joel's ex-girlfriend. We think she might be the reason he went off the deep end and started attacking women."

Hans nodded. "Let me know what you two come up with." He retreated to the back room and closed the door.

David sat down and placed the phone on the counter. "I'll put her on speaker so you can hear the conversation."

Maya took a chair, determined to stop thinking about David in a romantic way and focus on catching Joel. She hadn't come on board the ship to fall for someone—she'd been hired to do a job and she needed to get it done.

David punched in the number. He set the phone down on the counter by the security screens.

She did a quick study of the security screens, still hoping that Joel would make an appearance.

After three rings, a voice came on the line. "Hello?"

David leaned toward the phone. "Is this Tiffany Swarthout?"

"Yes, what's this about?"

"This is David Garrison, chief of security on the Alaska Dream cruise ship out of Seattle. I understand you used to be an employee here."

"That's right," Tiffany answered.

"May I ask why you quit?"

There was a long pause but then she said, "I quit to get away from my then boyfriend."

"Joel Morris?"

"Yes. Why do you ask? Has something happened?"

"We have reason to believe that Joel is responsible for some attacks on women on the ship…and a murder."

A gasp came across the line. "I'm so sorry to hear that! I knew I had to get away from him. He scared me. But I—I had no idea he would go after other women."

"Why did he scare you?"

"Joel was wonderful at first. The attention, the flattery and the gifts made me feel so special. But then if I even talked to another guy, even on the job, he would get mad. I started to see a side of him that made me afraid. He was possessive and controlling." A tense silence filled the air. When she spoke again Tiffany's voice was raw with pain. "But when he got physical, I knew I needed to get away fast."

That made sense to Maya. Joel had probably always been unstable, but it came out only in intimate relationships like a romance. "Hi Tiffany, this is Maya Rodriguez. I'm helping with the investigation. Had Joel said anything about past relationships?"

"He had nothing but negative things to say about other women, including his mother. That should have been a red flag," Tiffany said. "Please, if I had known he was going to hurt other women… I don't know, maybe I should have done something."

"Tiffany, don't beat yourself up," Maya said. "Right now, we want to focus on getting Joel into custody."

"Thank you for saying that. I want to help any way I can. It's important that Joel not hurt anyone ever again. What can I do?"

"Joel's hiding somewhere on the ship. We think that you might be able to help us find him. Was there any special place he may have taken you that he might be using as a hideout?"

Tiffany didn't answer right away. "We used to meet on the upper deck at night after our shifts. Hardly anyone goes up there. It was private."

Maya thought it would be better not to tell her about the attacks and murder on the upper deck. She seemed eaten up with guilt as it was. "Anything else you can remember would be helpful, Tiffany. Even if it doesn't seem important."

"I'm just trying to think of something that might be helpful," Tiffany said. "He had worked on that ship for a long time… He knew lots of clandestine places." The silence indicated that she was searching her memory. "Oh wait. I do remember something. You know that entertainment venue, the really big one where they have the musical reviews and concerts?"

"On deck seven?" David's voice held a note of hope.

"Yes, the one with a catwalk. Anyway, Joel took me up there late at night after the venue was shut down. He knew the code to get in there through the back way where the performers enter."

"Tiffany, that may help us," he said. "If you remember anything else, please get in touch with us right away."

"I will. I had no idea Joel was capable of killing someone." Tiffany's voice faltered.

It sounded like she was feeling a lot of anguish. "Tiffany, we don't blame you in any way. You did the right thing in protecting yourself."

They said their goodbyes and David clicked the phone off. "Go wake up Hans. We might need his help."

Maya hurried into the break room and shook Hans's shoulder. "So sorry to disturb you. We might have a lead on where Joel is hiding out."

Hans sat up, blinking rapidly. "Give me just a second."

When she returned to the main room of the security office, David was clicking away on the computer keyboard. He stared at the screen. "The last show for that theater shut down over two hours ago. They do family-friendly stuff, so they are not going all night." He grabbed his phone and pressed in a number. "I have a master key to get in. I just need to get the permission of the guy who manages that theater."

While David made the call, Hans stumbled out of the break room. Still looking a little sleepy.

"Long night for all of us, huh?" he said, glancing toward David who had just hung up the phone. "So what's the plan?"

David motioned for Maya and Hans to move in closer as he pointed at the computer screen. "I've got a rough map of the theater that is in all the guides for the ship. It's a big theater with two entrances for the public and two for the entertainment at the back."

Maya stared at the screen. In addition to the rows of seats, there was a balcony. "There must be dressing rooms, right?"

"Yes. They are not shown but they are off to either

side of the stage. Plus, there's a costume and prop storage room here next to the women's dressing room."

Hans leaned closer to the screen. "Lot of places someone could hide."

"Hans I want you to enter through one of the public entrances. Maya and I along with Sarge will each come through the back way."

"Got it," Maya and Hans spoke in unison.

As they got prepared to leave and head toward the theater, that familiar mixture of anticipation and fear coursed through Maya. When she worked with the rest of the K-9 team, the intensity of emotion was the same.

As they hurried down corridors toward the theater, she wished they had guns. Even though there were three of them and only one suspect, she was keenly aware of how vulnerable she felt going into a potentially volatile situation unarmed.

SEVENTEEN

As they got closer to the theater, they slowed down from a jog to a brisk walk. Though his injured leg was hurting, David relished the excitement of moving in on a suspect. He swiped the card that would open the door for Hans. He cupped the other man's shoulder. "Go in on my command. It's best that we all enter at the same time. Give Maya and me a few minutes to get around to the back. I'll radio you when we're in place. The doors have been reprogrammed so you can't get out without a card key. If he's in there, we can trap him."

Hans nodded while he held on to the door David had just swiped. He had it open less than an inch. Not enough so anyone would notice it was open. Hans gave David a quick salute. "Got it."

David's heart was already pounding from the run to the theater and the anticipation of catching Joel. He led Maya to the door she was to enter and unlocked it for her. "You don't have a radio, but I'll step back from the door and give you a hand signal that I'm going in."

She nodded and gazed at him with such trust in her

eyes. While Sarge stood at attention looking up at him. Maybe it was just the adrenaline coursing through his system, but he felt so drawn to her in the moment that he reached up and grazed her cheek with his fingers. "Stay safe."

He sprinted to the other door and unlocked it. With the door only ajar a sliver, he peered inside not seeing or hearing anything. He looked around for something to brace the door in place so he could signal Maya without losing time unlocking the door again. Just inside the door was an empty shoe box. He grabbed the top of the box to hold the door in place and then he radioed Hans. "We're in place, give me a five count before you go in. Go slow. If he is in there, we don't want to alarm him. Our best chance of catching him is if we can surprise him. Maybe we'll get lucky and he'll be sleeping. Let's keep radio silence for now unless you see him."

"Got it," Hans said.

David took several steps back and craned his neck. Maya was staring in his direction waiting for his signal. She must have braced her door as well.

He lifted and dropped his hand making as big a motion as possible so she could see him in the dim light. She disappeared. David bolted toward the door and eased his way inside where it was even darker. He had come in on the side of the men's dressing room. As his eyes adjusted to the dim light, he saw the sign on the door. The dressing room was unlocked. He eased the door open and peered inside. It was an open room with makeup tables and mirrors. Not many places to hide.

David stepped outside into the hall that led to the

backstage area. When he peered out onto the stage whose front curtain was open, he could just make out Hans as he searched the theater seats and then headed up to the balcony. David's gaze was drawn upward to the catwalk and the rows of lights. He didn't see movement anywhere.

Still remaining hidden behind the back curtain, he peered across the empty stage expecting to see Maya. He waited a few seconds more before becoming worried. She should have cleared both the dressing and costume rooms by now.

Aware that Joel could be anywhere in the theater, David slipped behind the back curtain to avoid being seen. Concerned, he hurried across the stage to check on Maya.

Maya cleared the women's dressing room fairly quickly, but the costume room proved to be more of a chore. There were a hundred nooks, crannies and closets where someone could hide. Sarge sniffed around, alerting to something in the corner behind a rack of costumes.

Even with Sarge to help her, she was keenly aware of how vulnerable she was without a weapon. Even though Joel had dropped the hunting knife, he worked in a kitchen and could have stolen one of the chef's knives easily enough.

She called toward where Sarge had alerted. "Ship security. Stay where you are."

Sarge sat back on his haunches and let out a single sharp bark. She relaxed a little. If there had been a person back there, he would have remained standing and kept barking. She hurried to where Sarge had alerted.

When she peered behind the rack of costumes, she found what looked like a makeshift bed fastened from some costumes and a blanket and a take-out food container. Evidence that Joel had probably been there recently. He'd have to be out by early afternoon the next day when the actors and tech people showed up to get ready for the evening shows. She was starting to get a picture of how Joel must be evading them by moving from place to place at different times of the day when he knew certain parts of the ship would be closed down. Her guess was that if he hadn't hidden the evidence of his staying here, he hadn't left. That meant that he was still somewhere in the theater. She tensed at the thought.

The door burst open.

She whirled around. Even though he was dressed in black just like she was, his stature gave David away.

"I was worried when you didn't show backstage."

"He's been here, and I think he's still in the theater." She pointed to the makeshift bed.

David stepped in to look. "Let me alert Hans." He pulled his radio off his belt, then spoke in a whisper. "Hans, are you there? We think the suspect is on the premises." David took his finger off the talk button. He glanced nervously at Maya. Sarge let out a yip. He spoke into the radio again. "Hans, are you there?"

A tension-filled silence fell between them.

"Do you think Joel got to him?"

David shook his head. "Not sure. But if Joel did get to Hans, it means he know we're in here looking for him."

"Maybe he silenced his radio because he saw Joel, and he didn't want the noise to mess with his chances of catching him."

"Maybe," David said. "We're dealing with a bunch of unknowns. All the same, move slowly and try not to be detected. I'm sure Sarge will sound the alarm if you find Joel. I'll get to you as fast as I can."

She nodded. "I'll take stage left and work my way up to the balcony. You can take stage right. We'll meet in the balcony."

David nodded. "Let's do this." He disappeared from sight. She could hear his feet padding softly as he hurried to the other side of the theater.

Maya searched the backstage area and then took the steps down to the auditorium where she pressed against a wall. Sarge remained close beside her as they inched along. She gazed down the rows of seats, knowing that Joel could be hiding in any one of them. A chill raced down her spine as flashes of his previous attacks assailed her, but nothing would deter her. She had a job to do.

Working her way to the end of the auditorium, she pushed open the swinging doors that led to the lobby. Maya could see David on the other side of the lobby though he was mostly a moving shadow. She saw him only because she was looking for him. Other than the ticket booth, there was no place in the lobby to hide. Heart pounding, she sprinted the short distance to the ticket booth. She peered through the window half expecting Joel to jump up at her. When she tried the door to the ticket booth it was locked. That settled that.

David came toward her. "We've got to find Hans. He's still not responding by radio. The last place I saw him was the balcony. Let's head up there."

They separated and Maya hurried back into the auditorium with Sarge. She found the winding staircase to the balcony and headed up. She stepped out onto the balcony and searched the seats while she moved toward the back. Opposite her, David had made his way to the very back of the balcony and was moving down row by row.

A light on the stage burst on. Maya turned around. Sarge growled. Someone lay face down on the stage with a spotlight on him. Maya froze in place. It was Hans and he wasn't moving.

Quelling a rising panic, David hurried down the balcony stairs and raced toward the stage where his colleague lay, maybe unconscious, maybe dead. It was clear now Joel was in the theater and he was playing a sick game with them.

He bolted toward the stage fully aware that Joel might be watching them.

David's primary concern was for Hans, but he also thought maybe the perp might be setting some kind of trap. His attention was drawn upward to the rows of stage lights that must weigh a ton. He got to the base of the stage, standing at the bottom of the stairs that led up. His gaze moved across the auditorium where Maya and Sarge were. They'd slowed down as well. Hans still had not moved. David's chest grew tight at the sight of his prone partner. And then he saw the pool of blood around Hans's head. Forgetting the risk, David bolted up the stage reaching out for the injured officer.

A force came at him from behind, knocking him off his feet while a bolt of electricity shot through him. David was momentarily paralyzed. He could hear Sarge barking and feel the sensation that Joel was reaching into his chest pocket.

As he lay unable to move, he heard retreating footsteps headed toward one of the backstage doors. Maya was right beside him. She shouted at him as she ran past him. "He took your card key. That was all he wanted."

David was still extremely disoriented. Joel had known he was trapped and outnumbered. Escape was the only option and now he had a master card key. Knowing that Maya and Sarge were in hot pursuit of Joel, David drew his attention to Hans as he waited for the effect of the stun gun to wear off.

With the spotlight on, he could see that the other man was still breathing. He reached out and touched the puddle of blood by Hans's head. He drew it up to his nose expecting that coppery smell. It wasn't blood at all, red dye or something like it from the prop room.

He reached out to Hans, lifting his closed eyelids. Something had caused him to lose consciousness even if he wasn't bleeding. Hans's radio was not on his belt. Joel must have taken it. David grabbed his own radio and called for a medic. "I've got an officer who needs medical attention. Deck seven. The stage of the main entertainment venue."

"We're on our way. Be there in five."

"Thanks."

He rose to his feet and stepped toward the door where Maya and Sarge had gone chasing after Joel. The hallway was dark, though he could see lights at the end of it where it connected with the public part of the ship. He ran to the end of the hallway and peered out, not seeing Maya or Joel. There were still a few people strolling around. Some of the shops stayed open late as did the bars and buffets.

He needed to get back and make sure Hans was taken care of. Once he was back on the stage where the officer still lay motionless, it took only a few more minutes before the EMTs arrived.

David leaned over while the medic was checking Hans out and taking his vitals. "Don't be alarmed. The blood is not real."

The EMT gave Hans a quick-once over. Then rolled Hans on his back and lifted his eyelids. "He might have sustained a blow to the head." The EMT turned back toward his partner. "Let's get him on the stretcher."

David watched them transport Hans. He'd have to check in with the doctor in a bit. Knowing that Joel would be privy to all radio communication, David called Noah on the phone and told him he needed to get back on shift. "Meet me in the security office and we'll come up with a strategy. He's got a master card key. That means he has access to a ton more places." Fortunately, it was a different master card key that gave David access to passenger rooms and could be used only if the safety of the passenger was at risk. The key that Joel had taken would get him into any shop or public area that was locked after hours. It also gave him access to supply closets where merchandise was stored.

He had just moved to step off the stage and head out the backstage entrance when Maya came through the door with Sarge right beside her. She spoke between breaths, shaking her head. "We lost him."

"Where at?"

"He went down a corridor where there are a bunch of niche shops that are not open late. He probably went into one of the shops and the door locked behind him. If Joel was still carrying that knife, Sarge could have sniffed him out."

David knew the area that Maya was talking about. Joel could have taken a side hallway as well. "Let's get up to the security office—maybe we can see him on camera. I'm going to send Noah out so we can catch our breath and grab a quick bite. This could take all night."

"How is Hans?"

"Not sure. I'll check in with the doctor later," David said. "Joel took Hans's radio. So all communication will be via phone. We don't want Joel knowing what our next step is."

They hurried back to the security office. David had communicated with Noah where to begin his search. David put on a pot of coffee and grabbed some granola bars from a cupboard above the microwave. Maya was already sitting in front of the security monitors clicking through them and shaking her head.

He placed the granola bar on the counter in front of her. "Thanks." Her fingers tapped the keyboard as she switched from one camera to another to see what was going on.

"Why are you shaking your head?"

"It feels like we're doing the same thing over and

over and Joel keeps getting the upper hand." She lifted her hands from the keyboard and leaned closer to the monitors. "Some of these screens are black." She put her fingers back on the keyboard and clicked around to bring up the different screens.

David drew his attention to the black screens. "He's disabling the cameras." He clenched his jaw. "At least we know where he's been. By the time we could get Noah there, Joel will have moved on."

"We're running out of time, David. What we're doing is not working." She looked back at the screens. "And now it's like he's toying with us."

"What are you suggesting?"

Maya swiveled in her chair. "I think we need to set a trap, and I think I need to be the bait."

EIGHTEEN

Even as Maya proposed the plan to catch Joel, she had to fend off the rising fear. Sarge looked up at her and made a whimpering noise.

David didn't answer right away. He straightened up and looked at the black screens. "I don't like the idea of putting you at risk."

"How many more hours do we have until we are in port?"

"We'll get in early morning in about six hours." David shook his head. "I don't know if it will even work to set a trap. All he has to do is hide out until we dock."

"So our last chance to get him would be before he leaves the ship?"

"Right. We can make sure security is high when we dock, but I'm concerned he'll be able to give us the slip, considering how much skill he has displayed so far."

"We know that he has a thing for that upper deck. It's been closed off and there are no cameras up there. What has it been… More than a day since he tried to attack a woman other than me? I say that his anger is mostly directed at me because I am trying to keep him from hurting other women. What I know about my training in criminal psychology tells me he will need to try to get to me again soon. It's like a compulsion."

David ran his hands through his hair.

She could tell he still wasn't convinced. "Look, David. I don't want to do this either. But I want to catch this guy. Which means I have to look totally vulnerable. So Sarge can't be there."

"I don't like it, Maya. You'll be risking your life."

The plan was becoming clearer in her mind. "He's smart enough to know to look for you and the rest of the security team. You can't be anywhere close. Is there a way we could set up hidden cameras so you guys see what was going on if I did need help?"

"How would we get to you fast enough? Besides, we don't have extra security cameras."

"All of that would have to be worked out." Maya felt an increasing tension in her muscles as she thought about what she was proposing. "I just don't know if there are any other options at this point."

David's phone buzzed. He took it out of his pocket. As Maya listened to one side of the conversation, it was clear that Noah had spotted either Joel or some evidence of the killer's whereabouts. David ended the conversation by saying. "Okay, we'll get there as fast as we can."

He clicked off his phone. "A passenger called in that they thought they saw someone in the bumper car area which is shut down right now. If it's Joel, it's going to take all three of us to catch him. Let's go. I need to think about your plan some more, Maya. There has to be another way."

She shoved Sarge's leash toward David. "You take him. That way while we're searching, I'll look super vulnerable. Joel cannot control his impulse to go after women who remind him of Tiffany. Maybe he'll come after me while we are looking for him."

"Maya, we've got to do this in an organized way. Security measures need to be in place to ensure you'll be safe."

"We're running out of time. And I do have self-defense training. All we need to do is lure him out." Given Joel's previous attacks, David's concerns were not unfounded. But the thing foremost in her thoughts was catching Joel. Maya hurried toward the elevator that would take them to the deck where the bumper cars were. She held the door for Sarge and David.

She was afraid the few minutes in the elevator would give David time to make more objections about the danger she was putting herself in. However, before he could speak, his phone rang again. It was clear it was Noah once more. David gave single word responses and then ended with. "Okay, we'll widen the search."

Clicking off his phone, he turned toward Maya. "Noah says he found disabled cameras in the bumper car area. We're going to widen the search to the areas around the bumper cars. He is searching the north end. We'll take south and east."

"We are running out of time David. We need to split up. I'll be okay."

David didn't answer right away. Finally, he nodded. "You move toward the arcade. Widen your search as you clear each area." David handed her the leash. "You're vulnerable enough as it is. Take your partner with you."

As she held Sarge's leash, Maya wrestled with a mixture of relief and frustration. If Joel saw that Sarge was with her, he would be less likely to come at her knowing that he'd been foiled by the dog before. But having her partner close made her feel that much safer. The elevator doors slid open.

"Remember, I'm a phone call away," David said as they stepped out.

"I know." Her throat went tight. The time it took to make the call was enough time for Joel to kill her. If she could even get to the phone fast enough.

David reached out and touched her arm. "I'm afraid for you."

She tilted her head to look into his eyes. The concern she saw in his expression compelled her to fall into his arms. "I'm scared too."

He held her for a long moment. Drawing strength from his embrace, she closed her eyes and relished how safe it felt to be in his arms. She pulled back.

He leaned and kissed her on the forehead. "We're in this together. I have your back."

Still reeling from the intensity of his hug and the light touch of his lips on her skin, she nodded. "You have to give me some credit. I do have police training."

They ran toward the bumper cars and then split off. Maya saw the sign for the arcade which was next to the bumper cars. She could see the bumper cars through the glass walls. Movement and shadow on the other side must be Noah searching the area.

She stepped toward the arcade but was surprised to find the door unlocked. Maya clicked David's number. She spoke in a whisper. "I'm outside the arcade. It's not locked."

"I'm coming your way."

She looked up to where a security camera was still in place. Maybe someone had just forgotten to lock the arcade. Most of the security cameras were up high enough that Joel must have some sort of long object to reach up and disable them. His motive was probably to make their search for him that much harder, but it also left a trail of where he'd been. It was like he was playing a game of cat and mouse with the security team.

She glanced through the windows of the arcade again. Lights flashed on one of the games that had a moment ago been dark. Her heart pounded as adrenaline surged through her body. Joel was in there or had been only seconds ago. If she was going to catch him, she couldn't wait for backup. Maya stepped inside with Sarge beside her. She searched for an exit door.

The arcade was long and narrow. She spotted the exit sign nearly hidden behind a tall game but could still see the flashing lights of the game in her peripheral vision. After running toward the exit, she pushed open the door, then found herself staring down the short hallway where she could see a sliver of the bumper car area. An odd banging sound caught her attention.

She took in a deep breath. Sarge stood at attention watching her and waiting for a command. Her partner's response gave her courage and quieted her fear. She moved toward the bumper car area. Through the glass, she could see that someone had started two of the bumper cars, so they were banging into each other over and over. Lights flashed on the cars each time they collided. Clearly, this was Joel's work. There was something menacing about the repetitive noise.

"Maya?"

David's voice reverberated behind her and she whirled around.

"I thought I could catch him." She had a feeling Joel was long gone by now.

David held a small piece of paper. "This was on the flashing game in the arcade." He handed her the piece of paper.

The message was in block letters with a red pen.

I will get you, Maya.

Even in the dim light, David could see all the color drain from Maya's face as she held the threatening note.

She kept her eyes on the note. "You know what I'm feeling right now?"

"Fear would be understandable," David said.

She looked up and shook her head. "What I feel now is righteous anger. Joel thinks he has the upper hand. And now he thinks he can torment me. He's a criminal and he needs to be behind bars."

Through the glass windows to the bumper cars, David could see Noah shutting off the two cars that were banging into each other. The other man shook his head, indicating that he had not found any sign of Joel.

"David, we *have* to set a trap for Joel with me as the bait. It's the only way."

He signaled for Noah to come join them. David knew what Maya was saying was true. He just didn't want to think about the risk she would be taking. "We have to find a way to make sure you will be safe."

"Don't you see? Joel isn't stupid. If you are close by, he'll figure it out. I have to look totally exposed." She held up the piece of paper. "This note indicates his obsession with me. We're dealing with a clever, unhinged man. The only thing we have working for us is his desire to hurt, even kill me. I believe if he sees a chance, he will take it."

Noah came over and joined them. "This guy knows the ship really well. There are too many places for him to hide until we get into port. David, we've got to do something different."

Maya turned toward Noah. "We were just talking about that." She handed him the threatening note. "We think if Joel gets a chance, he will come after me."

"What Maya wants to do though is very dangerous," David muttered. "Joel will figure out if protection is close by."

"So we have to come up with a way to trick him," Maya said. "If I go up to the upper deck alone, I believe that he will follow me up there and look for a chance to attack me."

David addressed his comments to Noah. "The upper deck is where Joel and his girlfriend who dumped him used to go. It's a triggering location. Given that the murder and a number of attacks took place up there, we believe he has almost an uncontrollable impulse to go after any woman who looks like his former girlfriend when he is up there."

Noah rubbed his chin. "So, we have to have a way to keep eyes on Maya and get to her quickly without Joel figuring out the setup."

David started walking. "Let's head back to the security office."

They all started walking while they brainstormed a plan.

"If we position cameras on the upper deck, he'll figure it out," Maya warned.

"We have almost no additional surveillance equipment anyway. We'd have to work with whatever the electronics shop had." David shook his head in frustration. "He'd figure out he was being watched anyway. I feel like our hands are really tied here."

They continued toward an open area with a view of the water and mountains in the distance. The light in the distance was their port city of Seward. Maya stopped and Sarge sat down beside her. "David what about the North Star? You would have a view of the upper deck from there if it was up high enough right?"

"Probably," he replied. "But I couldn't get down fast enough to come to help you."

"We'd have to create some sort of relay system. Noah up in the North Star where he has a view of the deck. And then you hiding somewhere so you could get to me as quickly as possible…but not where Joel would ever figure out where you were."

"That might work," Noah said. "We take the North Star up with me in it. Put out a notice that says it's broken and locked in place, so Joel doesn't make the connection. And if I stay up there an hour or so before Maya goes out on the upper deck…"

"We know that Joel stalks his victims and waits for an opportunity. Before I head to the upper deck, I'll give him plenty of opportunity to see that neither Sarge nor David are close, but I will try to stay in public areas."

"If I see that Maya is in danger, I can text you, David." Noah's inflection indicated excitement about the plan.

Maya could tell from David's body language that he still wasn't on board with the plan. He crossed his arms and his jaw hardened. "I don't like the idea of Maya being so vulnerable. And can we even find a place where *A*, Joel won't figure out I'm hiding and *B*, I can get to Maya fast enough."

They were standing outside the security office. David swiped his card key.

"Are there blueprints or a map of the ship that would show details, possible hiding places?" While she understood David's resistance and even was touched by how protective he was of her, she felt like they were running out of options and his stubbornness was costing them valuable time.

"The maps are very general, drawn up for the passengers. I would need to go up to the upper deck and scout it out."

David seemed to be coming around.

"You two figure out the details," Noah said. "I need to get into position. I've got to track down the operator for the North Star. Text me the exact plan. If I need to be up there for a while, we don't have a lot of time."

Noah took off.

They stepped into the security office. David shook his head. "I'm not totally on board with this plan."

She gazed at him. "It's the only way."

"I got a text from Hans that he is out of the infirmary. I'm going to have him watching the security cameras that are still operational. After what he's been through, I think he needs to be at a desk. He can contact us if he spots Joel. The safest thing for you would be to catch him before he even gets to the upper deck."

"I agree."

"After I check on Hans, Sarge and I are going to try to find a hiding place. Noah's only going to have a partial view of the upper deck, so you'll have to stay toward the east side."

"Got it," she said.

"I'm worried about you."

"Don't be. I can handle this."

He reached up and cupped her cheek. "I know but I care about you...a lot." His features softened as light came into his eyes. He leaned in and kissed her, brushing his lips over hers.

When he pulled away, she was breathless. He left the office with Sarge in tow not saying another word. Maya collapsed into a chair, still lightheaded from the kiss. What did David mean by *I care about you a lot*? And then a kiss. How ambiguous. It wasn't *I love you*. It wasn't *I want to be with you*. She shook her head. Maybe David didn't even know what he was really feeling.

She was still thinking about the effect David's kiss

had on her when Hans entered the security office ten minutes later.

"David called me. Guess my job is to watch the cameras," Hans said. "David hasn't texted you yet that he has a hiding place?"

She shook her head.

"Guess we wait then."

Maya took in a breath, trying to soften some of the tension in her muscles. "Yes, we wait. How are you doing?"

"I have a bit of a headache, but I'll be okay." Hans clicked through the screens turning on the ones that were not black. "We won't be able to replace the disabled cameras until we're in port."

She stared at the screens. One of them revealed that the North Star was already being fully elevated. She studied the other screens catching a glimpse of Sarge right before he was out of camera range as he trailed behind David on the leash. The location revealed that they were still about a five-minute walk from the upper deck.

She pointed to the screen where she'd seen David and Sarge. "There are no more cameras to show us where they have gone?"

"The only other one in that area has been disabled."

She pulled out her phone and set it on the counter. When she clicked on the screen, she saw she had a text from Helena Maddox, one of the other K-9 officers.

What a day I've had. Luna and I went looking for Eli's survivalist family that his godmother so desperately wants to locate. While looking in a remote area of

Chugach State Park, I ran into two men and showed them photos of the Seaver family. They said they didn't know the Seavers, but I think they were lying. Later when I was leaving, I was shot at. I think we are getting close and that is making someone nervous.

Luna was Helena's Norwegian elkhound. Maya stared at the phone for a long moment and said a silent prayer that she would get back to shore alive to help track down the Seaver family before it was too late.

David walked the upper deck with Sarge, not finding any hiding place that wouldn't be obvious. His only option was a supply closet filled with lounge chairs. The closet was around the corner and down a hallway from where Maya would be standing. He'd have no visual on her at all. At a dead run, he estimated it would take him about a minute to get to Maya if she needed help. Sixty seconds was time enough to kill someone. Plus, there would be an additional time delay if Noah had to communicate what he was seeing.

The closet was stuffed so full he and Sarge had to squeeze in. His hands were pressed close to his side. It took some maneuvering to get the phone to his face after he dialed Maya's number.

She answered right away, "Yes."

The sound of her voice renewed the memory of the kiss they'd shared. Without intending to, his voice took on a smoldering quality. "Hey, I'm in place. When you get to the upper deck if you think that Joel is near, I need you to press in my number and keep it on so I can hear what is happening."

"I might not have time to do that if I wait until I hear him coming. What if I just turn it on when I get to the upper deck?"

Not having radios was proving to be a challenge. "Okay, Noah can give me the play-by-play via text up to that point. If Joel does show, I am worried that the delay for Noah to communicate what is happening will be too great. I can't see you from my hiding place."

"David, I know you're worried, but remember I am a trained police officer."

The warmth in her voice made his heart beat faster. He had not lied when he said he cared about her, but was there something even deeper between them?

"I know you can take care of yourself, Maya. I'm just making sure every precaution is in place."

"I'll leave the security office in about two minutes. I'll make my way toward the upper deck slowly. If Joel is watching, he'll have every chance to see me."

David gripped his phone a little tighter and breathed in a wordless prayer. "I'll let Noah know the plan is in place and that you are on your way."

"Got it." A silence fell between them, but Maya stayed on the line. "I care about you too, David." She hung up.

Her words seemed to reverberate in his head. Had she confessed her feelings just in case she was killed?

NINETEEN

After saying goodbye to Hans, Maya left the security office and headed toward the upper deck. She chose a path that would make her visible from a distance and where there were still cameras so Hans would be able to track her and alert the rest of the team if she was attacked. It was hard to say if Joel would even take the bait.

She walked past a room with wide open doors. Classical music spilled out and when she glanced inside, she saw a strobe light and ballroom dancers moving across the floor. Her eyes traveled up to the balconies that looked down on the promenade.

Though most of the shops had closed down, some restaurants and bars were still open. There were enough people to ensure that Joel wouldn't try anything unless he could remain hidden.

By the time she made her way to the upper deck, her heart was racing and sweat trickled past her temple. Before she got to the upper deck where the railing was, and where Noah would have eyes on her, she passed a family. A mom and dad and two girls who looked to be under the age of five. The father held one of the girls in his arms.

"Have fun. We'd thought we'd come up for the view of the stars since they opened the deck up, but it's a little too windy and cold," the father said.

Maya drew her coat around her. "Still a nice night though."

The older of the two girls held her mother's hand. She pointed at Maya with her free hand. "I saw you with your dog."

"Yes, that's Sarge. He's with a friend right now."

As the voices of the family and footsteps echoed and faded, she was keenly aware of how vulnerable she was without Sarge. She walked more slowly. When she glanced around, she didn't see the supply closet David and Sarge were hidden in. That made her nervous. It must not be very close. Her heart pounded a little faster.

She could see the railing up ahead not far from the spot where Crystal Lynwood had been killed and the other woman had been attacked. She walked past the lounge chairs, stopping for a moment to look at the entry door where Joel had probably escaped after the attacks. There were multiple ways to get to the upper deck. Maybe Joel wouldn't follow her.

She stepped toward the railing and gripped it. A gust of wind made her jacket balloon and then deflate. She looked over her shoulder and up. Though the twilight made it into a silhouette, she could see the elevated North Star where Noah was. Lights of the port city they were headed toward glowed in the distance.

Maya thought she heard a noise behind her by the

lounge chairs where the other entrance to the upper deck was. She hurried back there but saw nothing in the dim light.

Returning to the railing, she peered out, listening to the sound of the waves. Her hand rested on the side pocket of her jacket where she'd put her phone. If Noah saw anyone moving toward her, he would alert David.

After waiting about five minutes, she began to wonder yet again if maybe Joel wasn't going to show. Would he just lie low until they were in port and then find a way to slip off the ship unnoticed? He had to know they would ramp up security as the passengers got off. But she had to believe that his compulsion to go after women who reminded him of the one who had rejected him would override common sense. It had so far. Attacking women on a ship where he could not hope to escape, only hide, held a high level of risk.

Maya stared up at the twinkling stars and the outlines of mountains in the distance. Why at such a moment did she wish David was standing beside her and that they were just sharing a tender moment together, not entrenched in a sting operation? Her feelings for him ran so deep. Would she go so far as to say she loved him? Maybe. The kiss had caught her off guard after all his resistance to anything romantic. She shook her head at the memory of how his lips felt on hers.

Her phone dinged. She pulled it out. The text was from Noah.

No sign of him from up here. You see anything?

She remembered the noise that had sounded like someone coming through the entryway by the lounge chairs. It could have been the wind jostling a lounge chair.

She texted back.

Not sure. Pretty quiet.

Maya stepped away from the railing. She'd never been good at doing nothing and that was what this operation had started to feel like. What if Joel had figured out they were setting him up and now he was stalking another woman on some other part of the ship? Yet as smart as he was, it didn't seem like he'd be able to decipher what they had in mind to catch him. If her classes on criminal psychology had taught her anything, the note he'd left in the arcade meant he was honed in on her.

Still, just standing around was hard to do.

After putting her phone in her pocket, Maya remembered the lounge where the other victim had been with the kind older couple. That was on the other side of the ship where the upper deck wrapped around. She glanced up at the North Star. Noah might not have a visual on her if she went over there.

She returned to the railing and stared out at the rolling sea. The wind had intensified. She thought she heard a banging sound somewhere close.

Maya ran to check the entrance by the lounge chairs and found the door was open and banging against the wall. The wind could have done that. All the same she

approached with caution. Noah would be able to see
her go toward the door, but she'd be hidden under the
eaves once she reached to close the door.

Why take the chance?

Let the door bang in the wind.

A voice as cold as ice pelted her eardrums. "I'd told
you I'd come for you."

She whirled around. Joel stood three feet from her
grinning. He must have used the entrance by the lounge,
or Noah would have seen him.

She reached into her jacket pocket, fumbling with
her phone. Then she put her other hand in her pocket
hoping Joel wouldn't figure out what she was doing.
She couldn't find the button right button without looking. Noah would see Joel and signal David. That was
her hope.

Joel lunged at her.

She angled away but her foot caught on a leg of the
lounge chair and she fell forward. The stumble gave Joel
the advantage. He grabbed her arm, yanking her back,
and then pushed her toward the open door. Now they
were both hidden by the eaves. Had Noah had time to
register what was going on?

"It's over for you."

Joel pulled a knife out of his pocket forcing her to
step backward through the open door or be stabbed. He
must have taken it from the kitchen where he worked.

She turned to run down the stairs, but Joel grabbed
the hem of her jacket. "Don't you dare run from me."

Still on the narrow landing, she turned, seeking to
get the knife out of his hand before he could do any

damage. She reached for it. They tussled. She managed to smash the back of his hand against the stairwell wall causing him to drop the knife. Metal banged on concrete as the knife slid down several stairs.

Joel's expression communicated rage. "You will die." He bared his teeth and slammed both hands against her chest and shoulder. She stumbled backward, unable to catch herself, and fell on her back.

Somewhere in the distance, she heard a dog barking. Sarge. The wind seemed to pick the bark up and carry it away. But they were coming for her.

Alarm spread across Joel's face. Turning, he grabbed the door and latched it. Probably some sort of emergency latch for when there was a storm.

The delay gave her time to get to her feet. She looked around for the knife but didn't see it. She hurried down the stairs. Above her, she heard banging noises that indicated David and Sarge were trying to open the door.

She had only run down four stairs when the banging stopped. David must have realized the futility of trying to break down the door. As she ran, she could hear Joel's footsteps behind her.

She saw a door up ahead, though she couldn't remember where it led. She pushed it open and as a gust of wind hit her, she realized she was on a tiny exposed viewing deck. She glanced one way and then the other, spotting the door that would allow her to escape. Joel grabbed her from behind before she could get to the door.

He yanked her around, so she was facing him. He shoved his arm under her chin, pressing hard and backing her against the wall.

Maya wheezed, unable to breath due the pressure he put on her neck.

His eyes were wild and unfocused. "Having trouble breathing, my dear?"

She lifted her leg to kick him. The blow felt weak and only seemed to enrage him more. Now he grabbed her and banged the back of her head against the wall.

Pain radiated through her skull. Knowing that his favorite thing to do was choke her, she was ready for him when his hands reached for her neck. Maya deflected the move. "You won't get away with this."

"That's what all the pretty girls say." He grabbed her hair.

She heard barking.

The door opened a sliver. Joel kicked it then swung her body around so her back was against the door and his hand pinned her there by pressing into her shoulders. His face was so close to hers she could hear him breathing.

David was on the other side of the door trying to open it while the weight of her body held it in place. Sarge's barking intensified.

She scratched and clawed at Joel's hands while she leaned forward, hoping to allow David to get the door open.

Joel reached for her neck choking her, pressing harder and harder. She saw black dots and felt light-headed.

The door separated from the frame then banged shut again. Joel's grip on her neck loosened momentarily. She took in a breath and pushed off the door.

It opened again not more than a few inches.

Sarge's barking was the last thing she heard before the darkness surrounded her.

David managed to get the door open far enough for Sarge to squeeze through. The barking was filled with menace and punctuated with growls. David pushed hard against the door, but it was held in place.

On the other side of the door he heard Joel yelp in pain. David grabbed the knob and pushed on the door again. There was still some sort of weight on the other side, but he was able to open it wide enough so he could get through. Once in, he saw that the weight was Maya's unconscious body. The sight of her lying there so still was like a blow to his stomach that knocked the wind out of him.

He knelt down. She still had a pulse.

Both Joel and Sarge were nowhere in sight. He hurried toward the entrance that led up the stairwell toward the sound of the muffled barking. He swung the door open. Sarge had cornered Joel on the landing.

"Call him off." Joel's voice was filled with terror.

David hurried up the stairs. Sarge stopped barking but licked his chops and kept his eyes on his prey.

David pulled Joel's hands behind him and secured them with zip ties they used as cuffs. "You're going to be locked up for a long time for what you've done."

Joel jerked and lifted his chin. "We'll see about that."

Noah appeared at the bottom of the stairs.

"Take him in please," David said. "I've got to take care of Maya. Come on, Sarge."

David returned to where Maya still lay unconscious.

Her head tilted to the side and her long dark hair covered her face.

He gathered her in his arms and brushed the hair away. Sarge whimpered and licked her face. "It's going to be all right. She's going to be okay. She has to be. I love her."

Sarge licked David's face and wagged his tail.

"It's true, buddy." He stared down at Maya's beautiful face. "I realized I loved her when I thought about a world without her if she didn't survive this operation to take down Joel..." He brushed his finger over her cheek.

Her eyes fluttered open. "David."

He gushed with joy. "So good to see you."

"Joel?"

"We caught him."

"Oh...good." Her voice was still very weak.

He cringed when he saw the bruises on her neck. "We almost lost you."

She looked directly at him. "Yes, but you didn't, and the important thing is that Joel has been apprehended."

"That is a great thing, but it's not the most important thing."

"What are you saying?"

David's throat constricted and his mouth went dry. He wanted to tell her he loved her but the words would not come. Sarge whimpered and licked David's hand as though offering support.

Maya lifted her head a little and then pushed herself into a sitting position. She glanced at the dog and then at David. "Is everything okay?"

"Great...fine."

"Well, once we're in port, Joel will be taken into custody and I can head back to headquarters in Anchorage. I missed everyone so much."

"I'm sure you're excited to get back." David rose to his feet and reached a hand down to help her to her feet.

"Sure of course."

They faced each other as the sun was coming up and the lights of Seward glowed in the distance. It was clear Maya had already shifted focus to getting back to work with her team. Even if he could find the words to tell her how he felt, she might not feel the same way.

TWENTY

The next day, before she could even make it to her office at headquarters with Sarge, Maya got a text from her boss.

Welcome back. We need you in the conference room ASAP.

Back to work. Though she was excited about seeing the rest of the team, she'd felt an emptiness ever since she'd said goodbye to David and left Seward. If he had truly cared about her, he would have said something, right?

Sarge trotted beside her as she headed to the conference room. "We just got to let him go, don't we? It wasn't meant to be."

Sarge whimpered in response.

When she entered the conference room, the first thing she saw was a banner that said Welcome Home, Maya.

Four team members stood around the conference table that held a box of cupcakes frosted in bright colors. Lorenza, her assistant Katie, Helena with her Norwegian elkhound Luna and Eli, the tech guy.

Helena stepped forward and gave Maya a hug. "The rest of the team is out on assignments. Otherwise everyone would have been here."

"It's good to be back," Maya said. Sarge let out a little yip. "He agrees."

Katie handed Maya a cupcake with yellow frosting. Maya looked up at the sign.

I am home. And then she looked at the people surrounding the table. *And this is my family.*

Katie's green eyes flashed. "So you'll have to tell us all about your adventures on the cruise ship." She took a bite of her cupcake.

The sudden pang inside surprised Maya. She couldn't just forget David and get on with her life. Because the truth was, she cared deeply for him. If only he felt the same way… "Maybe sometime over lunch we will talk about it."

"I hate to rush this along," Lorenza said, running her hands through her silver hair. "But we do need to get to work. Maya, I want you and Helena to go back out to Chugach State Park where she was shot at after she started asking questions about Eli's godmother's family." Lorenza rested her gaze on Eli. "I think we are getting closer to finding the Seavers. Given what happened to Helena, I'm sending you out in pairs to ask questions."

Maya nodded, glad to be able to dive right into work. Maybe that would help ease her broken heart.

She and Helena loaded up into the K-9 trooper vehicle and headed out to the park. The day went by quickly. Though they questioned several people who were close to where Helena had been shot at, no new evidence emerged. They headed home just as the sun was setting. Maya was grateful for the longer days of summer.

Helena was driving as they pulled back into the headquarters parking lot. "You want to grab a bite?"

"Sure." Maya looked through the windshield. She wondered if her eyes were playing tricks on her. David, still dressed in his uniform, stood on the sidewalk holding a bouquet of flowers.

Helena leaned a little closer to the windshield. "Who's that handsome guy?"

Joy flooded through Maya. "Someone I met on the cruise." She clicked open her door and then unloaded Sarge. She raced over to where David waited.

He handed her the flowers. "I didn't go back out with the ship. I knew I couldn't."

She shook her head. "What are you saying?"

"Maya, when I thought you might die I realized something. I love you. I don't want to live in a world without you."

"But David, your life is on this ship."

"I can take a leave of absence and we can figure it out together. I'm open to anything as long as it's with you. Wherever you are is my home, Maya."

"I agree. You and me, together is all that matters." She looked down at her partner. "And Sarge of course."

He smiled. "Of course."

"Why the change of heart? You love that ship and your job. I saw that would never force you away from that."

"That's one of the reasons I love you Maya. Cause you want me to be happy." Light danced in his blue eyes. "After you left, I felt this huge hole inside." He brushed her cheek with the back of his fingers.

His touch made her feel warm all the way through. "Me too."

"I realized that what was holding me back had nothing to do with who you are. I can't let the fear that I will be like my father keep me from having love in my life. And I don't want to miss out on a lifetime with someone as wonderful as you."

Joy surged through her, and she reached up and wrapped her arms around his neck. "Oh David."

Being in David's arms made her feel alive.

He pulled his head back, smiled and kissed her.

His hand rested on her cheek as he looked into her eyes. "I love you and I want to be with you. That is all that matters."

"I love you too."

Sarge gave his bark of approval. David drew Maya close and kissed her again.

* * * * *

Heather Woodhaven earned her pilot's license, rode a hot-air balloon over the safari lands of Kenya, parasailed over Caribbean seas, lived through an accidental detour onto a black-diamond ski trail in Aspen, and snorkeled among stingrays before becoming a mother of three and wife of one. She channels her love for adventure into writing characters who find themselves in extraordinary circumstances.

Books by Heather Woodhaven

Love Inspired Suspense

Calculated Risk
Surviving the Storm
Code of Silence
Countdown
Texas Takedown
Tracking Secrets
Credible Threat
Protected Secrets
Wilderness Sabotage
Deadly River Pursuit
Search and Defend

Visit the Author Profile page
at LoveInspired.com for more titles.

ARCTIC WITNESS

Heather Woodhaven

Fear thou not; for I am with thee: be not dismayed;
for I am thy God: I will strengthen thee;
yea, I will help thee; yea, I will uphold thee
with the right hand of my righteousness.
—*Isaiah* 41:10

To all the dogs who keep garden harvests
from going to the squirrels, thank you.

ONE

Someone was downstairs. Ivy West heard rushed foot-steps before the security alert pinged on her phone. She set down the adoption papers she'd started to fill out. So much for a lunch break in her upstairs apartment.

The bottom of her boots slapped each wooden step as she hurried down to her post at the Nome Survival Mis-sion, a small nonprofit store geared to help survivalists, preppers and anyone from the surrounding villages try-ing to withstand the harsh climate. Whoever was down there would hear her coming to help. She moved past the heavily stocked shelves of blankets and survival gear with a ready smile, only to find the room empty.

The wraparound windows provided ample views of the churning Bering Sea in front and the tundra of the Seward Peninsula on the sides. A few miles past the outskirts of Nome, the vast expanse brought a cer-tain amount of comfort. She could never be caught off guard, and yet she'd been certain she'd heard someone walking around. No vehicles were out front.

A current of crisp September air hit the back of her

neck. *Aha.* The back door wasn't fully closed. She opened
the door fully to step onto the deck. Sometimes her visitors were skittish and traveled on foot. The mission fre-
quently served as a first step for those who needed help
getting to a women's shelter. Except, no one was outside
but the musk oxen, grazing on the tundra brush. They
needed to eat up. The wildflowers of the summer had
already dwindled. Winter was at their front door.

She'd left Dylan's blanket in his car seat when she'd
dropped him off with the babysitter. At thirteen months
old, her foster child loved the messy teething biscuits.
If she threw the blanket in the wash now, it'd be ready
for when she picked him up this afternoon. She rushed
down the deck stairs to where her Jeep and snow machine were parked on the back incline.

A warbling voice sent a shiver up her spine. Ivy
reached for the pepper spray she kept fastened on the
belt loop of her jeans, but relaxed when she saw it was
a dog. With a gorgeous mix of gray and white, the thick
coat of a Siberian husky fluttered in the wind as the
animal stepped out from behind the vehicle. The dog's
eyes softened while its white fluffy tail wagged hesi-
tantly. Huskies rarely barked, preferring to howl or what
sounded like an attempt at speaking.

She grinned. "Are you lost?" The gray at the top of
its head formed a point on the forehead almost like a
widow's peak, a unique marking that should help connect the dog with the owner quickly. The husky trotted
toward the wild brush the musk oxen enjoyed. "Don't
get too close. They're quick to use those horns, you
know." She knew the canine couldn't understand her,

but if huskies went to the trouble of attempting to speak, she wanted to return the favor.

The husky might be a missing sled dog, since the end of the famous Iditarod Race was held in downtown Nome. The start of the race was in Anchorage, where her ex-husband still lived. Roughly a thousand miles away. What would Sean think when she told him she was adopting a baby? He'd recently called, wanting her survivalist knowledge for a case. Ivy craved hearing his voice again, but since one of the reasons they'd divorced was his refusal to have children, she also dreaded telling him about Dylan. Her chest tightened like every other time she'd forfeited her dream of raising a family together.

The dog looked over her shoulder and waited a beat. Ivy placed a hand on her chest. "You want me to follow?" The husky took a few more steps toward the brush and again turned to wait. "Fine." She walked forward. The dog disappeared into the tall grasses and bushes. "I'm telling you right now, if you stir up a swarm of mosquitoes, I'm leaving." She followed the grass movement until the husky stopped and faced her.

On the ground, dark hair spilled out over the matted-down grasses. Ivy rushed forward. She dropped to her knees and reached for the woman's neck to search for her pulse. "Good dog!" This had to be the husky's owner. "Ma'am? Can you hear me?" Her fingers couldn't find a pulse. No breath. She ripped open the woman's coat to begin compressions.

Her gaze caught a dark red circle that spread from the center of the woman's chest.

Murder. Ivy's own heart pounded harder. This woman had been killed… But when? Her skin chilled. She stood, reaching for her phone. The husky released a short howl. She spun to see why, but lightning struck the base of her skull. Her bones lost all strength.

The grass, the house, everything turned white, then fuzzy as she tried to blink through the blinding pain. How'd the dog suddenly get over her head? Something grabbed her ankle and pulled. She struggled to raise her head, but blackness draped over her vision until her mind went silent.

Sean West stepped into the Alaska K-9 Unit head-quarters with Grace, his Japanese Akita Inu partner, by his side. His bones felt heavy, having just returned from a recovery operation. They'd brought peace and closure to a missing man's family, and while he appre-ciated the purpose of handling a cadaver-seeking dog, success in such a mission brought a deep weariness. Being with the team, even in a boring meeting, would get his head back in the game.

Colonel Lorenza Gallo blocked his entrance to the meeting room. "You're back. I wasn't sure you would be in time. I need a quick word in private."

He tried to ignore feeling as if he were being sent to the principal's office. A quick glance over Lorenza's shoulders confirmed the rest of the team was waiting for the meeting to start. Grace tilted her fluffy fox-like head up at him as if wondering why they weren't allowed to join the rest of the K-9s. He shrugged and followed his boss a few steps down the hallway to her office.

"This will only take a minute," she said.

Sean wasn't sure if she was speaking to Denali, the retired K-9 husky who sat upright upon their entry, or him. Lorenza's silver pixie cut and tailored suit complemented the rest of her immaculate office, nothing out of place. She faced him and sat on the edge of her desk with her arms crossed. "Do you have your go bag ready?"

"Yes." Seemed like an odd question. He'd driven over two hundred miles early this morning, after the recovery case. He never knew where in Alaska he'd be assigned, as the elite K-9 Unit supplemented all law enforcement in the state. Sean's bag was always packed, though sometimes his extra uniforms awaited a wash, like now.

"We received a PD request for help. A missing woman, rural area, outside of police jurisdiction."

"You suspect a recovery is needed?"

The colonel stiffened. "I hope not. I've already assigned Helena and Gabriel to this case. I'll tell them to wait for you at the airstrip. They brought extra supplies for Grace just in case you're running low."

Sean tried to connect the dots. Lorenza wasn't supplying any of the details she usually loved.

"I didn't want to brief you over the phone," she said, as if seeing the silent question in his eyes. "And we're out of time. Helena will fill you in on the plane." She hesitated. "Sean, I'm sending you because if it were me… Well, that's what I would want."

His veins turned ice-cold, but his hunch could be off base. "Where?" he asked.

"Nome."

Sean's mouth went dry. She hadn't confirmed his suspicions, but he didn't want to take the time to discuss. He ran out of the building without another word. Grace trotted by his side. With the use of sirens, they made it to the airstrip within ten minutes. Helena Maddox and her Norwegian elkhound, Luna, stood outside of the cargo hold of the trooper-owned Cessna. Gabriel Runyon and his Saint Bernard, Bear, were already preparing to step into the aircraft.

Sean grabbed his two go bags, one specially equipped for Grace's needs, and jogged to the plane.

"You made it." Helena's shoulders dropped. "I wasn't sure you would. Are you okay?"

"The missing woman is Ivy?" He tensed the muscles in his jaw, determined to keep all emotion at bay at the thought of his ex-wife in danger.

Helena avoided making eye contact. "We don't know much except that a police rep went to drop off a donation and found the door open. Ivy was nowhere to be found. The PD thought it urgent enough to put in a call to Lorenza, partly as a courtesy to you."

Sean's heart went into overdrive. He nodded, glad for once that both Helena and Gabriel had gotten to know Ivy before the divorce. He wouldn't need to explain how out of character it would be for his ex to miss any meeting.

Gabriel gave Helena a side-glance. The man had an intimidating quality, no matter what expression, but that glance held a rebuke. Helena was supposed to tell him more, then.

"What?" Sean pressed. "What else?"

The other man's forehead creased. "PD spotted blood on the ground."

"We don't know if it's Ivy's," Helena added quickly. "It could be from an animal, for all we know."

Sean wouldn't allow himself to ruminate on a mission to find his own wife—ex-wife—dead. She *had* to be alive. He tapped the side of his leg, and Grace, without needing a command, jumped past the two troopers and their dogs into the plane. "Let's not waste any time."

Helena and Gabriel scrambled behind him into their seats. They each attached the special travel harnesses for the dogs into the seat belts. The pilot, another Alaska state trooper Sean didn't know, sat in the cockpit, checking instruments.

Roads across Alaska to Nome didn't exist. The only way there was by air, sea or dogsled. The ninety-minute plane ride was the fastest choice but torturous, as he feared his worst nightmare had become reality. As a search-and-rescue handler, Gabriel would take the lead on the case. Sean overheard his loud voice hollering over the noise of the propellers as he made calls throughout the journey to prepare for their arrival.

The wheels hit the tarmac and taxied up to three waiting trooper SUVs. The moment the pilot shut off the engine, Sean and Grace launched out of the plane. The vehicles weren't specially equipped for K-9s, but the dogs were trained for all manner of transportation, given the challenges the Alaska terrain could throw at them.

"Go east, and the Nome Survival Mission will be on

our left. Can't miss it," Helena hollered over the wind. She and Luna jogged next to them and made for the middle vehicle.

The keys were left on the dash of each vehicle, just as Gabriel had requested. Sean flipped on the emergency lights and followed the other man's lead at full speed, barely registering the transition of cement to gravel and the beauty of the sea on his right. In a missing person's case in Alaska, every minute counted. And as Nome's history suggested, it was too easy for someone to disappear, never to be seen again.

They pulled in front of the mission. This was where Ivy lived? This small house in the middle of nowhere? Sure, they'd divorced at the point of barely speaking to each other, but lately they'd found reasons to talk more often. Almost as if they were becoming friends again. He'd imagined her as part of a community, not with musk oxen as her only neighbors. His stomach tightened to the point he needed to blow out a slow breath to keep the pain from registering on his face.

Gabriel stepped out of his vehicle, a hand up in front of Sean. "We got here in record time. Now, it's imperative we don't rush. There might be a scent Bear can grab as long as we're careful not to disturb the scene."

Bear's search-and-rescue specialty included being able to track scents, even in permafrost. That was likely why the colonel had assigned him to this case.

Helena climbed the steps to the deck that wrapped around the building. A lot of the houses close to shore were set on stilts to endure the floods and snow throughout the year. Thankfully, they weren't up against either at the moment, though flurries drifted onto his jacket from the gray clouds above. Helena placed her hand on her weapon as she stepped toward the ajar back door, swaying with the wind. "We'll check inside."

"If you see anything belonging to Ivy, bring it out, please," Sean called up to her. Maybe Bear could find her easier with a fresh scent.

"Understood." Helena hesitated. Luna stood at the ready, specializing in suspect apprehension, so if there was someone inside, the dog would find them. Helena pointed in the southeast direction. "Up here, I can see a matted-down path in the tall grasses. Might be from animals, but—"

"That's probably where our contact spotted blood," Gabriel said. "On it."

Grace did a little dance with her paws. Was she trying to tell him she smelled Ivy? Would she even remember Ivy from her days as a puppy?

"Found one spot of blood," Gabriel announced. "Small amount, but looks relatively fresh." He glanced at Sean. "Are you up for this?"

His mouth went dry. He knew what his teammate wanted from him. If he put Grace to work and she alerted on the blood, then they'd know that whoever had been on the ground was already dead before they were moved.

"Time to work." His voice came out in a ragged whisper. Grace's ears swiveled higher and her mouth fell open, as if smiling. He and Grace were often called to scenes where loved ones waited for news, so Sean had decided to use a relatively innocuous phrase to cue

Grace. She dropped her nose to the ground and smelled the blood, then huffed, a sign she was annoyed.

Without alerting, Grace knew she wasn't going to get a reward. Sean fought against laughing. He'd never been so thankful. "If that's Ivy's blood, she was still alive before she left." Hope blossomed inside him with renewed vigor. "Can Bear track her?"

Before he could answer, Grace spun around and strained ahead, her nose frantically huffing and puffing in the matted path of grass. A second later, she sat down and looked over her shoulder at Sean.

Gabriel winced.

Sean pushed forward. A separate section of blood, dinner-plate in size, had caked in the grass underneath a pile of freshly pulled grass, as if someone had tried to hastily cover up its existence.

"Good work, girl," Sean said, but his voice shook. He produced her favorite chew toy, but as much as he tried, he couldn't offer a smile for his partner.

"It's two different people," Helena shouted from the deck. "I'm coming down. No one was inside the mission." Sean whirled around to see his colleague jogging toward them with a jacket in her hand that he recognized instantly. Gabriel took the jacket and offered it for Bear to start smelling.

"Why do you think it was two people?" Gabriel asked.

Helena pointed to the road. "From the deck, I could see a path through the grasses from here to the road." She pointed at the muddy areas. "It's more obvious with a view from above, but there were three people total.

Whoever did this dragged two people to a vehicle and drove through the grasses, likely on an ATV of some sort."

Grace dropped the toy and strained her nose east. Bear sniffed Ivy's jacket and immediately turned to the first spot of blood, not the second. Two different sets of blood meant there was still a chance his ex-wife was alive. "Best-case scenario, she's still with a murderer. We need to go now—southeast, it appears."

Helena studied the two men and nodded. "Someone needs to stay here and process the scene. You go ahead."

Sean fought against running through the grass to get to the car faster, as that might disturb the crime scene. He scooped up Grace's toy and moved to go. The dog stopped midgallop, sniffed something on the ground and sneezed. Sean leaned over. A pepper-spray can. He recognized the pink holder Ivy kept attached to her belt loop.

Helena grabbed her phone to start the lengthy process of photographing every angle and piece of evidence. "I see it. Go."

Sean ran the rest of the way to his vehicle and opened the door for Grace. He rolled down the window in the back seat to let his K-9 partner stick her nose out as they drove. It was unlikely she would catch scents while he drove at high speeds, but not impossible. She could smell a drop of blood from a long distance.

Miles of coastline shifted into miles of tundra. As far as the eye could see, there was nothing but land and grazing animals. No sign of any humans or ATVs. Grace continued to strain her nose forward, sniffing wildly. In the rearview mirror, he could see Bear doing the same out the back of Gabriel's SUV.

A line of trees rose up out of the vast expanse of nothingness. Sean slowed down as the road disappeared. He bumped over the dirt, pressing onward. The tree branches brushed up against the sides of the vehicle. In front of him, a river rushed over rocks and boulders.

No bridge. A dead end.

He hit the steering wheel in frustration and Grace barked, her eyes squinting and her ears pointing in opposite directions, like she was asking him, *What's your problem?* His shoulders sagged as he waited for Gabriel to park behind him.

When Sean first took the job in cadaver detection, he focused on the noble act of bringing people much-needed closure, the type of peace his mom had never received when his uncle went missing on the Pacific Crest Trail. He kept the rest of the implications about his job at the back of his mind, never letting it grow louder than a dull hum. But now...

He couldn't find Ivy dead. He'd never recover. *Please...please let her be alive.*

Sean stepped out of the vehicle to face Gabriel. "Don't suppose you have a boat handy?" His teammate offered Bear a smell of Ivy's jacket. The Saint Bernard rushed forward, nose to the ground, through the tall grasses close to the first set of tree trunks.

Grace lunged forward and blocked Bear. She uttered a low growl, staring right at Sean. His mouth dropped. She never acted like that unless—

A click sounded. Two logs swung from opposite

standing trees and smashed into each other, just above Grace's head. Sean crept forward, bending over until he saw the trip wire resting against the front of her legs.

"She was trying to warn us. Someone really doesn't want us to be out here," Gabriel said.

Sean blew out a breath, never more grateful for Grace. Because of the types of jobs they worked, she was trained to avoid a variety of dangers, usually wildlife and hunting-related. "Traps or not, we're Ivy's only chance."

Ivy's fingers moved and something soft brushed against her ankles. Weird physical sensations demanded she make the extra effort to open her eyes. A rotting wooden ceiling above her. A husky with a gray widow's peak stepped into view, looking down and sniffing her face. Ivy tried to twist away and sit up, but her hands refused to let her.

Her wrists were tied to a pole. Her heart jolted and her eyes widened, suddenly fully awake. She couldn't think clearly with the way her head throbbed. The husky shifted next to her. She managed to sit up and found herself staring into dark eyes surrounded by a black mask.

"So you're finally up." He was hunched over, his arms around a rolled-up rug. She didn't want to think about what was in the rug. The man dropped the rug and the tips of his fingers flopped over the edge. Ivy held back the scream building in her throat. He stepped forward and grabbed the collar of her sweater, pulling her close, her arms twisting against the pole. He studied her face.

She squirmed, trying to avoid looking into his eyes, to get away from his touch. The friction of the rope against her wrists burned.

His eyes crinkled as if he were smiling behind the mask. "She gave you something, didn't she?"

"What? No. I didn't know her."

His eyes narrowed, maybe at her confusion. "I think you're lying. Just like she did. You can either talk on your own or be made to. Is that what you want? To end up like her? I'll give you a minute to think about it." He released her and straightened. The bottom of his boot connected with her chest, sending her backward.

Her head hit the floor, straining her right shoulder socket as her hands remained attached to the pole. She closed her eyes, fighting against the waves of pain firing in her temples, neck and arms.

"Come," the man said. The sound of a dog's paws against the floor followed with a door slamming, then silence.

It was now or never. She *had* to escape. Dylan had no one else in the world but her. She gripped the pole and hoisted herself up. A moment later, her eyes adjusted to the dim light streaming through the front slats of the poorly constructed shack door. The man had tied her up with bowline knots.

She grabbed the spot to break the knot with her teeth while tugging on the loop with her strained right hand. The ropes fell away. The stiffness in her back and legs fought against her intention to jump up and run. She hobbled to the front of the shack, shaking the feeling back into her legs, and peeked out the door. Without a weapon for self-defense, she needed to be fast if she ran.

Tree branches hung down low, almost blocking her view of the husky and the killer's back. *Trees!* There were no trees in Nome unless someone counted the Nome Forest, a name jokingly referring to the pile of used Christmas trees collected in January. The permafrost prevented trees from growing deep enough roots. The closest place with trees was either Pilgrim Hot Springs or the Niukluk River. Pilgrim Hot Springs took hours to get to, so she would guess she was closer to Council, an abandoned townsite across the river. Still, miles away from her place. Even if she sprinted her heart out, she couldn't last long. She bit her lip to keep hopeless tears from rushing from her eyes.

Her racing mind could only settle on one prayer. *Help!* She nudged the door open a little wider. Her abductor hunkered over a metallic boat. The husky looked back at her and her breath caught. The dog jogged to the front of the boat, vocalizing a solemn warbling moan at the man but pointing in the opposite direction, almost as if creating a distraction for her.

He stood. "What? What is it?" The husky continued to make noise. "Stupid dog!"

Ivy pushed open the creaking door, hoping the husky's song covered up the noise. She ran around the backside of the shack with a quick look over her shoulder. The killer spun around, no longer wearing a mask. Their eyes met. Towering at roughly six foot three with auburn hair and pale skin, he lunged for a gun resting on a nearby boulder.

She screamed and darted into the tree line. Something snagged at her foot and she tripped. When she jumped up, she spotted a rope on the tree ahead, and another rope from a nearby tree. She grabbed a rock and tossed it forward. A ball made of spiked branches swung down, right where she had been about to run. She twisted and sidestepped the trap, her heart pounding in her throat. She had to keep moving or die trying.

Footsteps crunched over leaves behind her. If she ran much farther, she'd be out in the open again, an easy target for shooting practice. She dropped low, crouching behind a crowded grouping of trees. Maybe she could hide and wait until the cover of darkness. Footsteps grew closer. She held her breath, not daring to move a muscle.

A hand closed around her nose and mouth. "Shhh."

She flinched and struggled to breathe. If she could just lift her foot and strike the instep of whoever had grabbed her... A fox-like beast stepped into view. It *couldn't* be. Grace? She relaxed. The hand dropped and arms spun her around to face—

"Sean." She wrapped her arms around his chest and pulled him tight. "But how? How'd you—"

He patted her back. "Get behind me, Ivy. We're not out of danger yet."

TWO

Sean pointed at Ivy. "Grace, protect." He stepped around her with a hand on his weapon and gave a nod to Gabriel, who was peering through the trees. "What do you see?" His first priority was getting Ivy to safety. The shadow of a man filtered through the thick section of tree branches.

"Alaska State Troopers. Hands up!" Gabriel shouted.

A dog or wolf in the distance howled. Footsteps could be heard, but he couldn't get a visual. The trees and brush were too thick to see far here. Were there wolves in there?

"It's a Siberian husky," Ivy whispered.

Neither Grace nor Bear were trained in suspect apprehension, but even if Helena had come with them, she wouldn't have been able to send Luna through the woods after the suspect with possible traps hidden in the ground and trees. A splash sounded, followed by a boat motor revving. A few moments later, silence draped over the woods. They remained at the ready, a few minutes more, until absolutely sure it was safe.

"Did you get a look at your kidnapper?" Sean asked

softly. Now wasn't the time to reflect on the way she'd felt in his arms. He could feel her quivering hand at his back as she stayed close.

Her breath rushed past his neck. "Yes. Roughly six foot three, auburn hair, fair skin, maybe a little younger than us, but not by much. And he had a boat, but you probably figured that out by the sound of things."

"Was there only one man?"

"Yes. I mean, he was the only one I saw."

Gabriel blew out a breath and dropped his hand away from his weapon. "I think it's likely he just gave us the slip. Where does this river go?"

"It splits off into roughly sixteen creeks, but they get narrow pretty fast and some are dry by now."

"Your description will help a lot." Sean turned back around to face her. "We'll pass it to the troopers, the police—"

"The village safety officers," Gabriel interjected, swirling his finger around in the area like a lasso to indicate how far-reaching the description would go. There were so many native villages that a village officer was recruited at each one to keep in communication with state troopers.

"There are traps hidden around here," Ivy said. She pointed in the direction of the river. "I could show you where."

Sean had first met his ex-wife at a wilderness survival course. She'd been the instructor, and after the other participants had gone home, she'd run him through extra drills and answered all his questions. Traps were never part of the curriculum, but he believed in her ability to help find them. "Thankfully, Grace spotted something amiss on the way to find you and we missed one trap already. We'll catch this guy, Ivy."

"Sean, she's still bleeding." Gabriel took a step forward and peered around at the back of her head. "Ivy, we also found your blood back at your place. Did that man hit you?"

Fury radiated through his bones. He should've noticed she was hurt by now. It was his job to keep her safe, and he was failing her. Again.

She reached for the back of her head and groaned. "I think he hit me with a gun or something. I'm not sure. I blacked out, and when I woke up, my head was killing me." She pulled her hand back around, covered in fresh blood. "Must have reopened the wound when he kicked me down."

The pink-and-green flannel shirt his mom had given her for a birthday a couple of years back had bits of weeds and dirt all over it. Now it had blood on the shirttail as she tried to clean off her hand. Her hair, in a low ponytail like she had on their first date, was also streaked with red.

He should ask more questions. Instead, his face grew hot. He searched the woods behind him for any sign of life, any clue. The monster who had hurt and kidnapped Ivy needed to be thrown in jail. Now.

"How long do you think you were out?" Gabriel asked.

"I… I don't know."

Not a good sign. Sean focused on the ground for a moment before he faced her. Ivy's health was the most important thing now, and he shouldn't need a fellow

officer to remind him of that. Anytime a person lost
consciousness from trauma for more than a few seconds, there was the possibility of complications, which
meant the man could've killed her. Grace sidled up to
her and pressed against Ivy's leg, as if trying to support her. Many dogs could tell if a person were about
to have a seizure or a diabetic crash. Grace wasn't one
to seek out attention or someone to pet her. What if the
K-9 could tell Ivy was going to die soon?

"Hospital, now." He reached for Ivy's hand. Cold and
clammy. "We can get you there faster than waiting for
an ambulance."

"Agreed," Gabriel said. "We'll return tomorrow at
first light. Might have some more troopers available by
then to cover more ground." He twisted and headed in
the direction they'd come. "We'll lead the way."

"Remember, I can help you look for traps." Ivy's
voice was uncharacteristically faint. "If we step out of
the line of trees, we'll need to focus only on the ground
instead of both ground and branches. The farther away
from the shack, the safer it gets, I'd imagine."

Sean moved her hand to his arm so she could lean on
him for support. "He had you in a shack?" His words
were clipped, and judging by the way her eyes widened,
she could read his emotions. He stared ahead and made
his expression blank. The last thing she needed to worry
about was him. If they hadn't found her in time…

Gabriel waved them forward. "We'll come back
and investigate the shack tomorrow, then. Let's get her
that medical attention and get back to the SUVs before dark."

Ivy remained quiet as they walked. He had so many questions to ask, but he held his tongue. Gabriel would make sure to get the description of the suspect to the region's law enforcement. All the other questions could wait until Ivy was treated and feeling better.

They followed her advice and stuck to the tundra, far from the tree line and river. They weren't moving fast enough for his taste, but unless he was willing to ask Ivy to let him carry her, he would need to trust they'd get there in time.

The moment he spotted the cruiser, he rushed ahead to grab a blanket and some first-aid gear from the trunk. He ran back to Ivy. "Do you think you can add a little pressure to the back of your head while I drive, to slow the bleeding?"

"Probably a good idea." She seemed paler than she should in early fall, after a summer of enjoying nature. At least, the Ivy he knew would spend most of her waking moments outdoors. He helped her into the passenger seat and waited until she had the gauze and ice pack situated behind her head before turning his vehicle around. Gabriel set the pace in front of them. Within minutes, they'd hit the highest speed they could safely maneuver.

The only sounds in the vehicle were the occasional crunch of rocks underneath the tires. "I was surprised to see you," she said. "Happy but surprised." Ivy offered an encouraging smile in his direction.

"Same, but I'm not too fond of the circumstances." How many times had he almost taken a plane to Nome to see her but chickened out? He'd usually replay some of their most-repeated arguments in his head until it was no longer a temptation. Time and space were supposed to make her absence easier, but instead, his heart had never felt so raw and vulnerable. "Listen, uh, after we get you treated, I'd like you to take the first flight to Anchorage. You'll be safe there. You can stay at our place, our *old* place, I mean. At least until we catch this guy." He took a deep breath to slow the stammering.

"I can't, Sean." Her eyes were strained. Against pain, maybe?

"After you're feeling well enough to travel," he said. "I'll sleep on the couch." He'd overwhelmed her, then. "If you've seen the guy's face, you'll be much safer somewhere else. Doesn't have to be at our old place."

"Even if I wanted to, I can't. I have…" She worried her lip. "I have responsibilities here."

"The mission? I'm sure the nonprofit can find someone else to run the store." His peripheral caught her grimace. "I'm not saying you'd be easy to replace," he added with a quick side-glance. "I know that your survivalist expertise is sought—"

"Sean," she said again, this time her voice urgent. "It's not that. I have a child now."

He fought to keep his face neutral again, his focus on the road, even though his gut felt like it'd been used as a punching bag for half the day. She had a *child*? Since when?

He studied the road. Unless she'd changed personalities, Ivy West would not have moved on that fast with someone else. They'd signed the papers twenty-two months ago. People could change after divorce, though. He certainly had. A child, though?

Divorce had been the end of their marriage. But moving on and adding a child to the mix was like slamming the door on any potential hope for a rekindled relationship. Not that he had such hopes. He gripped the steering wheel and moved his foot from the gas to the brake as they crossed a bridge. So, she was taken. It'd take some getting used to, but the bottom line was he had a job to do. He could remove the personal nature of their relationship out of the equation. The bomb she'd just dropped changed nothing. He wasn't going to leave town until he knew she was safe.

"A foster child," Ivy said. Sean's forehead looked like it was doing push-ups with his hairline. She'd seen his face try to mask emotion a million times, but his forehead always revealed that he had opinions. He just wasn't ready to share them.

Her heart went into high gear. The pulsating feeling of heat at the back of her head distracted her. She faced forward in the car, trying to keep the gauze in the right place, but it stung too intensely to apply actual pressure.

Ivy tried to forget the way his jaw pulsed the moment she said the word *child*. He'd made his position on the matter abundantly clear when they were married. The world was too messed up to bring any children into it, he'd argued. Maybe on her darkest days she could agree to accept his argument, but she'd never truly understood his unwavering stance against fostering or adopting, especially since he was a natural around children.

"So you can see why I can't leave Nome," she finally said after the long silence. "I've been fostering for a while now, and I can't abandon him. There aren't near enough qualified foster parents around here as it is. They have to ship a lot of children to the lower forty-eight—" She closed her mouth tight. He didn't need to hear her rant on the subject, no matter how passionately she felt. The details of her life weren't his business anymore.

The memory of the man in the shack invaded her thoughts. No. She didn't want him in her brain ever again. She could barely think straight while her head throbbed.

Maybe Minnie Harkness, her babysitter, would be willing to let her stay the night. "You're probably right about tonight, though." The creep had attacked her at her home. He knew where she lived. "I think I'd feel more comfortable if Dylan and I stayed somewhere else, at least for tonight." She shifted slightly in her seat. "Can we stop at the mission just for a second? I really don't want to drive all the way back here after getting checked out of the hospital. I just need the car seat and a few supplies."

Thankfully, she was used to living on little and the stockroom below her apartment held everything they'd need. As a last resort, she could take Dylan to the bunker her parents had gifted her, east of town.

Sean said nothing, but his knuckles were turning white around the steering wheel. This was exactly why they could never work through any disagreement. Whenever he closed up like that, she knew it was better to move on rather than try to get him to open up. Which was exactly what she'd been trying to do in Nome before he'd shown up, wrapped his arms around her and—

Her shoulders sagged, remembering the relief of being rescued. And by him. *Why now, Lord?* "Wait. Were you already in town? On a mission? How did you end up finding me?"

"Someone came to give you a donation and noticed—" he cleared his throat with a cough "—your absence and the blood."

She didn't trust her judgment with the unrelenting pounding in her temples, but it almost seemed like his voice shook. They only sent Sean to the scene if they suspected… She felt her eyes widen as the matter-of-fact nature of his work hit her anew. "The troopers thought I was dead and sent you to find me?"

"No." He shook his head frantically. "Lorenza sent me as a personal favor. She wanted Helena and Gabriel to do the heavy lifting. I'm sure she thought I knew you well enough that maybe I could help locate you quickly. We didn't know about the murder victim at the time."

"Oh." The memories of the dark hair spread over the grass and the fingers that appeared out of the rolled-up rug caused an unbidden shiver up her spine.

"Did you see the victim?"

"Yes, but I don't know who she is." Her throat throbbed and she barely was able to whisper the answer. There were enough similarities in their appearance that it could've been her. "Shoulder-length hair, petite, approximately the same age as the man who attacked me." The desire to wrap her arms around her baby increased exponentially. The poor little guy probably wondered where she was. She never picked him up this late. Did Minnie have enough baby food for Dylan's dinner?

"It can wait for now," Sean said, his voice kinder, gentler. "We'll need to ask you for a full statement after you're treated."

The vehicle stopped moving. Ivy realized with a jolt that they were already back at the mission. This home she loved had darker windows than she remembered. Her shoulders hunched forward, hating the new vulnerability she felt. Mere hours had passed, but everything appeared different.

She was a strong woman, resilient and ready to be a single mother by choice. She couldn't afford to let a murderer ruin the new life she'd worked so hard to build. Her eyes stung as she continued to stare at the mission.

Sean rested a hand over hers. "Tell me what you need," he said softly. "I'll run in and get it."

The warmth and comfort enveloping her brought a different type of pain. She slipped her hand out from under his touch. "It'll be faster if I go. Sorry, I zoned out for a minute."

"You need to be seen."

"I will, but I'm sure the doctor is going to say I just need rest. Five more minutes won't kill me." Her breath caught at her careless use of the word. A woman had been *killed* here. Squaring her shoulders, she stepped out of the vehicle and flinched at movement in her peripheral.

It was only Helena, waving at her from inside the

tall grasses. Her hair was longer than the short cut she'd last seen two years ago, but at least Luna looked the same. Sean's team acted more like family when they worked big cases together. She'd gotten to know many of the troopers at the picnics and barbecues. Ivy's confidence faltered. Did they hold a grudge against her? Even though they'd mutually agreed that their marriage wasn't working, friends tended to pick sides in a divorce. They'd obviously side with their teammate, Sean.

Helena's kind smile didn't seem to hold any animosity, though. Luna rushed out of the grasses and her handler followed behind her. "I think I'm done processing the scene. Sean radioed that you need something inside?"

"I just need to grab some supplies." Ivy tried to hustle up the stairs, not wanting to think any more about the events of the day. She grabbed the first container on the edge of the shelf. Emergency Survival Supplies, a kit she put together for any women on the run, might prove useful. She also picked a backpack kit made specifically for toddlers, which would hold diapers, wipes and baby food.

Sean stepped inside the mission with Grace by his side. "I transferred our gear to your Jeep. I figured you might need to take your foster child somewhere after you're patched up at the hospital. Easier to drive your vehicle than try to put a car seat in the trooper SUV."

The man had a servant's heart. Even once they'd agreed to divorce, when they'd lived the remaining days of their marriage in separate rooms, he still made the coffee the way she liked it and took her Jeep to have the oil changed. Things were wonderful when they were in agreement, but when they weren't…

There was so much they could never see eye to eye on. Sometimes she wondered if she'd found Christ before their divorce, would things be different? Christian or not, people still divorced. She couldn't control his decisions. She turned away from Sean to give the stockroom one last look and refused to let her mind ruminate on what-ifs. "I think that's all I'll need for tonight, at least." Her gaze caught the front door. "The camera," she said, pointing. "I got an alert that someone had come inside. I don't usually check it because our internet is so slow out here, but if the attacker or the woman came through the front door, the camera should've saved the footage."

She reached for her pocket to pull up the camera app. *No phone, of course.* She glanced at the front counter where she usually kept her personal items, but her phone wasn't there, either. The murdered woman flashed in her head again. "I had my cell phone with me," she murmured, the memories becoming clearer. "To call 9-1-1. Did Helena find my phone in the grasses?"

"Not that I know of, but I'll ask."

Her stomach soured, and her muscles turned weak and shaky. She couldn't panic. "Sean, if you can't find my phone out there…" Her voice shook and she fought to gain control. "That man has it."

She remembered the sensation of her fingers moving of their own accord before she woke. Her wrists still showed angry purple marks from the rope. What if he had used her thumb to access her phone? He'd have gained access to photos of Dylan. She needed to get to her baby. *Now*. She hefted the backpack up on her shoulder. But her muscles refused to cooperate, and her legs gave way. Hands pressed against her back, pushing her upright.

"Ivy?" Sean's voice sounded panicked.

She blinked intentionally, trying to focus, but everything was blurry. His arms cradled her neck and knees, and he lifted her to his chest.

"Dylan." The only word she could whisper before her brain flipped a switch and all went black again.

THREE

Sean paced the empty waiting room. Grace kept rhythm with him, tapping four staccato beats for each of his strides. She stayed with him for five laps across the twenty-foot room until she flopped down with a harrumph. If she had eyebrows, one would have definitely been raised. He leaned over and ruffled the top of her head. "You've had a hard day, too. Sorry I'm not taking this well."

A woman in blue scrubs walked out from Ivy's room, stopped at the nurses' station and turned to face him. "You're the husband?"

"Yes." Sean gave a flick of his hand, a simple thumbs-up that let Grace know the doctor wasn't a threat. The Akita sat at attention while he crossed the room to meet the doctor. "Ex-husband, actually."

The doctor gave a cursory glance at Grace. Before they'd entered the hospital, Sean had slipped on the dog's official Alaska State Trooper K-9 Unit vest. Once on, Grace's uniform usually silenced any questions about a dog being in a hospital.

"Can you tell me Ivy's prognosis? She was in and out of consciousness on the way here…and likely hit on the head with a gun by her assailant at one point. Probably out for hours."

The doctor's forehead creased. "It's never good when someone has blacked out for that long. I can tell you she's extremely dehydrated. I'm waiting on the scans for any other diagnosis." She offered a kind smile. "Feel free to wait with her."

Grace padded along by his side as they walked down the hallway and into Ivy's room. Recessed lights glowed over the cabinets lining the wall. Ivy's head was wrapped in a bandage, and a tube extended from her arm. She waved her right fingers half-heartedly. Grace's tail flopped against the side of his leg. No doubt about it now—his partner remembered Ivy.

"You're awake. How are you feeling?"

"So much better."

He grabbed a chair and pulled it to her bedside. "You've got some color back."

She pressed her lips together and took a deep breath. "When I got knocked out, I hadn't had lunch yet."

Black coffee every morning, he remembered. She rarely ever ate anything before noon. Sean still enjoyed a big breakfast, but he'd appreciated the way she'd sit and sip from her favorite mug, two hands wrapped around the ceramic for warmth no matter the weather. Halfway through the mug, she'd pour in more coffee as a warm-up. She'd continue the routine for several more refills, but always set off to conquer the day with almost a full cup still left in the mug. It used to drive him nuts until he started turning her leftovers into iced coffee for the afternoons.

"What's so funny?" She tilted her head to the side. Grace did the same, mimicking her expression.

"Nothing." He'd forgotten moments like these. Strange, the small things he missed. He hadn't gone to the trouble of making iced coffee in almost two years.

"Can I use your phone? I'm really worried about Dylan." She glanced at the tube attached to her arm with a grimace.

"He's on his way here. I reached out to the foster care folks. Didn't take long before we found his social worker, and she had your babysitter on file. Helena should be escorting them both here as we speak."

Her shoulders relaxed and she sank into the pillow behind her. "Thank you." She shook her head. "They might not let me take care of him if I'm in danger."

"They know you won't be staying home. Helena assured them we'd be taking charge of your security. For now, they're fine with it."

The way her eyes passed over his face, silently studying him, set the hairs on the back of his neck on edge. What was she thinking?

"Thank you," she finally said. "I'm ready to give my statement. I'd rather get it done before Dylan gets here. He's thirteen months but picks up on everything. He'll be able to tell I'm upset." She took a deep breath.

Sean pressed the voice-record feature on his phone. "Are you sure you're ready?"

"It's like a nightmare. Some parts are more memorable than others. That husky I told you about helped me escape. They're really loyal animals, and looking back, I think she was trying to get help for her owner..."

Sean watched Ivy's forehead tighten and lips purse, fighting off emotion. He leaned forward and gave her hand a squeeze. It was too natural to reach for her. He released her fingers just as fast. "Are you sure you're up for this? We can wait for Helena and—"

"Yes, I'd like to get it over with while my memory is fresh. The Siberian husky made me wonder if the murder had something to do with the Iditarod. We have a few teams that train around here. Although, the killer didn't seem to have the type of fit physique most mushers have, so maybe the woman he killed was the musher. Or the husky was just a pet." Her eyes focused on the wall across from her as if the day's events were being projected there. "I think the woman came to the mission because she wanted survival gear from me. Maybe to run away from the killer. But he found her before that could happen."

"We'll investigate all those possibilities. We found your pepper spray. Did he attack you first before he knocked you out?"

"No. It was like he came out of nowhere. I was about to call 9-1-1."

"Maybe he was preparing to transport the body, or he hid in the grasses when he heard you approach."

"When I woke up, he said something strange. He wanted to know if she gave me something." She squeezed her eyes tight. "I can't remember his exact wording." She opened her eyes and shrugged. "I had no idea what he was talking about. For all I know, he was out of his mind."

"Bye-bye…bye-bye! *Bye-bye!*" A little boy's voice was getting louder and louder and rang through the hallway.

Ivy sat straight up, a smile radiating across her beautiful face. "Dylan? I think that's him." She laughed, her eyes bright. "When he starts shouting *bye-bye*, it means he doesn't want to be here."

An older woman with curly, shoulder-length black hair highlighted with silver streaks stepped inside the room. She was hunched over, holding a little boy's hand. "Would've been here sooner if he'd let me pick him up and carry him. He's in one of his independent moods today, Ivy. Just like his mama. You doing okay, sweetie?" Helena and Luna stood behind the sitter and child.

"Thanks, Minnie," Ivy said. "I think I'm going to be okay. Just a big knock on the head is all."

Understatement of the year. His own legs felt weak remembering the moment she pulled her hand away from her head, covered in blood. The boy ran forward in a waddle, tripping over his shoes, hands outstretched, determined to reach Ivy. Sean could see the same determination to reach him in Ivy's eyes. She sat up and tried to lean over the side of the bed. But she shouldn't be picking him up before the doctor gave the all clear. The boy froze midrun, blue eyes wide. "Doggy!"

Grace flopped her tail from side to side but remained in place, as Sean's splayed fingers directed. Most of the Akita Inu breed were only trained and used as guard dogs for law enforcement and not recommended as family dogs, but the troopers had rescued Grace from a shelter as a mixed-breed puppy. While mostly Akita Inu, especially in appearance, her DNA revealed a hearty mix of golden retriever, which probably accounted for her amazing smelling abilities and fondness for little people.

Sean scooped the boy up. The moment the bundle of energy was in his arms, the striking shade of Dylan's blue eyes and dark blond hair were hard to ignore. It was like looking at a photo of himself at that age. Sean froze. The toddler stared into his face, as well. Did the boy see the resemblance, too, or was he stunned into silence by the fact a strange man had picked him up?

Math wasn't Sean's strong suit, but they'd been divorced twenty-two months. If Dylan was thirteen months old, was there any possibility that—

"He's only been with me six months," Ivy said softly, reaching her hands out and offering a sweet smile Dylan's way. "But he's already got me wrapped around his little finger."

His ex-wife knew exactly where his mind had gone in that brief moment, Sean was certain. She'd read his thoughts and attempted to spare him from an embarrassing conversation in front of his coworkers. Whether he should thank her later or not, he hadn't decided. He preferred to avoid potential triggers that would reopen past disagreements.

The boy strained in his arms, eager to go to Ivy. Sean, careful to avoid the IV, rested Dylan in her lap. The little hands reached for Ivy's neck. He wrapped himself around her, while resting his chubby face against her chest. Sean's heart practically exploded out of his chest in a way he couldn't understand.

He'd decided three years ago that children would be out of the question. In his line of work, he didn't need any new vulnerabilities. At the time that he realized he'd need such strict boundaries, Ivy was already in his life, but his job required everything else of him. He'd turn down any new opportunities to make him susceptible to weakness.

It wasn't that he didn't like kids. He enjoyed them a lot. *Other* people's kids. He could make them laugh, then walk away without getting too attached…

Dylan and Ivy pulled back from their hug, beaming at each other. Despite himself, his heart melted again.

Sean turned to Grace to get his bearings. The dog, the team, the job. That was his life. And right now, he needed to focus on finding the murderer so he could leave Nome with the knowledge that Ivy was safe. The faster he did, the better.

Ivy followed Minnie down the hallway of the Golden Dreams Bed and Breakfast until she stopped at a door to the left. "Here's your room," the older woman said. She used an old-fashioned key to unlock the door. "I'll make sure someone brings down a portable crib for Dylan."

The room managed to feel bright and airy while capitalizing on Nome's other claim to fame, the rush. While most famous for the gold rush of the late 1800s, the past few years had brought a second rush of sorts. At least, enough to draw the attention of fortune hunters and reality shows. The lamps were crystal containers of what appeared to be gold glitter, the gold bedspread was complemented by the blue curtains that looked like rivers, and even the sink basin resembled a gold panning bowl. If it weren't almost midnight, combined with a bandaged head and painkillers in her system, she'd have been thrilled by the decor. "Thank you, Minnie. This is lovely, but are you sure I'm not taking business away from your daughter?"

"The troopers are paying for the lodging," Sean said, appearing behind Minnie with a backpack slung over each shoulder. "You are a witness to a homicide and a victim of kidnapping. We need to make sure you're safe. We take our job seriously." He stepped past Minnie and opened the adjoining door.

Helena appeared on the other side of the door. There were two beds in the female trooper's room and her K-9 had already commandeered one of them. "We'll be here. If you need anything, Luna and I can make another run into town." She pointed at Sean. "I just received some good news from the pilot we commissioned. He's already delivered the evidence to the lab, and I've given Tala a heads-up that we need this bumped up to priority status."

"Oh, I remember Tala," Ivy said without thinking. She might have been proud she remembered so many of their team members, but she doubted they cared if she knew who their go-to forensics scientist was. Tala Ekho worked for the Alaska State Crime Lab, only a couple of miles from the K-9 team headquarters, and she assisted with most of the K-9 cases. Ivy had been introduced to the woman at one of the picnics and was immediately drawn to her, perhaps because Tala seemed as if she was an outsider, too.

Sean's eyebrows rose. "You only met her once. I'm impressed."

"Hopefully, we'll have some new leads soon. And we're working on tracking your phone, Ivy." Helena offered a friendly smile. "So far no pings, but we'll keep at it. As soon as the phone is somewhere with a signal, we should get a lead."

"That is good news. I don't like the thought of him having my phone." She couldn't shake the weird memory of the man grabbing her hand before she was fully awake.

"I finally made it." Gabriel stepped past Helena, as if joining a late-night party in Ivy's room. The thought almost made her laugh aloud. The trooper carried a jug of milk and a bag of baby food and snacks, while also loosely holding a leash for Bear to stay at his side. He set down the items on the dresser. "Did you know they sell ATVs in the produce aisle? They're sitting right there in between the cucumbers and the shelves of bread. And *eight dollars* for a gallon of milk?"

Ivy snickered, imagining his reaction. "Thank you, Gabriel. Welcome to Nome." Such a beautiful and remote area came with a price. All groceries and supplies had high transport costs added. And their grocery store didn't only carry groceries. She'd gotten used to vehicles in the veggie aisle without much thought.

"Doggies, doggies, doggies." Dylan squirmed in her arms, reaching both hands out, opening and closing his fingers, as if he wanted to squeeze the K-9s like stuffed animals.

"Sorry, buddy. Bear's head is almost the same size as your entire body. I'm not sure he'd appreciate you pulling his hair out." Ivy perched on the edge of the bed so he could see the dogs better.

Sean threw a thumb over his shoulder. "Gabriel and I will be stationed in the rooms across the hall."

Minnie stepped back into the room. "I may not technically own the place, but being the mother of the owner does have its perks." Minnie's son-in-law, Ben Duncan, appeared with the folded-up portable crib. "It's been a slow tourism year, so they're happy to have you." Ivy knew Ben, but not very well. "Okay, we'll let you get your rest," Minnie said.

Ivy's cheeks heated as she faced the woman who was not only Dylan's babysitter but her closest friend in town. Minnie had actually been the one to lead her to Christ. The freedom and love that Ivy found in the Gospel was one of the reasons she wanted to spend her life helping others.

Everyone left the room except Sean and Grace. Helena's door remained slightly ajar as Sean set up the folding crib. Ivy sat down on the edge of the mattress. Her bones felt like they weighed twice as much as usual. Grace rested her chin on Ivy's free knee. "Oh, you really do remember me." Ivy helped Dylan hover his little hand on top of the Akita's head. "Gentle," she said.

While Sean had always warned Ivy that Grace was a partner and not a pet, the dog still had managed to steal her heart. It had been so hard to say goodbye to Grace.

"Is doggy?" Dylan asked, twisting his face until they were nose to nose. Dylan had developed the habit of getting in her face, making sure she had no choice but to answer him.

"Yes. Doggy's name is Grace."

"Yace!" Dylan attempted the name with a nod. Grace wagged her tail and let her tongue hang in response, sending him into a fit of giggles. He rubbed his eyes, so exhausted. Ivy snuggled her little boy and swayed side to side, too tired to stand.

"I think we're set here." Sean checked each rail of the crib to make sure it had locked correctly. The small attention to detail was like a punch in the gut she wasn't prepared for. This was what he would've been like as a father.

"Are you okay?"

"Fine," she answered, pushing past the tightness in her throat.

His eyes narrowed. "I'm familiar with traumatic brain injuries—"

"Mild," Ivy interjected. "The doctor said it was a mild injury. He said if I rest, I'll be fine."

"He said most likely. It's not a guarantee. You have to tell me or Helena if you have headaches or nausea. Promise me?" His eyebrows lifted and then lowered as if he realized he'd crossed a line. Her husband could ask her to promise, but it was plain odd for a trooper to ask in that way. "I mean, I hope you take your health seriously. Please ask for help if you need it."

She sighed. "I understand and I will. I'm about to fall asleep sitting up."

Thanks to Minnie, Dylan had already been fed and changed into pajamas.

"Then let me help you." Sean's expression softened, staring at the toddler. She glanced down to find him asleep on her chest. Sean bent over and lifted him from her arms. The coconut scent of his hair caused her to inhale automatically. She loved that smell.

Sean turned and lowered him down in the crib carefully. Dylan blinked his heavy eyelids and began babbling, half-awake, his normal routine to drift off to sleep. At least he hadn't started singing. He really enjoyed babbling songs, though she was probably the only one who could recognize them.

Grace turned and sniffed the mesh panels of the crib. "Not now, Grace," Sean whispered. Dylan giggled but thankfully didn't stand back up.

"I'm thankful, Sean. I really am. Now that I'm safe, I feel certain that when I interrupted that horrible man's plan, he acted in the heat of the moment when he abducted me. He's headed as far from here as he can if he's smart. I'm sure I'll never see him again." Even saying so aloud helped ease the hum of anxiety in her stomach.

Sean picked up the backpacks he'd left by the door. "I don't like to remind you, but you did see the man's face."

"And Alaska is *huge*. I want him behind bars just as much as you do, but the point is, he has a chance of never being caught. And if that's the case, I'm safe. I'll take you guys to the shack tomorrow and hopefully you'll find enough to track him down, but I don't think it'll be anywhere near here."

Sean tapped his leg and Grace returned to his side, a stark reminder that the dog's loyalty to Sean and the job always came first. "Get some rest, Ivy. We can discuss the next steps in the morning."

There was wisdom in waiting until morning to make any decisions, but old hurts and longings rose to the surface at his abrupt end to the conversation. Like pausing an old movie before she'd seen the ending. "Good night, Sean. Good night, Grace."

He slipped out the door, and within minutes, Ivy had put away the milk and groceries into the mini fridge and readied herself for bed. Focusing on tasks that needed to be done helped keep the churning thoughts at bay, though she feared it would be harder now that her head was no longer distracting her with throbbing pain.

Helena's hotel door was left an inch ajar, but her light was already out, as well. Ivy clicked off the lamp and snuggled under the covers. Minutes of sleeplessness turned into an hour of staring at the patterns in the ceiling. She was growing more awake, not less, despite the exhaustion. Maybe it was the painkillers' fault.

The whine of a door hinge sent a shiver up her spine. The moonlight seeped in between the sliver of the two curtains. A shadow moved across the wall closest to Dylan.

A man was making his way to her bed.

FOUR

Sean tightened his fists for a count of five and released. He'd already changed into his K-9 Unit sweatpants, but it was hard to relax when he kept replaying every interaction with Ivy. Fatigue finally won out. He focused on his breathing as sleep took his mind.

Grace growled, a low rumble in her throat that sent him jumping out of bed, all promise of slumber gone. She never made that kind of noise without a reason. "What is it?"

Grace trotted to the hotel door. She barked another deep and impressive growl. Sean grabbed the gun on the nightstand. His heart pounded in his head as he yanked the hotel room door open. The hallway was pitch-dark. Why? The hallway light was on when he'd gone into his room.

Another bark sounded, this one higher pitched, and not from Grace. A woman screamed.

Helena yelled, "Attack!"

A baby wailed. *Dylan?*

Sean lunged across the hall. A sliver of light led him to Ivy's door, left ajar. "Alaska State Trooper," he yelled as he burst into the room. The baby's cries accompanied Luna's frenzied barking. Light from the street streamed in from the open window. Luna was halfway through the window, her head poking out.

Helena tugged on her K-9's collar. "Off, Luna." The curtains fluttered into the room, along with the cold arctic breeze. The dog sat and Helena closed the window and flipped the lock.

While still dim, the light from the street highlighted Ivy's form, hunched over and pulling the screaming Dylan from out of the portable crib. She straightened and whispered, "Shh," in a soothing pattern.

Lights flooded the hallway. Sean spun around to find Gabriel and Bear in the doorway.

"What happened?" Gabe beat him to the question.

"A masked man entered through the hallway," Ivy said softly. "Shh, it's okay." She went back to comforting her baby boy.

"Ivy screamed. I ordered Luna to attack, but the assailant made it out the window." Helena spoke rapidly. "I think Luna bit his wrist but didn't get enough of a grab to hold him. By the time I got to the window, he was gone."

"Do you think we can find a scent? Should I go?" Gabe asked.

"Let's try. I'll go with you. If we catch sight of him, I'm sure Luna will want a second chance to take him down." Also dressed in her official sweatpants, Helena ran into her attached room with Luna by her side, presumably to slip on her shoes on the way out. Gabriel met her in the hallway, and they ran together, out the door.

The adrenaline pulsed hard and fast in Sean's veins, begging him to search with his team, but Ivy needed him. And Bear and Luna were more suited to the task.

"I know you probably want him to go to sleep, but I need to ask you some questions first." Sean found the light switch and lit up the room. Ivy dipped her head, her cheek pressed against Dylan's. "It's okay," she whispered. The baby's cries had faded into staccato sniffing and shuddering gasps.

She rubbed Dylan's back. "Oh, honey, I know. It was scary. You're safe now." She kissed the top of his head.

A memory of his first recovery with Grace, after an earthquake, made an unwelcome appearance in his mind. He blinked it away. "I need to know exactly what happened tonight."

Even as he asked for more details, he knew the most important fact. The killer definitely hadn't left the area, and Ivy was still in danger. All the other questions made background noise in his mind. The killer had figured out her room and how to get inside without being detected.

He'd driven Ivy's Jeep here, but her vehicle blended in with the many other Jeeps in the lot. Helena and Gabriel had also parked their trooper vehicles in the parking lot. Law enforcement vehicles were a deterrent for any "normal" criminal. In his experience, the more desperate a criminal, the more dangerous.

His boss would want him to make finding the murdered victim a priority tomorrow. But now that Ivy had been rescued, once he and Grace found the victim, the colonel would likely take him off the case and leave other troopers to track down the killer. The truth hit him in the gut. Even if he had to take time off, he wasn't leaving Nome until he knew Ivy and Dylan were safe.

She swayed from side to side, still attempting to lull Dylan back to sleep. "I need to keep my voice light, like I'm happy, or he'll get worked back up again."

"Give Dylan to someone else."

Her lips pursed. "Excuse me?"

"If you want to be a foster mom after we find the killer, you still can. But right now, you're not safe. The baby isn't safe. Let someone else foster him and go to Anchorage."

"Give him *back*?" Ivy's eyes went wild and she clenched her jaw. But when Dylan turned his face up to her, she forced a strained smile.

Sean's chest tightened. The words had come out without a filter, again. "I could've been a little more tactful, but the bottom line is still true."

"While I agree that Dylan's safety is paramount," Ivy replied stiffly, "I can't just *give him back*, as you say." She turned away from him and set the boy in the portable crib with a new bottle. Dylan, though, had no interest and climbed up to standing, reaching for Grace, whose tail was just out of reach.

Ivy took a step closer to Sean. "I will contact the social worker first thing in the morning to keep her updated and decide what is best for Dylan, but I'm not going back to Anchorage. I'll go to the bunker."

"In the middle of nowhere?"

"All the more difficult for that—" she gestured to the window "—man. No one knows about the bunker.

Which makes it almost impossible for any danger to find us." She blinked away the new sheen of tears forming in her eyes and stared at the golden carpet below her bare feet. "Sean," she said, almost in a whisper, "I appreciate you coming all this way and finding me. I really do. I know you're trying to keep me safe, but I'm a mother now, whether you like it or not. And I'm not your wife."

His internal temperature rose ten degrees on the spot. He'd let his desire to keep her safe rule his thoughts and feelings, instead of acting like the professional he was. At least Helena and Gabriel weren't there to witness his rash behavior, ordering her around like that. "You're right. I'm sorry."

Ivy's forehead wrinkled and her mouth dropped open. Grace looked up, her mouth also slightly agape at him. "Come on. It's not as if I've never apologized before." He chuckled, hoping his cheeks weren't turning red.

"True. Just a new speed record." She offered a small smile.

"I suppose I deserve that." One of his greatest regrets was how he'd handled disagreements in their marriage. He wanted to think he'd changed for the better, grown up since she'd left. And yet, the instant fear gripped his heart, he'd tried to lay down the law without so much as a conversation. Would he really have given a stranger the same advice? Maybe, but he would've asked a lot more questions. And he would've respected their input first and suggested a new course of action in a more delicate manner.

But even after the adrenaline of the incident and the

argument began to fade, he still thought his plan was best. "As your…" He didn't want to call himself *the ex*. But did he have the right to say they were friends? "…former husband," he finally said, "I am asking you to reconsider coming to Anchorage. I think tonight is proof this man has no plans of leaving a witness alive."

Her face paled. Dylan giggled, averting their attention. Grace swished her bushy white tail left and right, barely out of reach of the boy's greedy little fingers. He cackled, laughing so hard he fell down to sitting in the crib and reached for his bottle. It proved impossible not to smile in response, which made it harder to return to the subject at hand.

"As a state trooper responsible for your safety, I'd like to place Grace in your room for the rest of the night as added protection."

"And—" Helena's voice rang behind them "—you're switching rooms with me. Our search fizzled about two blocks away. He must have had a vehicle waiting."

Gabe and Bear appeared behind her and Luna. "The housekeeping keys were stolen from behind the front desk."

"Your babysitter, Minnie, signed us in," Helena added. "They do things old-school here. Paper and pen at the front desk. So when—"

"He managed to get her keys and her room number?" Sean crossed his arms across his chest.

"Oh, please don't tell Minnie it was her fault," Ivy said. "She would never forgive herself for putting us in danger. I know it wasn't on purpose."

Sean sighed. He agreed with a nod.

Gabe checked the window lock a second time. "Let's get the room switch done and see if we can catch a little shut-eye before sunrise. We'll look for new accommodations tomorrow."

Sean had several objections. He held up a finger. "But—"

"We've informed the local PD," Helena said. "They're putting a uniform in front, and they've got another officer canvassing the town." She flashed an encouraging smile. "If he does manage to come back again, he'll find Luna here instead of Ivy. We'll get him before you know it."

He couldn't share her enthusiasm. The killer had evaded three trained officers and their highly trained K-9s. Until he was caught, sleep wouldn't come easy.

Ivy woke to the sounds of a truck's backup beep outside her room. She sat up and glanced at the clock. Already nine in the morning? By the time she'd switched rooms with Helena, it had been after 1:00 a.m., but she never slept this late. Even though it had brought her comfort when Sean ordered Grace to protect her, hours had gone by before she'd finally drifted to sleep. A quick peek confirmed the dog still rested, spread eagle, from her spot in front of the door. She'd often wondered, even when Grace was a puppy, if she dreamed that she could fly while sleeping in that position.

Her stomach growled. Grace's eyes flashed open. "Sorry, girl." Just this once, Ivy planned to indulge in the biggest breakfast the B and B offered and didn't want to sleep away her chance. Careful to move quietly so Dylan would remain asleep, she tiptoed toward the bathroom to get ready. Grace popped up, took a few steps and turned sideways, her posture regal, effectively blocking Ivy's path.

Ivy tilted her head back and let out a breath of exasperation. Of course, Sean's dog would take the protection detail a little *too* seriously. Just like Sean would. "I promise I'm not trying to escape," she whispered. She pointed to the bathroom. Grace took a step backward and plopped down again, apparently satisfied.

After getting ready in record time, Dylan began to stir. Ivy heard a tap at the adjoining door, slightly ajar for Helena's easy access. "Come in," she called. Before the door could open, Grace sprinted across the room and sat at attention at the door, sticking her nose into the space.

"Just me, Grace. At ease." Helena poked her head inside. Luna's head thrust past the door right below her knee, and the two dogs huffed at each other, as if in greeting.

Dylan laughed at the exchange. "Yace and Doggy."

"That's right." Helena offered him a grin. "Sean is waiting in the hall to take Grace for her morning walk and meal. If you two are ready, I'm to accompany you to breakfast. We have today's logistics to discuss."

Ivy nodded. "No problem."

"Come on, Grace." Helena disappeared from view for a moment. Meanwhile, Ivy grabbed the diaper bag Minnie had returned to her last night. The zipper wouldn't close on the bag, overstocked with the baby food and snacks Gabriel had been kind enough to pick up last night. She had yet to open the emergency bag of supplies she'd brought from the mission. A relief, too, as she might need them once they got to the bunker. Dylan's rosy cheeks and beaming smile squeezed her heart tight. How long would they have to hide?

"Okay, Sean and Grace will meet us at breakfast in a few minutes. Ready?" Helena asked.

She looked past the trooper, fully dressed in the blue uniform, and remembered the shadow that had moved across the wall. Ivy had forced herself to wait until the intruder had creeped past the crib to make sure he wouldn't try to grab Dylan if she reacted. She'd bided her time as the man stepped closer, her heart in her throat, while praying fervently for help. Only when he'd reached the foot of her bed had she allowed herself to scream.

"Are you okay?" Helena reached out and touched her shoulder. "You turned white as a sheet."

"Yes. Sorry. I'm fine." Even though God had answered her prayer and help came in time, she still couldn't shake the helpless feeling. She'd always thought she was strong, but right now she wanted to do exactly as Sean suggested. *Run away.* Except she couldn't do that without Dylan, which took time and paperwork. Besides, she wasn't sure her heart could handle returning to the place she'd lived with Sean. So much hope and heartache experienced in one place. At least she could take Dylan to the bunker. She'd had the place approved during the foster application process since her parents stayed there when they visited. The bunker would be safe.

She kissed the smiling boy on the forehead, placed him on one hip and lifted the strap of the bag on her shoulder. "Rough night of sleep is all. Can't complain. You all got the same amount, too."

Helena laughed and stepped aside for Ivy and Dylan to walk with her to the door. "You'd think I'd be used to sleepless nights, but I'm not. I just appreciate the peaceful ones." Luna took a giant yawn, triggering another squeal of delight from Dylan.

"Great timing, Luna." Helena waved them forward and locked the door behind them. They walked down the hallway, a tight fit all together.

"With everything going on, I never got a chance to say it's good to see you again, Helena. How are you?" Ivy realized she was holding her breath, wondering if the other woman would give her a cold shoulder if she tried to get friendly.

Helena surprised her with a genuine smile. "I'm good. I recently got engaged."

Her jaw went slack. If Helena's raised eyebrows were any indication, Ivy's surprise seemed unwarranted. She'd been under the assumption that the only people on the team who were married must have met prior to their K-9 specialties. A few months into Sean's K-9 duty, he'd changed. Came home drained every night. It seemed hard to believe there'd be time or energy for any of the specialized troopers to start a new relationship. Obviously, Helena didn't have that problem. "Congratulations," Ivy said, recovering with a grin. "Who is the guy?"

"He's a police officer. We met on a case. His name is Everett."

Figured. They could probably relate to each other in a way Ivy never had a chance to with Sean. "I guess that means Luna approves."

Luna looked up at the mention.

"Oh, Ivy." Fiona Duncan, Minnie's daughter and the owner of the B and B, entered the hallway from a side room. "I'm sorry for the intrusion to your sleep last night."

Helena pursed her lips ever so slightly, and Ivy understood the silent message. Fiona didn't know the whole story, so Ivy should keep quiet.

Fiona stopped prematurely when she eyed Luna. The Norwegian elkhound looked fierce when it stared down a person. The innkeeper nodded a greeting at the dog. "We've never had any intruders before. The guests know the troopers prevented an altercation. That's all," she whispered conspiratorially. "And you can be assured that we're updating all our security and check-in protocols. The locks are getting changed today. That nice trooper, Gabriel, helped us see where we can improve."

Fiona spun around, beckoning them. "Follow me. I've got a big breakfast lined up for everyone. We pride ourselves on a family atmosphere. Everyone that stays here is always so friendly and fascinating. They come from all over the world, you know. Bird-watchers, gold hunters, yachters taking a break to check reports on ice before crossing the Northwest Passage… You'd be surprised how many different kinds of folks show up here!"

Helena exchanged an amused grin with Ivy but remained silent. Fiona was full of energy and had never met someone she wasn't able to wring out their life story. Maybe the troopers should consider using her as a confidential informant, as she knew everything and everyone in the Nome area. The woman reached the threshold of the dining room and paused. "See that man the trooper is talking to?" Fiona's voice had dropped back down to her juicy-news whisper that Ivy knew so well. Looking in the direction that the innkeeper indicated, she saw that Gabriel was already in the dining room, shaking hands with a scruffy-looking man among the half a dozen guests already seated at tables.

"Mark Gilles is his name. He's looking to buy some dogs from a husky breeder in the area. He's hoping to start an Iditarod team, training in Anchorage." Fiona's eyebrows waggled. "See what I mean? Fascinating people."

"I saw a loose husky yesterday." She glanced at Helena to confirm that the trooper understood the significance. Could it be the murdered woman had something to do with the man interested in starting a husky team?

"And then those two men in sweaters, Evan Rodgers and Hudson Campbell," Fiona said with a little nod. "They're the ones at the table for two. They've been keeping to themselves, but it's because they came here trying to buy a sizable set of mining claims. Those gold-seeking types try to stay on the down low, but don't you worry." She placed a hand on her heart and spoke so rapidly it was hard to keep up. "My Ben comes from a third-generation gold-mining family. We're giving those men tips to make sure they won't get swindled. Ever since the latest gold rush here, and the host of reality shows, we get all sorts trying to make their fortune."

"There's still active gold mining?" Helena asked.

"Oh, yes! In fact, my Ben built one of the largest working dredges in use today. He can tell you all about it, if you'd like. But be careful who you talk to around here. Everyone acts like they know how to mine gold, but they don't." She straightened. "Well, there's the missing member of your party. I set aside the extra dining room in case you troopers want privacy." She moved into the dining room, arms out in greeting, ready to mingle with her guests.

"I wonder if she's telling her guests about us in kind," Helena mused.

"I don't think she will," Ivy said. "Fiona's loyal and tight-lipped about locals. She would be about her guests as well if she thought the topic needed privacy." At least, she hoped so.

At the opposite end of the hallway, Sean and Grace approached. She'd always appreciated his dark blond hair, blue eyes and broad shoulders, but now he seemed more rugged, more mature. He was going to be one of those men who only got more attractive with age.

The dog opened her mouth as if in a smile. Helena and Luna followed Fiona into the dining area. The smell of bacon and sausage and freshly brewed coffee beckoned Ivy in farther. Sean accompanied her to the buffet table in the back of the room. "I'd be glad to help you get a plate for Dylan."

"That's very thoughtful, thank you, but—" Dylan reached out his arms and practically vaulted out of hers.

Sean easily accepted him and pressed him against his chest. She opened her hands to take him back. "I'm so sorry. He never does that."

"No, it's okay." He grinned down at Dylan. "Make your plates. We've got a little meeting room set aside in back to discuss today's plan. See you in there."

Dylan was busy messing with the badge on Sean's uniform, acting as if he didn't even notice Ivy wasn't with him. For a man who didn't want to have kids, he was frustratingly great with them. She sloppily piled a large plate of food she could share with Dylan and entered the side room where Helena had been watching for her. Helena closed the glass door behind her when she entered. A tablet sat on the center of the table with a live feed of Trooper Maya Rodriguez, if Ivy remembered the team member's name right.

"Not much of an update," Maya said. "We're still on the search to find the groom and best man from the missing-bride case."

Awareness hit Ivy. Months ago, back in April, Sean had called Ivy to ask her a series of questions about survivalists, specifically about the community in residence in Chugach State Park. Unfortunately, she didn't know much about that particular area, but she gave him general tips.

He'd said the park was at the center of two separate cases. First, the missing-bride case that had been all over the news. A wedding party had been in the park when the future bride had become murderous, according to the groom and best man, at least. Then the bride had disappeared, rumored to be pregnant with the groom's baby

and hiding somewhere in the state park with survivalists. The second case revolved around helping their team
tech, Eli Partridge, search for his godmother's survivalist relatives in order to relay news of her fight against
cancer.

Ivy had been curious to hear updates on both cases.
She put down her plates at the edge of the table where
she wouldn't be visible in the video feed and took Dylan
back from Sean. Thankfully, her sweet boy only had
eyes for the dogs and wasn't making too much noise.

"Sorry, this will only take a minute," Sean whispered. "A quick team update."

"I was able to track the groom, Lance Wells, to Anchorage," Trooper Hunter McCord said. Ivy recognized
his voice instantly. "The groom may have been a step
ahead of us, but disguises are not his strong suit. Unfortunately, there was some gunfire, and he managed
to get away. He won't next time."

The way the trooper spoke, it sounded like the real
villain was the groom instead of the missing bride.

"No sign of Jared Dennis, the best man," Maya
added. "And I believe Hunter also received news from
Ariel Potter, the maid of honor, or maybe I should refer
to her as the future Mrs. McCord."

Ivy could see a bit of the screen and Hunter flashed
a bashful grin, which seemed out of place for the man.
From the context, it seemed Hunter and Ariel were an
item now.

"Yes," Hunter said. "Ariel received a call from Violet James. I think it's safe to say she wouldn't call herself a bride-to-be anymore. She's grateful that everyone

knows she's not a murderer now, but she's not coming home until Lance and Jared are behind bars."

Ivy tried not to react, but she knew her face betrayed her. That was a big update. The bride was no longer a murder suspect. But the groom and best man were?

"Violet is too worried they'll find her and hurt her future baby," Hunter said. "So for now, she stays hidden. She didn't confirm or deny that she's found safe harbor with survivalists, but I think it's a good guess."

Sean had his arms crossed over his chest. "That makes it harder on us to wrap this case up."

Hunter agreed and the rest of the team members reported no other news. Helena tapped on the tablet and the team said their goodbyes. "Sorry about that. Normally, we would ask you to wait in another room while we had the meeting, but circumstances…"

"That's okay." Ivy took a seat. "I'd already heard about the other case in the news when Sean asked me about survivalists, so I was curious to hear updates. I'm sorry I wasn't able to offer more help about the missing survivalists in Chugach State Park."

Gabriel's eyebrows rose. "I'd forgotten we'd had Sean ask you. You're practically a consultant, then," he said, a teasing lilt in his voice, before he took a big bite of an egg sandwich.

"If the groom and the best man are the actual murderers of that tour guide, then I don't blame Violet for staying hidden until you guys catch them." She met Sean's gaze. "I would do anything to protect Dylan. Which is why I'm going to take you back to that shack today and help you catch that killer so he'll leave us alone once and for all."

FIVE

Sean took a deep breath. "If you could give us some landmarks to look for, I think that's all we'll need."

"It would be faster if I showed you," Ivy told him. "Besides, there is the matter of traps."

"Don't worry about that. Gabriel and I have been in this situation before. We sidestepped some nasty traps in Chugach, actually—"

"Barely, but technically that's true," Gabriel added.

Sean tossed a glare his way. His teammate wasn't helping his case. The last thing he wanted was Ivy to be put in danger again, but Gabriel folded his arms over his chest, seemingly nonplussed. "We also had a park ranger give us some tips on how to avoid them."

"And yet your dogs found the traps before you," Ivy said. "Not all the traps are at a dog's level. Did this park ranger give you some hands-on training?" Dylan wiggled in her arms as she studied both of their faces a moment. Sean tried to look confident, but Ivy nodded triumphantly. "That's what I thought. This is what I do, Sean. You know that."

"Of course I do." Before he became a trooper, he'd wanted a little extra wilderness training to prepare himself for the type of remote Alaskan locations he might find himself in. That was why he'd signed up to take a survivalist course all those years ago. Ivy had not only put him through the paces of making shelters and fires no matter the weather or topography, she'd also filled him with confidence that he'd make a great trooper. And here she was, sitting in front of him, more beautiful than the day he'd met her, despite the weariness in her features. If he couldn't keep his own wife— *ex-wife*, he corrected himself again—out of harm's way, then what good was he as a trooper?

"She'll be safer with us, anyway," Gabriel said.

Helena nodded. "Sorry, Sean. Gabriel is right. Why would our suspect return to the shack, knowing that's the first place we would most likely look for him? The guy would have to be bold or stupid to try anything else knowing Ivy has troopers on her right and left."

Sean's memory flickered with recognition. He'd said something similar to Trooper Will Stryker when he'd been trying to keep the woman Will was falling for safe. "I've had my fill of bold and stupid criminals lately."

Gabriel stood and paced the length of the room with Bear at his side. "Agreed, but Ivy also has a point. She's the most qualified to help us investigate the evidence without dogs or troopers getting maimed. If her babysitter is willing to watch Dylan in a new location for the morning, we might get what we need to wrap this case up by nightfall."

Despite his pessimism, hope sputtered to life in his chest. "All right. I give up. If Ivy's willing..."

"You know I am," Ivy murmured, bouncing Dylan on her knee.

The toddler smiled contentedly, then turned around and climbed up her shoulder. "Mama. Doggy." Her face glowed with joy as she kissed his cheek in response.

Sean's insides turned cold. He couldn't really pinpoint exactly why that happened every time she kissed her baby boy.

"Speaking of tracking our suspect down..." Helena interjected. "Gabriel, did you get the rundown about our guests from Fiona, too?"

Gabriel smirked. "Yes, along with a history of the best and finest visitors ever to grace the shores of the Golden Beaches. I don't believe any of the guests in the dining room are suspects. Bear or Luna would've given us some unusual behavior. Especially Luna if she got her teeth close to the man."

"That's true," Helena said.

Gabriel held up an index finger. "But I'd like to follow up with the man who wants to buy huskies for an Iditarod team. Ask him a few questions and perhaps interview the breeder he's here to see."

"Mark Gilles is his name," Helena said. "And I think that's a good idea."

Sean pondered the new information. "You want to interview him because of the husky Ivy spotted? Sounds like a peripheral lead, but I'm all for turning every stone." He nodded at Gabriel. "So you'll take the interview? I think Helena might be more useful at the shack if Luna really got that close to the suspect."

Helena stood and wiggled her fingers at Dylan. "Let's get this cute little guy somewhere safe with Minnie and hit the road."

Thirty minutes later, Sean drove the Jeep back in the direction of the shack. A quick glance in the rear-view mirror confirmed Helena trailed behind them in the SUV. In the back seat of the Jeep, Grace had settled her head into the now-empty car seat. He wanted to let off a joking warning about not getting too attached to the boy, but he had a feeling the commentary would fall flat. Ivy sat rigid in the passenger seat.

"Hey," he said softly. "You don't have to do this, you know?"

She blinked rapidly and pulled her shoulders back. "I'm actually glad to go back to the scene so soon, with you and Helena. It's like getting back on a horse after you've fallen. This is my home. I can't be scared to be here. I've always loved going until the road ends. Dad would take us to the Niukluk River to fish for fun."

Sean pulled his chin back. "For *fun*? You mean for food?"

"We usually went to the store for food. I mean we needed to know how to catch a fish in the event we needed to, but…" She eyed him. "You might have a different idea of my childhood than the reality of it."

"I'm just a little surprised, I guess. You said you didn't want to raise a child the same way you were raised."

"That was back when I was under the impression you

still wanted kids. Just because I don't want to repeat the choices my parents made doesn't mean I didn't learn a lot of valuable things from my childhood. Clearly, there are a lot of things I love about the survivalist way of life or I wouldn't have chosen the occupation I did." Her voice lost the earlier warmth. "Please stop at the mission first. I'd like to pick up some supplies that'll make it easier to spot the traps."

He flipped on the turn signal in advance to give Helena warning. Grace sat up in the back and stared right into the mirror. It seemed like she was shaking her head ever so slightly as if even she knew he'd put his foot in his mouth. He pulled into the gravel parking lot and parked right next to the trooper SUV he'd left in the lot the night before.

"Sean—"

The side door, ajar, waved back and forth in the arctic breeze. There was no way Helena would've left that open. "Stay here."

He stepped out of the Jeep and reached for his holster, with a glance at his colleague. "I see it," Helena said. "I know I locked up before I left. I'll lead with Luna to check it out."

"I'll be your backup." Sean turned around and led Ivy and Grace into his trooper vehicle. "You'll be safer inside here." Though, he hoped they wouldn't need the extra ballistic protection the vehicle offered. "Wait here until I give the all clear." Ivy wrapped her arms around herself and nodded. "Grace, protect." He flipped the locks and closed the door.

Helena waited on the stairs to the deck. He jogged

up behind her and they approached with renewed caution. She grabbed the swinging door, keeping it from slamming closed again.

He tapped her on the shoulder. "Let me peek through the windows before you go in." He kept his hand on his weapon as he stepped past the doorway. With an uneasy feeling in his gut, he flattened his back against the small strip of siding in between the doors and windows, then peeked inside. Great. Just as he'd suspected. The store was destroyed. Nothing left on the shelves. Everything scattered on the ground. "Ransacked. No sign of anyone, but I can't see the upstairs apartment."

Helena nodded and shouted inside. "State Troopers! Hands up and exit the building. I'm about to release the dog and she *will* bite you."

They waited, staring at the empty threshold for what seemed like forever. Then he gave the nod. Helena released Luna and the dog tore through the building at breakneck speed. She ran back, panting, the familiar look of disappointment. "No one's here."

"So, was the ransacking a statement? Or was he looking for something?" Helena placed her hands on her hips and stepped inside.

Sean followed her. "Assuming it's the same guy, I think he's after something." His heart pounded harder with the implication. "Ivy said the man demanded to know where something was. He never said what."

"I think it might be helpful to ask her again. She might remember something, a small detail, which could prove invaluable." Helena gingerly moved a backpack on the floor with her foot. Blankets, ropes, packaged food and every other necessity needed in the wild were strewn all over the floor. "We'll also need her to give us an inventory list and a statement. She might notice something missing. Maybe he got what he was looking for. Does she own this place?"

His neck heated. He wasn't 100 percent sure. Ivy had talked a lot about the mission and her life in Nome the last time they'd spoken on the phone, but she'd also never mentioned Dylan. There might be other things she'd held back. "A friend owns this, I believe. Ivy just manages the place and lives here." He nodded toward the stairs. "I want to do one more sweep upstairs before we bring her in."

Helena glanced at Luna but nodded.

"I'm not questioning Luna's skills. She would've let us know a person was here, but I want to make sure he didn't leave some gruesome kind of threat for Ivy anywhere."

Her eyebrows rose. "I'm sorry. I didn't think of that." She nodded to the door. "We'll start the inventory down here while you check."

The stairs creaked as he took the steps two at a time. Entering her living space was surreal. This was where Ivy lived, *without* him. The living room held a love seat with a purple afghan. Sean's lips quirked. She loved purple. The kitchen and dining room were adjacent in the open layout. He passed by the kitchen counter on the way to the two bedrooms. In the center was a stack of papers with a pen to the side. Had he been right? Had the man left a written threat?

His eyes drifted to the top of the sheet. *Adoption Application Letter of Intent.* His fingers rested on the papers. Foster care was one thing…but adoption? His insides churned. No wonder she refused to leave. She wouldn't go anywhere without her soon-to-be son.

He closed his eyes for the briefest of seconds. There was no going back. No trying again. She had a child, and he needed to accept it and shut the door on any what-ifs for their relationship. The only way to do that was to make sure she was safe. The man had gotten careless. They'd catch him, but he needed proof to make the murder charges stick. Ivy's and Helena's voices could be heard from below. Grace sprinted up the stairs to his side. Timely. They had a body to find.

Ivy tightened the paracord to the thin branch she'd found on the dirt road near the river.

"Are you—" Sean began.

"I haven't changed my mind, Sean. Besides, I need something to distract me from the state of the store and my apartment." Truth was her insides still vibrated as intensely as the two other times that man had violated her personal space. First, the kidnapping, then breaking into her room. And now…*this.* It was almost too much. Pawing through all her belongings and vandalizing the mission almost broke her. The back of her neck tingled as if the man was watching her still. She couldn't escape him. Ivy turned her back to Sean so she could squeeze her fists tight without his noticing. It was either that or scream in frustration. "This is the only thing I know to do. I'm also good at tracking."

"I know."

"Please let me do what I can." And if she didn't succeed today, she'd take Dylan to the bunker. Away from the world. Safe. They'd stay there as long as it took.

"So what's the plan?" Helena approached her with Luna at her side.

"I walk forward with this stick outstretched. The cord is weighted just enough to hang straight down but light enough it won't trigger any trip wires. We should be able to see if it catches on anything before we step into danger."

Sean reached out his hand. "I'll hold it, then." She opened her mouth to argue, but his eyes narrowed. "Ivy, I draw the line at you going into the trees first. Besides, you'll probably be able to notice faster if you're not the one holding the paracord." He offered Grace's leash. "Trade?" At her resigned nod, he glanced at Grace. "Heel. Ivy." He pointed.

Grace shuffled backward, her spine straight and her head perfectly aligned with Ivy's left foot. "I didn't think she'd be willing to work with anyone but you."

"She won't. She knows you, so I think she understands what I'm asking. Even without the leash, I'd expect her to remain in a heel with you until I release her." He tilted his head with a smile. "She's the best partner I've ever had."

Luna huffed behind them, prompting Helena to laugh.

"No need for jealousy, Luna. You're the best partner I've ever had, too."

Sean turned around and held his arm straight. The stick added a good four to five feet from his arm and the cord dangled just as Ivy had hoped. "Stay behind and be my eyes." He took a deep breath and squared his shoulders. "Here we go."

Ivy's heart rate sped up. Grace leaned against her leg for the briefest of moments. Was she trying to comfort her? Ivy fought against blinking, watching the string and scanning the environment for potential setups. There. The tip of the branch on the right tree hung down in a curve. *"Stop!"*

Despite it still being daylight, she'd found a flashlight on the floor of her shop and brought it along. She flipped it on and pointed its light at a branch. The beam produced a reflection off a thin filament. And while the line might seem like a spiderweb to most, she knew better. "Stay put a second." She dropped the leash, and Sean commanded Grace to stay. With a flick of her knife, she cut the line and located the spikes, hidden in the tall grasses, set to be used as projectiles. "Hopefully, the cord would've caught it, but if I can spot them before we get that far, even better. You were right. If I'm not holding the cord, I can see more."

She hated admitting her failures and weaknesses to Sean, no matter how small. Their divorce was like a giant F on her report card in marriage. He seemed to have changed in many ways. The old Sean would've stubbornly refused her help, even with her expert qualifications, and she would've defiantly refused his.

He seemed more thoughtful now, too, but maybe that was just because he was on the job. He brought his best to work. She always knew that. And besides, she was becoming a mom, so she really needed to stop caring what he thought of her.

She picked the leash back up and took a step forward, but Grace didn't budge. Sean grinned. "Heel to Ivy." The journey through the thick grasses was slow going. A few yards later, Grace whined before the dangling paracord had caught on anything.

"I think this is the trap she found last time," he said.

Grace made a noise two other times, the paracord revealed three more traps, and Ivy found another right before they reached a small clearing by the river. "There." She pointed. Through another set of trees, the shack blended in with the surrounding brush.

Her insides twisted, but she took a deep breath and looked around, wondering if the husky was still in the area. No movement, except the slight breeze. Her heartbeat pounded against her throat. She might miss something if she didn't get a grip. "I need you and Helena to keep an eye out, too, now," she told Sean. "There's a lot to watch for."

She spotted another set of traps identical to the log smasher she'd found the day she escaped. Luna helped Helena find a ground trap, and finally they made it to the front door of the shack. Sean reached around her for the handle.

Something didn't seem right. Ivy blocked his hand. "Not yet."

Grace whined and Sean raised an eyebrow. "It's best not to make contact with me like that. Grace might feel forced to choose her loyalty. She doesn't give a warning if she feels she needs to protect me."

Irritation coursed through her veins, but she didn't have time to examine why. Grace wasn't a pet, after all—she was Sean's partner—but she'd be lying if she said she didn't love the dog. "I had good reason. If the murderer takes the time to set traps, he's probably smart enough to know I'd bring you guys back here."

"Fair point," Helena said.

Ivy flipped on the flashlight and guided the beam along the peripheral of the door. Parallel to the doorknob there was the slightest change, but it could be simply part of the construction. "Might be light reflecting off the latch," she muttered before moving the beam around the outer perimeter. Grace whined again. "I can't see anything but—"

Luna also complained. "Okay, it's time to trust our instincts. Something definitely feels off," Helena said. "Maybe our guy really is still inside there."

"Stand back," Sean said, looking around for any potential projectile trap. "Put Luna on ready alert."

Helena guided Ivy and Grace to the side they'd already cleared of traps. They could see the door but were far enough away to miss any projectiles. "Ready," Helena declared both to Luna and Sean.

He moved to the opposite side of the doorknob and crouched down against the shack wall. "State Troopers!" He reached across the door and turned the knob until a click. He leaned back and used the stick with the paracord to shove the door wide open.

A gunshot rang out. The dogs barked and lunged forward, straining against the leashes. A cloud of dirt and Sean's prone body were all Ivy could see.

SIX

"State Troopers," Helena shouted, a slight tremble in her voice that only other troopers would be able to detect. "You have five seconds to leave the premises with your hands up or I send the dog in and she will bite. Five..."

"I'm fine," Sean yelled back. "He missed me." The jolt of hearing a shotgun at close range made him lose his balance and fall back. He was more on edge than he'd thought after discovering so many traps, but now they were going to get this guy. He popped back up on his feet, pressed his back against the wall and grabbed his weapon out of its holster. Helena's counting grew stronger, steadier.

"One." She took a deep breath as the threshold of the shack door remained empty. "Attack!"

Sean stepped inside immediately after Luna, his weapon raised. Helena stepped to the right. The shack was empty except for the gun, an old spring-loaded twenty-gauge shotgun rigged up to shoot in the corner. The K-9 still stood on guard, staring at the shotgun, while Helena sliced at the rig used to engage the trigger with the door's motion.

Sean moved cautiously in case there was another trap. His eyes roamed the interior, taking note of the rotting wooden roof, the structural beam, the ropes on the ground, the blood on the floor… His throat went dry.

"He knew we'd come back," Helena said.

"He meant to kill." Ivy stood at the door, her features unnaturally blank as she scanned the room. Grace passed her and stepped into the room, spinning and then sniffing the floor in front of him. Grace sat down and looked directly at Sean. A thick layer of dust formed a border, a perfect rectangle, around the K-9.

"Did she just alert?" Helena asked softly.

Sean didn't want to discuss it in Ivy's presence, but he nodded. Even if the body wasn't actively in the room, the cadaver dog would be able to smell death for up to two weeks, though never past a month. While it probably seemed rare to Helena for Grace to alert without prompting, they thankfully weren't accosted with the scent of recent death all the time.

He wanted Ivy out of here as fast as possible. He pointed at the border of dust around his K-9 partner. "A rug was here?"

She nodded but said nothing.

Helena placed a hand on Ivy's shoulder. "Are you okay? You don't have to stay in here."

"I'm fine." But her voice sounded barely over a whisper. "When I woke up, the man had already rolled the rug up." She pointed to where Grace still sat. "I didn't see the woman inside, but I… I saw a hand." Her eyes drifted to the pole behind Sean and her entire face went white. "Excuse me. The dust must be getting to me." She spun on her heel and stepped back outside.

Seeing where the man had kept her, what he had put her through, what could've happened... For a moment, he heard nothing but roaring in his ears until Helena stared him down.

"Did you hear me? I said she's safe now."

"I know."

Helena pulled out her phone and began taking photographs of the shotgun and of Grace sitting on the only clean portion of the floor, along with images of the ropes on the ground. Sean rewarded the K-9 with her favorite toy. Afterward, he walked out of the shack with Grace by his side to where Ivy waited, her arms wrapped around herself, staring toward the river.

Was she *really* safe?

"See that riverbank?" Ivy murmured. "That's where I saw him without his mask."

He didn't need her to repeat the description. The words were burned into his memory. Six foot three with auburn hair and pale skin. He hesitated, but he had to do it. "Do you remember any other details now?"

She shook her head. "If that husky hadn't distracted him..."

"We would've found you in time," Sean finished for her, an edge to his voice that he knew probably wasn't helpful. Every fiber of his being told him to pull her close, to tell her he was so thankful she was okay. But he couldn't. For so many reasons.

They stood together in silence for two minutes. Sean placed a hand on her shoulder, ever so gently. He couldn't stand to see her like this. Ivy turned into his touch and tilted her head, wordlessly studying him. She stepped closer, and it was like two magnets coming together. He wrapped his arms around her, ignoring the warning bells in his mind. Her hands gripped the back of his jacket, the comfort of her touch no match for the many layers. He missed being able to hold her this way. The feeling that nothing could topple them if they were together, leaning on each other. He had no right to think of them this way.

Sean abruptly stepped back. Grace dropped the toy at his feet, and he picked it up. "Grace, it's time to work. Lead."

The extra word meant everything to the K-9. It was her cue that she was to take him to the body she'd smelled in the shack. Her ears swiveled and her spine straightened, her nose straining forward. He had to focus on the case now. At least they'd already passed by this section and knew it was free from traps. Still, he didn't want to take any chances and kept his eyes trained for any potential areas traps may be hiding. He knew from the way Ivy followed his exact steps that she was doing the same.

Grace kept her nose down to the ground. A line in the dirt, roughly six inches wide and headed straight, indicated she was likely on the right track. Helena and Luna joined them, a few paces behind. "The river?" his colleague asked.

"He might've taken the body to a different location with the boat," Sean answered. "We heard a motor moments after we found Ivy. He could've changed his plan after her escape and gone far from here. I'm hoping Grace can lead us in the right direction."

"A metallic fishing boat," Ivy said. "That's what he put the rug in. I remember that much. It looked old and beat-up."

"That's good," Helena praised her. "Feel free to tell us anything from that day, even if you think it might not matter. Every detail has the potential to help."

Sean studied Grace as she paused, lifting her head. *Come on, Lord. Please help her tell us which way he took her next.* The dog turned in a full circle, her mouth hanging open, breathing in the air. She returned to the waterline and plunged her face into the river. Her head jerked back. She shook, water droplets flying from her ears and neck, but even after, she didn't sit. If she had sat, they would've called in divers and searched the bottom of the river. Sean knew they still might have to resort to that, but given the amount of tributaries, he didn't like the options. Besides, the riverbed seemed to get shallow in places with rocks jutting out and tree roots sticking out from the bank. Grace huffed and looked over her shoulder. Her eyes grew soft, and by the way she held her head, he knew she was disappointed. He patted his leg. "Good job." Her tail wagged in acknowledgment.

"Dead end?" Helena asked.

Sean hated that phrase in his specialty, even if it described the truth. "The trail is cold." As well as his hope that he'd be able to close the case anytime soon. He was going to have to beg for more resources that weren't there. Someone would need to take over in keeping Ivy safe because he and Grace would need to systematically comb every square inch of Alaskan tundra until they found the victim. The colonel might not understand, but Sean would have to *make* her understand. Ivy was one of their own. Well, she used to be. Begging may not buy him much time, but he'd be willing to take unpaid leave and keep going. If he discovered a body while he wasn't on duty, the corpse would still be evidence.

The clock was ticking. The longer they waited, the more chance the suspect got away with getting rid of the body. Sean couldn't live with himself if the killer succeeded.

Ivy missed her Jeep. The seats in the state trooper SUV weren't the most comfortable. "Do you often have to leave your car in Anchorage and use other troopers' vehicles?"

"Uh, not usually. Typically, I can drive to where I need to go." He followed behind Helena on the highway. They ascended a hill next to the sea. Movement in the peripheral caught her eye.

"What—" Sean's mouth hung open as he slammed on the brakes.

A massive herd of caribou—almost fifty, if she had to guess—ran into the road from the eastern tundra. A sea of brown in front of them made it hard to distinguish where one animal ended and another began. Their antlers held the answer to how many were in the herd, but at the moment, they were so close together, it would be impossible to count.

The radio squawked. "You guys okay?" Helena asked.

"I've never seen so many reindeer at once!" She'd been far enough ahead that the herd hadn't blocked her path.

"Should I tell her they're called caribou around here?" Ivy whispered to Sean.

"They're not reindeer?"

"Same animal, believe it or not. But if they're wild, they're technically called caribou. If they're domesticated, then they're called reindeer. People will know what you mean either way, but they might school you."

"Like you just did?" Sean winked and grabbed the radio. "We're fine, but the *caribou*," he emphasized, "don't appear in a hurry to go anywhere." He tested the horn and the herd jogged a few steps forward but then stopped again.

"I'll wait a few minutes," Helena said.

Ivy leaned her head back, trying to calm the butterflies in her stomach. All from something as innocent as Sean's wink. How often had that wink been used after a meal or a funny joke? It was an invitation to get closer, to snuggle up. It didn't mean that anymore. Just like that hug at the river didn't mean anything. Two people simply trying to get past thoughts of a horrible crime. That was all it signified. A few of the caribou turned, watching them. "I think they're used to vehicles and aren't too scared of them."

"Why not?" Sean leaned forward, his arms draped on top of the steering wheel. "Why are they in the road? And why all *guys*?"

Ivy laughed. "Both males and females have antlers when it comes to reindeer."

"Don't you mean caribou?" he teased.

"Same thing," she said in a deadpan, though she ended up smiling a second later. "And, to answer your question, this is actually common around here. When the road isn't covered in snow or water, it's easier for them to travel on than the tundra. You'll find lots of animal herds prefer to travel by road. Or—" she squinted into the distance, searching for any other animals "—they could be running from a grizzly."

"I have bear spray, but nothing to encourage caribou to move on. Not sure I'd want to anger anyone with antlers."

He grabbed his radio. "Think I should tell Katie where she can find more reindeer?"

Helena responded instantly. "Probably wouldn't be appreciated. Besides, her ranch only helps injured, orphaned or unwanted ones. These all look fine to me. If you don't want me to wait for you, I'll start processing the crime scene photos and meet you at the trooper headquarters."

"That's affirmative. See you soon." Sean clicked the radio off.

"Are you talking about the receptionist, Katie?" Ivy asked. "Why would she want to find reindeer?"

"She's actually the team director's assistant."

Ivy vaguely remembered the green-eyed petite young woman. Always businesslike and professional, even at team gatherings. "Katie Kapowski?"

"That's the one. Turns out her aunt Addie owns The Family K Reindeer Ranch Sanctuary. It's a mouthful. Like Helena was saying, it operates more like a rescue center for reindeer. I found the whole thing a little confusing when I see them out here in the wild, but your explanation makes sense. Maybe they aren't technically wild anymore. They've been abandoned or—"

"—lost their herd?"

"I'm sure Katie would know. It's been on the team's radar because lately someone has been stealing the reindeer."

"Why would anyone do that?" Ivy tried to focus on the good in the world, but this week seemed to be relentless in showing her the worst of humanity.

"That's one of many questions we have. She thought her aunt was her only living relative, but we've discovered an estranged uncle, Terrence Kapowski. Her aunt Addie hadn't acknowledged his existence to Katie until recently."

"Oh, wow. That's unexpected. Have they reunited?"

He raised his eyebrows. "Gabriel has actually been trying to locate him. Before he was called here, he'd been tracking Terrence's whereabouts near the ranch. A bunch of the locals recognized his photo, so we can place him nearby. Bringing him in for questioning has just become a high priority for the team."

"But why would Katie's uncle target the reindeer ranch? Why not reach out and try to make amends? Do you know why he was estranged?"

He glanced at her. "You're asking all the right questions. Miss shoptalk?"

She felt her cheeks heat. "More like I'm curious what makes people tick. I deal with all sorts who come to the mission, ready to try out the survivalist way of life." She did miss hearing about what was happening in the team's lives, though. Learning about cases like the reindeer ranch felt like a small connection to the old "how was your day?" chats they used to have at dinners.

"The team doesn't know the answers to any of your questions yet. Terrence, the estranged uncle, never showed at the funeral of his mom and dad. They passed away almost a decade ago. So we're working with the theory that maybe he just now found out that he wasn't included in the will. He could be lashing out."

"Katie's aunt inherited the reindeer sanctuary?"

"Sole inheritance. Though, none of us understands what Terrence hopes to accomplish by stealing orphaned reindeer. As soon as Gabriel gets back to Anchorage, he's going to take Bear and track the man down. Then hopefully we'll have some answers. Oh, look! They're moving." Sean rolled slowly after the herd, as they picked up speed down the road, and took a sharp right into a field.

"It struck me that I'd never seen your job in action before today."

He whipped his head in her direction, his eyebrows raised.

"Training, yes," she clarified, "but not working."

His shoulders sagged. "It can be draining, but I know what I do is important."

"I've always known that," she said softly. She truly had. Standing on that riverbank, she'd found herself hoping he and Grace would locate the victim, ensuring they'd have enough evidence to capture the murderer and lock him away forever. How many people had Sean's work brought justice and closure to? She'd never asked him, partly because he liked to leave his cases behind when he came home.

But after months of seeing him drained, she got aggravated. Day after day, promises unkept. Promises he probably shouldn't have ever made before he knew what the job would demand of him. Promises she maybe should've released him from.

The thought smacked her over the head. Was she softening toward him? Perhaps. She twisted her lips to the side. Her tenderhearted feelings toward Sean were natural, though, since they'd been a couple for so long. And it didn't mean she wanted to be back together with him...

In her foster parenting classes, she'd been learning about attachment hormones. They amplified senses and memories to ensure a parent and child bonded. Like the way she smelled Dylan's head and adored the clean shampoo scent from his hair before she laid him down for the night. There was probably something similar between exes. Which meant she should probably disregard the confusing feelings for him without a second's hesitation.

At least, she *hoped* that was the case...

"I'm sorry about all this," Sean said, nodding toward the mission as they passed by. "As soon as the investigation is wrapped up, I can help you tidy up inside." Another state trooper vehicle sat in the parking lot, a trooper she didn't recognize walking around the perimeter of the building.

After the excitement at the shack, she'd almost forgotten about the break-in. "Not your fault." She looked past Sean to the Bering Sea churning next to the highway. A spray of water shot up in the air. Likely beluga whales this time of year.

"When you moved out, I'd hoped that away from me you'd at least be safe." He blanched and pressed his lips together, as if he hadn't meant to say anything.

She blinked rapidly. Had he really worried about her while they were in Anchorage? "Safety was never our problem, was it?"

He shrugged, which seemed odd. Almost as if he thought that maybe it *was* part of their issues. That made no sense, though. They never had disagreements surrounding her safety.

She would head to the bunker tonight. The possibility that the man wouldn't stop trying to hunt her down was foremost in her mind, but she didn't have the emotional bandwidth to deal with any more today. Maybe tomorrow. Tonight, she would pretend she was on vacation with Dylan in the bunker, far away from even the hints of civilization. She'd refuse to think about anything else except enjoying her sweet little boy's company.

The ocean view disappeared as they rolled past houses and the downtown with the fake Western awnings, heading to where Minnie was watching Dylan. To the right, the largest parking lot in town was dedicated to portable gold dredges. The dredges were designed for the ocean, set on boats. The vessels had to be large enough to hold machinery to dig up the seafloor, carry it to filters and spit back the remaining dirt into the water, sans rock and gold. The boat on wheels closest to them stretched out almost two hundred feet and likely belonged to Minnie's family. The expense to rent or own a parking lot of this size must be high. A chain stretched from the tip of the boat to the ground and was attached to a husky's collar.

"Stop!" She pointed in the dog's direction.

Sean slammed on the brakes. The seat belt caught her momentum as she tipped forward and back. "What'd you see? Is it him?" Sean asked, eyes roaming the parking lot.

"It's the husky."

He frowned as Grace let out what sounded like a dissatisfied grunt. "Are you sure it's the same husky?" Sean asked.

"Around here, it's unusual to only have one. People always own more than one, and they're never chained up." She tapped the glass window. "Besides, it's a Siberian husky with a gray topcoat that ends with a widow's peak right about the eyes. It's the same dog, Sean."

He reached the radio and called for backup. The dog's attention swiveled their way as he spoke. She wasn't sure the husky could see her face through the tinted windows, but she held her stare. "Maybe the man tied her up and left her. I think she was the victim's dog, not his."

"For all we know, the victim and the suspect were a couple."

What a horrible thought. They sat in tense silence for a few minutes. After just one day, Ivy was already sick of the fear that gripped her heart with every thought of that man.

The side mirror revealed Helena and Gabriel pulling

up right behind them, forming a V-shaped barrier from the exit of the parking lot to the road.

"That was fast."

Sean opened his car door and placed a hand on his holster. "They're the best team there is."

It was a good thing the town wasn't busy right now, though they were at the outskirts, far from other houses. At the other end of the parking lot was an alley in between two tall buildings. She had no idea if actual businesses still occupied them. The other two SUVs flashed their lights without sirens.

Sean stepped to the back and released Grace to join him. Ivy opened her side and climbed out. "I'll see to the husky while you three check the area."

"Not yet, Ivy." His hands rose up. "Stay in the—"

Gunshots rang out. Asphalt kicked up at her feet.

SEVEN

Sean ran around the back of the vehicle, but Grace beat him to Ivy. The dog lunged in front of her, ready to protect and take the hit for her. She screamed and covered her head but appeared frozen. Sean wrapped his left arm around Ivy's waist, pulling her backward as another round of bullets fired in their direction. Grace hopped backward, the last shot barely missing her.

Every nanosecond counted when dealing with a shooter. The bullet could hit her or Grace at any moment. He flung open the back door and pulled Ivy behind the glass window. His whistle alerted Grace to follow them to safety. A bullet pinged the glass. The bulletproof protection held as more rounds were fired. Ivy turned and crawled into the back seat. Grace hopped in beside her. Sean remained hunkered down behind the open door.

Gabriel could be heard over the radio. "Requesting backup. Active shooter. At the edge of Nugget Alley and—"

Another round of bullets. Sirens pierced the air. The Nome police had to be on their way. Confident the open door served as a shield, he shifted to make sure Ivy wasn't hurt. Her arms and legs trembled.

"I'm sorry I got out, Sean."

She shouldn't have to worry about whether or not to get out of a vehicle. He knew her heart. The poor husky, who was now huddled underneath a long extension of the barge, had been her focus. "It's not your fault. Stay here while I take care of this guy." He grabbed his radio. "Anyone get a visual on the shooter?"

Ivy leaned forward, her arm grazing over his shoulder. "Sean, look! Straight through the window. To the right. I saw his red hair."

On the backside of the farthest dredge, closest to the alley, he caught sight of him as well before the head disappeared again. The bullets had stopped. The guy must be running for it. Sean clicked the radio. "At my seven o'clock. Any sign?"

"I thought I saw an elbow. There might be a ladder on the other side of that dredge. I'm switching to speaker," Helena said. She meant that she was about to turn the SUV's radio into a megaphone. "State Troopers! Drop your weapon and present yourself with hands up in five seconds or we will send the dog and she will bite."

A man leaped off the backside of the dredge, dropping to the ground from a good ten feet up. His hair was no longer visible, a ski mask covering his head. The Nome PD pulled up behind his vehicle, lights flashing but sirens off. The suspect straightened and pumped his arms and legs in a sprint, heading for the alley between the two buildings. Sean groaned inwardly. Why'd they always have to run?

"You'll be safe with the police here. Grace, protect Ivy." He hated to leave his partner behind when he might need her, but she'd serve him best by protecting the woman he— No, he wouldn't let feelings get in the mix at a time like this.

"Attack!" Helena yelled loud enough to be heard without a radio. Luna shot off like a rocket. Sean stepped out from his position of safety, then took off in a sprint right after the dog. Helena's feet rapidly hitting the pavement behind him spurred him on. He pressed harder, faster. Luna was mere feet from snatching the man. Once she grabbed on, they'd have him. The nightmare was about to be over.

The man reached the shadowed alley. Sean moved his hand tentatively to his waist but kept running. He'd only draw his weapon if fired upon. Luna was almost there. Sean had maybe a hundred feet to go. Luna had twenty.

"Freeze!" Sean yelled, expecting any second for Luna to leap and clutch the gunman's right arm.

The man spun to face them, only his eyes and mouth visible through the cutouts of the mask. Sean unlocked his holster to pull his weapon. The man lifted something resembling a shiny glass bauble—as if that'd stop Luna—and threw it down on the ground. Glass shattered before them. Smoke filled the spot in front of the man, obscuring Sean's view.

Luna skittered to a stop just before entering the alley. Sean darted to the far right, lest the gunman could still see him and take aim. What was going on? Luna never hesitated to run through danger. Then the horrific smell hit him. Like rotten eggs and ammonia, except concentrated. An involuntary cough racked his lungs, and he hovered in a squat, trying to hack up the rest of the irritation.

"Luna," Helena choked out. She also hit her knees, coughing.

Because they'd been running at a full steam, they couldn't help but inhale deeply, only to breathe in more irritants. The sound of a metal door closing echoed from within the alley.

"Step away. Walk with your arms up. That will get fresh air in faster. And get Luna out of there." Gabriel had caught up behind them with Bear. He clicked the radio on his shoulder. "We need immediate backup on other side of alley. Suspect is armed, wearing a ski mask. Over." The smoke had dissipated, but the man hadn't waited around in the long alley. Gabriel pointed at Luna. "If I had to guess, I'd say it's a homemade stink bomb. Hydrogen sulfide and ammonia are toxic together, but only dangerous in extreme amounts."

Sean accepted his analysis without question. His teammate had a broader education in scent work, given Bear's specialty.

"Which means?" Helena asked.

"Luna is safe to keep going as soon as she's ready." Gabriel leaned over just as Bear sneezed, and he offered his K-9 a scent cone. "The smoke bomb will only mess up their scent-tracking momentarily. Now that he's had a good sneeze, Bear's senses are going to be stronger than ever. Let's get this guy."

Sean didn't need to be told twice. He ran through the

alley, hand on his weapon. The smell still hung in the air. A nondescript metal door on the left building wasn't fully closed. He pulled at the handle, and it opened easily into a hallway. *"State Troopers!"* he yelled. His voice echoed off the cinder-block walls.

Gabriel, Bear, Helena and Luna stepped behind him. The building held the musty smell of being abandoned. They froze for a moment, all straining to hear any sounds that might lead them in the right direction. Bear put his nose to the ground for a moment. His head popped up and his tail rose higher. Gabriel nodded. "He's found something." They ran after the dogs. So far, every room they'd passed had been empty.

Bear turned to the right. Gabriel nodded. "Looks like the suspect hit the stairs."

Helena grabbed the stairway door and looked at Luna. "Feel well enough to get to work again, girl?" The dog wagged her tail in response. Unfortunately, they needed to make good and sure the building was actually empty before telling Luna to attack.

She sprinted up the stairs with her partner at her side. Once again, Sean was right behind Luna. If another smoke bomb was lobbed at them, he knew this time it wouldn't hurt him. The dogs might not be able to run through, but he wouldn't let the smoke stop him.

Except all the doors to the four landing areas were closed. Luna ran to the top of the building stairs and back again to the second floor, where Bear was still sniffing his way up the stairs. The Saint Bernard lifted his head again and pointed to the door. "He's down this hallway," Gabriel said.

Sean kicked at the door until it flung open. Luna charged like she'd been racing on slick floors her entire life. The dog knew what she was after but wouldn't attack until given the word. Helena and Sean ran after her at full speed.

He'd be lying to say he didn't want to be the one to bring the guy in, but the important thing was getting him. Luna darted in and out of each room, so far with no success. Years' worth of dust and grime layered on the windows provided very little light streaming into the building. The back of his neck tingled with the possibility that maybe the man would be able to hide in a darkened corner. Bear, though, was still on the trail, albeit behind them. His sneeze echoed down the hallway, the second time in the last five minutes.

"Dust holds the smell. Don't worry," Gabriel said, his eyes focused on the K-9.

Luna ran up and down the hallway a second time, darting into every single open room, frustration evident by her whine. Helena said the word for her to relax and praised her for the try.

"No." Sean shook his head. "He's got to be here. Bear smelled him. Let's start taking down the closed doors."

"Judging by the names on the doors, this used to be an old mining company," Gabriel said. "They must have had a lot of claims to manage back in the day."

Bear alerted on a closed door on the right. Sean and Gabriel stood on either side of the door. Helena grabbed her Taser while Gabriel and Sean kept their hands on the handles of their guns. She would attempt to detain the suspect peacefully with the help of Luna, but if the man aimed a gun, they would be forced to shoot. Bear stood behind Gabriel, and Sean ticked his fingers off silently. *One, two, three...*

Sean twisted in front of the door and kicked it open. Helena yelled, *"Attack!"*

Gabriel and Sean charged after Luna, instantly moving to opposite sides of the room to leave Helena space. The breeze hit Sean fully in the face. Luna rushed for the open window and dived through it, paws first, disappearing from view.

"No!" Helena yelled.

Sean gasped at the sight. The dog had jumped clean out the window. They raced forward, Helena leaning her torso over the window first. "She's okay!" Sean peered over her shoulder to find Luna on the third stair, descending a rickety steel fire escape. *"Stop, Luna."* The dog froze at Helena's command and looked up. The suspect was nowhere to be seen.

Sirens blared from below. A local Nome police cruiser sped down the street. As the vehicle passed by the building, Sean spotted the source of the chase. At the end of the street, an ATV vaulted over the curb and hopped over rough hills in the tundra. The cruiser screeched to a stop. An officer hopped out of the vehicle and sprinted after him on foot, shouting.

"The suspect is too far away now," Gabriel said. "No more roads out there."

The ATV kept bouncing up and over hills, the light from the headlights appearing dimmer and smaller. The officer stopped after about thirty feet of running and turned to return back to the cruiser.

"What about planes?" Sean asked. "Do we have a pilot back in the area? What about a certified drone operator?"

"I'll check, but I think the only ones that have those qualifications are still out on assignment," Helena said. She patted the side of her leg and Luna jumped back through the window. She walked off, clicking the radio and asking questions of the Nome PD to see if they had any new leads.

Sean felt paralyzed, squinting in the distance. The man who was determined to kill Ivy had slipped through his fingers once again.

Ivy couldn't keep her eyes off the alley the team had disappeared into, especially after seeing them run past a cloud of smoke. Whatever was happening, Sean was in danger. Was this a normal day's work for him? Had it *always* been?

The Nome police officer blocked her view now, pacing back and forth in the parking lot while speaking into his radio and holding it up to his ear to hear the replies. He'd made the mistake of getting too close to Sean's vehicle to ask Ivy if she needed medical care. Grace had stuck her face up to the window and released a warbled bark that almost sounded like, *Back off, buddy.* It startled the officer enough that he straightened and kept an eye on her from a distance. If Sean didn't return soon, she didn't know who Grace would allow to get near.

Something caught the cop's eye and he turned sideways enough that Ivy could see past him to the three team members with Luna and Bear striding back together. Their shoulders hunched, their heads bent—looking down at the ground as they walked—instead of their usual jovial banter. They appeared weary. Which meant it was doubtful they'd already handed off a handcuffed murderer to the local cops. "I don't think they have good news for us, Grace."

A moment later, Sean beckoned her out of the car with a wave. She pushed open the unlocked door and Grace trotted to Sean's side. "Are you okay?" he asked.

Physically, yes. Emotionally, her insides were vibrating so hard she was going to come unglued. She fought against crying at his question. When the bullets had been firing, she hadn't been able to think clearly. For all her training in survival, her brain had simply switched to panic mode. She looked up to the gray clouds gathering above her. "Unharmed," she said simply.

Only then did she notice Sean seemed to be avoiding eye contact, as well. After having known each other so fully, she was taken off guard at how vulnerable she still felt in his presence. Like if they looked at each other too long, they might see everything they were trying so hard not to say. Maybe he felt the same way? That seemed unlikely. Sean had always told her he was a simple man. Sure, he'd said it most often when they were trying to figure out what to have for dinner, but he wasn't one to gush.

"He got away, but you probably already figured that," Sean said. "I know you're eager to get Dylan. I'll need to do a sweep of the area with Grace and then we can go."

"With Grace? You think he might've hidden the victim here?" She didn't bother to camouflage the surprise in her tone. Why would the man drag a deceased woman all the way to the shack only to bring her back to town to hide the body? Unless he had a new motive to frame someone.

"It's precautionary," Sean said. "In case he's murdered someone else while here."

Her jaw dropped. She wouldn't have thought of that, though she'd heard that murderers found it easier to kill after the first time. An involuntary shudder worked up her spine. She quickly hugged herself, hoping Sean missed it.

"I hope that won't be the case, but we need to be sure." His eyes connected with hers. "I'm sorry." Maybe she was right to fear he'd see more in her, because his apology wasn't about not catching the guy. What exactly was he trying to say? He frowned and cleared his throat, and the moment was gone. "Grace and I won't be long. You can either stay with us or wait with Helena or Gabriel."

"I'd feel safer with you." The thought slipped out before she could filter it with less emotion.

His eyebrows jumped, but he nodded and turned around. "Time to get to work."

Grace's spine straightened and her tail curled over her back. The transformation from normal dog to working partner always amazed her.

Gabriel and Bear also sniffed each dredge from the parking lot. "Helena is working on finding out who the owners are. We'll start by asking their permission to search these—with warrants, if necessary. Grace shouldn't need to get on the boats to let me know she smells something inside."

His radio came to life. "Bear confirmed the man has recently been in the two largest dredges in the lot but none of the others," Gabriel said.

Sean clicked the button. "So far Grace hasn't alerted on anything."

The moment they got close to the still-chained husky, Ivy ran forward. She'd been dying to check on her condition. The two-toned fur seemed matted compared to yesterday and her striking blue eyes had a hollow, lifeless stare. Her ears flattened, though, and she let Ivy approach with only one warbled bark.

"She's stressed or anxious, huh?" Sean asked. "That's usually when the colonel's dog—also a Siberian husky—talks the most."

Ivy gingerly touched the dog's fur, watching for any signs that it might attack. So far, the dog was docile. Except her fingers touched something dried yet sticky. Her fingers pulled back the husky's thick coat. "There's blood."

Ten minutes later, Ivy paced the vet's lobby while Sean and Grace sat at ease in the chairs. She wanted to know if the husky was okay but simultaneously couldn't wait to get to Dylan. The vet entered from a door labeled Employees Only, and Ivy caught a glimpse of a tech loving on the husky. Her shoulders relaxed slightly. The dog was in good hands.

The vet appeared to be in his late forties with thick dark hair. "I collected the sample of blood. Likely a day old and not from any injury to the dog."

Ivy's head spun. Not from the dog? Could it be from his owner?

"Should I send the sample to the state troopers?"

"That'd be great," Sean said. "Any chip? Any identification of the dog's owner?"

"None, I'm afraid." The vet turned from Sean to Ivy. "I think she'll be fine, but she's underweight and very dehydrated. I'd like to keep her overnight for observation while I run a few tests. As long as she's healthy, I can release her to you tomorrow."

Ivy placed a hand on her chest. "To me?"

"Yes, since you brought her in. I know of no other owner. If you have no interest, animal control will be called. I have to warn you, though—they've been full and have been transferring stray dogs to Anchorage."

Her heart ached at the thought of the sweet animal getting shipped off. She hesitated. "Can I think about it? It's a big decision."

"Of course. Let's touch base tomorrow."

Sean clenched his jaw, clearly trying not to make a face. Ivy ignored the apparent disapproval and smiled at the vet. "Thank you."

They silently returned to the SUV. Grace turned and looked back at the building, as if she was concerned for the husky, as well. Inside the vehicle, Sean's expression remained stony.

She sighed. "I take it you're not happy I'm considering taking home the husky."

"Ivy, I know I don't have a right to make my opinion heard unless it directly pertains to this case." He shrugged. "That said, I can't help that it's still my instinct to keep your best interest in mind. So, if you want my opinion, I trust you'll ask for it. Right now, though, I'm guessing you want to pick up Dylan?"

Her mouth dropped open. It was a lovely speech, but she didn't believe it. What she wanted was to ask him how deciding a year into their marriage, unilaterally, that they wouldn't have kids could be in her *best interest*, but she knew that would only stir up the past and start a fight. "Yes, I'd like to go to Dylan," she said instead.

He'd made it clear he was trying to keep professional boundaries, and yet Ivy's curiosity would not be tamed. "Fine. I'm asking your opinion," she said, before she could change her mind.

He glanced at her, wide-eyed, before composing his features and returning his attention to the road. "It might be nice if you were no longer in danger before deciding to adopt a dog. I mean, you're committing to a forever home, right? In fact, I would think *all* major decisions would be off the table right now, considering that."

"Which is why I said I needed some time to think about it." She reflected on his words again. "But what do you mean by *all* decisions?" Her eyes narrowed. Did he know about the adoption? He'd come down the stairs when she was counting inventory at the mission, too distracted by the destruction of all the displays to have realized the implication. He'd been in her apartment. Had he seen Dylan's adoption papers?

"All I'm saying," Sean said, turning the vehicle around to head in the direction of where Minnie was caring for Dylan, "is that you're a single woman."

"I know that I'm a single woman." So many comments came to mind, but part of the process in becoming a foster parent was learning better communication skills. She couldn't claim that fighting fair came easy, especially with Sean, but the class had taught her that disagreements were useful if genuinely trying to understand the other person. She took a deep breath. "I'm a little confused what you mean by that statement. I would think having a big dog would be an advantage, not a weakness, given that I'm single."

"You're alone. If something happened to you, what would become of the dog? Or what if the killer decides to come after the dog? What if he's angry you have it and decides to hurt either of you? What if the dog is hurt or, worse, dies? How would you *ever recover*?"

His last two words reverberated with emotion. She pressed her lips together. Where had that come from? The rapid list of scenarios and the way he gripped the wheel until his knuckles turned white set off alarm bells. Was *Sean* scared about something?

Her mouth went dry. Her gut insisted this wasn't about the dog.

He blinked rapidly and shrugged. "Just some things to think about tonight, I guess."

"I guess so," she replied softly, her mind still reeling. "Thank you for telling me what was on your mind, but I think I need to tell you what's on mine. Would you be willing to pull over for a second?" She'd like to avoid arriving to pick up Dylan as an emotional wreck.

He gave her a side-glance and frowned. "Of course. It's been a big day." He pulled over to the side of the road.

Grace made a sound in the back that sounded like half a whine and half a question. "Still off duty," Sean said softly. He twisted his torso to face her.

"Would you have the same opinion, the same questions for me to consider, if I told you I was applying to adopt Dylan?"

His form remained statuesque, but his pupils widened, darkening his eyes. He blew out a breath and his torso sagged in front of her. "I think we both know I saw the adoption papers back at your apartment."

"If it bothered you, why didn't you say something earlier?"

"Instead of resting it all on the husky, you mean?" He shook his head and offered a small smile. "You could always see right through me."

"Funny because I always felt like you were a mystery most of the time."

"I have no right to tell you what to do, Ivy. We both know that. But I've said it before. I still care about you, so I have these knee-jerk reactions. I'm trying to work through it." He scratched the top of his head. "I think I finally need to tell you something."

She held her breath. The promise of a secret terrified her. Would she finally find out why he'd changed so drastically early in their marriage?

He folded his hands and rested them on the bottom half of the wheel. "On my first call out with Grace— an earthquake discovery—I was convinced we would find people alive."

"Oh." The word came out as a hushed breath. "I didn't think she was trained to find—"

"Grace is not a search-and-rescue dog, if that's what you mean. But if she comes across a person who is still alive while she's working, she's going to react in some way. And I'd notice." He offered a sheepish grin. "Newbie optimism, I guess. Anyway, we were called out within seconds of the earthquake and only five minutes away."

"I remember that day. The chandelier swung in our dining room for like five minutes. You called to check on me before you went out on the call."

He nodded. "I'd hoped that we'd arrive fast enough to the scene. Grace alerted almost right away. Rescuers swarmed the area. We dug and moved the rubble as fast as possible and found—" His voice broke and he cleared his throat. "We found a woman… She looked remarkably similar to you." He spoke in a low, gravelly monotone. "And she had her arms wrapped around a child. The woman had already passed away, but the child stirred—at least, I thought she might have." He coughed. "But I was told the child was also already gone, too. We weren't able to save either one."

It was as if a grainy home movie rewound in her mind and replayed. Ivy questioned every interaction they'd ever had after that moment. She'd always assumed he'd never found anyone in that earthquake. He'd said Grace did great on her first run. That was all. Was that when he started dragging his feet into their home each day, drained? She couldn't be sure when that had started. Had she misunderstood him most of their marriage? "Your first call out," she said weakly.

"I didn't tell you to upset you. In my specialty, officers aren't encouraged to talk a lot about what we discover, especially with our families. Besides, it's best if we don't dwell too long. I didn't want you to hate my job. I had to work through it and figure out how to cope. Just because it was hard didn't mean I wanted to quit."

She nodded, because she wasn't sure what to say. Surely, he could've at least told her that he was having a hard time coping. *Couldn't* he have?

"I've learned it's best to focus on the good things and move on, but that discovery was my first and the hardest. I'm only telling you now because if you'd experienced what I have, then maybe you'd agree."

"Agree about what?" she asked softly.

"That there's so much pain and sorrow out there." He waved his arms, gesturing to the world outside the window. "You have to know, Ivy, that you'll face that kind of sorrow if you agree to adopt. If it's not a murderer threatening you, then maybe it's the choices Dylan makes later on. It's not a matter of if but *when*. And I'm not sure you've ever understood that agreeing to parent is assenting to a broken heart, on purpose. Do you really want that for yourself? To end up broken?"

She'd heard his argument against having children so many times that she had it memorized, but this was new. Entirely different. This time she finally comprehended the moment that convinced him that he shouldn't become a parent. No wonder he'd changed his mind all of a sudden. Her eyes burned with unshed tears, but she refused to cry for him, for them, for that mother and the child he'd found. Even though she desperately wanted to be alone and do just that.

Instead, she focused on the crumbling building in front of them and took shallow breaths. The building was missing pieces of siding. Just like she'd been missing pieces in understanding Sean. It'd weakened them and led to their entire marriage crashing down around them. Her voice shook as she said the words that played in her head on a loop. "I guess I'm just in shock you didn't tell me about your first call out. That's a pretty big thing."

"To be fair, you never really asked me about that part of the job."

"I always asked about your day!" Her volume rose despite trying to stay calm. "I wanted to respect your professional boundaries if you couldn't tell me some things. What was I supposed to say? *Find any bodies today?*" She recoiled at her own words.

"Of course not." He shook his head. "I wasn't trying to start a fight. I was only trying to get you to realize how big a deal—"

"—having a child is. Yes, I heard you." All his other reasons he'd tried to convince her with over the years were overshadowed by this one. "I'm also hearing how much fear and control had a say in our marriage." She hung her head. "More than I'd thought. I'm sorry if that sounds harsh."

"What? No, I think you've misunderstood me. Ivy..." Radio static burst through the speakers.

"Sean, we need you at headquarters," Gabriel said. "Bring Ivy."

He let out an exasperated sigh. "Guess we're out of time." Sean shifted the SUV into Drive.

She faced forward, realizing his statement had more than one meaning.

EIGHT

Sean vibrated with energy as he parked in front of the trooper post. The few officers assigned to this post had to cover an area the size of West Virginia. So it wasn't unusual that the post was empty enough for the K-9 troopers to take an office. They shared the space with the Alaska National Guard Armory. The entire bottom section of the building was made of garages for the various vehicles needed, given the constant changing terrain. He led Ivy and Grace up a set of metal stairs to enter the main offices.

Each step on the metal stairs set his teeth on edge. He needed to let go of the last words Ivy had said to him, especially since he wasn't afforded the option to discuss it further. He should've never told her about that earthquake in the first place. Delving into things from the past was like stepping into an unmarked minefield. But he thought she'd understand that he was trying to keep her from making a mistake. A dog and a kid would make her even more vulnerable.

That first call had been on his mind more than usual

lately. They had a new rookie trooper getting ready to join their ranks, Ian McCaffrey, with his newly-trained cadaver dog. A German shepherd named Aurora. Sean would be assigned to help show him the ropes and let Ian shadow him from time to time. It'd forced Sean to reevaluate how he'd handled his first year before he could offer any advice.

The unpleasant conversation with Ivy had left a bad taste in his mouth. She couldn't be right about the control thing, though. *Could* she? He almost scoffed aloud. There were plenty of things in his life outside of his control, his job being a prime example. Not five minutes had gone by since they'd left the vet before a work call had interrupted their conversation. Control was only an illusion in life, something he'd fully admitted when he'd recently decided to believe in God.

He reached the top step and offered Ivy a forced smile as he opened the door for her. She'd misunderstood him, that was all. Understandable, considering how someone had tried to kill her only an hour before. If a quiet moment presented itself later that day, maybe he'd try again.

"Over here," Helena called, poking her head out into the hallway, the third door to the right.

Sean let the door close behind them as they hustled down the hallway. They stepped inside the office in time to hear the colonel speaking through the desktop monitor station on the countertop.

"We need you back in Anchorage." Lorenza glanced down at something off the video conferencing camera.

A muscle ticked in his jaw. He *knew* this would happen. Now more than ever, he couldn't leave Ivy. The gunman had specifically aimed his shots at her, not the rest of the team. Sean took a step forward and opened his mouth to speak.

But Gabriel placed a hand on his shoulder before he could utter a word. "You and Helena are staying here in Nome, on the case. I'm going back to help with the reindeer case."

"Sean, good to see you," the colonel said. "Yes, we don't want the lead on Terrence Kapowski to go cold. Katie's counting on us."

"Understood, ma'am." He blew out a breath, releasing all the pent-up energy from being prepared to argue.

"Lorenza has some news on Ivy's case," Helena said. "That's why we needed you both here."

"Yes." The colonel offered a friendly smile. "Good to see you, Ivy. Sorry that it's under these circumstances. Appreciated you helping us out with the survivalist case recently."

"Not sure I was much help, but thank you," Ivy said. "I'm always happy to offer what I know."

Lorenza's smile faded as she addressed her fellow team members. "Now to the news. We're sending the results on the victim your way. Check your fax machine. Tala was able to find a match on the blood DNA of the victim. Let me share the most recent photo we have in the system."

The screen switched to a zoomed-in version of a Washington driver's license photograph. "'Francine McMillan,'" Sean read aloud.

Ivy blanched. "That's her. A few years younger and with different hair, but definitely her."

The fax machine roared to life. Gabriel gathered the papers that spit out. "Arrested on shoplifting a few years back. Last known address was near San Francisco. Nothing else of note that I can see." He passed the stack of papers to Helena to review, as well.

"So, our victim wasn't a resident, and we have no idea why she was in Alaska," Sean said.

"No idea what motive our suspect could have yet, either," Gabriel told Lorenza.

"Could've just been the wrong place at the wrong time," Helena mused. She frowned, reading over the papers. "Not getting any clues from her record, either."

"Maybe she lifted something off our suspect," Sean said.

"That would explain why he kept asking me where she'd put it," Ivy added. "You think this is a theft and a violent retaliation?"

Lorenza's eyebrows shot up at Ivy's interjection. "I'll leave it to you guys to take it from here. Sean, make it your priority to find the deceased. Helena, take the lead. Gabriel, have a safe flight. Check in tomorrow morning with me."

Gabriel agreed and signed off the communication.

The muscles in Sean's back wouldn't relax. While he was glad that Lorenza wasn't ordering him back home, the message had been clear. She wanted him to find the body and leave Ivy's protection to others. And he knew the moment they found the victim, Lorenza wouldn't hesitate to bring him back to Anchorage, whether or not they'd found the murderer. Professional courtesy, given his relationship to Ivy, only went so far.

"Can you make a copy of the license for me to take?" Ivy asked, jarring Sean out of his thoughts.

Helena frowned. "What'd you have in mind?"

"I'd like to ask Minnie if she recognizes the victim. Fiona may have her pulse on all the visitors who stay at her B and B, but Minnie knows all the locals and several from the nearby villages. She's lived here for ages."

"It's a good idea," Sean acknowledged. But they couldn't just hand Ivy copies of the reports. "I can show Minnie."

Gabriel moved to a desk monitor and took a screenshot of the license, cropping the photo so it only showed Francine's face, and printed it. He handed the printed photo to Sean and shook his hand. "Hope I'll see you soon back at base. But not too soon."

At least his teammates understood the importance of finishing this case. He gestured to the door with the photo. "Shall we?"

Gabriel flashed her a grin as she turned to leave with Sean. "And don't worry," he said. "These guys don't need *me* to solve the case."

"I wasn't worried until you said that," Ivy said, a teasing lilt to her voice. It didn't disguise the strain in her eyes and forehead.

Helena handed them each a hoagie from the sub shop across the street. "You need to keep your strength up. And say the word if you need to take a rest, Ivy. You still are recovering from a nasty bump on the head."

Sean studied the loose bun she had at the nape of her

neck. He should've noticed it wasn't her usual style. Her head likely hurt too much to pull it back into her standard tight ponytail.

"Oh, and before I forget, there are a few empty rooms with cots and blankets down the hall, reserved for traveling troopers. They're available to us. This won't be luxury accommodations, but it'll be safe."

He nodded. "Agreed."

"I'm staying at the bunker," Ivy said.

"We can't force you, of course," Helena cut in before Sean could object. "But we do highly recommend you allow one or both of us to stay in the same location for your safety. At least until we have the shooter behind bars. This office is well protected."

"Yes, and as you mentioned, it's bare-bones. No offense to anyone, but it's not well suited for a toddler's needs. The bunker is already childproofed. There's plenty of room for you and Sean, if you're willing."

Helena raised an eyebrow but said nothing as she exchanged a glance with him. Judging by her expression, she was just as apprehensive as he was about the bunker scenario. He'd had enough dealing with survivalists lately; he didn't want to live like one, too.

"Give us until the end of the day before you decide, please," Sean said. "Maybe neither will be necessary."

"Okay. I think I'll take my sandwich to go. I'd really like to be with Dylan now."

"Of course." He was just as anxious to leave, but not for the same reason. Though, the thought of seeing Dylan again eased some of the tension in his muscles. Didn't mean he was changing his stance on having kids.

He could find them amusing without wanting one of his own. It was human nature to enjoy a baby's laugh. It was in a dog's nature as well, if Grace was any indication.

Neither of them ended up eating their sandwiches, though, despite nearing late afternoon. Sean, for his part, knew the bread would taste like cardboard until the day was done. Now that the danger of the morning had fully passed, his brain replayed the shooting on a loop. He'd almost lost Grace and Ivy in one go. But it hadn't happened. Maybe his prayers were being heard. Though, why God couldn't have also stopped the man from kidnapping Ivy and murdering Francine was something he might never understand. *That's why they call it faith.* Eli Partridge, their tech guru, had answered that to quite a few of Sean's questions.

He pulled up to the house they'd escorted Minnie to that morning. An unmarked police car sat on the corner with an officer who waved at them. "See? He was safe the entire time."

She strode ahead of him to the porch and knocked. Minnie answered with Dylan in her arms. "Doggy. Mama," the boy said, rubbing his eyes.

"I see where I am in the order of things," she said with a laugh and leaned over to kiss his cheek.

"Just woke up from his nap," Minnie said.

Sean turned around slowly, examining the houses and street around them. He was searching for any movement, any sign they'd been followed. "Do you mind if we come in and ask you a few questions?"

Minnie arched an eyebrow. "Am I a suspect now?"

Ivy laughed, pulling Dylan into her arms and snuggling her cheek against his. "No. We just need to know if you recognize someone."

The babysitter led them into a kitchen decked out in cow-themed decor. A canvas at the far edge of the room featured a smiling cow whose eyes appeared to follow him with every move. "Dylan loves this house," Minnie said. "My friend Charla said we can use it all week if we need to." She reached out and squeezed Ivy's wrist. "For your sake, honey, I hope that's not true."

Sean held up the printout of Francine's photo. "Do you recognize her?"

"Oh, yes." Minnie squinted and stared at the ceiling. "Her name's on the tip of my tongue. She came to town a while back, can't say for sure how long, though. At least a few months. Saw her at one of the town meetings. She was asking around for seasonal work. Struck me as a snooty city girl at first, to be honest, but she said she had dredge experience. Was willing to do the cleaning and work her way up." The older woman shook her head and whistled. "Hard work, that job, and the least glamorous to volunteer for. You can't help but end the day soaked to the bone and covered in mud when you're first learning the ropes. And even then, it doesn't get much better." Minnie walked across the kitchen, opened the top of a cookie jar and waved at it. "Want one?"

Ivy shook her head. "Is that all you remember?"

Minnie's exhalation carried a hint of sadness. "I've seen loads of desperate hopefuls come around here searching for gold and find themselves exhausted, cold and dirty, with little to show for it. But she—oh, her name will come to me—she seemed ready to work.

Demonstrated more knowledge than most who try to characterize themselves as experienced."

"Do you know if anyone hired her?"

Minnie finally selected a cookie from the jar and took a bite. "If she was still around, I imagine someone did. Most people know you, Ivy. They'll talk to you." She gave a side-eye to him as if to say, *Avoid bringing the stiff.*

Sean fought against rolling his eyes. He would do anything to keep Ivy safe, but the last thing he wanted to do was ask for her help in this case. *Again.* He held up the photo again. "Was she with a man?"

Ivy shot him a surprised look.

Minnie tapped her chin. "Maybe. Um…"

Ivy set Dylan back down next to the diaper bag of toys, but the boy reached for Grace. The K-9 sat down without Sean's command and allowed Dylan to pat her head, a bit intensely. Sean took a knee to make sure the pats didn't turn to pulling out fur.

Minnie shrugged. "Having a hard time remembering anything about a guy."

Ivy blinked rapidly and straightened, lifting her hand above her head. "Was he about this tall and auburn hair—"

"Sorry, no. At least, I never saw her with anyone like that." An electronic buzzing filled the room. Minnie set down her half-eaten cookie and picked up the phone from the counter. "I don't recognize this number."

To Sean's surprise, she still answered it. "Hello?"

The woman had the volume of the phone on high, because the caller's deep voice rang through the room.

"Good afternoon, ma'am. I'm an Alaskan State Trooper calling on behalf of Ivy West. She's running late, answering questions after today's incident. She would like you to bring Dylan and meet her—"

"Oh, is that right? She does, huh?" Minnie's outraged voice practically shook the walls. "That's funny since she's standing right in front of me! How *dare* you try—" She pulled her chin back. "He hung up!"

Sean scooped up Dylan, lest there be any fur pulling while he wasn't looking, and crossed the room in two strides, taking the phone from Minnie. The sound of a disconnected line hit his ears.

The older woman crossed her arms across her chest. "Can you believe the nerve?"

Sean hit the button to look at the list of recent callers and took a heartbeat to memorize the number. He clicked the radio at his shoulder. "I need a trace."

Helena answered his call and took the number. A few moments later, she was back on the line. "Must've been a burner phone. Got nowhere."

He looked toward Ivy. Her skin had turned paler than a piece of chalk, and she grabbed a chair to steady herself. "He's after Dylan now," she whispered.

With all his precautions, his worst nightmares were coming to life before his eyes. Even though he hated it, deep down he knew it was time to go to the bunker.

Ivy rushed forward to hold Dylan. Sean's eyebrows rose, as if he'd forgotten he was holding him, even as the toddler repeatedly smacked the shiny name tag above

Sean's uniform pocket. She wrapped her hands around Dylan's waist and pulled him to her.

He whined, which prompted Grace to mimic the whine. Dylan laughed so hard his forehead hit her chest hard. But physical pain was welcome compared to the chaotic thoughts running through her head.

"We need to know how he found out about Dylan, got Minnie's number..." he began.

"My phone. He used my phone." Her mouth went dry, imagining that man sifting slowly, methodically through every text, email and photo. "I wasn't sure it was real but had a vague memory of him using my thumb to touch something. He could've turned off the lock screen then and wouldn't need a cell signal to go through everything. Easy to take that information and use a different phone." She should've thought of that before. She'd let her hopes get up that Helena and the team would be able to track her phone down. "He already knew about Dylan because he saw him in the B and B. A quick read of my texts and anyone would be able to figure out Minnie was his sitter."

The store break-in was nothing compared to a murderer having access to what amounted to her digital diary. She imagined the auburn-haired man yanking Dylan from her arms. A chill went through her. Then her mind darted to the memory of the woman's fingers sticking out of the rolled-up rug, and she nearly keeled over.

Sean reached for her, his strong hands on either of her arms. "I think you need to sit down and eat that cookie Minnie offered, whether you want to or not. You haven't had anything since breakfast."

She'd eaten a huge breakfast, a rarity for her, so she didn't think that was the cause. The weariness in her bones kept her from arguing. She sat in the kitchen chair and allowed Dylan to go back to toddling around the room. He gave chase to Grace, who trotted just out of reach, then waited. Within seconds, the boy and the dog were in an epic game of keep-away.

She was watching something hilarious, something she'd love to remember someday. But her mind refused to cooperate and revel in Dylan's delight. She took shallow breaths as she nibbled on the cookie Sean had placed in her palm. A *cookie*! This was no time to be eating a treat when someone was intent on taking her son from her. Maybe he wasn't officially her son yet, but…

Her eyes burned and she placed her tongue firmly against the inside of her teeth to keep from crying. How would this affect the adoption? At the very least, she had to let the social worker know that the gunman was after Dylan. There was no time to allow herself to be scared or angry or even violated, despite being hit over the head with all three…

Sean clicked the radio, but his eyes didn't so much as flicker away from her face. "Any progress on pinging Ivy's phone?"

"Double-checking," Helena answered.

He crouched in front of Ivy and held her hand. "I know this is difficult, but we need to be careful not to make any knee-jerk reactions. We can't even assume it was the murderer on the phone."

"It *was* him." A cold sensation trickled from the top of her head and worked its way down, as if allowing her body to go numb.

Sean frowned and pulled her hands together, placing his other hand on top of hers, while two fingers slid to the inside of her right wrist. "Take deep breaths for me, Ivy, before we discuss this more. Your heart is working so hard right now you might be going into shock."

Shock would be welcome compared to the sensation before. Still, she needed her wits right now. Ivy knew she wouldn't be any use to Dylan if she succumbed to fear. So she pulled her hands from his and forced herself to eat the stupid cookie. Minnie rushed to the kettle and had a cup of tea in her hands three minutes later.

"You've got a little color again," she commented, nodding.

"Why'd you have to taunt him, Minnie?" Ivy's question slipped from her mouth without a filter. "We might've been able to keep him talking, trace him, set up a trap..."

The woman took a step back, hand to her reddening neck. "I wasn't trying to taunt him. I was furious he would even—"

Ivy set the tea down. Of *course* she didn't mean to. She dropped her forehead into her hands. "I know."

"I'm sorry. I didn't think of trying to keep him talking."

"Please forget I said anything. I didn't even think of it until now." All threads of civility had begun to unravel after the day's events. If she didn't get some time to herself soon, she feared what she might say next.

"I really am sorry, hon." Minnie reached for her

shoulder and gave it a squeeze. "Don't lose hope. God is with you. Even now."

Ivy flattened her lips together and avoided eye contact as she nodded.

"You don't want to hear it now. Understood. I know it doesn't feel like it, but knowing He's with you is everything. Believing isn't a onetime thing. And you need that faith more now than ever, even when you can't see Him working."

Her eyes stung with hot unshed tears. Sean's phone rang and they both swiveled in his direction. He answered and mouthed Helena's name. "Okay," he said into the receiver. "No big surprise since so much of the area doesn't have a cell signal."

In other words, Helena wasn't finding any leads on her phone. Despite Minnie's encouragement, Ivy couldn't stay put anymore. Being kidnapped and shot at was one thing, but now the killer was after her son. She scooped up the diaper-bag strap and lifted it over her shoulder. "I need to go." She shifted Dylan to her left hip and walked out the door.

Grace ran in front of her path and stared, a challenge in her eyes.

"Seriously, Grace? He didn't tell you to protect."

"I think she's taken it upon herself to protect Dylan," Sean said softly. He nodded at Minnie. "Block that number. I don't want you answering again if he calls. And we need to discuss your safety. Maybe stay with your daughter tonight."

Ivy's gut grew hot. She hadn't thought of Minnie's safety.

"I think I'll do that," she said. "You two go on. I'll be fine."

"I'll let the officer know to stay here and follow you to your daughter's." Sean shook a thumbs-up sign at Grace. She ran around the back of Ivy's legs and moved to his side. They walked down the porch steps together.

Sean reached across her to open the door. "I know you're upset—rightfully so—but at least he doesn't know where we are."

"Let's keep it that way. Tell Helena if she wants to come with us, she needs to meet up with us at the hospital."

His eyes narrowed. "Your head injury? You *have* been looking really pale."

"I'm fine. The hospital is on the outskirts of town and the easiest place to meet up before heading to the bunker. I'm not giving directions over the phone. Not after what happened earlier."

"If you're worried about him following us, we are trained to spot—"

She held up a hand, fighting to keep a tight rein on her emotions. Like a frayed rope, the rein was barely intact. Before she could explain herself, Sean waved her to the SUV. "Helena says there are a couple of unmarked SUVs in the garage. How about we use those for extra protection. Then you don't need to worry that someone will recognize our trooper vehicles."

Nothing other than that creep being behind bars would help the worry go away, but she forced herself to nod. Ten minutes later, they hit the road in the two black SUVS. While better than having trooper logos on the side, two black vehicles still seemed suspicious in her mind.

They headed northeast toward Anvil Mountain, directly for the White Alice antennae, a now-abandoned and obsolete communications system the air force built during the Cold War in the '50s. There were apparently thirty other stations like it throughout Alaska, but Ivy was only familiar with this one.

The four antennae that made up White Alice stood massive in size, their own Stonehenge in appearance. The SUV bounced from side to side on the rough gravel road, lulling Dylan to sleep. Her own eyes grew heavy the farther they drove from town, but she was the one who needed to give directions. Just as they neared White Alice—which caused Sean to whistle low in appreciation—she pointed to what would easily be mistaken as an animal-trampled path to the left.

"That's not a road," he said.

"I'm aware, but it's flat and solid and you're already in four-wheel drive." In fact, no one could make it this far in a normal car, as the road wasn't maintained.

Sean made the sharp, bumpy turn and drove in between two hills. Only then could Ivy see the front of the bunker. The stairs led to the open tunnel near the top of the hill. The bunker had been built within the hill but had to be high enough to avoid getting buried in the snow during winter. Permafrost prevented anything from getting built underground. If a wayward backpacker came this far, they'd likely think the tunnel to be old and abandoned.

Dylan stirred in the car seat. Grace leaned forward

and casually licked the top of his hand. "No. Doggy wet!" But judging by his smile, he was quite pleased the K-9 had licked him. If their caseworker said she could stay with him here on a more permanent basis, what would raising him in a bunker be like? This wasn't how she wanted to raise her own child, even though there was a lot she loved about survivalist living.

She'd been young, having just started middle school, when her parents hastily packed her and her siblings in an RV two days after a bombing in New York City. They'd traveled cross-country to the West Coast. From there, they took a boat to Alaska.

She stared back out the window at Anvil Mountain once again. At least she didn't have to run away to the other end of the country. But had she taken Dylan far enough away to keep them safe?

NINE

Sean cringed at the echo each step created. It was like walking inside a corrugated tin can that once had held baked beans. "Was this really the type of place you grew up in?"

Ivy shrugged. "The one we grew up in was built pre-fab. My parents had this one customized. I would say this one is a little better."

He tried to keep his jaw from dropping but couldn't. This was *nicer* than the one she'd been raised in? Ivy reached for the rust-covered door handle and pulled on it without using a key. "You don't lock the door before you leave?" They might have different definitions of what constituted as safe. He looked over his shoulder to see Helena mirror his apprehension. The hard cots at the trooper post were sounding better all the time.

The door creaked open and revealed another more modern white-covered steel door. Ivy flipped open a black lid above the doorknob, typed in a code, reciting it aloud for Sean and Helena's benefit, and pressed Enter. The sound of hydraulic locks opening preceded her shoving open the door with her foot. A gleaming white hallway with shoe cubbies, coat hooks and mats greeted them. Surprisingly modern.

Ivy kicked off her shoes underneath a bench and flipped on some switches for the air purifier, active electric, heat and water. She walked in farther to an open kitchen and living room complete with a rug, stainless-steel appliances and a wooden dining room table. Several wall hangings of various picturesque Alaska landscapes glowed with light, giving the appearance of looking outside through windows. Even though Sean knew the bunker was built into the hill, the fake windows offered him an odd sense of comfort. Like he wasn't actually at risk of being buried alive.

"This wasn't at all what I expected," Helena said, dropping her travel bag on a dining room chair and spinning around. "I feel like I've stepped inside a futuristic home. This isn't what comes to mind when I think of survival bunkers."

"The size of everything, including the toilet and laundry, is smaller and works a little different than what you're used to, but it's relatively comfortable," Ivy murmured. "My parents purchased a luxury model. This is on the lower end of that spectrum. I'd keep your coats on for a little while. The heat should catch up soon."

"What would be on the higher end of luxury bunkers?" Sean asked.

"Some millionaires have ones with aquaponics, fitness centers like rock walls, movie theaters, pools and…" She placed Dylan down on the rug and put a hand on her head. Her eyelids drooped. "Um…"

Sean rushed forward and placed his hand on her back. "I think it's time for you to take a rest." At least she wasn't as sickly white as she'd been back at Minnie's, but the exhaustion still strained her features.

Helena nodded. "Yes, the doctor said you should avoid too much excitement and concentrated focus. We've inundated you with both in one day."

"But I need to take care of Dylan and make dinner and…"

"We'll take care of both of those," he assured her. "I saw you struggle to stay awake during the drive. Take a short rest." When they were dating, they often took short day trips on his day off. Ivy had always been a night owl at heart, something that probably helped her in Alaska during the months when the sun never set. He'd taken it as a compliment when on their third day-trip date she'd fallen asleep while he was driving. He wasn't much of a conversationalist, so he wasn't offended, but he'd seen it as an indication she felt safe around him.

Ivy didn't look safe now. She glanced between both Sean and Helena. "Are you sure you can take care of Dylan?"

Helena sat in a squat next to Dylan and Grace. Luna had decided to take a snooze herself in the far corner of the room. "I've recently had experience with babies— well, *one* baby. My sister's. Go rest, Ivy. Between the two of us, we'll prep some dinner, and then we can re-evaluate."

Sean looked into her eyes. "Please let us know if you need to go back to the hospital." Her shoulders sagged, and she nodded. There appeared to be four bedrooms.

Three had queen beds and one had four bunk beds, so he suggested Ivy take the middle queen. That way Sean would stay closest to the front entrance and Helena would be closest to the emergency exit, which turned out to be a ladder leading to the top of the hill that the bunker was burrowed inside.

After seeing Ivy settled, Sean searched through the pantry. Helena found what appeared to be a trapdoor, labeled as Frozen Foods in the kitchen floor. They twisted the hydraulic lock open and lifted the heavily insulated panel to reveal a chest freezer, half buried. The permafrost nestled around the freezer in layers. Inside the chest, an assortment of frozen meats and vegetables were rock-hard.

Sean selected a package of ground beef and offered to cook dinner while his teammate took the first round of playing with Dylan. Mostly that involved making sure the eager toddler didn't get too rowdy with the dogs. It was amazing how much strength those little fingers could have when they locked down on something. As he browned the meat for dinner, he was reminded of all the little ones he'd interacted with over the last few months with the team.

His mind threatened to question every decision in the past, so he focused harder on the frozen beef. Amazing that the permafrost could work in a survivalist's favor here. Granted, most survivalists probably didn't have the luxury of such an upscale bunker.

The permafrost intrigued him. Even though there was grass and sage brush on the top layer outside, permafrost was frozen ground. Any type of frozen earth, whether soil or sediment or rock, all bound together as ice could make up permafrost. Near Anchorage, permafrost could be found, but only in isolated patches. In the Arctic, it was likely to be everywhere. Grace had worked in avalanches, but he couldn't recall a case with permafrost. She should still be able to detect through it. From what he could tell, the stuff looked rock-hard. How would that affect where the victim's body could be buried...?

"I'm feeling much better," Ivy said. She stepped into the kitchen, now dressed in light pink sweatpants and a sweatshirt that read Parenting Style: Survivalist.

"Nice sweatshirt."

She cringed. "I thought it was funnier before we actually headed over to the bunker. You were right, though. I just needed a few minutes to close my eyes. Smells delicious."

"Dinner's almost ready." He just about flinched. It sounded too natural to be in the kitchen together.

She didn't seem bothered. She picked up Dylan and nuzzled his nose. "Any new developments?" she asked in a singsong way as she grinned.

Sean stilled, wooden spoon in hand. It was like seeing a distorted version of the dream life they'd spent hours imagining in those early months of marriage. He loved seeing her smile like that, in her element as a mother, loving on their boy. *Their* boy? He poured a can of crushed tomatoes in the skillet and stirred faster. Sauce splashed on his hand. He took a deep breath. He had no right to even think such a thing. Maybe he also needed a nap.

"Sean filled me in on what Minnie said when you

showed her the victim's photograph," Helena said. "We'll go interview the dredge companies in operation tomorrow. Starting with the ones that parked in that lot."

Ivy nodded slowly. "That's good, but Minnie was right that I should go with you. People get touchy when you start asking too many questions about their gold operations. I know some of the employees already. Seasonal workers—usually new to the job and the area—can't afford to get a place to live, so they pick up gear at the mission until they make enough money to afford housing. The majority end up going back home." She sighed. "But I don't know if Minnie will be willing to watch Dylan again after what happened today." Her lighthearted tone turned somber. "Especially with how I reacted…"

"She will," Helena said. "I spoke to her on the phone while I was waiting for you to pick up the unmarked cars at the trooper post. And we have a uniformed officer willing to guard her friend's house again while she watches him."

Ivy shook her head. "She's a true friend. I don't deserve her."

"You didn't deserve to be kidnapped or targeted, either." Sean was struggling to keep his own thoughts positive, as well. The dredge operator interviews had potential, but the colonel made it clear his first priority was finding the victim's body. After their time near the shack, he was feeling hopeless on where to even start. But right *now*, he had a meal to put on the table. Sean used a fork to check the tenderness of the spaghetti noodles. "Dinner is ready."

Eating spaghetti with a thirteen-month-old proved a training exercise for Grace and Luna since the food was flung to all four corners of the bunker. The K-9 partners weren't allowed to eat on duty and were only allowed to enjoy their special food. Helena finished first and took care of their meals and a quick walk outside while Sean cleaned the kitchen. Ivy wiped up the considerable mess on Dylan and the walls. He began to fuss and whine.

"Did he even eat anything?"

She put her hands on her hips and studied him for a second. "If only food by osmosis worked." She laughed and their eyes connected. The warmth in his gut sobered him immediately. He turned back to find something else to clean. Except Dylan's fussing turned into full-on crying. Ivy offered him his favorite foods from the diaper bag and there was no interest. The dogs came back inside, but not even their appearance stopped his crying.

"I'm sorry," Ivy said over the noise, pacing with him in her arms. "Sometimes he does this. It's usually when he's overtired. And everything has been different the past two days. No routine. I don't think he had his full nap time today."

Grace moved to Sean's pack and placed her nose on the side pocket. His partner always surprised him with her intuition. "Good idea, girl." He hadn't intended to train Grace to perform whenever a child was unhappy, but after the past few months, they had performed for quite a few unhappy little ones while working cases.

"Uh-oh, I think this is my cue to get my earplugs and go to bed," Helena said. She grabbed her pack. "No offense, Sean. Come on, Luna. I'm not sure you'll appreciate this, either."

"Everyone's a critic," Sean said, causing Ivy to raise her eyebrows. "Grace and I have been alone a lot—often somewhere remote—and we sort of picked up a new hobby." He pulled out the harmonica.

Ivy's mouth dropped. "You learned to play?"

"That's *debatable*," Helena called out with a chuckle. She disappeared into her room and closed the door.

"You're not my target audience," Sean told Helena. He glanced down at Grace. "Ready? Here goes nothing." He took a deep breath and began to play the only song he really knew. The notes to "Twinkle, Twinkle, Little Star" amplified in the bunker as Grace howled along. She lifted her nose to the sky and managed to look as if she were crooning the notes. Dylan silenced midcry, staring at them both, wet cheeks and all. His little lip quivered, and then the smallest of smiles appeared.

Sean took a step back and stood with his legs apart, Grace's cue for the next part of the routine. The dog darted in between his legs and around in a figure eight while singing. Then it was Grace's turn to stand still while Sean marched around her. He tried to focus on only Dylan, but couldn't help but enjoy the way Ivy leaned back and watched him. By the time they reached the long final note, the toddler was giggling and clapping.

"Shall I play the 'ABCs' now?" Sean asked. "Or how about 'Baa Baa Black Sheep'?"

Ivy tilted her head, her eyes glistening. For a small

second, he felt like her hero again and not the one who had caused her pain. "Don't those all have the same melody?" she asked.

He raised his hands. "Busted. We only know one song. Grace does the singing and dancing, and I provide backup."

Dylan yawned and rubbed his eyes. In a swift motion, Ivy offered him a blanket and slipped away to put him to sleep for the night. She returned in five minutes, beaming. "That was better than any bedtime story I could've told him. Thank you, Sean."

"You're welcome." He sat on the couch, reorganizing and repacking the contents of his pack. Even though the mood was much lighter between them now, he still hated how they'd left their last conversation about Dylan.

Sean blew out a breath. He needed to ask her a question but didn't want to cause any more emotional upheaval in one day. Still, it *had* to be asked before they called it a night. "I need to know everyone who knows this location."

"My parents, the social worker, and now you and Helena."

His eyebrows rose. "And that's all? You haven't talked about it with anyone else?"

Ivy leaned back into the couch cushion and reached up to dim the light coming from the faux window above her. "They're the only ones that know the actual location and have been here. I mean, Minnie knows *of* the bunker." Her eyes widened. "And I guess my friend Marcella knows."

"Marcella?" It took him a moment to remember Ivy's friend. "The one that still lives in Fairbanks?" He knew it'd been hard on Ivy to live so far from her good friend.

"You remembered. She actually owns the mission. When she heard we'd…" Ivy hesitated. "…*divorced*," she continued, in a softer tone, "well, she knew I was planning to live in the bunker. She offered me the job. She visits in the summer and during the Iditarod, and I'm happy to share the apartment during those times."

Sean walked to the front door and checked the security panel. It was reassuring that her parents had made safety a priority. In addition to the armed security system, there was a perimeter alarm engaged and a gun case. He hesitated. "You really haven't talked about this place to anyone else?" He turned to face her. "Just in passing, even? A date, maybe?"

Her eyes widened and she quickly looked down at her clasped hands. "No."

"Is there anyone in Nome that might be wondering why you've dropped off the grid?"

Her lips curled up. "Are you still asking me because of the case, or is this conversation of a more *personal* nature?"

"What if it's a little of both?"

"I haven't been seeing anyone. Is…uh…anyone waiting for you to get back to Anchorage?"

He hated that her asking pleased him so much. "No."

An awkward silence hung in the air before she smiled. "I think I better get as much rest as I can before Dylan wakes up."

"Okay. Only one more question. Does the social worker know you're here right now?"

She pulled her knees up to her chest on the couch and wrapped her arms around them. "I used the burner phone Helena gave me and called her at the trooper post while you were installing Dylan's car seat in the SUV. She said as long as you were offering us protection, there shouldn't be a problem, but—" her voice cracked "—I'm still only a foster mom, so I can't really make a decision to run away with him. Even if it is for his own safety. I'm a realist. I know if that man isn't caught soon, you'll get called back—"

The pain in her voice was like a vise grip on his heart. "Ivy, I promise you I'm not leaving until that man is behind bars."

"*Don't.* I'm not holding you to that." She stood and offered him a sad smile. "We've been down the road of promises we couldn't keep. Let's not do that to ourselves again. Good night, Sean."

His breath caught, taken off guard that a simple good-night punched him in the gut with the same intensity as the moment he'd signed the divorce papers.

Ivy slid out from under the quilt with regret. The bunker never got hot, despite the heater running. She blamed the permafrost just underneath the flooring, which also was heated. Dylan's outstretched arms warmed her, though. She hesitated at the threshold. She needed Sean, yet she bristled anytime he came to her rescue. Once he got the guy, he'd be leaving. If she let her guard down, it would be harder to patch her heart up for the second time.

Shoulders back and head on straight, she stepped into the kitchen to find Helena hard at work, making waffles. The smell of maple, sugar and coffee brewing could almost fool her into believing everyone was gathered for fun. They worked around each other as Ivy prepped Dylan's oatmeal. Sean joined them just as they sat down at the table, though Ivy found it hard to sit so close to him. It was too much of a reminder of all the times they'd shared breakfast together in years past.

She felt Helena's stare before finally looking up. The trooper was alternating her stare between Ivy and Sean. "Did I miss anything last night?" she asked.

"Nope," Sean said, a little too quickly to sound normal. Ivy shrugged, unsure of what to say.

Helena raised her left eyebrow. "Okay, then. I'm curious about this survivalist lifestyle. Did you really grow up like this?"

She got the question often in her line of work. And there was no textbook answer for what she found they really wanted to know. "There are different types of survivalists. The type often depends on the motivation that inspired the change of lifestyle. For instance, my dad was a hedge fund manager who missed country life and my mom was an anthropology professor who wanted to be a homesteader. We lived in New York, and when there was a bombing, they suddenly believed moving out here would be the only way we'd survive. They cashed out their retirement savings and we made our way to Alaska. When things calmed down, they decided they liked living in the middle of nowhere. After my sisters and brother left for college, they decided to go back to the lower forty-eight and build up their retirement again." Ivy gestured at their surroundings. "They vacation here every summer, though."

"Did all your siblings stay in Alaska?"

"Spread out, but yes. Aside from the mosquito swarms, we love it here. Other survivalists are motivated by staying off the grid, distrustful of government. Some just have a love of living off the land, and then you have those who are running away from something. Like that missing-bride case you mentioned."

For the first time, it struck her that her parents really fell into the category of running away from something. They'd always focused on how they wanted to try living off the land anyway, but the reason they had was because they were fleeing from potential danger. Wasn't that her first instinct whenever trouble came her way, too?

She'd been a hypocrite. The thought smacked her fully awake. She'd been angry with Sean for letting fear have the deciding vote in their marriage, yet she let fear rule her heart plenty of times. She didn't want to disregard wisdom, though. Getting enough distance from the issues to figure out which was which proved almost impossible. She lifted up a silent prayer. *I need Your help.*

Helena pulled her hair back into a ponytail. "Sean mentioned you were a survivalist instructor but didn't want to raise Dylan the same way. Is hiding here hard for you?"

His neck turned red, a sure indication that he was worried Ivy wouldn't be pleased he'd shared that tidbit. "Well, Sean isn't wrong, but I wouldn't mind bringing Dylan here under different circumstances. I suppose that may seem contradictory, given my line of work. I still think they're useful skills, but the isolation and some of the hardships I experienced seemed unnecessary. A lot of benefits came from it, too."

Ivy gestured at the glowing images of the tundra on the walls. "You have to appreciate your surroundings wherever you are in order to stay alive. A certain amount of flexibility is required. Thinking outside of the box. And I love the quiet of nature."

She sighed, remembering the constant hum of traffic in Anchorage that set her teeth on edge. "In college, I discovered I enjoyed teaching those skills to others. There's something about being in nature. It's much easier to believe that God's in control and I'm not when I'm out there. And a little overwhelming to realize that such beauty was all created for more than our survival but also our pleasure." Ivy cradled her coffee mug. She'd gotten carried away and probably had said too much. "Anyway, I worked for the college fitness center, taking students on weekend adventure trips in the area. I loved it so much I took a job as a survival instructor after graduation."

"And that's how I met you." Sean beamed at her as if he were proud. The expression caught her off guard. "I knew I'd be in all sorts of remote areas as a trooper and wanted to be sure I had what it takes."

The memories of that week hit her in the gut. She

had to tone down the emotions and keep the conversation professional. "That's right. You were an excellent student. Ever had to do a waterfall jump as a trooper?"

His eyes twinkled as he leaned forward on his elbows. "Can't say that I have."

Heat filled her cheeks. She shouldn't have alluded to that afternoon. Shortly after that practice jump, he'd kissed her behind the waterfall. *What* a first kiss!

Ivy stood and moved to attend Dylan, except he was perfectly content for once. She stood there, unsure of how to busy herself, her cheeks on fire.

Helena also left the table. "Come on, Grace. Do your morning walk with us."

Sean straightened. "Oh, you don't have—"

Grace and Luna flanked her on both sides. "We'll be able to pack up and leave faster. You can help Ivy clean up."

Ivy didn't miss the sly smile on Helena's lips as she stepped out of the bunker with the dogs. If Sean's teammate was trying to play *re*-matchmaker, she was barking up the wrong tree.

"Do you remember when you called to ask me for forgiveness, back in March?"

Sean's question only increased her discomfort. She nodded. Dwelling on the humbling moment wasn't the most pleasant, but her reasons had been. "I needed to let go of some unresolved stuff keeping my heart hard. Owning up to my part of the divorce helped." She wondered now, though, if her heart was really resolved.

"Really surprised me. You didn't ask me to apologize for my part, even though…" He cleared his throat.

"Well, we both know I could've handled things better, too." Dylan began to fuss. Ivy turned to pick him up, but Sean scooped him up first, much to the boy's delight. She blinked rapidly, warring emotions building in her chest. What was he *doing*? Where was this headed?

"I went to work the next day and told Eli about your call." Sean made a funny face at Dylan, who tried to mimic him by scrunching up his nose. "I hadn't noticed the cross on Eli's desk before—at least, not consciously. He helped me understand. I've been wanting to tell you, but I don't know what's been holding me back."

"Are you trying to tell me you're a believer now?"

"Back in April." Sean turned to face her, and Dylan followed his gaze. "I guess I can't help but wonder if we had both…"

The two most important guys in her life watching her, together, took her breath away. She knew what Sean meant. If they'd both had faith, would they have handled things differently? "I've asked myself that, as well."

Sean set the boy down with a couple of toys from the diaper bag. "And about yesterday. I think you misunderstood me if you thought it was about control—"

"Sean, I'm not sure I'm ready for this conversation." Like a switch being flipped, her entire body tensed. He wouldn't dare try to convince her not to adopt again, would he? "I'm going to need a little more time to process what you told me. Don't get me wrong. I'm glad you told me about your first recovery and how it affected you. I always wondered why the sudden change—"

"It wasn't sudden." He stood and crossed his arms

over his chest. "All the reasons I listed had always been issues."

"Yes, ones we'd discussed before we married, and yet agreed, *together*, that they weren't enough to deter us from starting a family. So, when you went back to those same bullet points a year into our marriage, I thought you were trying to hide that the real reason you didn't want kids was because of me."

He pulled his chin back. "What? What do you mean?"

"You thought I'd be a bad mother since I couldn't even handle city living." The words slipped out, words she'd been determined never to voice aloud.

"No. Why would you think that?" He moved forward, closer to her.

She automatically took a step back, her legs pressing against the edge of the table. "You are amazing with children." She waved at Dylan. "You clearly love kids, and they love you. So, I thought it had to be me. I was never a needy mess in small towns, but all my strengths seemed useless in a city." She whispered, "And you were never there."

"Ivy, I'm sorry I ever made you feel that way." He straightened and ran a hand through his hair. "I admit I got frustrated, but it was at myself. I knew I was failing you. We never went backpacking and adventuring like I said we would. That first year of working recoveries, I… I didn't handle the transition well. I think I was depressed but wasn't ready to acknowledge it, even though it'd been my dream to be part of the K-9 Unit." He pulled in a breath. "But it was never about not wanting to have a child with *you*."

They stared at each other, and Ivy couldn't look away, despite how blurry her vision had become. Her perspective shifted once more, coloring the memories different shades than they had been before. "All our arguments seem to have different meanings now." Her breath shuddered.

He reached for her and wrapped his arms around her. "I'm starting to feel the same." His voice, low and soft, made her stomach flip.

She closed her eyes, willing the burning sensation to go away. She wouldn't cry. Instead, she rested her cheek on his chest. The uncomfortable stiffness in her muscles and bones suddenly evaporated, her entire body relaxing into his strength. Oh, how she'd missed being wrapped up in his strong embrace. This was how it was at their happiest. To be with him, to be married. He was always eager to touch her, comfort her. In his arms, everything was okay.

And she knew she could face anything as long as they were together.

But they *weren't*. She stepped back and offered him a small smile. They could've handled things so much differently, but it was too late. He still didn't want a family, despite the impression he loved being with Dylan. "And yet…some things haven't changed at all."

His mouth dropped open, but he seemed at a loss for words.

"I'm glad we both have changed for the better," she whispered. "We can be happy for each other." The front bunker door slammed. She couldn't bear to continue this conversation in front of Helena. She moved to the pack she'd brought from the survivalist mission. There had to be some tissues handy there.

She clumsily opened the bag and it tipped over. A canister resembling a giant tin of coffee fell out of the sack, and the lid popped off and rolled across the room. Packets of powdered water purification packets tumbled out, along with a glass jar that rolled to the tip of Ivy's feet. A glass jar shouldn't have been in there. She stretched to pick it up but froze before her fingers reached the glass. The light caught the contents and reflected yellow hues around the room. "Sean, I think I know what the man is searching for."

TEN

Gold. Everything about this case pointed to gold. He felt more like a sheriff in an old Western than a trooper trying to solve a murder case. The jar contained the purest flakes he'd ever seen, as well as pebble nuggets. Gold had reached almost two thousand dollars an ounce, so that hefty jar had to be worth a pretty penny. Helena had the jar right now, though, processing it for evidence and checking the glass and lid for fingerprints.

"So Francine must have wanted to escape with the gold. Why else would she have come to the mission?" Ivy tapped her knee with her finger as they drove through the streets of Nome, having already settled Dylan and Minnie back at a safe location. "Except the mission is practically made of windows. So maybe she came inside to get gear, but saw the man coming, so she stuffed the jar in one of the closest containers, thinking she could come back for it after she got rid of the guy."

"Your theory means she had to know her murderer," he said.

"She must have, otherwise why hide it?"

"Maybe he saw her with the jar of gold somewhere else and had been stalking her from her previous location. We can't rule out any possibilities without more evidence."

He pulled into the parking lot, noting the dredge the man had shot at them from. No sign of movement. "Let's start with the dredge that Minnie's son and daughter own."

Ivy pointed to the eighty-foot-long one. "It's the biggest one. They have the most employees, so that's a good choice."

"It's gigantic."

"They use it in the Norton Sound. Minnie said they spent over a million dollars to get it fixed up recently."

Sean whistled. "They find that much gold each year to make that a safe investment?"

"I can only assume so," she replied. "Minnie says they're like third- or fourth-generation miners, so they know what they're doing."

He parked in a way that would ensure he'd be the first to take any hit if someone was hiding on any of the other dredges. He escorted Ivy and Grace around the backside of the first dredge. Two men stepped out onto the top deck of the boat, twenty feet above them. Sean placed an arm out and Grace uttered a warning growl. "I know them," Ivy said, reaching her arm up and waving. "It's Ben, Fiona's husband, from the inn. And his son, Nathan."

"Hi, Ivy. Minnie said you'd be stopping by."

They climbed up the ramp that was still on the back end of the boat. The smells of fish and bleach warred with each other. Grace opened her mouth and scrunched up her nose, her teeth bared. "I know, girl," he said softly. She didn't like the smell of bleach, but it also wouldn't stop her from smelling the scent of death. "Get to work."

They maneuvered in between the equipment that seemed to fill every nook and cranny. So far, other than her huffs, Grace didn't alert on anything. The aluminum stairs led them to the top deck and, thankfully, to fresh air.

The lines in the older gentleman's face indicated the man had either been smiling or squinting most of his life. He offered a beefy hand to Sean. "So your Ivy's…" He let go and let the unsaid words hang.

"My ex," Ivy finished for him. "And he's kept me safe this past week."

"I know Minnie said we might be able to help you, but I don't really see how. She said you're in some kind of trouble, but she wouldn't tell us much more."

Sean pulled out the photograph of the victim, Francine. "Actually, we only need help in identifying this woman. Have you seen her before?"

The two men exchanged a meaningful glance after scanning the picture but didn't say anything.

"You know her, then," Ivy pressed. "It really would be a help if you told me about her."

Nathan scratched his head. "She was a big mistake, that's what. She worked for us for a couple months. Came highly recommended and knew how to talk the talk."

"Until she walked away with almost a hundred thousand dollars' worth of gold," Ben muttered. "She swindle you, too, Ivy?"

Her jaw dropped. Sean reached over and gave her hand the smallest of squeezes to indicate she shouldn't answer. The touch, though, sent warmth shooting up his arm, and he let go of her fingers at once.

"To be fair, we don't know if she robbed us," Nathan said. "Not for sure. It's not as if we saw her do it."

Ben rolled his eyes. "Olivia had our Nathan wrapped around her little finger."

Nathan's neck reddened. "Dad, she didn't. She was a decent employee, then one day disappeared."

"Olivia?" Sean asked. If Francine McMillan was her real name, the woman had used an alias here.

"Yeah. Olivia Truby."

"If you were worried, why didn't you report her missing?" Ivy asked.

"We did, but the local cops told us we'd been duped." Ben turned back to the hoses he'd been wrangling when they had boarded. "Apparently, her driver's license and Social Security number were fakes."

"You said she came recommended," Sean said.

"Yeah, by one of the top mining district companies." Nathan turned to his father. "I did my due diligence. Her references checked out."

Sean felt like they were hearing an argument that had been played many times before. "Can I get those phone numbers from you?"

Nathan's shoulders sagged. "Sure, but they won't do you any good. Used to be one of the top mining district companies until their claims dried up a few years back. That's why I thought she was looking for work elsewhere, but when I called them after she went missing, all the numbers had been disconnected."

Ben shook his head in disgust. "Come to find out the owner had died several months before we hired her. Who knows who Nathan actually was discussing Olivia's references with."

Maybe they were dealing with a con gone wrong, then. "Ever see another man with her? Maybe a fellow employee with auburn hair?"

Nathan's eyebrows shot up. "No. That her boyfriend or something?"

His dad seemed to have pegged him right. The man had been smitten, which made it easier to be fooled.

"We're not sure. But do you know who owns the claims, the district, now?" Ivy asked.

"No. We figured the cops were right and left it at that." Ben wagged his finger. "But you could always check the Alaska Mapper."

"Of course," Ivy said, nodding. Sean had heard the name before but couldn't remember what it was. They said their goodbyes and left, without Grace having alerted.

Once back in the SUV, he turned to Ivy. "Alaska Mapper?"

"All gold claims have a paper trail now. I believe they went digital when the Department of Natural Resources started auctioning mining leases again, roughly ten years ago. Ben works in the Norton Sound, but there are still lots of smaller claims around all the rivers and creeks throughout the tundra. You can buy, sell or inherit claims as long as the permit fees are kept up to date. If we can use your computer at the trooper post, I can show you in person."

Sean headed for the post as she'd suggested. He needed to do a quick run on the Olivia Truby alias, as well.

"At least we know Francine was up to no good, otherwise why the fake name? And why couldn't we tell them that we found their gold?"

"It's evidence and we don't know they're the owners for sure yet."

"No assumptions." She nodded. "Right."

Her words hit him funny. While it was his motto while he worked a case, he'd certainly failed to do the same in their marriage. But right now he had to focus on the matter at hand. "Since Ben reported the missing gold to the local police, it's likely they'll get it back when we're done with it."

"Does any of this help us get closer to getting the guy? Maybe we could use the jar of gold as bait and you can lure him out."

"Maybe." He pulled into the trooper post and they found Helena in the office, hanging up a phone.

"Just touched base with the team," she said. "No fingerprints on the jar of gold except for the murder victim. It was a fast match since we'd just identified her." Helena pointed at Sean. "I'm eager to hear how the interview went, but excuse us, Ivy. I need to update Sean on some things in private."

Ivy pointed to another desktop computer. "May I? I'd like to start looking at Alaska Mapper."

Sean reached over and clicked a guest account that would keep her from clicking on any classified information and followed Helena into the hallway. "Sensitive news?"

"Possibly." Helena pulled her lips back in an apologetic grimace. "The troopers that've been on location in Little Diomede have wrapped up. They're on their way back here late this afternoon. The colonel says she'll give us another twenty-four hours. Then she needs us back. The troopers at this post can take over for us."

A sour taste rose up in his mouth. Ivy's assurances that he shouldn't promise anything came to mind. "Thanks for telling me." He didn't know how Lorenza would respond to his request for leave. Ivy might not even agree to let him protect her without Helena's presence, as well. If he thought about it too much, he wouldn't be able to focus on using the time they had left. His teammate eyed him for a second as if she didn't believe he was taking the news well before they walked back into the office.

"I think I've found something," Ivy said. He and Helena hovered over her shoulder as she zoomed into an online map with a box labeling the area as Bozsan mining district. "Ben and Nathan should've checked the Mapper before they called those numbers. They would've seen beforehand that the ownership was recently transferred to a trustee." She turned around. "Maybe you guys can get somewhere with that?"

Helena grabbed a notepad and jotted down the information. Then Sean moved to the computer next to Ivy and did a search for the mining district itself. A mining journal website filled with personal ads for gold claims filled the screen. *Top-tier gold deposit. For sale. Twenty State of Alaska placer and lode claims encompassing nine hundred acres. Recently mined forty troy ounces in one week. Proof of gold to serious buyers. Start mining gold nuggets immediately. $2,000,000.00 for recent mine, claims, camp and equipment. Contact Marty Macquoid. Agent.*

The ancient clacking keyboard Helena's fingers were tapping stilled. "That name isn't in our system. No Marty Macquoid. But—" she inhaled sharply "—the district used to own that building next to the dredge parking lot."

"The one that our suspect ran into?" Sean blew out a breath. "Ben and Nathan Duncan indicated this mining district had dried up."

"True," Ivy said. "But if I follow your advice not to assume anything, then I can tell you that just because a claim dried up a few years ago doesn't mean they can't find more gold. This district surrounds a few creeks. They can also do hard-rock exploration." She paused. "You can't dig up the whole land, though. They only own the mineral rights of gold, so there are restrictions. This also uses a different type of dredging than Ben and Nathan do in the sea. It's possible there's potential for more gold to be found, but it's suspicious."

He stepped closer to her and looked at the mining map still on the screen. "I can't really tell where these claims are. This is an unusual map."

Ivy squinted at the screen. "I think I can help you with that." She turned to the map of the area the troopers post had laid out on the table in the center of the office. "See this?" Her finger traveled from the sea up a river. "This is the Niukluk River. There are countless creeks stemming from it, though you never know when they'll be dry or flowing during this time of year. It depends on how hot the summer was. The claims start—" Her finger froze in the air and her face paled.

Sean stepped closer. "Is this as close to where you were kidnapped as I think?"

"It's on the other side of the river." She inhaled and nodded. "But yes. Fairly close."

"So, if he took the body on the boat—"

"Like we thought, the body would've likely been discovered on a bank nearby by now. With the low water levels in places, something would've snagged it."

"Let's explore the theory that this is about the gold claims," Sean said. "The ad indicates there would be proof of mined gold."

"Olivia—I mean, *Francine*—could've stolen the gold for him." Ivy's eyes widened. "Maybe she double-crossed him and decided to run off with the gold instead of letting him use it to swindle some buyers."

"You think he was planning to pass off the stolen gold as gold recently found, even though the claims are actually dry." Helena tapped her finger on her chin. "If our suspect thinks he can scam someone out of two million dollars, that's motive for murder and reason enough to stick around until a sale," she said. "Let's keep working this angle."

Sean paced the space in front of the door, with Grace by his side. He often had his best ideas while moving around. "What if the body was buried somewhere on the land he currently owns?"

"He doesn't own the land, though. Only the claims." Ivy shrugged. "But it's not like anyone is living on the land, so it would be deserted."

Hope rose and quickly crashed. "If he's strategic about where he buried the body, it's possible it could never be discovered."

"Perhaps. But if he doesn't know the area well enough, then the body will be discovered on its own during the summer."

"What?" Sean stopped pacing and tried to decipher what she'd just said. He remembered the way the food kept cold underneath the bunker. "Permafrost?"

"Exactly. You can only dig about two feet before hitting rock-hard permafrost. Even the cemetery in town has to use an excavator. If it's not buried deep enough when the warm months hit the top layer, some frost melts and the waterlogged soil lifts up…" She shrugged. "Well, let's just say they've learned how deep they need to dig to prevent unpleasant surprises."

Sean didn't want to imagine that scenario. "But the riverbank has trees, so the soil there must be softer."

"Except the river surges every spring." Ivy tapped the map. "Ice chunks float toward the sea but get caught up all the time. Flooding is inevitable. Unless the murderer was fine with risking the body appearing after winter—"

"Which he wouldn't be if there was a way to trace him after the sale of the gold claims," Helena said. "If he had shown up with the jar of gold and sold the claims, there'd be no way to prove he scammed the buyers out of their money. Gold dredges flop all the time. It's a known risk."

Ivy gasped. "I should've realized."

"What?"

"On the opposite side of the river is the abandoned townsite I told you about. Even though it's not recommended, a number of foolhardy tourists try to drive across. Nome keeps an excavator over there specifically to help pull stuck tourists out. The gold claim intersects close to where they keep the excavator."

"Is it possible the suspect is hiding out somewhere on the thousand acres?" Helena asked. "The ad mentioned a camp."

Sean joined Ivy at the map. "I need to get Grace there. Time to be foolhardy and try to get across that river, too."

Ivy glanced at him. "Good thing you used to be married to an expert."

Ivy reversed and maneuvered the SUV for a third time. Grace grumbled a warbly commentary. "I don't need back-seat drivers, Grace."

"Welcome to my world," Sean said, laughing.

"It's imperative to get the best entry and exit points of the river for a crossing. Put Helena on the radio and make sure she follows my exact wheel movements as she follows us." Ivy geared up right to the edge of the gravel and thought through her technique. She'd already disconnected the fan belts in both vehicles and checked the air intake to ensure water wouldn't flood the engines.

The river's water levels were constantly fluctuating as well as the currents, developing class one and two rapids at various times of the year. At the moment, the waterway seemed calm with ripples over the rocks. "I think the murderer knows the area well."

"Something new convince you?"

"All of this is happening after September fifteenth, when fishing is no longer allowed. You won't see locals from nearby villages rafting down here anymore." She accelerated and felt the give in the steering wheel as she moved slow and steady through the waters, watching the bow wave move from front to back. "Tell Helena to take a sharp turn left after the rock on the right." They swayed side to side with the movement, driving over rocks below the surface.

Sean parroted her instructions on the radio as she reached the other side of the river. "You want to tell her anything else?"

"Gas up slow and steady up the incline. Stop immediately once out of the water."

Ivy parked at a diagonal, ensuring Helena had space to get past the mud, and hopped out. Rivulets poured out from the wheelbases like mini waterfalls. Stopping so soon helped prevent erosion of the exit point. She reattached both the fan belts and made quick work to get them driving again. Once again, the day was moving faster than anticipated.

Her thoughts drifted to her little boy. Even with an unmarked patrol car keeping an eye on the house where Minnie watched Dylan, none of it settled her nerves. She fought to keep her focus on what was right in front of her because Sean would be leaving tomorrow. Except he didn't know that she knew. She'd always teased him that he didn't know how to properly whisper, and it seemed Helena shared the same affliction.

He was being ordered home.

She'd be alone. *Again.* And Dylan wouldn't have Sean to pick him up and smile at him and play his harmonica…

She swallowed against the tightness in her throat. With his departure, her chances of being able to keep Dylan while a crazed man was still after her would dwindle. Her nose began to burn. Helena said the other troopers would take over her case, but they wouldn't spend every waking minute making sure Ivy and Dylan were safe. The least she could do was adopt that husky. Then Dylan would have a dog and a live security system.

She pulled up to the side of the abandoned warehouse where the excavator was parked.

"Stay in the vehicle, please. I'll only be a moment." Sean leaned forward as if to give her a quick peck goodbye and froze, inches from her lips. His eyes widened and he reached his hand out to tap the steering wheel. "Uh, I guess I don't need the keys. Be right back." He jumped out of the vehicle and released Grace to run by his side.

Ivy sat stunned. He had been about to kiss her. As if they were married again, like part of a daily routine to kiss his wife every time he said hi and goodbye. Ivy's pulse hammered against her chest. Her imagination could be exaggerating. She flicked the key ignition to roll down the driver's-side window for some air.

"Look at the control panel." Helena's voice carried. "I'd guess someone hot-wired this recently."

Grace trotted to the portion with the claw and bucket. The dog sat down and stared at Sean. "She alerted," Ivy whispered aloud.

Sean and Helena ran back to the vehicles, their dogs beside them. He stopped at the door. "I'd like to drive now. Grace has the scent and she pointed north."

"To the mining claims." Ivy ran around to the passenger door, and within seconds, Sean gunned the SUV down a gravel path, past several buildings. A glimpse of something red caught her peripheral vision, and she twisted to find an ATV with a helmeted driver sitting, watching them. "Sean…there!"

He glanced in his mirror and slammed on his brakes. The ATV revved and turned due north on a gravel road, kicking up mud as it vaulted up and over a hill. Sean hit the radio button. "It might just be a joyride coincidence, but it's too suspicious not to at least ask a few questions."

He flipped on his sirens, but the ATV made no signs of stopping. After half a mile, the path abruptly stopped. Sean hit his palm against the dash. "Is this really another dead end?"

Ivy strained to look out the window. "No. Tracks in the tundra due northwest." She hesitated a second to get her bearings and confirm they were where she thought. "He's heading directly to that set of mining claims."

Sean gunned the vehicle northwest. The radio squawked. "I'm calling for backup," Helena said. "Let's hope we have some off-road support available to join us."

Ivy tensed, gripping the handle on the ceiling of the SUV, as they bounced over a particularly rocky terrain. "Sean, there are so many creeks in the area the ground is unreliable. It can be rocky, then covered in brush, then suddenly go sof—"

"Got it."

She wasn't so sure he really understood the unique natures of tundra. While much drier than the spring, there were still marshes and bogs. Her teeth chattered at the speed he was navigating, following the ATV's path. They rounded a foothill and the ATV was in their sights.

"Can you tell if it's him?" Sean asked, his focus never veering from the windshield, a challenge considering the increasing mud splatters. She squinted at the retreating form but had no way of knowing how tall a man was when he was sitting and bouncing over rough terrain. The black helmet covered all signs of his hair color, and they were too far away to notice his shoes.

"No," she said. "I'm sorry." They drove parallel with a creek on their left and a creek on their right, roughly six hundred feet apart. Worrisome. She wondered if Sean noticed as well, but as long as he was careful to stay on firm ground and the two creeks didn't intersect anytime soon, they should be okay. The ATV driver twisted to see them and changed direction suddenly, veering up and over another hill and disappearing. Sean accelerated and mud spattered the side windows, obscuring their visibility.

"Sean, maybe we should wait for—" Gravity took hold, and they dropped several feet. A scream escaped her at the sudden plunge. Grace barked until the vehicle stilled.

Sean turned to her, white as a sheet. "What just happened?"

"I think the ground just gave way." She pressed her forehead against the window and found the mud had already risen up to the middle of her door. "We're stuck in a mud hole."

Sean glanced in the rearview mirror. "We've lost Helena!" He grabbed the radio. "Helena? Are you okay?"

"Yes. Popped a tire before you rounded that last bend."

"We've lost him, but we will need a tow truck."

Ivy shook her head. "You need the dozer. It's the only thing with enough power to pull us out, just like the tourists who get themselves in trouble. Ask for Max. He volunteers his time to do this." She dropped her forehead in her hands. As soon as the locals got word she needed saving like this, she would never live it down.

Sean gritted out the request. They sat in awkward silence for a minute, though he was constantly twisting in his seat, presumably trying to come up with another solution.

"Dispatch said they had already called Max on standby when I asked for backup here," Helena relayed through the radio. "Guess it's common to get stuck."

"I should have known better," Ivy said with a groan. She'd worked so hard to get accepted as a true local instead of the transplant she'd first been considered. "ATVs are easier to get unstuck without calling in help. I shouldn't have encouraged you to follow him."

Sean tilted his chin to look straight up as if he could see into the sky. "It's not your fault. I really thought we had him."

"I know," she said softly.

"This whole faith thing can get hard to keep up when I see so many bad things happening around me. I try to stop it and…" He leaned his head against the backrest. "I thought this whole relationship-with-God thing would mean life would go a little more in my favor."

"I know." Ivy sighed. "I pretty much complained the same sentiment to Minnie a couple months back."

He raised his left eyebrow, always the left one when he was surprised. "Did she have any words of wisdom?"

The memory made her laugh. "She said *as long as I've already made my requests known to Him, I try not to complain with the same mouth and lungs He created for me.*" Ivy tapped her knee. "The rest I can't quote verbatim. It was classic Minnie. Maybe I'm not mature enough in my faith, because it's still pretty hard to remember that I'm not alone."

The last word caused her voice to crack. Sean eyed her, as if suspicious of the cause.

"Sean, I should tell—"

"Ivy, there's something—"

The use of each other's names when they'd simultaneously spoken caused them both to stare at each other. "You first?" she asked.

A gunshot suddenly rang out and the impact hit the window. A white circular bit of plastic bulged inside, and the glass fractured around it like a spiderweb. Grace's bark stung her eardrum. She flinched and pressed back into the seat. Then another bullet hit the windshield, and she sent a panicked look Sean's way.

"Don't worry. The windows are bulletproof." He grabbed his radio. "Under fire! Need assistance. Now!"

Helena replied, but Ivy couldn't make out anything she said because of Grace's barking. Two more bullets impacted the shield. Nothing but white on the windshield now, and the plastic-looking layer warped inside.

Her insides shook involuntarily. She kept telling herself Sean was right. It was bulletproof, but it was hard to stop flinching.

"Grace, quiet!" The dog whined but obeyed Sean's order. He clicked the side of the radio. "ETA?"

"Dispatch says five more minutes, and I'm changing my tire. Hang on," Helena said.

The color in his face drained as he slowly put the radio back in its holder. The glass pinged with three more shots. He reached for Ivy's hand.

She wrapped her fingers around his, and the tension around her gut eased slightly. "How many bullets can this withstand?"

He squeezed her fingers, then quickly released. "Five," he whispered. He moved his hand to the gun on his holster.

"He's already shot more than that!"

"Stay in the vehicle with Grace." His voice sounded strangled.

"But you can't even open the door."

He nodded and pressed the button to roll down the window.

ELEVEN

Sean's heart pounded in his chest. He should've never admitted to knowing how many bullets the window was certified to withstand. "It's the minimum amount. Don't worry." He didn't have time to see if she believed him. He was worrying enough for the both of them. The layers of glass and plastic that molded together to absorb the impact of each bullet made it impossible to see out the windshield. Add the mud splatters to the mix on the side windows, and he felt blind. The shooting had stopped, which meant there was a possibility the ATV driver was approaching. Sean couldn't let that happen.

The driver's-side window rolled down enough for the breeze to hit him fully in the face. He planted his elbow on the window seal and used it as a pivot point to launch up and out of the car, instantly training his weapon to the west, where he'd last seen the ATV. The sun reflected off the black shield of the helmet, the driver pointing his weapon in his direction. Sean didn't hesitate. He shot three bullets. The driver twisted and dived off the ATV. Had he hit his mark?

Sirens reached his ears, but he couldn't afford to look back and see how far away Helena was. He kept his weapon trained on the driver. He really needed to get out of the vehicle to get a better shot and approach.

"State Troopers," Helena's voice announced through the megaphone-speaker function of the SUV radio. *"Put your weapon down!"*

The driver popped up on one knee with his arm raised. He wasn't surrendering. Sean fired two more shots. At this distance, no wonder he was missing. He could barely make out his form. The driver jumped up and hopped back on his ATV.

A car door slammed. Grace whined and scratched at the back door. The ATV engine revved and took off up and over a hill and vaulted over a creek. Luna took off like a shot, her legs extending and recoiling like a powerful spring. She was practically flying, but Sean knew in his gut that the driver was too far off for her to catch him.

A knock at Ivy's window caused them both to flinch. He twisted enough, still hanging partly out of the window, to see Helena gesture on the other side of the hood. "I see now why some people call it mudding instead of four-wheeling."

Ivy rolled down her window. Grace whined again. Taking pity on her, Sean lowered the back window. The K-9 immediately jumped out and nuzzled her nose underneath his neck, a sure sign she was worried. He rarely ever had to unholster his gun, as that, in and of itself, was considered a use of force. Discharging his weapon was something Grace had only seen him do at the ranges. Working discoveries typically meant the majority of the danger had passed already. Though, given the last few months with the number of traps and assignments he'd been sent on with the team, he was starting to feel there was no longer any normal.

He shimmied his entire body out the window. The wet mud seeped through his pants as he hopped up to standing. Luna was trotting back their way. Helena helped pull Ivy out of the vehicle without Ivy having to sit in the mud as he had. At least there was that. He'd made a bad call pursuing in that way on the unstable terrain. He'd been so desperate.

Why can't You let me catch him? Don't You want Ivy safe? What possible priority could You have that outweighs stopping this man, Lord? He blew out a breath and patted his K-9 partner's head. "Good girl, Grace." Eli had told him that when the job weighed him down, he had to remember to make his requests known but then acknowledge he wasn't God and move on. That was basically what Minnie was trying to tell Ivy, wasn't it? Just with different words. Saying it sure was easier than living it. *Lord, please help someone—even if it's not me—catch this guy.*

His shoes fought against the pull of the mud as he stomped around the back of the SUV. He wasn't sure he was ready to handle what the sight of the windshield looked like up close. If he let himself imagine what would've happened... No, he wouldn't let his mind go there. He focused on the ground and tried to stay on rocks as he moved to slightly higher and much firmer ground. Ivy caught his gaze. "It's amazing how much difference even six feet makes in the tundra."

A hard-earned lesson. "I suppose that's why you have to be a certified pilot to get stationed out here."

The dogs both perked their ears. Helena smiled. "The Nome police agreed to send out their helicopter to help us out."

"Is that our only backup?"

She avoided his eyes. "At the moment." In the far distance, a dozer approached but came to a stop a good hundred feet before Helena's SUV, parked behind them and to the south. "He's waiting to see if it's safe to help out, I think."

Sean glanced out at the hills. "I didn't see a long-range rifle on the suspect, but let's have him approach with caution."

Helena nodded, patted her leg, so Luna would stay by her side, and moved toward the dozer. Grace spun suddenly and her entire back went rigid.

"That's the same scent you caught before, isn't it, girl?" The question being, was it coming from the dozer again or closer?

"Sean, I think we're right in the middle of the mining claim mentioned in that ad," Ivy told him, her eyes wide.

Grace didn't relax, though. "Time to go to work," he said softly, testing to see if she really had something. Grace opened her mouth, catching all the scents in the breeze, twisted and then took off like a shot due west.

"Helena, keep Ivy safe." Sean pressed off the muddy ball of his shoe and sprinted, attempting to keep up with Grace. He hurdled over bushes and thorny patches while she glided across the terrain as if it were a smooth track. She paused at a creek and waited for him to catch up.

The sound of the helicopter's rhythmic patter of rotors in the wind grew stronger. He grabbed his shoulder radio and asked Helena to relay to the Nome PD pilot the direction the ATV went and let them know he was pursuing a cadaver discovery to the west. "Please have them do a sweep around us to make sure we can work safely."

Not even a minute later, the helicopter did just that, circling them from a far radius and then a tighter circle before taking off in a diagonal line to where they suspected the ATV driver had gone. He helped Grace find a shallow point of the creek. Once they crossed, the vegetation grew sparse. Not enough water, perhaps, which was a good sign. His eyes caught wheel tracks, wide enough to indicate heavy machinery. Was it possible the killer had hot-wired the dozer and buried the body over here?

Grace ran to the tracks. The hairs on the back of her neck stuck straight up. The scent was stronger apparently. They ran across the tundra for what seemed like a good mile. Grace stopped right in front of a sage bush and circled it three times, before she plopped down to sitting and panted, her tongue flopping out to the left side. Had she found the body?

Sean took a knee. The dirt didn't look disturbed here, though the tire tracks of the dozer were only a few feet away. He peeked under a gangly sage brush and saw packed dirt, almost as if it'd been planted by hand. The man must have used the dozer to bury his victim here and also taken the time to transplant bushes right over the site. In the wild. Where the disturbed earth wouldn't easily bc seen by helicopter or drone.

He hated smart criminals.

"Good girl," Sean said in the happiest voice he could muster. He retrieved her toy and let her run off with it, only a few feet away. "Helena," he said gruffly. "I'm going to need the dozer to follow my coordinates. I think we've found something."

"I hope you're right, because it's about time something good happened. The helicopter found a campground and landed to investigate, but there's no sign of the suspect. It appears he's disappeared again."

Sean remained on his knees near the sage because it finally hit him. While he had likely succeeded in his assigned mission to find the victim, he'd just made it harder to convince the colonel he should stay in Nome.

The landscape she usually enjoyed watching flew past her without her really seeing it. "Do you think Grace has really found the victim?" Ivy finally asked.

Helena sighed, hands at the wheel as she drove over the bridge that crossed Safety Sound. The name seemed ironic now. "We'll find out soon enough."

Ivy turned in her seat to fully face Helena even though the woman kept her gaze on the road. "What's your instinct?"

She glanced at her, eyes soft. "I think so, yes."

Ivy faced forward. That was her instinct, too, which meant that Sean had finished what he needed to do. She needed to stop relying on her ex to be her safety net and prepare for what came next. She'd pick up the husky first and then Dylan. Neither one could fit well in the SUV with Luna taking up the entire back seat. "I need you to stop at the mission and let me retrieve my Jeep."

Helena slowed down and pulled off the highway into the parking lot but hesitated to unlock the doors.

"I need my own wheels again. I doubt Luna is the type of dog that likes to share a back seat with a husky."

"I knew you'd end up adopting the husky. I saw that look in your eyes when we found her at the dredge lot."

"You don't approve," Ivy said.

"What you decide is none of my business," Helena replied. "If I pulled a face, it's only because I know Sean won't like it, but—"

"He won't be here to have a say in that, will he?"

"He told you, then." Helena sighed. "If they've found the body like I think they have, no. The trooper assigned to this post knows this case is high priority, Ivy. The moment he arrives, he's going straight to the campsite they've found to gather evidence and potential leads. We're going to get him."

Ivy folded her arms across her chest. She'd heard that reassurance used too many times to mean anything. "Is the mission cleared for use now? Would I even be allowed to move back in?" She'd loved her little home, but now the cozy store and apartment brought her a shiver of trepidation, and she hated it.

"As soon as we know you're safe."

Ivy grabbed the Jeep keys she'd kept in her purse. "Okay."

"I'll follow behind you all the way until we get you settled back at the bunker."

Ivy stepped out. The sound of tires on gravel made her spin on a dime. A mud-covered SUV with the windshield missing pulled to a stop. Sean stepped out with Grace trotting behind him.

"Looks like a pretty chilly ride." Her attempt at humor failed.

He shrugged as he strode up to her. "Grace and I both have coats. She seemed to enjoy the wind in her fur. What's happening here? Another break-in?"

"No, she's getting *her* Jeep," Helena said, one foot out of the intact black SUV. "I was going to follow her, but if you want to, we can switch vehicles. I'll take that back to post."

Ivy held up her hands. "That's not necess—"

"That'd be great," Sean said.

Helena looked between the two of them and settled on Sean. "News?"

"Grace has never been wrong." His voice sounded ragged. "The stationed trooper arrived with a couple of Nome PD deputies. They're processing the scene and asking the helicopter pilot to stick around a couple more hours. See if they'll spot anything."

"So we were right, then. This is about gold. The mining claims…" Ivy's words trailed off as she tried to connect the dots.

"Likely, but we still aren't sure how."

"The mining claims were for sale, right?" Ivy turned to Helena, whose eyes lit up.

"The two men in the B and B."

Sean frowned. "The guys that wanted to buy…" His confusion cleared. "Oh, the men that were looking to invest in some gold mines."

"Exactly." Helena beamed. "I can stop by the B and B after I pick up a new vehicle from post. I'll see if they are still in town and let you know." She led Luna to the shot-up SUV, carefully backed up and moved on down the highway.

"It was definitely her?" She felt silly the moment she asked, but some part of her needed to hear it.

He gave a curt nod. "The rolled-up rug just as you described."

Ivy felt a tug in her gut. She crossed the space between them and wrapped her arms around him. His back stiffened, but his hands slipped around her waist.

"I'm okay, Ivy," he rasped. "It's my job." But she felt his spine and shoulders relax. His arms wrapped tighter around her, and he sighed deeply.

"Maybe it's more for me, then," she whispered. They stayed in the embrace, and she rested her chin on the top of his shoulder. "I don't think I'll ever forget seeing Francine and the realization it was too late to save her. But I knew I couldn't focus on that if I was going to get her justice." She straightened and stepped slightly back. "Is that a little what it's like for you?"

"Almost exactly." His hands dropped from her waist, and it was as if they were on their first date again. Awkward and unsure of what to say or do next. He turned and walked to the Jeep.

"Did you find it odd the way Helena emphasized that it was *my* Jeep?"

Sean shook his head and bent over to peek underneath the vehicle. "No. It was her way of reminding me that we're not married. I can't boss you around."

For some reason, the notion tickled her. "Have you ever really bossed me around? You had strong opinions, of course—"

Sean dropped in a squat and looked up at her, the beginnings of a smile at the edge of his lips. "No. I knew you well enough to know you'd make up your own mind and do what you wanted." He stood and wandered to the other side of the Jeep, taking a look underneath again. "Besides, you had me wrapped around your little finger and you knew it."

The sentiment evaporated all humor. "I think it was obvious I couldn't boss you around, either."

He moved to open the back door, peering inside. "No," he said quietly. "I suppose you're right about that. We both were too stubborn." He lifted his gaze to meet hers. "I thought my job as your husband was to keep you safe, and I'm sorry that didn't extend to more than your physical safety. I know I didn't cherish your heart like I should have." He coughed and moved to check underneath the hood. "The Jeep doesn't appear to have been compromised. I'll follow you."

Ivy got into the Jeep and focused on the musk oxen that were grazing a few hundred feet away. They offered her a sense of normalcy when her stomach twisted into knots. His apology should've brought her peace, but instead her throat tightened, fighting off tears. She turned the ignition on and spun the car onto the highway. A husky and a toddler boy were waiting for her. They were her true home now.

Twenty minutes later, she walked out of the vet's office with the beautiful husky. "What should I name you?" she asked, letting her fingers sink into the dog's soft fur, gently massaging away the tension in the husky's neck. The dog looked up adoringly and twisted to lick her arm.

Sean waited in the parking lot, leaning against the black SUV. "You're sure about this?"

"I don't understand why you're so against it."

He rolled his eyes. "You're hiding out from a killer in a survival bunker with a foster baby. Why not adopt a dog, too?" His sarcasm was evident, but he shook his head as if he'd disappointed himself. "Sorry."

The only thing she was sure about was not letting this beautiful animal go another day without good care and love. And, selfishly, the dog would help her feel safer after Sean left. Grace harrumphed but remained firmly at Sean's side, even as the husky strained against the leash to smell her.

"Ivy?" a man called out. She looked up to see Nathan gesturing to her from across the street. After she waved back, he jogged in her direction.

Nathan's forehead was creased and sweat gathered in the hollow of his neck, presumably from the run he appeared to be taking. "Is it true? Mom said they found her…"

Ivy glanced at Sean for permission. She didn't want to make a mistake in revealing something she shouldn't.

"I'm afraid so," Sean answered, compassion in his eyes. "Can I ask how you heard?"

"My mother knows the helicopter pilot's wife. She knows everyone." Nathan's head fell, sorrow written all over his features. His bright eyes focused on the husky Ivy fought to keep by her side. "Sky?" he asked.

"You know her?"

"It was her dog." His voice cracked. "Sky never warmed up to me, though. Olivia said she wasn't that fond of guys in general."

"You were a little closer to her than we knew." Sean regarded him with a shrewd eye.

Nathan's eyebrows pulled in tight. "Yes, we were close. I didn't want to upset my dad further."

"Did you know she was planning to steal gold from your family's business?"

Nathan gave a side-glance to Sean, then turned back to Ivy. "Olivia said she wasn't going to go through with it. She'd gotten herself entangled in a mess, but she said she was taking care of it. On the day she went missing, she left me a text—" His voice broke and he pressed his free hand against his eyes for a moment.

"What'd the text say?" Ivy asked gently.

"She needed to disappear and lie low, but she'd text me where to meet her. She said she'd make things right and not to worry." Nathan squatted and reached out to pet Sky, who rested her chin on Nathan's knee, the dog's soulful eyes looking up at the man. "She told me to keep my dad calm."

"That's why you were trying to convince your dad that maybe she didn't steal anything."

"I tried to cover for her as long as I could, but my dad…" He sighed. "I tried to get her to tell me what kind of trouble she was in, but she wouldn't tell me. I should've insisted."

"Did she mention any other details? Any names?"

He shook his head and turned his face away. "No. Nothing like that."

"Did you know her before you hired her?" Ivy asked.

He cleared his throat. "No. I think she'd never had a good employer before. Or she didn't want to get too close to us before she stole from us, but I watched her change before my eyes. Her heart changed." He exhaled a long breath. "I have to believe she would've done the right thing in the end."

"You can help us get her justice by giving us your statement," Sean said.

Nathan nodded rapidly. "I should've done that earlier. This will hurt my family, knowing I essentially let someone steal from them. I really did think she was going to bring it back in a day or two."

Sean's stern expression softened. "We may have what she stole. Your testimony should help get it back more quickly."

The other man's eyes widened, but it didn't ease the tormented expression on his face. "I'll stop by the trooper post today." He glanced down at Sky. "I'm glad you're getting a good home." He turned and jogged away, albeit at a slower pace.

Ivy turned to pat Sky on the head. "I'm glad I know your name now. It suits you."

Sean's radio came to life. He picked it up to answer.

Helena's voice was coated with static but still clear. "The two men are still here. How fast can you get Ivy to the B and B? I could use her help."

Sean looked to Ivy, the question in his eyes. What possible reason could they need her? But she would never turn down a chance to help end this nightmare, so she nodded. "We'll be right there."

TWELVE

"I've been thinking. That's twice now our suspect has gotten away by ATV." Sean walked with Ivy from their parking spots on the side of the road to the B and B. Sky remained on Ivy's left side as Grace stayed on his left. "As a survivalist expert, how—"

"Is he able to hide? He knows the area well. If you do, it's easy to disappear," she told him. "Given his knowledge of traps, he definitely has survivalist skills. I imagine he only learned the skills to evade law enforcement, but that's going against your rule of making assumptions. I also can't claim to know what he'll do or where he'll hide next. Sorry."

"I should've argued for Gabriel to stay longer."

She quirked a brow. "Isn't he helping with Katie's case?"

"Yes, and I want that solved for her sake, but if we'd had Bear here, we might have gotten the suspect's scent at the campsite."

Ivy gestured in front of her. "There are hundreds of miles of hiding spots around here. An ATV can cover more ground than Bear could possibly in one day. I'm sure Gabriel would tell you the same thing."

"Arguable."

"Fine, but Gabriel even told me that he and Bear do more rescues than tracking bad guys. Don't beat yourself up." Ivy smiled. "I know you're doing everything you can to help me."

Was she softening toward him? The more time he spent with her, the less he remembered the reasons for their divorce and the more he remembered the good times. His thoughts kept ruminating on Ivy and Dylan. He couldn't stop thinking about both of them. How would he be able to focus on any other case if he was sent back?

They stepped inside the inn's lobby. Helena and Luna rounded the corner. "Oh, good. I'm not sure how much longer they're willing to stay. It's Evan Rodgers and Hudson Campbell. The same two men Fiona pointed out to us at breakfast, Ivy." Helena gave a quick nod of acknowledgment, but her eyes drifted down to the husky. "Is she trained?"

Ivy shrugged. "I assume so? She only strained when she saw someone she knew. Otherwise, she's stayed by my side."

Helena raised an eyebrow. "I told the men I had a few questions, and they wanted to know if they needed a lawyer."

Sean took a step forward. "I thought they were city types. Either that, or they have reason to be nervous."

"I've assured them they aren't under investigation." Helena's eyes twinkled with mischief. "*Yet.* In any event, they've agreed to wait a few more minutes. I told them I needed to check on something."

"We know from Fiona they're here to buy mining claims," Ivy said. "Have they told you which one? The Bozsan district?"

Sean shook his head. "We can't use any leading questions."

"Besides, they were tight-lipped," Helena added. "Here's why I needed you, Ivy. Because of our time crunch, I'd like you to make the emotional plea. Reveal you're in danger and make them feel like heroes if they help with information."

Ivy pulled her chin back and blinked. "That wasn't what I was expecting. Are you asking me to flirt?"

"No," Sean answered quickly. His neck felt hot. "I'm sure she wasn't."

Helena shrugged, a laugh playing on her features. "I was thinking more about having you describe the suspect for them."

Fiona rounded the corner with a stack of white towels in her arms.

Ivy approached and took the top half off the stack to see Fiona's glowing face. "Let me help you with that." She set the towels on top of the countertop. "Fiona, can you tell us any more about those two men interested in gold claims?"

The innkeeper leaned forward and peeked left and right. "Well, I don't know much about our guests, but my Ben did try to give them some advice. Mostly, they wanted to know where to find reputable employees." Fiona threw her hands up in the air and rolled her eyes.

"If that were easy, everyone in Nome would be rich and never get swindled."

Sean studied Fiona's countenance. So the woman knew about the gold stolen from her husband's dredge. Did she know her son had been in love with the thief?

"Between you and me," Fiona continued, her voice hushed, "it seems those two have just come into some money and thought it would be an easy way to multiply their fortune, but Ben gave them the hard truth. They've been holding interviews in my dining room for a crew leader. I've weeded out quite a few that would be no good for them."

"Oh, they asked you to screen the applicants?" Ivy asked.

"No, but I'm sure they appreciated it."

Grace snorted, and while Sean was sure it had to be from the fabric softener smell wafting from the towels, her timing was perfect.

"Anyone come to interview with red hair?" Helena asked.

"Auburn," Ivy corrected. "Over six feet tall."

"No," Fiona said slowly, her curiosity piqued. "The men have also been gathering price quotes for equipment, trailers, that sort of thing. I think they're stepbrothers, but they both must have been in their father's will. Evan wasn't as hot on making their fortune in gold as Hudson, but he's recently broken up with his girlfriend—sounds like she looked a little like you, Ivy—so he was eager to come to Alaska and get his mind off things, you know."

Ivy grinned and shared a smile with Helena. "I suppose that's good to know."

"Sorry I couldn't be more help. Like I said, I don't know much about them." Fiona turned around and went back to stuffing the towels in the back closet. If only every witness *didn't know* as much as Fiona knew.

"Thank you, Fiona," Helena said. "We'll only need the dining room for a few more minutes."

Sean gestured for Grace to stand back up from her seated pose. "How about I take the lead?" He walked ahead, mumbling under his breath. "No flirting necessary."

"What was that?" Helena asked.

He shot her a glare. "Nothing."

The two men in the dining room wore loudly colored sweaters and sat on opposite sides of a table, both on laptops with their phones also in their hands. They looked nothing alike, one with blond curly hair and the other with straight jet-black hair, but their mannerisms hinted at a familial resemblance.

"State Trooper Sean West. I understand you've been speaking to my partner, Helena." He gestured. "And this is Ivy West." He'd let them draw their own conclusions about having the same last name. "Ivy was a recent witness and kidnapping victim. We were hoping a quick dialogue might help us get closer to finding our suspect."

The man on the right, Evan, if he remembered right, jumped up. "We don't know anything about a kidnapping." He ran his hands through his thick hair. "What'd you get us involved with, Hudson?"

"Nothing." Hudson's voice rose, genuine surprise on his face, as well. Which was exactly the mindset Sean wanted when he asked his next questions, all thoughts of lawyers replaced with shock and curiosity.

"To be clear, we have no proof that the Bozsan mining district is related to these alleged crimes…" He paused a moment as the two men looked at each other, recognition and questions in their eyes. Helena had said they'd been tight-lipped as to what mining claims they'd been interested in buying, but this was the confirmation he needed. "We could use your help in arranging a meeting with the district's contact to ask a few questions."

"Are your dogs here to sniff us? See if we helped the kidnappers or something?"

Helena opened her mouth to answer but Sean beat her to it. "The K-9 helped me sniff out a murdered victim in the Bozsan mining district."

Their jaws somehow dropped even farther. Evan blinked rapidly. "I… I…don't know. Maybe we should call a lawyer just to be safe. I wasn't sure about investing in gold, anyway!"

Sean cringed. He'd gone too far and scared them.

"We're only asking you to help us arrange a meeting with the owner of the claims. If it turns out not to be the guy we want, then you can carry on with business as usual," Helena said, shooting Sean a glare this time.

The two men stared at each other, clearly unsure.

"You'd be helping me," Ivy added softly. "This man keeps threatening me and my…" Her voice cracked, and Sean could see the strain in her face was no act.

"She has a little boy." He pulled out his phone and showed them one of the photos he'd taken the other night. "The suspect tried to trick this little one away from his sitter. So you can see why we're asking the public for help."

Evan gawked at the sweet boy's smile. In that moment, Sean knew they would help. "It was an agent of the trustee. That's what we were told. Somebody inherited the district and didn't have the know-how or experience to run it. We don't, either, but we were going to hire people who did."

"We were supposed to meet him here," Hudson admitted. "Marty Macquoid."

Sean shared a glance with Helena. That name had no leads, which made it highly probable it was an alias. "When?"

"Tomorrow. Ten in the morning. He's bringing proof of the gold found recently. We have someone lined up to see if it's legit. After that, he was going to take us to see the claim sites before we signed the papers and wired the money to the trustee."

"That's very helpful," Helena said. "I'd like to ask that you don't change a thing about your plans. With your permission, we'll have some plainclothes waiting for Mr. Macquoid outside the B and B for tomorrow. We'll talk to him, and if he's not our suspect, he'll come inside for your meeting."

Evan and Hudson nodded dejectedly.

"We'll be in touch," Sean said. "Thanks for your cooperation."

The moment they stepped into the hallway, Ivy's eyes went wide. "You have a photo of Dylan?"

He pulled out his phone. "I meant to send it to you, but then I got busy with cooking. Grace and Dylan were practically posing for the camera." Even now, the sight of the little boy's bright grin was contagious. Grace apparently thought so, too, as she practically smiled whenever the boy was in sight. "We should probably go pick him up now, right?"

Ivy blinked slowly, staring at him as if he'd grown two heads. "I'd like that."

Ivy kept Dylan on her lap as Sky approached on a leash that Sean held. Grace sat alert but passive. Even if it was their last night together, she wasn't about to refuse his training tips. Helena had offered to make dinner and Luna was snoozing, blocking the entire kitchen entrance.

Dylan squealed with laughter the moment Sky's nose sniffed his bare feet. The dog wagged her tail and sat, eager for someone to pet her. Ivy helped Dylan pat her head. "Gentle," she said, easing the force of the boy's taps.

"We may not know Sky's history, but she seems to like people." Sean patted the husky, as well. "I'd like to see how the other dogs interact with her inside the bunker before I take off the leash."

Ivy nodded. While the bunker was a luxury model, they still had limited space. Three adults, a baby and three dogs felt a little tight.

Sean asked Grace to come. She approached and

waited. Sky sniffed her and then tried to place her head on top of Grace's neck. Grace huffed, spun and put a paw on top of the husky's head, slowly pushing her down in a seated position. Ivy snickered. "Did Grace just tell her to lie down?"

Sky was now on the ground, panting, a smile appearing to be on her face. Helena laughed, looking on from behind the kitchen counter. "I think that's exactly what happened. The husky is used to a pack leader. Seems to me she's accepted Grace as that leader without a fight."

"I'm glad for that."

"Dinner's served," Helena said. She put out a pot of soup and a set of bowls on the countertop. Ivy eagerly scooped a ladle's worth in a bowl. Once it cooled, Dylan would be able to enjoy it. As they sat at the round table and ate in silence for a few minutes, Ivy wondered at how the awkwardness of sharing such tight quarters was lessening so quickly. Maybe because she'd known Helena prior to this, but it was almost like having a family dinner.

"So maybe we should discuss tomorrow's plan," Sean said. "Do you mind if I call the team to discuss this?"

"Of course not," Ivy answered. She stared at the swirling carrots and potatoes in her bowl, stirring them faster with her spoon. Every time she allowed herself to feel peace amid the circumstances, the reminder of the incredibly high stakes, and that her time with Sean was coming to an end, came at her like flashing neon lights.

Helena opened a tablet and called Gabriel, who had already spent the day searching for Katie's estranged uncle, suspected of kidnapping the reindeer. They dialogued about tactical suggestions for tomorrow and steps to take for Nome police cooperation.

By the time they hung up, Ivy had fed Dylan his cooled-off soup and a banana puree for dessert. The faux windows on the walls shifted to a nighttime scene. While it seemed like an extravagant addition, she'd been thankful her dad had paid for such amenities to prevent the stir-crazy feeling she sometimes experienced as a child, particularly during long snowstorms.

Dylan's bright blues eyes watered as he yawned. Luna yawned, as well. Dylan giggled, then scrunched up his face and let out a wail. The cranky bedtime blues. She should've known. Minnie had warned her that his naps had been shorter lately.

"Thanks for dinner, Helena. Sean and I will wash up." She wiped Dylan's face and tried to keep the heat from her cheeks.

Helena stood up. "Then I think that's our cue to head for a quick walk before bed." She left the bunker with Luna.

"I didn't mean to speak for you," Ivy said softly. She unlatched Dylan and lifted him to her chest, the smell of bananas and carrots still wafting from his soft hair.

Sean shrugged. "I was about to offer." He picked up the bowls and walked to the kitchen. Ivy tried to set Dylan down with his toys, but he cried and kicked.

"He's so tired." She tried to hold him in her arms, but Dylan refused to rest his head against her, straining to sit up and move around. These were the most trying parts of motherhood. The moments where he didn't want to sit, didn't want to lie down, didn't know what he wanted.

"Here. I'm happy to take a turn." Sean slipped his hands underneath hers to take Dylan. "What do you think about that, buddy?" The little boy smiled.

"He adores you." The admission slipped out in a whisper.

Sean stared into her eyes. "I think he just likes my low voice." He dramatically lowered the last two words with a grin. "And I think it shocked him enough when I picked him up that he forgot what he was crying about." Sean beamed, and the little boy grinned back at him.

Helena came back inside and stopped midstride, spine taut, as if she'd stepped into a private moment. Ivy realized they were standing so close together, as if sandwiching Dylan in a hug. "Thank you for taking him," Ivy said politely. She moved back, allowing Sean to fully hold him without her. He squirmed in Sean's arms, fussing slightly, but not to the extent he had been.

"Maybe he just needs another rousing performance from the musical stylings of Grace and—"

"Oh, please *don't*," Ivy said.

Helena tilted her head back in a laugh. "I feel the same way. It's so special that once is enough." She winked and passed them. "Good night, everyone." Helena pulled her lips in tight underneath her teeth, as if fighting off another laugh. Then she disappeared into her room and closed the door.

Sean's shoulders dropped as he bent down and placed Dylan in his portable crib with some toys. This time the toddler grabbed his blanket and snuggled it, pressing his chubby fingers against the fabric of the crib. Sky was closest to him and flopped against the mesh, as if to accommodate. Grace took the opposite side of the crib and also lay down against it. Smart dogs. "I thought you were a fan of our musical number," Sean said. His tone held a forced playfulness to it, but when he straightened, she saw the slight hurt in his eyes.

"It's not that I'm not," she said. "Dylan usually loves his nighttime routines, and I don't want to get his hopes up that it's a new one that will happen every night." She turned back to the sink, blinking rapidly. It was going to be hard enough to say goodbye to Sean again.

"Oh." His voice sounded as dejected as hers.

"He normally settles down pretty fast in his own crib, but with all the changes…"

Sean joined her at the sink. "I think he picks up on the stress everyone is feeling, even though we try to hide it."

She picked up the dishrag and rinsed out each bowl. The two of them worked side by side, cleaning and putting away dishes. Everything was okay until the moment they brushed up against each other trying to get to the refrigerator and compost bin. Her throat ached with longing for his arms to wrap around her again, like he used to do in the kitchen after a long workday. She'd listen to the beating of his heart with one ear while the other listened to the tidbits of his day. Only now, she realized just how much he'd kept to himself.

Sean spun around and grabbed her hands. "You're shaking."

Her trembling hands were betraying her. "I…uh… must be more tired than I thought."

"Understandable." Sean took a step closer, his fingers still gently wrapped around hers. He looked over her head. "Dylan and the dogs both seem to be sleeping now." His eyes lowered to her lips.

Her heart snapped to high speed, the pulse vibrating in her throat. His right hand lifted, and he trailed his fingertips along her jaw. She leaned forward and slid her hands around his neck and into his hair. Why did his touch have to feel like she'd finally returned home? His eyes met hers and he lowered his head, his lips brushing against hers ever so softly. She leaned into the kiss, refusing to think of the consequences.

Grace whined. They broke apart, her heart racing. Grace's eyes were still closed, but her paws were moving in unison. Sean chuckled. "She's probably dreaming she's running after a squirrel."

Wherever the dog was running, Ivy knew Grace was alongside Sean, even in her dreams. Reality settled in the pit of her stomach. "I know you're leaving tomorrow."

His face blanched. "You heard?" He shook his head. "You always had good hearing."

"And you never learned to whisper properly." She did her best to offer him a grin. Why'd she let her guard down? Kissing him was the last thing she should've done.

"I don't have to go. I'm definitely not going if we don't catch the guy at the sting." His forehead creased. "Not right away, at least."

And there it was. "We both know you can't abandon your team. And with the missing pregnant woman and killers on the loose, Katie's missing reindeer and Eli's godmother's final request, I think it's fair to say you're very much needed."

"You're right, but…" His sigh hinted at conflicted emotions. Were they the same feelings she battled? "I made some calls when I followed you back here. Did you know you can apply to foster Dylan elsewhere? Given the situation and with a trooper recommendation, I'm hopeful the request might be expedited."

"Where would I go?" She watched him carefully. She did not want to have the same fight about Anchorage.

"What if you went back to working that job you loved?"

Her jaw dropped. "Survival instructor?" She didn't think he'd suggest that. "I have thought about that in the past, but I need something more conducive to motherhood. I couldn't go on trips."

"Like I said, I made some calls. There's a company that needs a training instructor, on site, days only. And I don't need to live in Anchorage. I didn't understand that when I first took the job with the K-9 Unit. I get sent everywhere. As long as my home base is within an hour or so from the headquarters, that's good enough."

"What are you saying?" Ivy's voice cracked.

"I saw you light up whenever you were out in nature. You'll want to share that love with Dylan. That survivalist company is in Palmer, less than an hour from Anchorage. Super small town surrounded by wilderness, next to Lazy Mountain and the Matanuska River."

She held her breath, refusing to consider what really did sound perfect. Rose-colored glasses, likely. She needed some time away from him. She braced herself, determined to ask the question most on her mind. "And how does where you live factor into this conversation? Dylan and I are a package deal, Sean. He calls me Mama—" She turned away to get a glass of water.

"I'm not asking you to give up being a mom, Ivy." His voice sounded more tender than she'd heard in years.

She couldn't look at him, so she continued to face the sink. "Then what—" She shook her head. "Even if you've come to your senses and realized you'd be a great father, we still had problems. I mean, look at us now, arguing…"

He placed his hands on the back of her shoulders. "We're not yelling at each other. We never have. We've disagreed, sure—"

"They were *fights*, Sean." She turned to face him, a little caught off guard that he didn't step farther back. "Let's call them what they were, and face the fact that happy couples don't…" She let her words fail her, shocked by what had almost slipped out of her mouth.

Sean raised an eyebrow. "Happy couples don't fight? Is that what you were going to say? Ivy, is that what you thought about us? Was that part of our problem?"

"No. I mean, I know it's good for couples to disagree." Ivy averted her eyes. Logically, she knew that, but she didn't want to admit how recently she'd learned, thanks to her foster parenting classes, disagreements were actually healthy. How would their marriage have been different? Not that the answer would do any good now.

"I know I was guilty of not telling the whole story when we did argue." He exhaled. "That wasn't fair."

She braced herself to meet his eyes. "Are you telling the whole story now? What exactly are you implying about moving? What are you asking me?"

His eyes dropped and eyebrows drew together. "I... I'm not sure yet. I just know that I want to keep you safe. I want to keep *both* of you safe."

Despite her best intentions to keep her guard up, his admission was like a knife spearing her heart. The only reason he wanted her to move was for their safety. She'd hoped for things she could never have.

A door creaked open behind them. Helena stepped out, her lips pinched. "I'm sorry if I'm interrupting."

They both faced her. Ivy plastered a fake smile on her face. "No, we were done talking. Can I get you anything?"

Helena shook her head and turned to Sean. "Fiona just called me. The two businessmen just checked out of the inn and left town."

Sean bolted into action. He threw his uniformed shirt back on over the navy T-shirt he'd been wearing during dinner. "I'll see if they're still at the airport."

"We can't force them to help us, Sean," Helena said.

"I'm fully aware, but I at least have to try to convince them." He grabbed his holster and made fast work of wrapping it around his waist.

Grace looked at Dylan before glancing at Sky. Her eyes seemed to say, *Take care of him while I'm gone.* Her white tail curled and her spine was alert. The Akita clearly understood she needed to go to work. She leaped after Sean before he even tapped his side, and they disappeared out the bunker door.

Ivy didn't need further explanation. The sting operation wasn't happening. She wasn't safe in Nome, and her heart wasn't safe with Sean. The only way to survive would be to take Dylan and run away. But even then, would they really ever be out of danger?

THIRTEEN

Sean paced outside the bunker. The morning air and movement helped him think, especially since he was short on sleep after the late night at the Nome airport. The two investors had already grabbed the last commercial flight to head back to Anchorage that only happened twice a day. And from there, they would journey on to Seattle.

He wasn't even afforded the chance to ask who they'd told about the sting before they left. For now, he would stick to the plan and hope there was a chance that their suspect would still show at the B and B. As he stewed on it, he realized the B and B owner might be able to shed light on the investors' fast departure. He texted Helena, who was still packing up in the bunker. She replied with Fiona's number.

"Well," Fiona said after answering, "we pride ourselves on guest privacy, but I will say they seemed awfully spooked before they left here last night."

"Spooked? How so?"

"It was odd. They had dinner, and I applauded them

on all the research and hard work they'd done. Told them maybe if all the miners had done their due diligence, then maybe there wouldn't be so many failures. Then I listed all the recent districts that have shut down. Next thing I knew, they were giving each other looks like daggers. Hudson said something about danger and cons and stormed out of the room, mumbling about mutual funds looking better every second. They left thirty minutes after, clearly annoyed with each other."

Sean didn't know whether to laugh or scream. "Did you by chance mention anything about the Bozsan mining district?"

"Oh, yes! That was probably the third one. It's an interesting one because it used to be a huge success, but it's all dried up now. Sad. The owner was a respected man but a loner. No family that I knew of. Died alone after spending his fortune on trying to find more gold, ironically."

"Do you know if Evan and Hudson met or talked with anyone in the last hours they were there?" he asked.

"Just you."

"You've been a great help, Fiona. Thank you."

"I don't know how I could've helped, but you're welcome. After you and the officers are done with your little stakeout, you come in and get some hot cocoa, okay? It's supposed to snow today."

Sean shook his head in disbelief and signed off. At least Minnie had kept her promise and not shared with the family the details surrounding the case. If Fiona knew they were after a murderer, surely she wouldn't refer to it as their *little stakeout*. And yet he already felt fondness for everyone he'd met in the community. No wonder Ivy enjoyed small-town life.

At the thought of losing her, his insides twisted in knots. So why couldn't he ask her to give them another chance? Why did he have to dance around it?

The door opened and Helena and Luna strode out, heading for their SUV. Ivy ran out behind her, Dylan on her hip and Sky on one side. Grace made a pawing action. The husky reacted by sitting at attention, waiting patiently, as if it were perfectly normal to take orders from a K-9.

Ivy thrust a thermos toward him. "I wanted you to take this with you. It's full of hot cocoa. It's supposed to snow later this morning."

"Would it surprise you to know Fiona offered me hot cocoa, as well?"

She laughed. "First snow of the season demands cocoa."

Dylan beamed at him, then turned and put his palm on Ivy's cheek. Sean's insides melted at seeing the interaction. He wanted nothing more than to pull them both into his arms. Instead, he nodded curtly. "Are you sure you feel safe here?"

"I'll put the security system on the moment I'm back inside. I have Sky with me and weapons." They stared at each other for a second until Ivy's eyes widened and she tipped over, straight into his arms. He caught her easily, pulling them both to his chest. "Something pressed into the back of my knees. I think Grace pushed me over!"

He peered over her shoulder to find Grace avoiding eye contact, standing directly behind her feet. "That move is only for taking down dangerous suspects, Grace." The dog seemed to roll her eyes and sway her hips as she took a long arc of a walk around until finally back next to him.

Ivy straightened but Sean hesitated to fully release his arms from around them. The kiss they'd shared had been burned into his memory. "Are you sure you're okay?"

She nodded, her blue eyes peering into his. Dylan had twisted so he could stare at the two dogs below them. Sean felt the tug to draw her closer once more, and he lowered his face toward hers...

"You better get going," she said softly.

Her words jolted him. He dropped his arms and stepped away. "Sorry about Grace." Affection had never been their problem. Ivy had always been his biggest cheerleader. Until she stopped. But she hadn't just stopped cheering him on, had she? She'd stopped living her days with joy altogether. Was it at the same time as he'd started putting walls around his heart?

"I'm sure it was an accident." Her cheeks flushed a glowing pink that matched her lips. She waved and ran back into the bunker. Sky jumped up and trotted after Ivy without being beckoned. Maybe the husky was the right choice for them. She certainly was a smart dog.

Sean waited until he heard the grinding of metal to be certain the extra door was sealed before turning to his partner. "I don't need any matchmaking skills from you." It was hard enough not to kiss Ivy without his dog throwing them together.

Grace harrumphed, clearly unconvinced, and trotted

back to their waiting SUV. Helena offered a thumbs-up from the inside of her SUV and started her engine.

Sean opened the door for Grace. "Let's go get this guy."

Ivy cleaned to the sounds of Sky's paws tapping across the length of the bunker, running after the tennis ball Dylan had thrown from inside his portable crib, followed by the tyke's giggles when Sky dropped the ball back inside the crib. Good thing she had a change of fresh sheets on hand before he took his nap. But the extra work was worth the smiles and bonding time between the dog and Dylan. At least it confirmed her suspicions that Sky loved people. She knew it the moment the poor thing had tried to find help for her owner.

Even Sean had seemed to recognize that it was a good decision. She spun around in a slow circle. Wasn't there something else she could clean? She didn't want to think about her conversation with him last night, the danger he was in today. Her fingers drifted to her lips.

He had almost kissed her. *Again.* And she was ashamed about how disappointed she was that he hadn't. They had unintentionally gotten back to a few of the routines they used to share. Cleaning the kitchen together, for instance. They'd done that whenever he was home for dinner. It was habit to kiss back then. Plain and simple. Didn't mean anything.

Then why wouldn't her racing heart slow down whenever she replayed that kiss in her mind? How many times would she allow her heart to soften? She'd almost thought he was about to ask them for a second chance last night. Only to find he wanted to serve as a part-time security guard for them. For a split second, she'd allowed herself to believe they could truly try again.

Why do I want that but also want to grab Dylan and run away? She closed her eyes ever so briefly in prayer. The tennis ball hit the top of Ivy's shoe and bounced to the back of the bunker, close to the laundry. "Mama!" Dylan laughed so hard that he lost his grip on the edge of the crib and fell back to sitting. He rolled over, still laughing, and crawled back up to standing.

Her heart burst and she picked up the little boy and kissed his head. "I love you."

Dylan's humor disappeared, only to be replaced with an intense frown. "Doggy?"

The dog backed away from the ball at the back and turned tail and ran past them, scratching at the front door. She studied the dog. That was odd. Maybe the laundry room scared her? "Do you really need to go out?"

It hadn't been that long since Sky had been out before Sean left, and Sky had definitely taken the opportunity to get things done. Ivy had promised Sean and Helena that she'd stay indoors while they were gone, with the security system engaged. She glanced at the lit panel that operated the system. It was still lit as secure. She leaned closer to examine it. Yes, both the front door and the emergency hatch in the back showed as locked and engaged.

Still, it was a very weird reaction from the dog. Ivy unlocked the gun case, mainly to calm her own nerves. It would only take her a second now to grab a weapon if needed. She lifted a silent prayer that it wouldn't come to that.

Sky's voice continued to warble in sorrowful, urgent tones. She turned and scratched at the door a second time. "Okay, fine. I need to call Sean like I promised, and if he says okay, you'll have to wear a leash. It'll need to be fast, and I can't go chasing after you if you see a moose you want to meet."

She grabbed the satellite phone to dial Sean, but it started vibrating and released a shrill ring. She almost dropped it in surprise. The number wasn't one she recognized, but it could be someone from the trooper post giving her an update. Dylan was also getting increasingly annoyed that Sky wasn't playing fetch anymore. She placed him back in the crib and apologized to the very nervous husky. "One more minute." She picked up the phone. "Hello?"

"Ivy? Oh, good, I finally reached you!" The voice sounded vaguely familiar, but the satellite phone didn't offer the best reception. Sky practically howled.

"Sorry, it's a bit busy here. Who is this?" Ivy picked up the leash and hooked it to Sky's collar. Maybe that would calm her down for just a second until she was given the all clear to take her out. Any moment now, her kidnapper would be caught.

"Anastasia." The phone cut in and out. "Social worker?"

Ah, that was why the voice was familiar. "Of course. Listen, I don't have the best connection, but I have been meaning to talk to you." Ivy rolled her head from side to side, the knot in the back of her shoulder starting to make a reappearance. "Even if the troopers catch the suspect today, I'm considering taking a job in a different area of Alaska. Just to be safe and start somewhere fresh." She paced as she spoke.

Even though she wasn't taking Sean's suggestion to move to Palmer and apply for that survivalist training position, the idea of getting back to the job she loved in a new area was strongly appealing. Besides, she really wanted Dylan to grow up somewhere closer to people. Ideally, she sought a small-town community located near vast expanses of wilderness but not as remote as the mission apartment. Nome simply didn't have that type of employment for her within the town limits. "Can we talk later about the process of how I would relocate while still fostering Dylan?"

She glanced at Sky, who had at least given her the courtesy of stopping the howl but was scratching with newfound tenacity at the door. Maybe she should put down a towel, just in case. Poor thing. She wanted to let her out, but she didn't want to be foolish with their safety, either.

"Of course. Just some paperwork, but that's not why I need to talk to you. I received a call a while back and I'm starting to second-guess myself. You said your ex-husband was a state trooper, right? And he was the one who was taking up your protection detail."

"Yes."

"He called and said you weren't picking up. Which I can see now is pretty valid since it took me a couple times until you answered."

"The satellite phone doesn't always work flawlessly,"

she admitted. The tension in her neck increased and now her stomach joined in. Something didn't sit right. Sean had been trying to call? Why would he contact the social worker?

"He said he needed directions to meet up with you. And that he knew you were headed north out of town but lost you."

Ivy's mouth went dry. "You gave him directions to the bunker?"

"Yes. I hope that was okay?"

Ivy's eyes darted to Sky again. She knew something. She was trying to warn her. Could Sky smell the murderer? "No, no, no. It wasn't my ex-husband."

"What? Oh, Ivy, what should I do?"

"I… I have to go." She hung up and her shaking fingers hit the preprogrammed number for Helena instead of Sean by accident. The call didn't go through. She cried out in frustration and Dylan's face crumpled in fear. "Oh, sweetie. I'm sorry. Mommy is just a little stressed."

She moved to press Sean's number again, but the security panel lights flickered. If she hadn't been standing right next to the door, she would've missed it entirely, especially since the perimeter alarm hadn't gone off. Ivy felt her eyes widen as she leaned forward. The lights of the security system flickered again and then went dark.

Sky spun around, looking past her, and released a deep, guttural bark that echoed against the steel walls. No sign of anyone inside. Could Sky hear him approaching from outside? Ivy dropped the satellite phone and wrenched open the gun case. She would trust her instincts. And this time, there was no option to run away and hide. She needed to stay and protect her son no matter what the cost. She grabbed the loaded weapon and stuffed it in the pocket of her jeans. She stepped forward to gather Dylan. Then she'd try again to call Sean.

"I'd put that gun down if I were you." The man stepped out of the shadows from the laundry room, holding his own gun, aimed directly at Dylan.

FOURTEEN

Sean kept his eyes trained on the two men passing each other in front of the B and B. The plainclothes officers didn't so much as glance at each other or the unmarked vehicles stationed around the place. They'd walk around the back where another Nome PD car awaited before making the same loop around the place, this time on the opposite side of the sidewalk.

His right leg bounced up and down. Enough waiting. The guy was almost ten minutes late at this rate, and yet he clung to hope. This stakeout *had* to work.

"When do we call it?" Helena asked through the radio. She was parked at the opposite side of the block. "And you're practically bouncing the vehicle with all your fidgeting."

He rolled his eyes in her direction. "No need to train the binoculars on me. Let's give it a little longer."

"Lorenza wants a status update. They're about to start a staff meeting. We can join as audio only while we keep our eyes peeled. The team might have some ideas we haven't thought of."

His first instinct was to argue. In the last couple of years, he'd learned to tame the first instinct that claimed his way was the best way. Besides, if he needed to plead his case to stay in Nome longer, then he should stay on the colonel's good side. "Yeah, okay."

He clicked on the tablet mounted on his dash and turned his camera off. The plainclothes officers rounded the corner. So nothing in the back, either. What if there was another way to enter the B and B? One he hadn't thought of. He was so focused he didn't fully register Helena's update to the team.

"It would be satisfying to still be there when you catch the guy," Gabriel replied to Helena. "But a few more locals have spotted Terrence Kapowski. I think we're getting close."

"If the guy was hiding underwater, we'd already have him," Brayden Ford said, in jest. His Newfoundland, Ella, specialized in underwater search and rescue.

"Hey," Gabriel objected with a good-natured laugh. "Maybe if you hadn't needed my help getting unstuck out of the mud, I would have him by now."

Sean cracked his first real smile of the day. Brayden had the reputation of getting a little messy, but he always got the job done. His radio squawked. Sean hit the mute button on the team feed and answered.

"Nome Police Dispatch to Trooper West. Patching through an emergency call made about an Ivy West. It's from her social worker?" The dispatcher sounded confused.

"Put it through." He leaned forward, his chest constricting as a click was made over the radio. The sound of sniffing filled the speaker. "This is Trooper Sean West," he said.

"I… I thought you called me earlier." The woman's voice trembled. "I called Ivy. She said you didn't call, though. Then she hung up and there was no answer when I tried calling again to make sure she was okay."

He cranked the ignition and turned the SUV around at high speed. He wasn't sure he fully understood the woman, but one thing seemed certain. Ivy was in danger. "What exactly happened?" He flipped on the lights without sirens.

"I gave you—not you, as it turns out—directions to the bunker."

His foot pressed the pedal to the floor, and he struggled to speak. "Thanks for your call, ma'am. I'll check on her now." He disconnected and swerved around other cars to get to the north exit of town. A quick glance in his rearview mirror revealed Helena's lights flashing.

"What's going on?" she asked through the radio. "You're still muted on the team meeting."

He untapped mute just before initiating a ninety-degree turn at full speed. "Possible hostage situation," he said to the team, straining to keep his breathing even. "Our suspect presumably found enough information on Ivy's phone to convince the social worker to give out her whereabouts. She's not responding on her sat phone."

Helena made up the distance between them, taking each sharp curve with him. Another set of lights blinked behind her. "I've got a Nome PD car remaining at the scene in case our suspect arrives. I've instructed the trooper stationed here to assist as backup."

"I'll put the Crisis Negotiation Team on standby until you've assessed the situation," Lorenza added. "Keep us updated."

"Yes, ma'am. About to lose signal." Before he even disconnected the call, the feed ended. He bumped over the large rocks and ruts in the gravel road as he drove at top speed toward the unusual sight of White Alice on Anvil Mountain.

He grabbed his satellite phone, narrowly maintaining control with one hand, steering as he dialed the number that he'd left with Ivy. His heart raced. First ring. His stomach clenched. Second ring. His breathing grew hot and shallow. Third ring.

"Hello?" Ivy's voice answered.

His foot slipped off the gas momentarily. He blinked rapidly in confusion. "Are you okay?"

"Sure, sure. Just about to get Dylan some watermelon." The toddler wailed in the background and Ivy breathed heavily. "I should go now. He's hungry. Have a safe trip." Her voice sounded monotone.

He paused. She had no watermelon. That had been the prank she'd tried to pull on Gabriel until he found out they were eighty dollars with transport fees. And Sean wasn't about to go on a trip. Someone was listening. "Thanks. I will," he said gruffly.

"Bye." Her voice caught and the line went dead.

He hit the radio. "He's there. We're likely dealing with a hostage situation. Proceed with caution and tell Lorenza to get that negotiation team on the line."

Grace released a mournful whine in the back seat. She may not have understood what he had said on the radio, but she knew when he was hurting. "It's going to be okay, girl. We're going to get her back." He exhaled. *"Please,"* he added as a one-word prayer.

The turn to the bunker was in sight. He couldn't do it anymore. He couldn't keep the shield up around his heart. What had all his caution brought him except heart-wrenching agony, anyway? It had made perfect sense when he decided fatherhood wasn't for him. He could still love Ivy and his parents because they'd already existed, but he didn't need to add new vulnerabilities to his life. Especially given his career.

Now it all seemed like rationale to cover up fear. He needed a different kind of shield around his heart. Faith was supposed to be like a shield, but it didn't mean there wouldn't be suffering. He'd have to cling to the faith that God was with him whatever may come. Easier said than done. But he wanted Him there with him not just in the hard times, but also the joyful times. Sean was tired of running from the good to avoid the bad. He just hoped he got to Ivy in time to tell her.

Ivy felt like she'd run a marathon, as hard as she was shivering. She dropped the phone. "Why? Why'd you have me answer?"

"It was the only way you were getting Dylan back." The man's smile turned her stomach.

"I've dropped my gun. I've pretended I'm fine. Let me pick him up."

He shrugged but didn't step away from the crib. She would have to approach, get close to the man in order to get Dylan. Ivy moved her eyes to her baby and his tearstained cheeks. She focused on him, *only* him, as she strode to the crib. Then, taking a deep, bolstering breath, she bent over and picked him up. The man grabbed the back of her hair and pulled, sending shards of pain through her skull. She screamed and Dylan's own cries echoed hers. The man laughed and finally let go. Her head throbbed.

"I thought you might still have a little sensitive spot there." He tilted his head and considered her. "I could've made it hurt worse."

"What if I get you the jar of gold? You can go on your way."

"You and your trooper ex-husband have cost me millions and you think a hundred grand will make up for it?" His laugh sounded hollow. "Oh, yeah, I know everything about you. Amazing what you can find out about a person by going through their phone." He grinned. "Just takes a little technical know-how."

Sky pressed herself against the front door. She'd stopped vocalizing but clearly didn't want to be any closer to the vile man than Ivy did.

"I see you've stolen my dog and turned her against me?"

"Was she really your dog?"

He shrugged. "She became mine after her owner tried to double-cross me, didn't she?" His bloodshot eyes stared at her. "But I'm sick of traitors, so she can stay here and starve to death. You're coming with me."

She hugged Dylan closer.

"Make him stop crying."

Ivy continued to take steps back. She repeated her

plea. "I'll get you the gold. You can take it and go far away."

"You're going to get me the gold *and* help me get out of here, sweetheart. And we both know the only way I'm getting away now is with a hostage. You helped the troopers, didn't you? Only a local would've figured it out. You scared away my investors. Yeah, that's right. I've been keeping an eye on them."

"It was your inheritance, right?" she volleyed back. "You tried to cover it up with a trustee and agent—"

"All me." He smiled as if proud.

"Maybe there's still gold there. If you'd just worked the land maybe—"

"That inheritance was a slap in the face!" he shouted. "My father never gave my mom any money while he had it. Not when she was dying, either. Didn't so much as meet me. Ever. I'm taking my fair share one way or another." His voice reverberated on the walls. "Those people you ran off had money to spare, and they don't deserve it if they're stupid, anyway." He pointed the gun at her. "Get the gold and head for the door."

He thought she had the gold in the bunker? She hesitated. If she clarified, he might shoot them. She lifted the diaper bag up and over her shoulder and let him assume it was in there until they were out of the bunker, with more options. He narrowed his eyes. He was questioning if she had it.

"Did you know Francine hid the gold in the gear I needed for him?" She nodded at Dylan. "At the mission. Before she met you outside."

His lips thinned. "I knew she must have hidden it in your shop. I'd followed her straight from the dredge. She thought she could bargain with me *after* she betrayed me. Enough talk. Go."

Please, Lord, help me see a way out.

She turned to the door, opened the first one and looked over her shoulder before opening the second. He'd put on a mask. Her stomach threatened to heave. He'd been lying. This man had no intention of letting them live if he had a mask on. She'd been the only one to see his face.

The perimeter alarm rang out.

"What's that?"

She felt her pulse in her throat. Dylan clung to her shirt, unusually silent, clearly terrified. Sky still shook against the door. The beep had to indicate Sean had come. She didn't know how he would have made it back so quickly, but she needed to buy some time. "Maybe it's the security system rebooting. What'd you do to it, anyway?"

His jaw clenched. "Shouldn't have been able to reboot," he mumbled. "Move!"

He'd also mentioned he would leave poor Sky here to starve. But Sean would return. He'd find her and make sure she was adopted by a good home. Her throat tightened from the tension of not being able to cry. He pushed her back and she rushed out of the bunker.

The moment her feet touched earth his arm snaked around her shoulders. A sharp point pressed into her lower back. It had to be the gun. Dylan wailed.

"Do exactly as I say." The man's loud voice directly in her ear made her flinch. His foul breath turned her stomach.

"State Troopers! Put your hands up!" Sean's voice rang out loud and clear.

The man twisted, forcing her to turn with him. Three SUVs barricaded the only way out, and three officers poked their heads slightly above the open driver's doors they hunkered behind. She couldn't see any way for this to end peacefully. She couldn't turn her head far enough to meet Sean's eyes. Someone was going to get hurt. She prayed it wouldn't be Sean or Dylan. *Let it be me.*

Sean kept his hands firmly on the gun, his finger off the trigger, but only a fraction of an inch away. The man kept his head and most of his body behind Ivy and Dylan. He might as well have been pointing a gun at his heart.

Grace whined inside the SUV.

The first and most important step to hostage negotiation was to establish a communication, a rapport of sorts. He was supposed to use empathy and build trust. How was he supposed to do that when the man held a gun to the love of his life? The rest of the steps included things like patience and active listening and staying calm.

"You still want to take the lead in negotiations?" Helena said in his ear.

The one thing he wanted most was their safety. And despite trying so hard, here was proof that ultimately that was out of his control once again. The wise thing would be to give up that control. He felt it in his bones. *Help me be alert and see our chance to save her, Lord.*

He reached up and touched the earpiece. "No. We

need someone to stay calm and keep him calm until the crisis team gets here."

Helena offered the negotiation to Phil, the trooper stationed in Nome who had arrived last. Even though this moment seemed like the biggest failure in his life, an odd peace slowed his heart rate.

The armed captor swiveled, waving his gun angrily. Sean stepped a touch closer to the edge of the door. Ivy's gaze reached Sean, and his skin felt electric. Oh, how he loved this woman, and he'd never told her properly.

He felt Grace brush against the back of his legs. At least, he thought it was her. Sean didn't dare shift his attention away from the gunman, in case he lowered his guard, in case they got a safe shot. It would be extremely unlikely Grace would maneuver herself through the small space between the front and back seats in the unmarked SUV. This one was a normal Ford Explorer, not a police utility meant for transporting prisoners, but Grace never got out unless he asked her to.

His peripheral caught a flash of fur to his right. She'd just proved him wrong.

"Did I just see Grace make a run for it?" Helena asked.

Sean darted his eyes to the right for a split second. Grace stayed low, running far to the east side of the small foothill. She was going up and over the back end of the bunker. What was she doing? The first day he'd brought her home flashed in his mind, and the way Ivy had loved on her. He'd ordered Grace to protect Ivy and Dylan a few times over the last few days. She knew the command wasn't still in play, but she still seemed determined to protect.

Grace only did that without a verbal command for him.

And his family. The realization took his breath away. Grace knew he loved them.

"If we just got him to lower his gun for a split second, I would tell Luna to attack," Helena murmured.

"Crisis team has just left. Ninety minutes away," Phil said in the earpiece. "I've been given the clear to start dialogue." The crackle of the trooper's external radio speaker being activated caused the gunman to swivel slightly in Phil's direction. "This is—"

"Don't even try talking!" The man waved the gun. "Just back your cars up and get out of our way."

A ferocious growl echoed throughout the valley of foothills. Ivy screamed and the gunman flinched. A blur of fur lunged at the back of the assailant's knees. He momentarily stumbled. Grace then jumped off her back legs and latched on to the man's hand that held the gun.

Ivy glanced down and elbowed the guy in the gut with her right arm. She was able to step away with Dylan still in her left arm.

"Ivy! Run!" Sean stepped out from behind the safety of his door. He sprinted like never before. If he could just get in front of them… The gun was still in the man's hands, despite his shouts for Grace to get off.

Halfway there. He pumped his arms as hard as possible, his focus on Ivy's wide, fearful eyes and Dylan's head, buried in her chest.

"Drop your weapon or another dog will attack," Helena shouted.

Grace continued her low growl, whipping her head left and right until the gun dropped to the gravel. Sean wanted nothing more than to continue running for Ivy, to wrap his arms around her and Dylan, but instead he turned to the suspect. The man could have more than one gun.

Grace was still latched on to the guy's wrist. He'd never trained her to attack, so asking her to release the same way Helena did with Luna wouldn't work. Helena and Luna and Phil ran up behind him. "Grace," Sean yelled. "Come!"

Thankfully, Grace heard him call over the man's hollers, let go and ran his way, her mouth hanging open, as close to a real smile as he'd ever seen. She was proud of herself. "Good dog!"

Helena grabbed the man's arms, and Phil kicked the gun far away. The moment the man's hands were behind his back, Helena began reading him his rights.

Sean whirled around to reach for Ivy, but she was already stooped over, lavishing praise and thanks on Grace. "Thank you, Grace! Good protect. Thank you." She glanced up, tears in her eyes. "Thank you, too. I have no idea how you found out or got here so fast—"

"Yace," Dylan said, half laughing with shuddering breaths.

Sean turned toward a warbling bark. Sky bounded in their direction from the bunker, a leash trailing behind her. Someone must have let her out. With so much commotion, had he missed his chance to pull Ivy into his arms and tell her how he felt? Would she even consider giving him a second chance? He didn't deserve one, and he knew it.

She looked up at him shyly. He needed to grab the moment before it was lost forever.

"Ivy..." He wasn't sure how to start, but he couldn't go back to normal.

Her eyes widened, and she dived for him with her free arm. He caught her and Dylan easily. But he felt an unnatural tightening around the back of his legs. At once, he spotted the problem. Sky's leash had wrapped around both their legs, but Grace held Sky's leash in her mouth, with that same fox-like smile. Helena's laughter reached their ears. Phil had placed the suspect in the back of his trooper vehicle. The danger had passed. Finally.

"A little help?" Ivy called out.

Helena waved. "I think you and Sean can figure this one out yourselves. See you back at the trooper post."

"Grace," Sean said. "I told you I didn't need extra help."

His K-9 released the leash from her mouth, and it was easy enough to loosen until Ivy stood straight.

"What did you mean by that?" she asked.

"I suspect Grace is trying to help me find a way to say I love you. That I love you both." He kissed the top of Dylan's head. "I love you and..." His throat went dry as he looked Ivy directly in the face. Her eyes misted, and he forged on before he lost his nerve, before she could let him down without hearing him out. "I love you, Ivy. And I know I'm asking a lot, but if you're willing to give me a second chance, I'd like to take some foster classes and adopt Dylan and Sky *with* you. I'd like to do life as a team and—"

She placed a hand on the side of his face, her fingertips alone making his heart race. She searched his eyes and lifted her chin until their lips were only an inch apart. "I love you, too. With my whole heart." He pressed his mouth to hers, soft and sure. She released the sweetest of sighs and straightened, her face radiant. Sean's chest felt like it was going to explode. Dylan patted Sean's head, laughing, yet trying to peer below Ivy's arms.

Her eyes twinkled. "How do we get out of this?"

Sean twisted to look down. Grace was pressed against their right side, and Sky was pressed against their left side. "I think this is what is known as a group hug."

Ivy tilted her head back and laughed. Sean pointed to the car. Grace stood and ran off. With a few well-timed lifts of his feet, Sky's leash was loosened from around their legs, and she ran after Grace. Sean held Ivy's hand and walked back to the car. His heart had never been so full.

EPILOGUE

Two weeks later

Someone was downstairs. Sky's warbled voice alerted her before the security alert beeped. She was all packed and ready, though. Ivy picked up Dylan and eagerly opened the apartment door to find Sean on the stairs.

"I've already loaded everything you've asked for from the bunker. You packed up here?"

"Should only take a load or two. All the furniture stays for my replacement."

Sean nodded and picked up two suitcases. She followed him down the stairs and outside, where a small trailer waited. She peered in to find the pack-and-play crib and toys she usually kept at Minnie's already loaded. "We should have plenty of time to get it to the dock. My friend who transports cars here says this will all be in Anchorage within a week."

She tilted her head into the sky and looked out toward the back, where the musk oxen grazed. "It smells like snow."

Dylan reached for Sean and he eagerly accepted.

"Doggy and Dada." Dylan said each word with a nod on each syllable, as if introducing Sean and the dogs to Ivy for the first time.

Sean kissed the top of his head. "Not quite yet, little man, but soon. Hopefully very soon."

She laughed, her eyes sparking with joy for what felt like the millionth time. Foster transfer papers had been approved, along with Sean's intent-to-adopt papers, as well. He had already started attending classes a week ago. Thankfully, they allowed him to attend a couple of classes virtually while out on location. And since the Alaska K-9 Unit had added Ian McCaffrey and his German shepherd, Aurora, a cadaver dog, Sean had someone to share on-call duty with. Ivy could scarcely believe it was happening.

"I realized something, though," Sean said to Dylan. "I've forgotten one key thing before I move you and your mom."

She racked her brain about what they might've forgotten. They'd tried to talk every night while Sean was back in Anchorage, and she'd made list upon list of what they needed. Sean pulled his harmonica out of his shirt pocket. Grace trotted to his side and Sky plopped beside her. Ivy couldn't help but laugh. "Another round of 'Twinkle, Twinkle' before we go?"

He began playing the worst rendition of "Here Comes the Bride" she'd ever heard. He swayed with Dylan, who was situated to face her in Sean's left arm. Her baby boy patted Sean's forearm as if it were a set of drums. Grace walked around Sean twice and Sky followed her. On Sean's final note, Grace and Sky both warbled a horrible off-tune finishing howl. Ivy clapped and Sean's face sobered. He bent over and set Dylan down on a small patch of grass nearest the building. "One second, little man. I need to ask your mom a question. Ivy, I know we've talked about this, but I want to ask *properly*." He sank to one knee and lifted his face up to Ivy. "Will you marry me—again?"

Her breath caught. "I will."

He stood and reached for her, his hands on her waist, pulling her close. Her fingers slipped behind his neck. He searched her eyes, as if wanting to see proof that they were in agreement. She grinned and met him halfway. Their lips touched. She pulled him closer, reveling in the kiss as peace flowed from her head to her toes. Even though they were moving to a different town, being with Sean was like returning home. Dylan's hands found their pant legs. They broke apart to find him grinning up at them with the surety of a child who knew his parents loved him and each other. Grace and Sky stood, wagging their tails. Then Sean swooped down and picked Dylan up for a group hug as the fat snowflakes, promising hints of a beautiful arctic winter, floated down from the clouds above.

* * * * *

Get 4 FREE REWARDS!

We'll send you 2 FREE Books plus 2 FREE Mystery Gifts.

FREE Value Over **$20**

Both the **Harlequin® Special Edition** and **Harlequin® Heartwarming™** series feature compelling novels filled with stories of love and strength where the bonds of friendship, family and community unite.

YES! Please send me 2 FREE novels from the Harlequin Special Edition or Harlequin Heartwarming series and my 2 FREE gifts (gifts are worth about $10 retail). After receiving them, if I don't wish to receive any more books, I can return the shipping statement marked "cancel." If I don't cancel, I will receive 6 brand-new Harlequin Special Edition books every month and be billed just $5.49 each in the U.S. or $6.24 each in Canada, a savings of at least 12% off the cover price, or 4 brand-new Harlequin Heartwarming Larger-Print books every month and be billed just $6.24 each in the U.S. or $6.74 each in Canada, a savings of at least 19% off the cover price. It's quite a bargain! Shipping and handling is just 50¢ per book in the U.S. and $1.25 per book in Canada.* I understand that accepting the 2 free books and gifts places me under no obligation to buy anything. I can always return a shipment and cancel at any time by calling the number below. The free books and gifts are mine to keep no matter what I decide.

Choose one: ☐ **Harlequin Special Edition**
(235/335 HDN GRJV)

☐ **Harlequin Heartwarming**
Larger-Print
(161/361 HDN GRJV)

Name (please print)

Address   Apt. #

City   State/Province   Zip/Postal Code

Email: Please check this box ☐ if you would like to receive newsletters and promotional emails from Harlequin Enterprises ULC and its affiliates. You can unsubscribe anytime.

Mail to the Harlequin Reader Service:
IN U.S.A.: P.O. Box 1341, Buffalo, NY 14240-8531
IN CANADA: P.O. Box 603, Fort Erie, Ontario L2A 5X3

Want to try 2 free books from another series? Call 1-800-873-8635 or visit www.ReaderService.com.

*Terms and prices subject to change without notice. Prices do not include sales taxes, which will be charged (if applicable) based on your state or country of residence. Canadian residents will be charged applicable taxes. Offer not valid in Quebec. This offer is limited to one order per household. Books received may not be as shown. Not valid for current subscribers to the Harlequin Special Edition or Harlequin Heartwarming series. All orders subject to approval. Credit or debit balances in a customer's account(s) may be offset by any other outstanding balance owed by or to the customer. Please allow 4 to 6 weeks for delivery. Offer available while quantities last.

Your Privacy—Your information is being collected by Harlequin Enterprises ULC, operating as Harlequin Reader Service. For a complete summary of the information we collect, how we use this information and to whom it is disclosed, please visit our privacy notice located at corporate.harlequin.com/privacy-notice. From time to time we may also exchange your personal information with reputable third parties. If you wish to opt out of this sharing of your personal information, please visit readerservice.com/consumerschoice or call 1-800-873-8635. **Notice to California Residents**—Under California law, you have specific rights to control and access your data. For more information on these rights and how to exercise them, visit corporate.harlequin.com/california-privacy.

HSEHW

HARLEQUIN
PLUS

Try the best multimedia
subscription service for romance
readers like you!

Read, Watch and Play.

Experience the easiest way to get
the romance content you crave.

Start your **FREE TRIAL** at
harlequinplus.com/freetrial.